I0788864

THE DRUMMER GIRL

Tim Boiteau

Branching Realities
Independent Publishing

The Drummer Girl
Tim Boiteau

The Drummer Girl is a work of fiction. Names, characters, places, and incidents are products of the author's imagination. Any resemblance to actual events or persons, living or dead, is entirely coincidental.

First Printing
June 2020

Branching Realities Independent Publishing aims to find the best in fiction of all genres from independent authors all over the world. To find more about us visit our website or send us an email. Please support the independents of publishing and writing.

Website: branchingrealitiespublishing.com
Email: branchingrealities@yahoo.com
Store: irbstore.co

For Dongfang

CHAPTER 1

The alarm clock crumbles when I touch it, and the music stops. Confused by the unexpected grittiness, I open my eyes and find I'm outdoors, my jeans and panties are pulled down, tangled around one calf, bra twisted about my stomach beneath my t-shirt. Pulse quickening, I rise to my knees and examine myself—no soreness, no blood or bruising, my inner thighs and pubic hair clean. Breathing a sigh of relief, I shimmy and shift my clothes back into place with a quick glance around.

No one in sight. Thank God.

I settle back down, shutting my eyes and massaging my temples. My head throbs. A chalky and bitter taste fills my mouth.

I squint at my digital watch, but the battery has died, the face blank.

Where is this?

I scan my surroundings. The ground sweeps up to the crest of high, glittery dunes. The sky is marigold, the air cool; feels like evening.

The river maybe?

No sign of water, no buildings, not even a scrap of litter—nothing but the dazzling sand waves arcing and humping into the distance, the rush of wind.

Several yards away I spot a spiky, black lump porcupining out of the sand—my purse. I crawl over and unearth it. Flick open the clasp, check for my bank cards, pull out my cash.

I count it—three hundred and change. All there. Wasn't robbed.

I pull out my compact and shake my short black hair

free of sand, brush a caking of it from my face, and clean the various facial piercings.

I snap it shut and stow it away. My fingers graze against the snakewood handle of the straight razor at the bottom of my purse and linger there a moment, then they shift to the mashed pack of Camels. I coax out a cigarette—only three more misshapen smokes left—fish around for my lighter, and shield from the wind as I light it.

I study the dunes. The things are huge, big as buildings. Hell, they could *be* buildings. I probably dropped some acid after the show. This could all be happening in one room of the Compound or my apartment or anywhere.

Part of me wants to get up and explore, but it's probably safer to wait until all of this sand melts back into graffitied sprawl or whatever reality underlies it. Then I'll take a cab home, clean up, call Bower and explain what happened. Should have been packed and at the Compound by 6AM to load the bus—but, then, it's only an hour drive from Detroit to Toledo anyway, and the first gig of the tour isn't until tomorrow.

Gathering my knees into my chest, I take a deep drag off the cigarette and gaze up at the sky, at a thrilling show of planetoids floating and spinning across the sky.

Seems selective what the LSD has metamorphosed—everything but me. I smell old beer on my t-shirt, taste the thickening of smoke on my lips, feel the solidity of the tongue stud pressing against my palate.

As if to stress this point, tongues of rainbow aurorae lick their way into life on the horizon.

Another voice whispers *Ma* to me, wanting me to turn my mind towards her, but I'm not willing to follow it there. Not yet.

The taste of the cigarette begins to rankle, the smoke stinging my eyes. Extinguish it. Return it to the pack. By now mounds of wind-shifted sand have pooled around my red sneakers. If I linger here too much longer, I'll be buried alive in this stuff—whatever it is.

I look back up towards the lights on the horizon, and it strikes me that what I'm seeing is the neon breath of the city—bars, music clubs, strip joints. Nightlife. Young woman tripping balls at night in one of the desolate burbs... I should move.

I stand and approach the nearest dune. About a hundred feet tall. I scramble up on all fours, expecting any moment for the sand to reassemble into brick or stone, but it stays obdurate and beautiful—like the detritus of an eroded pearl mountain. The snow-crunch of my feet and palms against the fine sand sends shivers up my spine.

Snakes of sandy wind whip up and past me, to the apex, where they fork and merge and slither over the hump. When I reach the peak, my eyes track across the countless dunes shrinking into the distance, drawn beyond them, towards the aurorae, to a crystalline mountainscape breathing in the light of the setting sun and singing it back into the sky in shimmering bands.

The sight is so gorgeous, I unconsciously plop down on my ass, my eyes scrabbling for purchase on the peculiar angles of the jeweled frostwork, and getting lost in the circuitry of light.

Detroit refracted through the acid lens.

How I'd wandered so far from downtown during the blackout is beyond me, but what matters now is to try and get my bearings at some landmark within the city. Work out the path home from there.

The first handful of dunes make for a fun journey—climbing up to the peaks and then bounding down. The novelty of this acid world is enough to entertain me—corkscrew horns of opalescent rock jutting out of the ground; caterpillars the size of trains, bedecked in spiny sails, coursing over the desert, ejecting sand spray out of their blowholes; a giant horse napping in a dune valley, regarding me dreamily as I pass by.

Up and down dune after dune, minutes of walking turn to hours—or they seem to. The sky, the sun, resist the advances of time. The sun has swept across the ice bloom horizon, casting everything in rainbow, but it looks no closer to setting than it had when I had set out.

The fun starts to flag.

Walking devolves into trudging.

By the time the sun has traversed the entire distance of crystal and re-emerged, my throat is parched; I'm queasy with hunger.

Search my purse. In the far corner, a hoary cough drop has become entangled in the lining. I unstick it, prune as much lint and hair off as possible, then pop it into my mouth. Tastes grainy and metallic at first, but eventually the soothing menthol bursts forth. Keeps hunger at bay a while longer.

Time drags on.

Despite the cool air, a light sweat has blossomed under my arms and down my back.

My feet stumble along, then stop working altogether.

I drop down at the base of a dune and close my eyes for a few minutes, massaging the pressure points around them with thumb and forefinger the way Ma had taught me.

How could I have walked so far and gotten nowhere? It must have been ten miles at least, half a day of walking, and yet the city/mountains seem no nearer than when I'd set out.

When I didn't show up for the bus this morning, the others must have gone knocking at my apartment, circled around my neighborhood, called around. Would they have reported me missing to the police? Maybe it hasn't been as long as I sense it has. Maybe the acid has mucked with my sense of time. Desolate as it is, it must still be late into the night.

I consider smoking the second half of the cigarette,

but my lips are far too cracked to make the experience enjoyable.

Then I remember my lipstick.

I turn over on my side, take it from my purse, twist up the angled, electric purple column. Can't remember if this is also a balm, but it's worth a try.

I lick my stinging, papery-white lips, spit out sand, then apply the lipstick, shifting around my lip ring with practiced ease, press my lips together, and pucker up for the warped reflection in the worn metal cap. It alleviates the pain somewhat.

I pull out the half-smoked cigarette, light it up, and knead my hands into the painful knot of my stomach.

A sunlit, bare stairwell, the landing sky blue linoleum.

A girl is seated in an Oriel window, smoking, reading a novel, now and again glancing up at the courtyard beyond, where wind stirs the falling leaves. She's slim, with large black eyes and small pug nose, her short hair uneven, the color of squid ink. A constellation of facial piercings glint in the autumn light. She wears black jeans, red sneakers, and hoodie, the rolled-up sleeves revealing a bandage wrapped around her left wrist. Tattoos sprout around its edges—alien flowers and color exploding out of intricate, black liana.

A man calls out from below, the words indistinct.

The girl snuffs out the cigarette in the ashtray on the windowsill, gathers up her things, and dissolves.

The sun has set, the sky aglow with a glitter spill of stars—no industrial-brown night. I've been half-buried, the cigarette butt glued to my sand-encrusted lips, ember a warm memory.

That was me in that sublimely mundane dream.

How long was I asleep?

Disinterring my arms, I pull at the butt, stretching the flesh an inch away from my face before it snaps off, and my lip recoils, stinging and offended with the coppery heat of blood.

I stretch out my arms. Something pricks my left hand. Stiffly propping myself up on one elbow, I dig up the spiked purse, empty out all the sand. I find my compact and open it.

Maybe it was some kind of wish-fulfilment fantasy, a dream of safety and normalcy.

Now back to this weirdness.

I examine my lip in the reflection. A black pearl of blood has beaded out of the crusted blue of my mouth, limned in a turquoise light.

Light?

I turn my head towards the source of this illumination. Several moments of blinking brings the phosphorescent aura into focus—a glowing copse nestled in the dune valley a hundred yards away, teeming with outlandish fungi and plants and stones.

I put away my compact and zip up my purse, rise and start approaching the inviting glow, when my footsteps falter.

Not stones, I realize—bones.

The flora-camouflaged skeleton—a bull's—is enormous, its horns spanning forty feet or more. Massive roots fork out of its gaping mouth; tangles of vines and cacti weave skyward through the overturned rib cage in a sumptuous tapestry; pink sunflowers gopher out of its eye sockets and the cracks in its fallen god skull.

I continue forward and at the verge of the oasis breathe in the thick, living air, a welcome relief from the biting dry of the white sands. The place sounds alive too—clicking and skittering, humming and chirping— and is riddled with fabulous insects: jellyfish spiders; scuttling anemones; glowing, roly-poly-like worms, some big as cats, staring at me out of milky eyes, flexing their bizarre mouthparts as if in greeting.

I wander inward, winding between the bone pillars, steering away from the curious insects. Ahead, it opens up into a small clearing—very few bugs here—a good place to study the flora, maybe find some food. I was under the impression that desert oases flourish around a water source, but it doesn't seem to be the case here.

In the clearing, I scan to see what my options are. Difficult to choose what might be edible: polyhedral fruits, elephantine mushrooms, rubbery flowers. One of the latter catches my eye. A red spider lily. Leafless, taller than me, its bloom a knot of fiery snakes.

I pluck one of the oversized petals, remembering how as a child I'd seen Ma in the garden stuffing one of these flowers into her mouth—during one of her lucid seasons.

Then it occurs to me I've abandoned all reason, taking the acid world at face value. On the tail of this thought, I searchingly re-examine my surroundings, attempting to link the components of the oasis to the layout of a more mundane place.

A convenience store maybe?

The bones might be shelving or architecture, the fruits goods on the shelves, the maggots... Christ knows. But what about a cashier? Other customers?

"Hello?" I say, voice rasping.

The only response is the scurrying of insects, the clatter of the tendril tree branches waving in the wind, and beneath it all the whispered promise of erosion.

"I'm going to eat this now," I announce, creaking my way back into a more human tone. I take a five-dollar bill out of my purse. "I've got money. Anyone? I'm dropping the cash here."

The folded bill flutters out of my hand, and I stuff the petal into my mouth, probe the texture and flavor: silky, a little tangy. After swallowing, I pause, monitoring my body for a reaction. When the most that happens is a few questioning grumbles from my stomach, I strip off more petals and continue eating, chewing with more gusto than before. After three petals I'm not full but have at least staved off hunger for a little longer.

Whatever it is I just ate, it hasn't killed me.

Saw off several short stalks of the umbel with my razor and begin to head back the way I'd entered.

Several feet into the return journey, a queasiness hits; a numbness spreads down my limbs; a seed begins to grow in my head, right behind the eyes. It balloons into a lemony cloud, lifting, relieving my feet of the weight of my limp body, filling me with the visceral thrill of soaring.

For several yards I float along, mind pulsing with a sense of harmony and love for this wondrous oasis— before collapsing head first into the ground.

The woman, elegant, with short gray hair and a slightly masculine face, smokes as much as Jing.

A small office, the sound of their conversation muffled, the image of the two of them is scrambled, colors wavering, moments superimposed over each other. Jing is sparing with her words.

All of her piercings have been removed.

She no longer wears her studded, faux-leather belt.

The woman lights cigarettes for her.

The vision flickers out.

Hundreds of pinpricks jolt me back into the oasis.

Glowing worms are swarming over my body, chewing through my clothes, through my skin.

I whip and writhe, flinging the things from me, then struggle to my feet and swat at my chest and limbs and beat them out of my hair. Someone is screaming, keening. It's me, my voice, fleeing my body like some exorcized demon. The woods quiver in pandemonium as more and more bugs flash out of the darkness, mouthparts flittering hysterically. One ferret-sized worm has burrowed into my thigh, sucking with zest, pulses of red spiraling through the semi-translucent maze of its innards. I yank at the thing, the flesh pulling away, then it rips loose, a piece of me clamped in its mandibles, blood gurgling out of the wound. The creature flip-flops out of my grasp, circling back and latching onto my arm. I try to shake it, wrench it off, but it has me in a vise-like grip, dangling there, guzzling my life.

The razor.

On the ground by my bag and the lily stalks.

I drop to one knee, trap the wriggling thing beneath my free foot, flick open the blade, and hack away. The exoskeleton is tough as thick, plastic packaging, but I manage to slice it open, releasing a stream of ripe, blood-streaked juice. Jab inward, twist back and forth, exacerbating the fountain. The thing squeals, loosening its grip. When it does, I stand and stomp down, popping its head open, then snatch up my purse and bolt.

Everything has turned carnivorous, grown lunging and chattering mouthparts.

I dodge and scrape up against boles of coral and powdery mushroom stalks, knocking the things off me.

Then I'm out in the cool, dry air. A star-dusted sky. Lovely, lovely, lovely barren sand.

I strip down, shaking with revulsion. Inspect every inch of my clothes and naked body. I find and kill twenty or so of the creatures, some as tiny as grains of rice, before finally reclothing. Even then I'm not satisfied—can't shake the feeling that maybe one of them had managed to tunnel its way inside. A microscopic one. Maybe it's laying eggs in there.

No. No. No.

After minutes of retching and deep breathing and gagging the panicky inner monologue, my hands steady out.

I'm Zen.

Back at the oasis, the worms have congregated near the bones at the tree line, facing out towards me, mouthparts chattering.

Blood is still spurting weakly from both my arm and leg, but they're the only bites that demand any attention. I rip the left sleeve off my t-shirt. Split it lengthwise. Bind both wounds as well as I can, mind working back over what had happened.

Ate a flower.

Had a seizure.

Weaker now than before the poison test.

What's more vexing is my inability to link this event to the real world, assuming, of course, that all this is just a phantasmal gauze over reality.

In which case, I just stripped naked in public.

Christ, Jing.

I yell out into the night for help, for anyone that can hear me to call an ambulance. I scream myself hoarse, but only the wind and the distant chatter of insects answer—mockingly, I think. I stare out at the desert, towards the city/mountains, their snowflake spires glimmering in a vista between dune peaks, no closer now than they had been when I started out.

After several hours of walking, the sun rises behind me, no longer skirting the horizon as it had once done but moving in a wide arc, the sky at long last brightening into a friendly blue with scudding clouds. The day grows hot, then sizzling. I retreat into the shadow of a rock outcropping and wait out the sun. The sand is blinding. When I squeeze my eyes shut and stare into a black and orange nightmarescape behind my eyelids, I fear it has burned a permanent afterimage onto my retina.

I get snatches of sleep, dreaming of television static and ribbons of distorted space, and wake at sunset.

Continue wandering.

No secret cough drop to be found in my purse, I try eating a dollar bill, till my tongue ejects the mushy gray-green wad of fiber. Every hour or so I peer into my bag and feel the pockets of my ever-loosening jeans, expecting to discover something missed. There's a scrap of paper with a guy's phone number on it. Name doesn't ring a bell. Stuff it into my mouth. Not as bad as the money, easier to chew, but it leaves me slobbering and more nauseated. Later I try the ticket stub from a show and gag.

The night suddenly grows cold, and I bury myself in the sand, breathing down the collar of my tattered shirt to warm myself. More static dreams.

I wake with bitter surprise, and a touch of diss-ociated fascination—how long can this go on?

Should have stayed by the oasis. Stayed there and systematically tried a little of each type of plant. Maybe even a worm.

But it's too late for that now.

My jeans have begun to slip down my waist, forcing me to tighten my belt to the very last hole—still not quite tight enough.

Night and day come and go, seeming with no con-sistency in duration. Sometimes the sun never sets. Sometimes the night stretches on so long, frost films the sand.

The pain of hunger and fatigue and worm bites burn down to faint, morning campfire embers hidden beneath fine, gray ash. My throat is parched and sealed, a layer of grit cemented over every inch of me, eyes sun-dazzled. The only thing keeping me staggering forward is a hair's breadth of obstinacy, but at last even that hair's breadth snaps, and when it does, my white-caked sneakers cease shuffling, my remains sway in the wind, a wheeze issuing from my constricted throat, then my worm-bitten leg buckles, bringing me to my hands and knees, the shifting sand beginning to bury my limbs, foreshadowing what I'll become—a sister dune to all the other wanderers that drowned in the sand.

Still, though, the faint embers of sentience glow on in the ash.

When I move, it's from a far-off place, like in the dreams I had many days ago—removed a few steps from myself. Pull out the razor, unfold it, then sit back and draw it down the tattoo of the exposed left wrist.

Blood gushes out onto the sand. A startling garnet. The only color in the world.

The white sand drinks it up darkly.

The wind petrifies its shine.

I topple over.

My lips are wet. Something is dripping onto them.

I lick at it.

Sweet, cool.

It sparks the drive in me, and I open my eyes to a confusing sight—as if some desert plant had sprouted out of my mouth, a cactus, chartreuse and smooth, with sporadic spine clumps.

Dangling over my head, its juices trickling into my mouth.

Beyond the cactus, planted in a field of snow, a large black eye watches me. I incline my head to let the juice wash down my throat, body returning to life, then reach up and grab the arm, pricking my fingers, and pull it down to my mouth. The full weight of it transfers into my hands as the eye recedes, and the beast comes into focus—a white Alsatian massive as a truck, black bowling ball eyes ringed orange in the dying light.

I study her as I replenish myself. When it's emptied, I drop the cactus arm, then lie back down—a flash of pain. Remembering suddenly that I'd been... did I actually do it? I shift the weight off my throbbing left arm and look down.

Split flesh and pinkish black grit. I curse, gritting my teeth, a complex of embarrassment and remorse heating my face. I fight the urge to touch the grisly fissure and verify it isn't some horror-movie make-up job.

Can't be real. I can't have done that to myself.

The dog approaches, sniffing with the hot force of a blow-dryer, its animal odor rolling over me. Too weak to escape, I can only cringe, eyes shut, as it licks my wounded wrist. I moan and grimace at the pain, but let it continue. After suffering several buffets of the tongue, I open my eyes and watch the giant, purple alien washing over the bloodied, skinny arm, the bifurcated arabesque, each slather clearing away more blood-pink sand.

I reach out with my good arm and stroke the dog's head, hand disappearing into the velvety, white fur. Too busy with its cleaning work, the dog doesn't seem to mind. It blinks rapidly with each tongue lash. In between each blink I spot my reflection: emaciated beneath the ghostly patina of sand, ripped jeans marbled with blood, one-armed t-shirt loose and worm-eaten, hair matted down against the head with the ashy plaster of oil and desert, purple lips blanched to periwinkle. There's something else in the large eyes besides me, in the distance, colors strident even through the obsidian lens, its size and elongated shape distorted by the fish-eye reflection.

"I know what you're thinking." The serpentine form stirs in the eye mirror. "'How is it I'm still alive?' Well, you have me to thank for that." At once soothing and unctuous, the voice speaks in subtly-intoned Chinese.

The dog growls as I turn.

Coiled on the sand, its crocodile jaws resting on interdigitating claws, eyes a marble of roiling white and celeste fire half-shaded by scaly lids, steam curling out of every orifice of its body, spiny tail flicking up a cloud of sand—the dragon stares back at me.

As I cower back against the dog, wide-eyed, the rainbow-scaled monster unfolds its claws, revealing a bamboo leaf cigar, places it in the corner of its mouth, and puffs luxuriantly.

"It wasn't my intention to startle you."

I open my mouth to speak, but no sound escapes.

"A 'thank you' would be in order. If it were not for my intervention, you would certainly have become oasis food. The dog helped, of course, but only with my strong encouragement."

Viewed from the front, it's difficult to read the dragon's expression, all that's visible being the teeth, the fiery white mane and wispy beard, and those eyes with their mesmerizing purls of fire, but as it turns its head, blowing the cigar smoke away from me, I can see its broad, toothy smile—row after row of bone swords.

"Okay." I clear my throat. "In that case: thanks." My eyes wander over the many loops and knots of its endless body, failing to grasp its full length.

"Dog, go and fetch our friend something to eat."

Though seeming reluctant to obey orders, the dog finally huffs and saunters off, the earth trembling beneath its massive paws. It soon reaches a distant floral grove, which I don't recall having seen before when I'd fallen to my knees and slit my wrist, but at the time I hadn't been aware of much else besides the plodding movement of my body up and down the dunes. Remembering what had happened, I have the impression of viewing a black and white film; silent, grainy, devoid of any sense but the simple flickering square of vision.

While the Alsatian busies itself with its task, the dragon rests its head in the crook of a dwarfish arm, its smoldering eyes still locked onto me. Unsettled by its gaze, I rip off a portion of my right sleeve, beat as much sand out of it as possible, and wrap up the cleaned wound, securing one end with clenched teeth and using my right hand to tie a snug knot. I use the opportunity to scan the ground around me for the razor.

Nowhere in sight.

The dog returns with a beach ball of a mushroom clenched in its jaws, drops it on the ground, and nudges it towards me. In the dying light of the day, the fungus glows only weakly. I remember having seen such mushrooms before when I'd ventured into the oasis of the dead bull—large, pockmarked puffballs growing in bulbous clumps—and hadn't for a second considered eating one.

"Well, go ahead and eat up. It won't hurt you, and you do look famished."

I lift the mushroom, spongy and unexpectedly lightweight, rotating it to find an area clear of drool and sand. When at last I settle on a dry spot, for good measure I wipe it with my hand, then start to take a bite, when my lips sting from stretching too wide. Instead, I pinch off a piece and place it on my tongue, testing the texture and flavor.

Chewy, woody.

"Tastes like a mushroom," I mumble, relieved, then tear off more pieces to pop into my mouth.

"Your first?" The dragon holds in the cigar smoke, then lets it drift out of its nostrils and eyes.

"Not exactly," I manage in between mouthfuls, watching as the dog returns to the grove to gobble up her own dinner. I turn back to the dragon. "I've had mushrooms before. Just nothing like this. Saw these earlier but wasn't sure if they were safe. I suppose I still might not know for a while." Each word stings, but it's nice to talk. How long, how many days has it been since I spoke with someone—or some*thing*?

"The dog seems to likes them, but then again, dogs do not discriminate when it comes to food."

"I guess I'm feeling a little gun shy." I stuff in a piece of puffball. "I ate a flower a few days back. Didn't go so well." Another bite. "I've been wandering for days it seems with nothing to eat or drink. I should've been dead long ago.”

“Well, you’d better eat your fill.” It points its cigar at me, the blue of its unblinking eyes deepening.

“Okay…” Something in the look makes my skin crawl. I lapse into silence and continue eating, listening to the slurping and gnashing of the dog at the oasis, wishing it would hurry and return, all the while watching the dragon out of the corner of my eye. What the hell is this thing I’m conversing with? A freight truck?

“By the way”—I turn to the dragon—“do you know how to get to Jefferson Avenue from here? I’m trying to find my apartment building.”

“Jefferson Avenue?” it laughs. “How long did you say you’ve been wandering around? Days?”

My chewing slows. “What do you mean? Are we not near… I haven’t entered Canada, have I?”

“Canada? That’s even better.” The dragon puffs. “You wards are so full of surprises, but I have to say that you, girl, have been particularly slow to catch on.”

I gulp down a large bit of unchewed mushroom. My throat feels thick, resistant.

The gourmand’s soundtrack ends, and the dog trots back over and lies down beside me, resting her muzzle on her forepaws. I look over at the dog, wondering if she can understand the conversation. She had, after all, followed instructions more complicated than a simple “Fetch!”

“Well, where am I?”

“How about I give you a hint and test how clever you are? A hint, mind you, about where we are *not*.” Without waiting for a response, it gestures towards the sky. “Look up. That’s right. Away from the mountains, towards those dunes on the horizon. You see those three bright stars in succession? Directly above the middle one surrounded by a pentagon of stars, what do you see?”

A sapphire star. No, not a star. It doesn’t blink.

The word is on my lips, though I hesitate uttering it. I'm afraid to. It's absurd.

"Earth?" I whisper finally. "You mean this isn't Earth?"

"I'm impressed. That was rather quick, though perhaps the hint was too obvious."

"No, wait. It's the acid, Jing. The acid. Did I even really slit my wrist?" I probe my arm beneath the makeshift bandage. The throbbing pain is all too real.

"Yes, the slitting of the wrist did happen."

"Okay… then it must be that I'm in the hospital—*that's* what it is I've been seeing!—and you're a doctor or nurse or something—or I'm in a coma—I don't know."

"Wrong again. Let's give you a hand and end this tedious guessing game. This is Psyche." It waves its cigar in a wide, encompassing circle.

"Of course it is." I click my tongue stud against the back of my teeth. "My psyche, altered by drugs."

"No, no. You misunderstand me: Psyche the asteroid, not psyche the mind of a solipsistic girl."

I blink.

"It's in the *asteroid belt*."

"Asteroid belt." I run my fingers through my sand-caked hair, disturbing an eye-stinging white rain. "Assuming I am on some asteroid, how exactly did I get here from Earth?"

"Oh, there are ways."

I pause to consider this vague response. The dog, body slumping, begins to snore. I look up at the darkening sky, the splendor of satellites, then turn back towards the dragon.

"Go ahead and ask," it sighs.

"It's just that the atmosphere here… Earth is the only planet with an atmosphere that can sustain life, at least the only one I'm aware of. If there were another in the Solar System—"

"The tedium is creeping back in, girl. Clearly there's an atmosphere, or else we would not be having this conversation."

I shake my head. "I've lost my mind. Simple as that."

"My advice would be for you to accept the situation you're in and move on from there. The sooner you stop questioning everything, the sooner we will begin to enjoy ourselves."

My chewing slows.

Enjoy ourselves. Enjoy ourselves.

"You said there are ways to get to Psyche from Earth. How exactly? And what about going back? How do I get out of this place?"

"I've not personally looked into these matters, but I imagine if you can come, you can leave. But anyway, let's not rush to parting when we've only just met. For example, we haven't even begun to discuss how you plan on repaying me."

"'Repaying you?'"

"Yes. For having saved your life. Surely there must be something owed for that tiniest of favors." It smiles, relishing the cigar smoke, over-pleased with itself.

"Well, I don't have anything to offer you, except three cigarettes"—I glance around and pick up my purse, eyes darting over the ground again, desperate to land on the razor—"a few hundred dollars Earth money"—no sign of it, probably the wind buried it along with the puddle of blood—"lipstick—"

"You do yourself little credit. You have plenty more to offer than these trivialities, and you are going to give me what is owed whether you want to or not. Don't worry: I won't hurt you as long as you acquiesce to my conditions."

"What conditions?"

It tosses the cigar stub, cracks the knuckles of its claws, and then rears up on its short hind legs, its sinuous back popping as it stretches up to its full height, tall as a mature oak, much larger than I had judged it when it had only been knotted in comfort on the sand. The idea of defending myself with a razor officially becomes ludicrous.

"I want you to feed me."

My heart skips. Of course. It's going to eat me. I've known this all along. Known it since I first laid eyes on those vicious crocodile jaws, the way the saliva glistens on them.

"Feed you?" At some point my hands had clawed into the sand. I manage to dislodge them. "You mean, like, um, give you mushrooms to eat?"

"Mushrooms?"

It twists back down with a flair. Standing on all four of its stunted arms and legs, it arches and shakes off the languor, then flicks a long, narrow tongue across the points of its teeth.

"No, not mushrooms," I whisper.

Those fangs would be wasted on mushrooms. However, even as this thought occurs to me, the dragon surprises me: "You will feed me consciousness, visions, your Earth energy."

It begins to slither around the dog and me, arms and legs tucked into its sides, an intense heat radiating out with it.

Consciousness? The vein in my temple begins to throb.

"The condition is this"—it disappears behind the hulking mound of the dog—"if you do not give me what I ask, I will suck your cortex out through your eye socket." Its head pokes around from behind the dog, gnashing teeth inches from my nose, the heat building.

The dog stirs, growling, hackles bristling.

The dragon shifts course and rotates onto its back while still somehow managing to worm over the sand, then begins to coil around on top of the ring its long body has created. "Now, on the other hand, if you do feed me as requested, I will allow you to live on together with me on Psyche."

"Wonderful. Thanks."

"I do not prefer the excerebration route—it is rather messy—but I have no qualms with doing what is necessary."

It snakes under itself, creating a mesmerizing wall of shifting rainbow, the air roasting and reeking of sulfur. Drops of sweat start to bead my brow. Then it coils past, settling back down at its previous, more decorous, distance, eyes wide and burning. The sizzling heat washes away on the blessed wind.

"You may begin," it says, eyes flashing brighter than ever.

I look away, trying to clear my mind of thoughts of dragons, staring out towards the crystal blooms barely cresting the nearest dune.

Consciousness, visions, Earth energy...

The dwarf stars of its eyes have burned a hole in my mind, a black hole leaking out all thought, all reality... then it occurs to me—the visions of me.

Without realizing how it happens, I feel my mind swell, hear voices burbling out of the silence, watch as colors occlude my mind's eye. Something clenches and squeezes my head, and the flood of consciousness, suddenly much stronger and clearer than it had been before, overbears me, and the energy blasts out of me and into the dragon:

CHAPTER 2

In the conservatory cafeteria a tray of food clatters onto the red steel table in front of Jing, startling her out of her book.

"I've figured it out, Drummer Girl," a wiry black guy with rectangular glasses says as he slides into the chair across from Jing's. In his mid-20s, wearing a maroon cable-knit sweater and loose jeans, his eyes have somehow evaded the medicated gray fog that so characterizes other patients.

She puts the book down, one hopeful finger saving her place. "Hi, Henry."

"It's the Muzak."

She listens a moment to the jaunty, interweaving melodies of a movement from *The Brandenburg Concertos,* her eyes straying to the glass wall beside them, framing a parkscape of autumn-burned trees and a lily-bearded pond. The wall radiates cold.

"It's the editing." Henry spears a piece of lettuce from the salad compartment of his tray. "And the order of movement presentation." He tests a corner of the lettuce. "Haven't you wondered why they've pared the pieces down and rearranged them?" Satisfied, he proceeds to scarf down the salad.

She continues to listen and wrinkles her nose when she detects an editorial seam, eyes flicking to Henry's for confirmation. He nods, his high hair shaking.

She spoons up some cold tomato soup. "Maybe they ran some experiments on what types of rhythms and melodies stimulate the appetite—without, you know, *exciting* anyone. Seems the most reasonable explanation to me. What do you think?"

"No, Drummer Girl, their aim isn't stimulating our appetites: it's sealing up our neural wormholes."

"Sorry? Our… neural wormholes?" Her hopeful finger at last relents and lets the book go. She leans back and takes a sip of coffee. "That's a new one."

"William told me about them. Before. They're like eyes but responsive to subliminal signals instead of light."

"And those signals are hidden in the Muzak?"

He nods, finishing off his salad, glancing around warily.

"Well, who cares if mine's sealed?"

"Who *cares?* Jing, neural wormholes are of vital importance. Your spiritual livelihood is at stake! If you continue down this path the psychoengineers have laid out for us, it will end in total cleavage from your spirit form. Once that happens you'll be nothing more than a medicated robot like all the rest of—"

"Henry, lower your voice, dude," Jing whispers, noticing his voice already aroused the attention of one of the techs, difficult not to with the place so deserted.

"I've been developing a system to counteract the effects of the Muzak. Four hours of meditation a day, plus listening to as much atonal music as possible— Stockhausen, specifically."

She conceals her mouth with a bite of grilled cheese. "Waters is coming."

"You two doing all right here?" the man says, making marks on his clipboard, pausing halfway up the steps to their level. He has a linebacker's build, with a thick beard.

"Fine, Waters," Jing says.

"Henry?"

"What?" Henry says, with no attempt to mask his animosity.

"You sounded a little excited from below." He mounts the remaining steps.

"Just a fly in his salad," Jing cuts in, her foot

nudging Henry's.

"Fly, huh?" He scrutinizes the plate.

"I removed the distasteful thing," Henry snaps, a quiver escaping through his hair.

"Easy, man." Waters straightens and jots something on his clipboard. "Keep it down. Might disturb somebody. You know how these things are. One little fillip, the whole place is a frenzy."

"We'll keep it down," Jing says.

"Please do."

As Waters leaves them, Henry pulls out a cigarette with his pampered, long-fingered hands. Ghost lights it.

Jing, on cue, fishes her lighter out of her pocket and provides fire.

Henry leans in close, taking a long drag off his cigarette, and then shrouds them in a curtain of smoke. When he continues, a quieter conspirator has emerged. "Just hear me out, Jing. The meds, the therapy, all of the various methods they push on us here, it's all a ruse. All that matters is the music—the *Muzak*. Goldfield, Murai, Conway, they're all a part of this. Psycho-engineers. They want to sever us from our spirits. But there's another way—my way, *our* way. We're getting out of here, spiritual connections intact and fuck everyone else. How do you like that?"

"I'm intrigued, at least, but..." *You're unhinged, Henry.* She doesn't know how to speak the words.

"I need to teach you the proper techniques to open your mind and counteract the detrimental effects of the Muzak. Tomorrow evening during movie time, slip away, come to my room."

"Fine. Will do. Now, can we talk about something normal for once? Like books. Read anything interesting lately?"

"The library here is filled with nothing but propaganda," he scoffs.

"You want to borrow this one? *The Mind of a Mnemonist.* It's from the *outside.* Should be done by dinnertime."

"Forget it. From this point on, we shouldn't be seen too much together anyway. People might get ideas."

He extinguishes his cigarette in the puddle of salad dressing in his tray, then hops off, the majority of his food untouched.

She takes her time finishing her own meal, looking around at the scatter of patients, the barren garden plots and the bold-colored tables, like some inhabitable Mondrian. After, she cleans out her tray in the waste room, then winds down a twisting corridor to the front hall rotunda, a room from a much earlier era than the cafeteria—double staircases that weave in and out in a helix, chandelier like an inverted art deco skyscraper, intricately-patterned ceiling tiles of cream and ebony. She turns off down another hallway to the meds station and downs her pills in front of the nurse. Then she threads a meandering path by offices and vacant rooms, through abandoned courtyards and glass umbilicals, arriving at last at a stairwell tucked away in a far corner of the complex. There she nestles into the Oriel window seat extending over the courtyard, smoking and reading in the sunlight. The sounds of Glenbrook—footsteps, calming but authoritative tones of the techs, the ravings, the odd cathartic scream—are reduced to muted echoes here.

Several cigarettes fill the ashtray. The end of the book looms near, when reality breaks in with cold breath: the door on the second floor landing opens. Jing glances up to find a squat nurse leaning through the doorway.

Jing smiles questioningly, lip ring glinting. "What's up, Diaz?"

She pauses for suspense. "You have a visitor."

It takes her a moment to process this, and she frowns, stubbing out her cigarette. "Really? Who?"

"Didn't catch her name."

Jing freezes when she sees the girl seated before a coffee table in the visitation room, long mahogany hair gathered loosely over one shoulder, shining in the October sun. Absorbed in a thick book, brow furrowed, long legs crossed, all decked out in white—sweater, slacks, sneakers, even nail polish—she doesn't notice Jing. Her hands recoil into the sleeves of her hoodie. Through the arched windows beyond columns of smoke rise out of the Detroit skyline, a few of the building fires visible from here, others veiled in the valleys of the city. The window panes pulse with the forceful tugs of lake wind. Finally, Jing walks over and sits on the sofa across from her, watching her leaf through the book.

"I don't know how you can read this... Ooh, I recognize this one," she laughs, pointing at one of the Chinese characters. "You really failed me as a teacher, you know." She looks up at Jing and tosses the book down on the coffee table.

"You came."

"Surprise." The girl shrugs. She's tall, her shrugs exaggerated.

"Yeah, surprise. Traffic must have been terrible."

The girl's emerald eyes sparkle. "This place hasn't changed you, I'm glad to see."

"You're supposed to say something like 'Oh, you're looking much better these days'—some shit like that."

"What's with the hair?"

Jing runs a hand through the unevenly cropped hair. "Did it myself. The beautician that comes here doesn't quite get what I'm going for. No good?"

"They let you have scissors?"

"Believe me, Penn, anytime I want to shave my legs or cut my hair, there's a team of supervisors standing around to make it awkward."

"Fun stuff. I swung by your place to pick up some goodies." She nods towards the book and leans over to rifle through a bag beside the chair. "By the way, your jungle was on the brink of desiccation. I gave it a good soaking."

"Thanks," Jing says, picking up the book and flipping through it. "I'd forgotten all about the jungle."

Penn tucks a wayward strand of hair behind her ear. "I also brought your Walkman, Discman, CDs, tapes, sheet music, got you a couple of sweaters, green tea (which, I might add, the guard downstairs nearly confiscated), chocolate, cigarettes." At the end of the inventory, she pulls out a carton of Camels and makes it dance. "If you need anything else…"

"This is great."

"I know it… took me a while—"

"Forget it. I mean, I get it." She pauses. "You have no idea how good it is looking at you—a different face from the loopy ones they furnish this place with."

"How is it then—you know—*in here*?"

"Not so bad. You know Henry's here? Small world, right?" She pulls out her cigarettes, lights one, and tosses the pack to Penn. "What about you? What's going on back in reality?"

"Nothing much. For a while I was playing with a few people." Penn flicks the pack, fishes a cigarette out with her mouth, and leans across the table, adding between clenched lips: "Nothing serious."

Jing meets Penn halfway over the coffee table, distracted by the warmth of lavender as she lights the cigarette. "With whom?"

"No one you know. No one from the Compound." Penn exhales, reclining back. "Just a temporary diversion.

Jing clicks the tongue stud against her teeth as she ashes.

Penn clears her throat. "Anyone else come to see you?"

"You're my first."

"Family?"

"They tell me my dad was here right after I was 'initiated' into the Glenbrook fold. I was still at my worst then; really don't remember much. Guess he hasn't had time to come back. Anyway, forget that. Why don't I give you the grand tour?"

As they descend the rotunda helix, the contrapuntal meandering of violas and violins drifts up to greet them. Penn dons a pair of noise-cancelling headphones, and their conversation comes to a momentary halt. They maze down through the north wing to a nurses' station at a hallway junction, where Diaz is monitoring the dayroom across the way. There, a gameshow blares out of a rabbit-eared television for the benefit of several glassy-eyed patients. White daylight streams in through the picture window, outlining their rigid faces. A few others sit crinkling newspapers or fanning out hands of cards. Plastered onto the wall in the back of the room, a white banner stresses in green cursive:

> The Glenbrook philosophy:
> -Biopsychosocial integration
> -Proactive attitude
> -Team trust

"I'm going to show my friend around for a few minutes. Also, I'll probably be skipping group therapy today."

"Just sign her in," is Diaz's automated reply. Then, registering the latter part of what Jing has said, the shade of scrutiny descends. "Did you request permission through your team?"

"No."

"Then you're attending group."

Jing checks the clock on the wall, then she snaps her fingers in front of Penn's face to direct her attention from the dayroom to the sign-in sheet. While Penn's signing in, Jing removes the headphones for her and says,

"You're safe."

Penn smiles conscientiously.

They walk down the corridor. Most of the doors are shut, but through the few open ones they glimpse catatonics frozen in bizarre postures or wrinkle their noses at the cloaked stench of excrement.

"It feels freer than I imagined it would," Penn notes. "I mean they just let me in here like this?"

"Well, it's a bit more complicated than that. This is me."

Jing unlocks the door and lets her friend in. Penn stands on the threshold for a few seconds, scanning the room before entering. It's furnished with two single beds set against opposite walls and generally two of everything, giving it a college dorm flavor—with the exception of the double-grated prison windows overlooking the brick wall of another wing of the Glenbrook complex.

Penn explores the tiny bathroom first, flicking the light on and off. "What do you mean by 'complicated?'"

"There's this... level system. Very video gamey. The higher up you are, the more privileges you have."

"Yeah? What's your level?"

"B2. Don't I look like a B2 to you?"

Penn's head pops out of the bathroom. "Is B good?"

"Like in school. All the Fs are upstairs in the Clouds, where they dope you up to the eyeballs. If it weren't for my B, I couldn't light my own cigarettes or take you outside the visitation room. And the numbers indicate how much money I'm allotted per week, though there's nothing interesting to spend your money on here—batteries, candy bars."

"Quite a little society they've got going on here." Penn wanders into the bedroom and compares the two sides of the room. Masses of dark clothes lesion the bed and bedside table on the left, and a puzzle of books on the windowsill blot out the window behind them, in contrast to the austerity of the right side, the stripped-down bed. "Where's your roommate?"

"No roommate—more rooms than patients here."

Penn goes to Jing's bedside, cocking her head to read the book titles in their various orientations. At that moment the distant background noise from the dayroom disrupts into commotion, first one patient shouting obscenities, then another bursting into tears, and several more joining into a chorus of yelling and accusations. Jing shuts the door, though doing so fails to keep out the discord. Her friend sits on the bed, listening. Jing sets the bag Penn brought on the opposite bed. Several minutes pass before quiet prevails.

"I'd apologize, but I suspect you've been waiting for something like that to happen since you arrived."

Penn nods, eyes wide, the brightest points in the room. "You need to get out of here. Is that... in the works?

"That's up to my treatment team. They have me on a bunch of different meds right now—antidepressants, anticonvulsants, antipsychotics, anti-you-name-its—but my doctor hasn't discussed diagnosis or prognosis with me."

"Really?" Penn sets back on her elbows. "It's been nearly two months already, and they haven't told you what's wrong with you yet?"

Jing nods, suppressing a smile. "Man, good thing the Thought Police didn't just hear that."

Penn shrugs, turning back to the books and withdrawing a slender, red piece from the puzzle. "*The Glenbrook Bible*," she reads. Flips through it. "'No physical contact between patients aside from handshakes and high-fives.' You get a lot of high-fives, Jingy?"

"I can't tell if you're mocking this place in general or just me in particular."

She rolls over onto her stomach, engrossed in the book. "I'm just trying to get a sense of what your world is like."

As she continues reading, Jing walks over and sits beside her on the bed, grabs a pen off the desk, takes a hold of Penn's wrist, and carefully writes a string of Chinese characters on the pale flesh all the way down to the elbow. Penn looks up from the patient manual, watching Jing write and at last notices the tip of the scar edging beyond her sweatshirt cuff. She hooks the sleeve with her finger and lowers it, slowly revealing more and more, eyes widening as she stretches it all the way down to the elbow. Then she rotates the wrist to study it better, caressing the tattooed skin, the intricate jungle split into two.

Jing puts the pen down, the writing unfinished. Covering her own arm back up, she turns away and lights a cigarette.

"I'm sorry," Penn whispers, studying the characters Jing had written. "It took me so long to come."

"You're here now. That means a lot."

"I'm such a shitty friend. It wasn't easy for me. I mean, do you want to... do you want to talk about what happened?"

Jing shakes her head.

"Sorry. I don't know what I'm supposed to say or not say. I feel like I needed somebody to coach me before I came to visit you."

"Stop apologizing. Honestly, say anything you like. Believe me, it's a relief to hear your voice, unfiltered—not the child-safety-locked euphemism they pad around here."

Penn sits up, leans her head into Jing's line of sight, wrinkling her angular nose. "What next, crazy?"

Jing waves her cigarette in a circle. "The tour resumes."

"Dope. High-five?" She holds up her hand.

Jing misses, smacking Penn on the forehead. "High-five."

By the time the two girls reach the nurses' station,

the dayroom excitement has quelled, several of the patients conspicuously absent.

"Diaz, can we walk around the grounds?" Jing asks.

The nurse frowns. "What level are you, Jing?"

"I take that as a no?"

"Just wait a few minutes. All the techs are... otherwise engaged right now." She glances meaningfully towards the disordered dayroom.

Eventually, Waters returns from the Clouds. A curious look passes between Penn and Waters, but when Penn opens her mouth to speak, Waters turns towards Diaz to report on the state of the two patients he'd brought upstairs. Diaz relays Jing's request, and with some relief at the prospect of getting some fresh air, he agrees to escort the two girls around the grounds.

As they amble down the stairs, back in the music-ridden zone, Penn dons her headphones again.

"What is that?" she asks, voice overloud.

"J. S. B.," Jing shouts back. "*The Brandenburg Massacres*. They pipe it in here and the cafeteria twenty-four seven."

More sheets to sign at the front desk, then they exit into the brisk, windy autumn. Jing, pulling up her hood and looping her arm through Penn's, guides her over the gravel driveway to one of the walking paths that rambles over the extensive grounds, Waters hanging back to allow them some privacy.

They walk first past the west wing of the main building, where the cafeteria and most of the offices are located, turn around the far edge and past two squat, detached buildings, both built in a more utilitarian style than the main building.

"Gym and community center," Jing informs her friend. "And over there is the staff residence," she adds, pointing beyond to a Queen Anne-style house with wraparound front porch and round tower. From here they walk behind the sprawling brownstone structure of the main building, past the murky pond and continue across a field, into a village of bungalows. Doors hanging off their hinges. Geese waddling in and out, excreting where they please. Visible through the shattered windows are overturned mattresses, empty refrigerators, faded walls spotted with vivid squares of color where art had once absorbed the sunshine.

"The Rota Wellness Village."

The path weaves on into the woods, past the shattered frame of a greenhouse, and beneath a colonnade of sugar maple supporting a brilliant yellow ceiling. Their footsteps crunch and sweep through the thick layer of freshly-fallen leaves, circumambulating a rope's course and an outdoor retreat with log seats and a small stage. During the walk, Jing catches faint smears of classical music like glimmers of sunshine through the canopy.

The Brandenburg Concertos? she wonders, remembering her conversation with Henry earlier that day. The music seems to be too faint to irritate Penn.

They cross a stream and then wind along a razor-wire-topped stone wall. Here, with the polite buffer of the babbling creek, Jing casts a look over her shoulder to find Waters still maintaining his polite distance, holding his clipboard behind his back, club tucked into his belt, keen on the metallic flashes of fish in the water.

Clearing her throat, Jing turns back to Penn. "You went to the funeral?"

Penn nods.

A pause as they continue on.

"Bet it was well-attended."

"Understatement of the year."

Jing feels around for the appropriate thing to say. "Did you play something?" she manages through her constricting throat.

Penn nods. "Some acoustic stuff. Too bad you couldn't've been there."

"Yeah, you say that but—"

"But nothing. You had just as much a right to be

there as anyone else. More so.”

Jing falls into silence, gazing at the rippling water, the slick stones, the spongy moss.

“Jing, do you remember any of the details from that night?”

“Not really.” Jing clicks the tongue stud and shuffles around some leaves.

“You don’t remember the show?” Penn pursues.

“I have sort of... vague impressions of it.”

“And afterwards?”

“Mmm...”

“You don’t remember what you said to me?”

“I bet it was something insane, right?”

“You could say that.”

“Well, what was it? Maybe it’ll help me remember other details.”

Penn takes too long replying, and when she does finally speak, she looks away from Jing, ahead into the woods.

“You mentioned something called a memoryfish.”

The word guides both sets of their eyes to the stream. The water crests over the stones so thinly, they seem to be encased in trembling gelatin.

“Memoryfish?”

“You asked me to keep something safe for you, something you’d ‘need to return.’ Your words. I should’ve known then.”

“What are you talking about?”

“I could tell something was wrong, should have done something, prevented what was going to happen, but I was ill—you know how it is after shows. I’d seen you before drunk, high, tripping, coked up, whatever-the-fucking—but that night... something else entirely—”

CHAPTER 3

The stream of visions severs, leaving me breathless, sprawled against the dog. It's unclear how much time has passed. The sun has set behind the mountains, the first stars beginning to shine, the air cold. Not sure if it had been on the verge of setting or rising when I'd begun feeding the dragon.

The dog is fast asleep, a low, rhythmic snore soothing me as I prop myself up against her side. Similarly, the dragon, flattened out on the sand, breathes deep, expelling twin curls of smoke, eyes sealed. The visions must have rendered both of us unconscious.

The celeste orbs flash open, head whirling towards me, upsetting an eddy of sand, but it regains its composure. "You've stopped. Please continue. I've digested your consciousness and am ready for more."

"I-I can't." My lips part like a crusted wound splitting open. "I'm exhausted. I need to sleep."

"Nonsense." It reaches into a small, black satchel tied around its wrist; it pulses and ripples, alive. The dragon's dinky tyrannosaur fingers pull out a long red leaf and drop into it some dried grass. "Sleep now and I might lose you for good." It rolls a cigarette, clamps it between its teeth, blows a thin jet of fire out of its nose, igniting the tip, and samples the smoke.

"I must've lost a lot of blood. A few more meals, a day's rest, then I can probably give you more."

"I need something more substantial than what you've given me." It licks its lips, eyes paling to a white burn.

"Don't worry. There's more. Much more. I can feel it back there... pressing against me, but I need more time, need to fully recover."

It lapses into silence, eyes narrowing to slits of light, smoke (whether cigar or dragon, I cannot tell) spilling out of the crevices between its long, needle-like teeth, then says, "Very well"—it ripples up onto its short haunches and stretches out its sinuous body to full length—"I'm going for a fly. When I return, you'll feed me until I'm satisfied." Then the impressive mass of the dragon stirs, the knot loosening, and lifts impossibly into the air, flipping and coiling, upsetting eddies of sand around us. Then it streams off like a ribbon of silk held aloft on the wind.

As the air settles, the dog whimpers a low whimper.

I turn and find her large, black eyes half-opened, regarding me. As I settle down against her thigh, the fluffy tail blankets me, the fur cool at first but gradually warming against my body, a relief against the gathering chill. It's the first time I've felt truly comfortable, even secure, since waking in this strange place.

Morning is announced by the lifting of the tail.

As the dog gathers up its bulk, I plop down. She stretches over me, shaking off a layer of hoarfrost from snout to tail, then seeks out the oasis, its glow dulled in the grayish-pink morning. I roll over and cling to the circle of unfrozen, dog-smelling sand for some time, shivering in the ice-barbed wind.

I tuck my sleeveless arms inside my shirt, the left flashing pain from the worm bite and razor cut. I rub them as they cradle my breasts, careful not to aggravate the wounds.

With a few abortive attempts, I manage to stand, huddling slantwise into the wind.

A hot shower, coffee, hoodie—Xanadu.

The barren view stretches before me, flat, veined with rivulets of wind, the occasional weathered rock out-cropping dotting the landscape like victims of exposure devoured by insects, and beyond everything those dizzying crystalline peaks with their now gentle emanations of color. Behind me are the shores of the rolling white dunes, the oasis fringing the shoreline.

The dragon is still gone, I find with relief. Whatever it was that had happened last night—mind- or consciousness-feeding—had felt uncomfortably intimate. I wonder if the dragon had seen and heard what I had, every secret detail about Jing/me. And how exactly had I fed it? Afterwards, I'd felt hollowed out, even more exhausted than I'd been after several days of traversing the desert.

I snatch up my purse and limp over to the rime-candied oasis, sneakers cracking the sand's icy pall. Indifferent to my approach, the dog continues to scarf down ice-capped mushrooms, glassy grasses, and glazed flowers. I find a cactus resembling the one I'd suckled from the previous evening. The arm tears away with a satisfying rip, and an icy slush oozes out. I drink and drink, lips screaming in pain, pausing only for a brain freeze to melt away. I forage for mushrooms, careful to stick to the puffballs I now know won't kill me, tearing off small bits to stuff between my cracked lips; my body starts to come alive again.

During breakfast, my mind sorts through what I'd experienced last night. A hallucination? A dream?

It certainly wasn't memory. It had been full of familiar details, but transplanted into an alien environment. Penn and Jing/me had discussed a funeral and a number of other things that didn't quite connect, and when Penn had prompted her, Jing had been just as unclear about what had happened "that night" (the night of the show) as I am now. In addition to Penn, Henry was a familiar face, but the others I'd seen, all of which registered with mundanity in Jing's mind, failed to spark anything inside me.

One curious point about this dream or vision, perhaps the point that had made it wholly unlike a memory or any dream I've ever had, is that I'd experienced it outside myself, almost as if I'd been cast off shadow-like. Despite this fact, I'd been privy to more than just the overt conversation and behaviors of the version of me I'd seen, sometimes experiencing her thoughts as if they were my own. I could almost see the shine or dimness of her memories as mind mists grew dense or dispersed with the various topics discussed. During lunch I could at times taste the creamy tomato soup, the buttery grilled cheese, and the bitter coffee. However, there'd been no such sensation-sharing with others around her; I could not taste the other patients' meals nor read Penn's thoughts. Clearly, it was this other Jing I was tethered to.

As for the location, the name "Glenbrook" was stamped into every wall and book in the place like a cattleman's brand on his drove. Glenbrook, the name of a mental institution in the outskirts of Detroit. That's where they'd taken Henry after his brother died, and not knowing him very well, I'd never paid him a visit. Thought about it (for what that's worth), but could never bring myself to go.

I ruminate on a bite of mushroom, staring into the oasis's sparkling rose echoes of dawn. If the cold or something else doesn't kill me, if I live to see another vision, maybe I'll learn more.

After eating, I extract a long fiber from the cactus arm and floss my teeth with it, then rinse with more of the viscous cactus juice. Mouth clean, I search the oasis for something to help with my hair. After all, if I had just spent the night in some abandoned urban lot hallucinating about dragons and giant insects and mental asylums, and am not actually stranded on an asteroid, I should try to make myself look as non-deranged as possible for when I do finally run into another human.

Need to balance both options until I'm sure of the truth.

An enormous succulent with complex blue dendrites beckons to me amongst the rest of the brush. I tear off one of the branching clumps and work it through my hair, unknotting the tangles and clearing out much of the sand, then store the makeshift comb in my purse. Finally, I apply some lipstick to my mouth, wincing, but to be fair, the pain has improved since last night.

When the dog finishes eating, she relieves herself, and I do the same in the densest part of the oasis. As I squat there, on vigilant lookout for worms, I notice a stone on the ground beneath the melting frost, flashing in the morning light.

When I attempt to pick it up, I find it anchored in the sand. After a little digging, I recognize the mottled pattern of the polished snakewood.

My knife.

"How in the hell..." I wonder, unearthing it and brushing off the few small bugs feeding on the caked blood of the blade.

It takes some effort to scrape off the stubborn coating of blood, but when it's done I study my reflection, fixing the edges of my lips and inspecting my teeth. I notice the background flanking me in the narrow slit and slowly maneuver the razor so I can see more—spidery jellyfish, stalagmite fungi, scurrying vermin that resemble the decapitated heads of chess pieces. If mirrors hold the power to dispel illusions, then... but of course they don't.

Suddenly, I notice an eerie quiet has settled over the oasis. I fold up the knife and return it to my purse. Light up a cigarette, wondering what it is that's wrong.

The dog. I can't hear it anymore.

The oasis is much too small to hide a beast as large as the Alsatian, so I rush out to the edge of the oasis, covering my mouth and nose to filter out the overpowering reek of piss, and scan the horizon. Sure enough, there it is, trotting at a good clip towards the mountains.

"Hey! Wait up!"

It either ignores or can't hear me.

I extinguish the cigarette and tuck it behind my ear. Not knowing when I'll next encounter another of these oases, I hurriedly gather up several more arms of cacti and hack to pieces a number of puffballs, and stuff them into my purse. By the time I've finished, the dog has shrunk to a pale blob on the horizon, nearly absorbed into the shining white plane of ice and sand.

Limping as fast as I can, I manage to catch up after about an hour. She lopes along at an easy canter, but with our size disparity, and me plagued by wounds, this pace won't be possible for me to sustain for long. Even so, I push myself to jog at her side, determined to stick with this creature.

In this slow dawn, the frost lingers over the sand.

Every crunch of ice beneath my thin sneakers excites waves of gooseflesh. The wind brutalizes with ice- and sand-flecked lashes. My sinuses burn with each breath, but the exercise keeps me warm.

"I'm freezing," I say at last to the dog, unable to contain myself any longer.

The beast doesn't even blink, gaze set on the mountains.

"And my bite is bothering me. I think it might be infected."

No response.

We continue on in silence for some time, while the many questions about my situation eat away at me. Although relentless with its pace, I can't forget that the dog (despite the dragon's claim) seemed to be the one that brought me back from the dead—licked my wounds, fed me, provided me with warmth throughout the night. Thus, I can't help feeling it might have my best interests at heart.

"Why are you heading towards the mountains?"

No response.

"This place, Psyche, it's not really an asteroid, is it? It must be part of Detroit."

Silence.

"Well, if this is Psyche, how did I get here? For that matter, how did *you* get here? Were you born here? Do you have a family or friends, I mean aside from the dragon? You know, other elephant dogs or something? *Is* the dragon even your friend?"

No response.

"How is it that the dragon can speak and you can't? And Chinese? Why Chinese?" My voice races, mind trying to outdistance the pain and discomfort. "Why won't you speak to me? I know you can understand what I'm saying... Can we rest? Or maybe you could let me ride on your back for a while. I know that sounds rude, but... you probably wouldn't even notice, small as I am."

And so I rattle on, childish frustration compounded by the overwhelming number of questions I have spiraling down into the dog's stony silence. Perhaps, after all, I wouldn't mind the return of the dragon. So many more things I need to know about this place. After having come to the conclusion that questioning reality is pointless (and tedious, in the dragon's words), my only choice is to work with whatever bizarre logic Psyche throws my way.

Fantasy or reality, I need to start learning about this place if I want to figure out how to escape.

Hours of trekking later, the sun finally clears the horizon but still only drifts low to the south.

The frost melts.

I breathe easier.

Cold, at least for now, can be marked off the list of problems.

Occasionally I eat puffball bits or pull out a cactus arm and drink. When the arms are bled dry, I salvage some of the long fibers to floss with later and toss the rest to lighten the load. Attempts to offer the dog a snack are met with rebuffs (of course, the bitesize mushrooms would be plankton in the massive dog's jaws), but by what seems to be midday, at the sight of a small copse, the dog veers off course and approaches a clump of ferns with leaves that coil and straighten as if on a timer. She scarfs them down with grotesque, canine zeal, then advances onto a curtain of seaweedy vines. Then a patch of apricot-colored grass. When she's had her fill, she paws over a cactus, pokes her snout into the well-like base, lapping up the juices, then eats the cactus itself, spines and all. Afterwards, she gluts on mushrooms, not merely the puffballs, but massive toadstools as well.

After my own much more restrained meal, I restock my purse with what edible bits the dog has missed. Then I undress my wounds, clean the bandages with cactus juice, and rewrap them. Afterwards I take a seat on a rock and smoke the rest of my morning cigarette, captivated by the feeding beast, who has already cleared out many square yards of vegetation. Wondering if the meal will ever end, I decide to explore the oasis a bit. Maybe I can find something useful, a weapon perhaps or material to cover my body for when the cold returns.

Inside the dense, vibrant copse, a fetid reek assaults my nose. My tongue sticks in my throat, and I draw my shirt collar over my face as I continue onward. The worms are not particularly active here, most of them small and lethargic. Deeper and deeper into the oasis, past giant flowers with droopy black petals, trees covered in pulsating gossamer, puddles of inching gelatin, green hedges reminiscent of sushi grass, the underbrush grows thicker, the putrescence stronger; I'm careful to keep a line of sight with the dog, listening throughout the excursion for its constant snorting and slurping as its feast stretches on.

Soon I became aware of the chatter of those flesh-eating worms and spot ahead a towering, frenzied mass of them.

A nest?

Though the sound of their gnashing mouthparts is what initially attracts my attention to the luminescent worms, I notice something even more curious at the peak of the mound staring out at me: a human-sized skull. Beyond its size, however, the resemblance with a human ends. Judging by the shape of its snout, this creature must have relied far more on its sense of smell than a human would have. The spacing of the teeth is striking: four giant incisors crowded together in the front, a gap in the jawbone, then rows of smaller molars and premolars towards the back.

"Hello."

The nasal voice oozes out of the rattling skull. The skeleton limps bipedally out of the thick underbrush, hunched over, a moldy brown pelt hanging off its deformed frame, waves of feasting insects cascading off the side of its body. As it swats at the worms, the putrescence lashes me anew, thick, hot tendrils of it. Eyes watering, gagging, I press the crook of my elbow into my nose and mouth, and fumble for the razor.

Then I hesitate.

Its claws raised as a show of peace, I realize it's not a skeleton after all, but a two-headed rat, its right head intact, the other skeletal and hanging limp. The flesh surrounding the skull has decayed almost completely, and the entire left side of its body has wilted, bone exposed in places, rotten, grainy viscera slopping through.

"Easy. Easy. We don't mean you any harm." Hobbling, the rat experiments toward me.

"No closer," I warn. I could simply run, yet something fixes me to the spot: The rat can talk, and despite its grotesque appearance, it seems... friendly?

"We thought we would shake hands—that's all. We realize that is how you humans greet one another."

"I-I don't think so."

"Oh, we see. It must be the chatterboxes that bother you," it muses, the right head talking while the left shakes, its teeth clacking together. As if in confirmation, a few more chattering worms tumble out of the skull and scatter when it tries to stomp them. "Our apologies. It happens quite often these days. We sit for a spell to rest and then wake up covered in the pests. It was all barren rock when we sat down to rest yesterday. Here, let us rid ourselves of these worms, then we can make proper introductions."

It continues to swat at the worms, inspecting itself all over, lurching hemiplegically. Each effort on its part, of course, dispatches fresh waves of olfactory horror my way, and I take this chance to quickly and quietly take my leave, back through the oasis the way I'd come.

Emerging from the brush and gasping for air, I find the dog stretching and content, her food orgy at last concluded. Once I've reached the verge, I glance back into the neon-fissured shadows of the oasis.

All barren rock yesterday? Is that what it had said?

Glimpsing its shiny fur through the branches of the exotic plants, prattling on as if it had not yet noticed I had left, I'm overcome with a strange admixture of revulsion and pity for this rat so inexplicably lingering on at the brink of death.

It is at first with relief that I follow the dog onward, wanting to put as much distance between us and the spreading stench of the oasis. But soon, my provisions consumed, I'm not so sure I've made the right choice.

We've reached a region of bitter flats, not an oasis in sight. The day has grown hot, but an unnatural chill runs through me, my hands clammy. At some point the wrist wound has reopened, and I tighten the wet bandages and press it against my belly. My leg has stiffened, too excruciating to flex, my foot raking along the ground. I focus on the expansive crown of mountains, hovering footless out of the empty waver of heat, try to shut out all else, but it's a losing battle. The dog tireless.

Still, I keep pushing myself on, treading through a mire of pain, each step laden with pounds of extra, mucky weight. My mind cycles back through the scene from the oasis, see the horrendous worm guzzling my blood. The more my leg agonizes, the more wild the image becomes, the worm mutating, sprouting spines and tentacles like that monstrous caterpillar I'd seen days ago. The wound, too, grows and grows—at least it does so in my mind. I don't have the courage to inspect it, what must be glowing red branches of infection splintering down my leg.

I want to return to Glenbrook, even if it means I have to stand outside myself for the rest of my life—that's fine—doesn't hurt that way—can't feel pain if you're not inside yourself—God, I can feel it coming—going to be sick, going to collapse, going to be buried by the wind and sand.

I look down at the left arm, now pressed tight against my body, see the pus-pink blood stain spreading over my shirt and down my jeans, and fall onto the sand and vomit. Light-headed, I lift my unsteady gaze towards the horizon. Everything is doubled, the crystalline mountains two rows of titanic teeth grinding away at the world, the setting suns a pair of flaming eyes, the twin dogs fleeting sunspots.

"Hey..."

The dogs do not hear, fading into the sunsets. The suns finally touch down on the mountains, and the world is set ablaze with rainbow fire. The sand and sky and the dogs blacken in contrast, then the suns peer out from behind the peaks—the world set aright again.

What will happen if the dragon returns without the

dog nearby?

Feels like the first lucid thought I've had in hours. Refocuses my vision.

Maybe last night it was the dog's presence that had kept the dragon at bay.

What was the word the dragon had used? Excerebration. Didn't want to take the excerebration route. I'm not quite clear on what it means, but sounds like it involves brains exiting my head.

The giant creature mounts the slope of a high dune in the distance, the first such dune we've met all day, the end of the hard flats and the beginning of softer sand. Beyond that peak, it'll be out of sight for good.

"Hey, dog!"

Nothing.

Brains shooting out of my eye sockets and nostrils and mouth. Excerebration. Such a dusty word for such gruesomeness.

"Dog!" I grunt with more force.

It pauses, glancing back, but then continues on unconcerned over the dune's apex.

"Stop! For fuck's sake!"

For a minute there's nothing but wind and dying light, a gorgeous final curtain to my life. Then, her infinitesimal form germinates, and though I can't make out her features, the speck, the seed, seems to consider me, consider whether it's worth turning around.

I roll onto my back, away from the vomit, cursing myself, unwrapping the bandage to survey the throbbing wreckage—my arm is spread ghastly wide, the fire of infection burning all the surrounding tattoo.

I'm sick again.

Time smears.

The dog's giant head looms into my field of view; with a huff she gathers me into the hot biome of her jaws, the rounded tips of her large, slick teeth jutting into my back. As she carries me, I stare up at her impassive eye and pat the side of her snout with its fishbone-thick, black whiskers. After several minutes of the rocking, up-down motion, she deposits me near an oasis full of twisting cacti and towering redcap mushrooms, giant tapeworms waving flag-like from their stalks. The dog licks my troubling wound for a bit. Then the white head disappears again, leaving me with the citrine floral glow and the chorus of alien insects.

I've nearly dozed off by the time she returns, but she licks my face till I've roused. She then pushes a large puffball onto my chest. Ravenous, I bury my face into it, ignoring the sting of my cracked lips. She's also brought another cactus arm dripping cool water. Starved as I am, the few bites I take merely make me queasy, and I lie back against the dog as she munches on various bits, pull the tail over my shivering body, unable to decide if warmth or cool feels better.

The red sun has all this time clung to the mountain peaks like a jewel set into a crown, waiting there with suspense, passing in and out of lacy arches of crystal, the world by turns cast in opaline glaze, and a red and black chiaroscuro horrorshow. The darkness and cold continue to gather as other satellites careen through the golden sky, forms I'd seen earlier on in Psyche but had failed to make sense of at the time. Now, I realize with feverish amazement that what I'm seeing is a pod of a hundred or so irregularly-shaped planetoids—other asteroids, covered in craters and planes of frost and forests of golden lichen—so close I can almost hear them drifting along, rotating, revolving around each other in complex gravitational hierarchies. Impossible. The tableau is impossible, the planetoids sunlit from varying angles, sometimes intersecting each other without celestial catastrophe.

A rush of wind, the crisp snapping of a sail, they bring me back down to Psyche. An odor washes over me—smoke stacks, industrial waste, melted plastic—a dystopian bouquet.

"A smooth flight and all in all a productive journey. I

have returned as promised. Now, if you would be so kind as to continue to feed me, the night will be a pleasant one for all."

I continue staring at the sky, watching what seems to be a herd of mammoth trilobites roaming across a field of black gelatin, but now I'm mindful of those rainbow scales glinting in the farthest reaches of my peripheral vision. The dragon slithers in closer, ignoring the somnolent, warning growls of the dog, and rests its long jaws on its clawed fingers. Puffing on its cigar, it crafts smoke microcosms mirroring the complexity of the sky.

As I gaze above, I feel that strange sensation I'd felt the night before: not remembering, more like hearing an echo and then following along behind the echo as it passes by, being towed in its wake and at the same time reeling it in towards me, till my mind and the force synchronize, every nerve ending scintillated, every pathway seized in riot. As I relay them out towards the dragon, the visions of Earth overtake my senses:

CHAPTER 4

Fifteen or so patients sit in a circle of fold-out chairs in rec room north, behind them a stage and a stand-up piano, along one wall a blackboard where patients have vented their frustrations in writing, and along the other a jigsaw of artwork, like some architectural baleen filtering out the patients' disturbing thoughts. Dr. Lindgren, a pert woman with glasses and long blonde hair, sits several seats down from Jing, looking over her notes from last meeting, fingers fidgeting. They begin with a recitation of the Glenbrook philosophy, a recap of the takeaways from last meeting, then Lindgren introduces the main purpose of today's meeting: coping with delusional thinking.

A middle-aged woman with mousy hair raises a tentative hand.

Lindgren nods eagerly towards her. "Would you like to get us started, Catherine?"

She clears her throat. "For me, it's either I'm a patient in Glenbrook or I've been abducted by vampire aliens and placed in a simulation of a mental hospital on their spaceship. And the voices are constantly pointing out little flaws in everything: people seem dim-ensionless; food is blander than you remember it being; music seems over-repetitious and out of date, like it's been mined out of some ancient library. There are other things the voices tell me as well: the rumors about how Dr. Rota harvested organs from his patients—maybe the vampires spread the rumor to test how you'd respond to reality; and there's the frequency with which they do bloodwork. Everything can be interpreted as reinforcing the delusion—even this meeting, populated by fake patients following scripts in order to assure me that my delusion is not reality so I can continue on in Glenbrook being studied and giving the vampire aliens sufficient data and blood." She titters, fretting her hair.

Silence blankets the group, the memory of Catherine's neurotic cadence dancing around on the air.

"This is what we refer to as internal consistency, one of the devastating characteristics of delusions," Lindgren says after a pause long enough to determine no one else intends to respond, "a cognitive trap of sorts, because any evidence that seems to challenge the delusion can be explained away by the fluid rule system of that same delusion. However, it's important to note that anyone outside of the delusional system instantly recognizes aspects of it as being invalid. Even so, it's easy for outsiders to recognize the internal consistency, almost like it would be for a scientist to view the layout of a maze a rat is running through. So, what kind of strategies have you developed to deal with these thoughts, Catherine?"

"Well, I know that tin corrodes the vampires' machines—at least, that's what the voices tell me—so, before having my blood drawn, I'll stick a tab of tinfoil under my tongue. Then, when the nurse takes a blood sample, I can see for myself that they're using normal, manmade equipment because the tin absorbed into my bloodstream doesn't melt the equipment. When I see that, irrefutable proof that the vampire alien stuff is bogus, the voices, so deafening before, go apologetic and quiet and there's all this uncomfortable shuffling, sort of like a courtroom after the judge has hammered the gavel for order. It's amazing. Then I'll be fine for a while, until one of the voices figures out that the vampire aliens must have seen me slip the foil tab beneath my tongue and so brought in a type of machinery imported from Earth. Then they all pipe up again in agreement, and I'm back to square one. Even so, it's nice how quiet and peaceful it is in the interim. Don't know if it works like that for everyone, though."

As the Governor follows up with his own story—how he began using his job as a telemarketer to campaign for gubernatorial office of Ra8noololo, the hidden state— Jing's mind begins to wander. She finds herself staring at the piano by the stage, wondering how it would sound in this room with its unflattering acoustics. She can't recall having heard anyone try it out, not even Henry. She assumes the various missing keys and stripped faux ivory are symptoms of some graver internal disease. She glances over at her friend, at the moment nodding off beside the Time Traveler, a stooping Hispanic man with facial tattoos, and finds herself remembering one of the shows he and his brother had put on—before Glenbrook. Both were musical savants, spending all of their time in piano composition and performance. Yet from what Jing can tell, since being committed to the hospital Henry has completely abandoned music.

So, for that matter, had Jing. However, spurred on by Penn's visit, she had decided it was time to reconnect with this un-deniable part of herself. Over the past week she had constantly been tuned into the Discman, listening to various CDs Penn had made her, finding herself adrift in musical reveries when the rest of the world was silent.

After group, Jing lingers behind, waiting for the room to empty. Then, for the first time since her arrival, she approaches the piano, sits down at the bench, and explores the keyboard, finding it as dilapidated and out-of-tune as the rest of Glenbrook (the highest three keys play the exact same thriller soundtrack tone), with a wobbly jangle of strings that echo close and jarring in this room.

Soon the door creaks open. Startled, she releases her

fingers as if electricity had just surged through the keyboard, and turns to find Waters leaning in the doorway.

"Sorry, didn't mean to barge in," he says. "I was wondering when you two would get acquainted."

Jing smiles. "I'm usually not this shy. It's just... lots of rust, both on me and the piano." She demonstrates with an unsettling, discordant chord. "That's supposed to be a major G, by the way."

Waters laughs. "Yikes. I don't remember the last time it was played. If you're interested, I'll see if we can get it tuned up for you. But in the meantime you got a phone call."

Jing settles into the creaky leather chair beside the phone in the dayroom, a vacant-eyed audience watching her—picks up the headset

"Jing. It's Leif." The voice grates over the phone.

"Leif." She sits up, stiffening. "Uh, hey, what's up?"

"How they treating you in there?"

"Can't complain, I guess."

"P.C. told me you were looking well."

"That was charitable of her. How you doing?"

"Busy. You can imagine." A gust of wind rattles the elder tree in the courtyard outside. "Been quite a mess to deal with."

She pauses. "Yeah."

"Are you, uh, getting out soon?" He sounds as if he's moving on to the next item of a list of questions he'd written out beforehand.

"That's still an unknown."

"Great."

"What's on your mind, Leif?"

"Two things," Leif says with noticeable relief. "First, 'The Pineal Eye': there's interest in buying advertising rights. These are opportunities we need to jump on; I don't need to tell you that they won't be around for long. We would make a fucking killing, but we need all Autoscope members on board. P.C.'s agreed to it already."

"What about Bower?" Finger toying with the phone cord spirals, she turns from the window and looks from vacant eye to vacant eye of the litter of patients.

A pause. "Bower's endgame was always maximizing exposure. No doubt about that. If P.C.'s in, I'm confident Bower would've been as well, and it's really only a courtesy I'm asking you—"

"I thought you said we all had to be on board."

"Ideally—not necessarily. You can make it easy or complicated for us."

She clicks. "How much exactly is a killing, by the way?"

"I'll fax you the details. Second, 'Hypercrystal' has been selected for the second single. There'll be a radio edit and a few B-sides for the EP. Since you're" — cough— "indisposed right now, P.C. would supervise editing. But according to the... contract... we again need everyone's written consent." Every time he says the word *contract*, there's a padded gap as if it were necessary to quarantine the taboo word from the rest of the sentence.

"Fine, but I'd like to hear it before signing anything."

"That's fair. Great talking to you. Glad to hear you're doing okay. Give me back to the nurse. I'll go ahead and fax over some stuff."

Dr. Goldfield's office is tucked away in a remote corner of the west wing of Glenbrook, a cramped room full of high bookcases overloaded with psychiatric and medical journals dating back to the 70s, each shelf reflecting the passage of time with the retrograde yellowing and fraying of journal spines. Behind an ornate desk, a narrow casement window peers into a small courtyard with a fountain choked with brown leaves and a black oak with only the most tenacious of leaves still clinging to its branches, twitching beneath a light rainfall. Across from Jing, smoking as they talk randomly for a few minutes, sits Dr. Goldfield, tall and narrow, with short gray hair and sapphire eyes, dressed in a long, dahlia-patterned skirt and black sweater, and decked out with chunky gold jewelry.

"How is everything going?" she asks, putting out her cigarette, opening her notebook.

"Good."

"Good is good." Goldfield taps her ring against the nailhead trim of the armchair. "Anything you want to talk about?"

"Not really."

"I heard you had a visitor last week."

"Uh huh."

"A friend of yours?"

"Yeah. An old friend. Her name's Penn. A bandmate. We went to college together."

"Well, tell me about it. How was it seeing her?" Goldfield starts making a few notes.

Jing idly turns her lip ring. "Great. Mostly great. Also, a little depressing."

"How so?"

She shrugs, taking the last drag of her cigarette. "I guess it got me thinking about how my life has been stagnating since I came here."

Goldfield smiles. "I wouldn't think of it as stagnation, Jing. It's healing, self-improvement."

"It's just"—Jing tucks her legs under her butt, striking an odd perch in the chair—"I got the sense she wasn't being totally forthcoming with me. A lot of vague responses to my questions about what she's been doing. Maybe she was being careful with my feelings. I don't know. But it raises the poignant question of what's waiting for me when I leave. She was my introduction into the Detroit alternative scene, and given everything that happened, I'm not really sure where I'll stand when

I'm discharged."

"What about your other friends?"

"Well, as you and everyone else at Glenbrook are well aware, this is my first visitor since my dad. I think that probably says enough about my friends." She pulls another Camel out of her hoodie pouch and lights it, remembering Leif's brusque tone.

Goldfield sets down her notes. "Even aside from the particular circumstances surrounding your case, this is not an unusual experience for psychiatric patients, and there are many reasons why friends may opt against visiting you. It may take a long time for some of them to come around, and others may never get there. At the same time, you may find that you'll have to take the initiative to repair these relationships if they are indeed broken. The important thing is not to brood about it. If you want to know where you stand with people, call them and talk. Very simple."

Jing trims the tip of her cigarette on the fluted lip of the ashtray. "Simple... You're probably right. Unfortunately, all of these people worshipped Bower, so I expect my network is going to be small-to-nonexistent in the future."

"What else did you two talk about?"

"Nothing much."

"Not Bower?"

"Oh, he came up." She clicks. "In every margin. Every silence. To be honest, of all the people that got hurt, she got it the worst. In fact, I assumed she would be the last one to forgive me. It was kind of a shock when I first saw her: my hands were shaking, I wanted to flee."

"Jing, you shouldn't blame yourself—"

"I'm not saying I do, but everyone else obviously does."

"Well, then this is certainly a big breakthrough for you, something to smile about, but I think it's important you discuss him with Penn directly and not just 'in the margins,' as you put it. What was your relationship with Bower like?"

Jing shrugs. "I don't know… I really don't want to talk about him today."

"That's fine. I won't make you talk," Goldfield concedes, then shifts her posture. "How about your meds?"

"Nothing new to report there."

"How about your physical health?" She shuffles her notes and starts moving her pen down a list of questions.

"Five."

"Why five?"

"I feel weirdly… empty inside, in my chest."

Goldfield jots something down. "How is your energy level?"

"Five."

"Mood?"

"Five."

"Sensing a pattern here. Appetite?"

"Five."

"Sleep?"

"Four."

"How bad would you describe a Four?"

"Just a few hours a night. When I close my eyes, they flutter around like moths."

"Could be the Clonazepam," Goldfield says, making some notes. "You also might consider cutting back"—a gesture towards Jing's cigarette—"and no coffee or tea after lunch. What about your concentration, memory, etc.?"

"Yeah, I find myself staring off into space a lot these days."

"Clonazepam again most likely. Expecting zero side effects isn't realistic, but I think we could experiment with lowering your dosage. Clear out all the moths. I wouldn't recommend switching meds. I have to say, you look much better physically—so much more full of life than you did a month ago."

"Thanks." Her voice is deadpan.

"What about hallucinations?"

"No."

"Delusions?"

"Nope."

"No third-person?"

Jing flushes, mouth tightening, and clicks.

Goldfield continues when Jing fails to respond: "Suicidal thoughts?"

Jing takes a drag and exhales. "No."

The doctor nods. "And what about your memory of that night?"

"Vague impressions. I know there was a show; that's about it." Her gaze drifts down to the tip of scar, and reflexively she retracts her hand into her hoodie sleeve.

Goldfield follows her gaze. "Is there something on your mind?"

"I think I would really benefit from having gym access. I'd like to become an A-level."

Goldfield nods, smile fading. "Well, you need to fill out a formal request with Waters, he'll present it at the team meeting, and then we'll all vote."

Jing smiles bitterly. "Okay, and if I were to do so *again*, would you vote 'yes' this time?"

Goldfield pauses. "I'm sorry, Jing. No, I would not."

"But why? I thought I was being an ideal patient here, and I have to say, what happened yesterday was really embarrassing."

"I'm not going to apologize for yesterday, and there's no reason to feel embarrassed about it. You expressed your wishes; the team considered and rejected them. A very normal event at Glenbrook."

"Well, to be fair, Devon and Billie just follow your lead. I hope you realize that. Waters is the only one I've ever seen go against you, but even he seems reluctant to do so."

"That's not how treatment teams work. Every member is allowed to hold and act upon their own opinion. They all know that."

"Well, then, what is your opinion?"

Goldfield takes a breath. "I really think you've made great progress, but there are several things that give me pause. First, your performance during group therapy is subpar."

"Wait, what? Are you shitting me?"

"Dr. Lindgren tells me you're not very forthcoming about discussing your own issues and tend to be dismissive of other patients' emotional needs."

"Lindgren said that about me?"

Goldfield nods, flipping back through her notes. "A-level is reserved only for those exemplary patients that live and breathe the Glenbrook philosophy. When I see those qualities in you—especially that key one 'Biopsychosocial integration'—you'll be sure to have my vote. For now, before you leave for lunch, is there anything else you want to discuss?"

Jing takes a deep breath, expelling her frustration, puts out the cigarette and studies the wisp of smoke curling out of the ashtray before continuing. "One last thing. When Penn was here we talked a little about my treatment. She was surprised to hear you guys hadn't yet given me an official diagnosis. Yeah, I agree. So, anyway, here I am having a"—she makes air quotes—"'Proactive attitude' and requesting my diagnosis."

Goldfield's jaw clenches. "Okay, but first I want to warn you: a diagnosis carries a lot of baggage with it. We find it difficult to predict how patients will react to their own diagnoses. Sometimes it negatively affects self-confidence; other times it becomes a source of pride. Personally, I didn't want to add undue anxiety to everything else in your life."

"Well it is my right, at least according to *The Glenbrook Bible*."

Goldfield nods. "Of course. You have every right to know. Now, it is still potentially too early to tell, and given your recent stability it's possible we will need to revise your diagnosis, but in the meantime I've settled on comorbid schizoaffective disorder and epilepsy. The choice schizoaffective disorder over schizophrenia is based mainly on your suicide attempt and depression, essentially a co-occurrence of a mood and psychotic disorder. The epilepsy seems to be unrelated, but we're not one hundred percent certain."

"Oh," she says. *Ma,* she thinks.

Goldfield's hand frets a page of notes. "Jing, this is not necessarily damning, and there's a lot of uncertainty in any diagnosis. There have certainly been cases of patients experiencing brief psychotic episodes such as the one you went through who never experience such things again, and lately I think things have been looking very positive for you. But what we need is more time together. You need a safe environment, regular psychotherapy, and to be good with your meds. I think after a few more months here, maybe we could move you to a halfway house, a place where you can be supervised and surrounded by a supportive group of people. But even so, this should not and will not be something that defines you. Just keep up with the meds and don't brood over the diagnosis and other issues. Communicate with those around you. If there's a problem, you can always come talk to me or other members of the team."

Jing nods, starts to pull out another cigarette, then stops herself.

"Jing?"

"Yeah."

"Talk to me."

"I don't... I don't know how to feel. I'm not all that surprised. You have me attending the psychotics group, doped up to the eyeballs. I just... I thought it was just some freak blip on the radar, maybe just the drugs... and maybe you were just keeping me around to monitor me, make sure I hadn't done any permanent brain damage. Thought I was just sitting around waiting for my discharge date."

"The worst of it may very well be over. It's sort of a

waiting game for us now."

"Does my dad know?"

"No, he doesn't know. Telling loved ones about this is something you need to do yourself, or if you prefer, with your written authorization I can tell him for you."

Jing clicks. "I need to think about this first. Christ." She rakes her face with a claw.

"Okay, but friends and family are important. Isolation has been known to exacerbate both mood disorders and psychoses."

Jing glances at the clock on the wall and then stands. "Lunch time. Guess I'll see you around."

"Wait. Sit down. We can't end on this kind of note. Just a few more minutes and you can go."

Jing sits, folding one of her legs underneath her.

"Thank you. Now, it would be grossly negligent of me to give you a diagnosis without also making sure you are equipped with a detailed knowledge of the condition, treatment, etc. There are many false beliefs about schizophrenia and related disorders floating around out there. For example, although the word itself implies a division of the mind, patients with this disorder do not have multiple personalities. The main thing is—"

"Hallucinations, delusions: I have gotten something out of group, after all"—*and from being my mother's daughter*—"but, for the record, none of those things apply to me. I don't hear voices. I don't purport to be the disciple of Christ or the Governor of never-never land."

Goldfield holds firm. "Maybe not now, but when you first came here—"

"Well, I was fucked up then. It was clearly the drugs talking."

"Just be patient with me, Jing. First, it's imperative you keep taking your meds. I can't stress that enough. Second, I would like to see you socializing more: reach out to other patients; participate more in group; keep in touch with Penn; call your father; but, at the same time, there are some patients at Glenbrook with whom you should limit your one-on-one contact."

"You mean... Henry?" Jing says, perking up, body tensing, but careful to mask a sudden wave of suspicion, recalling snippets of Henry's paranoid tirade in the cafeteria from a week before.

"Bingo. For a patient such as yourself whose symptoms have stabilized, frequent, unsupervised interaction with other psychotic patients could be unhealthy. For example, there's a condition known as *folie à deux*, where the delusions of one psychotic affect another, resulting in mutual reinforcement of the delusion. Now, Henry I can't talk specifics about, but his progress has been much slower than yours. Of course, it's more complicated with him, what with his twin brother." She turns the wedding ring with the pad of her thumb. "I can't imagine the staggering loss of growing up with a twin, having that constant confidante and companion, and then to have them taken away. So, he's a bit more alienated now than before and needs someone to fill the role in his life that William used to fill. I would in no way suggest cutting him out completely because that could be devastating for him when all he is trying to do is rebuild a structure that feels normal. However, for your own sake I do urge you not be the one to take up William's torch. Stay friendly, but try to avoid being alone with him too much."

"Okay," Jing murmurs.

"And the third thing is this"—Goldfield rummages around her desk and pulls out a pamphlet—"promise me you'll read it."

Jing takes it and reads: "'Coping with Schizophrenia.'"

"It may not all apply to you, but there's useful information in there and guidelines about how to discuss the disorder with family and friends for when you're ready to take that step. And you should *really* be more forthcoming in group. We're all here to help you, but you have to be open to receiving our help."

Jing studies Goldfield for a moment, wondering if the doctor is being candid with her or if there is some truth in Henry's ravings, not about neural wormholes, of course, but... There's something Goldfield isn't telling her.

"All right. I'll look at it," she says at last, folding up the pamphlet and stuffing it into the back pocket of her jeans.

"Great." Goldfield straightens in her chair, the leather creaking. She sets the notebook and pen aside, exchanging them for a cigarette. "This has been a very productive session, I think. Enjoy your lunch."

Jing is prodding her candied yams with a spork, watching the violent waterfall behind the glass wall—dark as dusk outside—when Henry's voice jolts her back into the cafeteria.

"You've gotta hear this. Last night, I was meditating and—"

"Wait," Jing cuts him off. "If this is about that Muzak conspiracy theory of yours, I'm really not in the mood."

"Jing, it's not a conspiracy theory; this is important."

"No, it's not. You're delusional. I'm delusional. Eighty percent of the brains in this cafeteria are."

"What are you talking about?" He sips his coffee. "There's nothing wrong with you."

"Thanks, but"—*no third-person?*—"if you want to tell anyone about your Muzak idea, why not share at the next group?"

He adjusts his glasses, shaking his head and hair, face ashen, blinking furiously as if he could change her mind by refreshing her image enough times. "Because Lindgren is a psychoengineer; some of the other patients might be as well. I thought you were on my side with this. You"—he glances around—"lied to Waters for me. You agreed with me about the Muzak—"

"Not true."

"And I saw you staring at the piano today in group, saw you were trying to signal something to me."

"What? I wasn't signaling anything. I was staring at it because I was wondering how horribly out of tune it might be—*very,* incidentally—and I was... I was curious about why you don't play anymore."

"Jing, you have to listen to me. We can't stay here. A week ago you said you'd come to my room for instruction—"

"Henry, I told you already: Don't care. No more theories."

"I'm disappointed in you." He leans back in his chair. "I thought we were buddies."

"Yeah, well if being buddies with you means I have to drink your wonky Kool-Aid, then no thanks." She stands, then feeling she was too harsh, adds: "Sorry."

She goes to the waste room to dump her tray, where a tech takes note of what she hasn't eaten—fodder for the clipboard. Gets a Styrofoam cup of coffee and jacks into her Walkman.

To a soundtrack of pulsing ambient music she winds her way over to the meds station in the north wing.

She carries the cup of coffee and meds to her retreat in the north wing stairwell, overlooking the elder tree courtyard, now just distorted shadows beyond the torrent.

She lights up a cigarette and digs the pamphlet out of her back pocket, glancing through it.

History.

Diagnostic criteria.

Treatment.

Having the conversation.

Patient interviews.

The over-concerned expressions on the actors' faces in the pamphlet aggravate her.

She folds it up and stuffs it back in her jeans.

She ashes into the limpid remnants of her coffee,

feeling a surge of resentment towards Dr. Goldfield, a delicious sensation which she lets burn unchecked, and it sets fire to everyone—Henry, Lindgren, Penn, Leif, Bower, the strange and ponderous weight of Glenbrook itself—and when the smoke finally clears, her mindscape is littered with ash and slag.

She regards the meds, three different pills: a chalky, white tablet; a round, green pill; and a white-and-green capsule. Clozaril, Klonopin, Prozac.

She brings the pills up to her lips, pauses—

CHAPTER 5

"You've stopped again. That was barely enough for two days of flight, and that's if I'm sparing with my fire."

My eyes pop open upon hearing the voice, thick and smug. It takes me several moments to remember where I am. I'd been so long inside Glenbrook, it had started to feel like reality—muted, but reality nonetheless. It is, thus, with disappointment that I am reintroduced by turns to various elements of the Psyche fantasy—the hard cold ground, jeweled night sky, distant dunes. Must've passed out while feeding the dragon just as I had last night. As I shift my body against the dog, disturbing a light frost, every muscle throbs with fatigue.

The dragon has tied itself into a self-indulgent knot, cerulean eyes beacons in the dark. Every so often, its bear trap of a head glowing with the flame it tends in its bowels, it puffs out smoke, not of the cigar, which I barely discern on the ground before it, now nothing more than an indentation of ash. Must have fallen out of its jaws once I began feeding it the visions.

I stretch, knead the small of my back, and massage my sore legs. The left flashes with pain.

"My body aches, my head is murky, I collapsed earlier during our trek. Just leave me alone for a little while. *Please.*" My voice sharpens with agitation.

"First it was the wrist: not enough blood to fuel your brain. Now it's fatigue. My patience is running thin, Drummer Girl. If I were to consume your brains now, I could fly for weeks digesting those nutrients."

"So fucking eat me all ready! Christ, you're tiresome."

The dragon begins to resolve its tangles and slither forward as if to make good on its threat. However, when the dog growls, yet again the dragon just winds around us, coiling into a stifling wall. As I watch the hypnotic dance for the second time, ending as before with the dragon knotting back down into its original spot, where it rolls a new cigar, I turn over in my mind what it had just now said.

Eat me now and fly for a few weeks. A slip of information.

Then it occurs to me that it's all been an empty threat.

"You won't do it, will you? And not because of the dog, though that is a convenient excuse."

"Careful with that tongue of yours," it snaps, lighting the cigar with nasal flame.

"You've clearly done the math: I'm worth more to you alive than dead. You need either brains or Earth energy to sustain you. If you eat my brains now, they'll give you a powerful kick, but then you'll miss out on years and years of these nighttime feedings. I get it. There's no need for the show anymore. I can feed you, but you need to be considerate—you know?—maybe pamper me a little, fly me out of this godforsaken desert, take me someplace comfortable, a cave full of mushrooms or something. Then, every evening I'll feed you to your heart's delight. I'm twenty-two now. With your protection maybe I'll live much longer, another fifty years or so. You could stand to gain a lot. Even better: let me live as long as possible, and then when I'm on my deathbed, you suck out my brains anyway. That would be the most bang for your buck."

The dragon smiles its dagger-toothed smile.

Undaunted, I continue: "You and I could potentially form a powerful alliance—you protect me, I feed you— but you need to respect the fragile state my body's in right now. So please just let me sleep."

I pull the tail over me and nestle against the dog's soft abdomen, my heart racing. Eyes refuse to close. It's a struggle to keep from shaking.

I prick my ears to listen for some movement, anything, but there is only the wind, the rumbly snores of the dog, a dead air from the dragon's direction. Any second I expect a wave of fire to wash over me—charring, crackling my skin, melting my insides—but it never comes.

After several minutes of silent prayer, I turn and see those marbled orbs of fire glaring at me out of the darkness.

At sunrise the dog rises, its warm tail swishing off my body. I try to burrow down deeper into the warm depression of sand that served as our bed, but the air is too bitter cold for sleep, the wind biting through the thin fabric of my clothes.

Exercise is the only way to warm up.

The dog grazes while I scavenge around for some puffballs, shivering violently. As I eat, mouth imprecise in the cold, I watch the morning rainbow aurorae undulating on the horizon. A few stars still linger in the pink sky. A distant cavalcade of planetoids spangle the horizon.

—So Bower is dead. Jesus Christ. Every past tense reference to him had been ice in my stomach—

My eyes stray from the horizon, and I notice the tract of sand where the dragon had lain last night—not a trace of having been slept on.

—That must be whose funeral Penn and Earth Jing had discussed in the earlier vision. But how?—

Thinking, waiting for the dog to finish, I venture into the oasis and here, sheltered from the wind, strip down, pour the desert out of my shoes and hang up my clothes to beat the sand out of them with a white tree limb. My body is a horrendous sight: ribs poking through, leg and arm swollen, everything chafed red and raw.

—It seems I've found another (or perhaps *the*) viable

explanation about the meaning of Psyche—a psychotic disorder, not an interminable acid trip—

Most of the sand comes off easily enough, but even with all the beating, a fine white powder clings to the fabric.

—The scenes I observe on the edge of sleep are simply brief moments of sanity; the rest of the time I'm trapped in a complex of delusions and hallucinations—

I unwrap my bandages, clean and wring them dry, re-wrap the wounds, and get dressed.

—If this is true, according to what Dr. Lindgren had said, it seems any sensory information that reaches my mind will be distorted by the lens of Psyche—

I pull out my compact and examine my reflection— skin as powdery as my clothes, mouth cracked and flaky. I tame my sand-gray hair with the dendrite comb I'd found yesterday, clean my mouth, apply the soothing lipstick.

—Yesterday I'd tried a mirror as a method of dispelling hallucination, but there is no test possible I could perform to prove Psyche is or is not real—

A large worm edges out of the brush. I put away my things and stand, gripping the stick two-handed.

—Only an entity outside of myself could judge the validity of my experience, but they couldn't discuss the issue with me—

Stave it in. Juices blast out of its mouth and anus.

—Because as soon as they were to attempt to communicate, the information would again be rendered unreliable—

I look down at the pulverized worm, goo bubbling with an acrid, chemical odor.

—In other words, I am doomed to wonder—

On the verge of tossing the stick back into the brush, I'm suddenly struck by its bizarre shape: pointed and long, curved and grooved. At its thick end (the part I'd used for bludgeoning the worm) a large concavity funnels down to a tiny hole which then coils through the body and into the groove.

"A fang."

I turn back towards the brush from where I'd fished out the tooth, and displacing the thick, orange-leaved branches, find another hooking down from the foliage, much more firmly rooted than the one I'd broken off. Two others jut out of the ground. I move apart more of the brush and discover the base of the jaw, spirited of all its flesh.

I set down the fang, light up the half-cigarette, and study the gigantic skeleton.

The two sides of the base of the jaw are disconnected, giving the creature an odd, insectoid appearance. Its tunnel of a ribcage recedes into the hoarfrost-coated thicket. A snake, I realize suddenly: the groove in the fang designed to let venom course down to the tip, the disconnected jaw for swallowing enormous prey.

I become aware of the silence and turn back to find that the dog has yet again, rudely, set out ahead of me. I stuff my purse with supplies, and start off, then sprint back into the oasis, pick up the femur-sized fang, and tuck it into the back of my belt.

What was it they had discussed in group therapy? Fighting the delusion on its own terms?

I stick as close to the dog as possible as we trek, its massive shoulders and chest screening out the wind. As the sun continues to rise and the day warms, the chill leaves us. I feel fresher and stronger than yesterday. Despite my distress over the situation on Earth/reality, my mood elevates. Not only have my baser needs been met, I've also made progress in my relationship with the dragon. In demonstrating that I know it knows how valuable I am to it, there has been a shift in the dynamic: the dragon will not be able to coerce me any longer, will have to work as a team. A symbiotic relationship with the dragon and transportation airborne or otherwise would improve the Psyche experience a thousand-fold. The dog doesn't seem to be inclined to let me ride, but then again I'm no pilot fish to the dog: she thrives on vegetation and insects, not on consciousness or whatever it is the dragon eats; I can't protect her; and she either can't or isn't inclined to converse with me. She seems only to tolerate my presence. The dragon, on the other hand, surely it would not be too proud to refuse my offer of a partnership, not when we could so clearly benefit one another.

As we plod on, I begin to hum. Some of Autoscope's music. The first song that pops into my mind is "The Pineal Eye." As the song evolves, I shift from humming to snapping and lightly tattooing rhythms against my stomach, a habit I'd developed when I'd taught myself the drums, a way to extend practice beyond the trap set and to carry on throughout the length of the day. When the song ends, I jump right into another. It's the set list from that night, *the* night. How many hours and days did we practice to perfect the transitions between songs? So ingrained now, it requires zero thought: a mandala unfolding in my mind, blown clean, then unfolding again, blossoms on the tails of blossoms. I hear Bower's warble and thumping bass, Penn's jangly guitar, a soundscape of electronics building behind it. The music feels so alive, a blanket of electricity, I can't believe there's any truth in the visions.

Bower can't be dead.

My sounds at first intrigue the dog, but as my form of expression disintegrates from humming to snapping and then finally to a minimal whisper of gesture and voice, it loses all interest and wanders farther from my side.

The heat of the day soon rises to a swelter. Ahead the glare of the opaline mountainscape needles the eyes, coercing their focus onto the watery mirage of the sub-horizon. The ancient stronghold of music provides the only shelter, where the cool, dark walls echo harmony from non-musical sounds.

For hours I trot alongside the dog in this distracted state of mind—until the bite in my leg begins to flare, shining harsh light into the peaceful, musical recesses, and it yanks me back, limping, into Psyche.

The farther we go, the wider spans the gap between canine and human, and before long, the distance is so great across the flat stretch of rough desert, the dog's legs appear as detached quivers in the sizzling miasma. Then we reenter the fluctuating dune-lands, more forgiving on the feet but tougher on the legs with the endless peaks and dips. At times I can make out the wavering white blob rising up one side of a dune, but at others there is no trace of the white specter on the horizon. So I must study its tracks in the sand. Even these paw prints are difficult to gaze at for too long, the minerals a blinding glamour beneath the sun's nadir. The sand is not white as I had once thought it: it is a cosmos of jeweled stars—ruby and emerald, sapphire and topaz, onyx and pearl, each glorious ray searing my retinas.

Despite the heat, the sky has cooled into royal blue, planetoids and puffy clouds mustered up into an armada skirmishing with the cruel sun. The day has stretched on into a harsh, sweat-drinking heat. It feels longer than yesterday, much longer. Again, though, all there is to gauge this observation by is my internal clock, faulty mechanism that it may be, especially in its relation to the motions of an alien planet (real or imagined).

In the midst of asteroid-gazing and pondering whether it is possible for my circadian rhythm to shed millions of years of evolution to adapt to a new environment, a novel idea suddenly occurs to me:

Seasons.

Though for a while now I've presumed the varying lengths of days here to be an aberration of my hallucinating mind, I see at least that there's a simple logic to the length of day problem: very short, day-length seasons. Indeed, these changes in the length of days have been accompanied by dramatic shifts in temperature. If this theory is correct, then following the recent long nights and frosty mornings, I should be headed towards longer, summer-length days.

This idea so consumes me that by the time I realize I'd been walking on auto-pilot, I find the dog is nowhere to be seen. Its tracks, too, have vanished. I stare at the cracked ground around me, a playa with the impressive sweeping dunes flanking its distant shores.

Did I veer off course?

I scan the surroundings.

In the far distance, in the depths of the once-upon-a-time lake, a small oasis twists and dances in the heat, beyond it a butte, osseous and malformed, its base wiped out of existence in the mirage. All around me the ground is as tough as fired clay, no paw prints.

"Fucking hell," I mutter, clicking the tongue stud.

I call out to the dog.

No response, of course.

Sweeping the hair out of my eyes and cursing, I turn to regard the landscape behind me, an impressive cliff of dunes.

"Okay, Jingy, retrace your steps. Back the way you came, then you'll find where the two of you forked."

A sensible idea. If only I could make out my own tracks. Everything appears illusorily splotched from sun-scorching.

Admitting the futility of this approach to myself, I head over to the oasis; I should at least restock my dwindling cactus arm and puffball supplies and allow the blindness to fade while I come up with a feasible plan. In approaching the copse, the not-unexpected fetid odor of death assaults my senses. I restock, scanning the meager oasis and finally spot it sitting against a rock, lightly napping: the two-headed rat from yesterday. Not only is it once again being assaulted by a clew of worms, flora has also begun to invade the creature—creepers spilling out of its skull, roots tangled up in its decaying foot. As I watch, I can *see* the plants creeping over it, hear them rustle and creak as they move. Fighting down an upsurge of sick in the back of my throat, I pull out the large fang and, one hand cupped over my mouth and nose, reach out and poke it in the side with the polite end.

Its eyes snap open as it cries out in surprise and pops up.

The rat sniffs. "It's you again, is it?" It shakes all manner of strange insects out of its skull along with rotten bits of itself, eyeing the long fang in my hand.

"I was just…" I return the fang to my side. "Sorry, I just thought I should rouse you."

"We thank you. It is rather tiresome, the tenacity of these things." The rat begins to weed itself with the thoroughness of daily ritual.

"So, it's true? The oases sprout up around the dead?"

"Not only the dead, but the dying."

As it speaks, I go back over in my mind the oases I'd encountered—the snake this morning, the bull a long time ago—realizing that one of them had *not* contained anything dead. That was the day after I'd slit my wrists. I'd seen no bones in the oasis where I recovered my bloodied razor. The thing must have effloresced around me after I'd done the deed. So the dog—or the dragon—had saved me from this fate of being eaten alive by those worms and being drawn and quartered by the plants. Idiosyncratic as they may be, I feel a swell of gratitude towards my saviors.

This rat has, incidentally and in just a few words, resolved one of the many mysteries of Psyche, and I consider again if I should engage it in more conversation. However, again the odor it gives off is so nauseating, its appearance so grotesque, like a walking disease, I am once again deterred. "I have to get going," I say. "I'm trying to catch up to my... umm... friend-pet-thing. It was, uh, lovely."

I move out of sight and smell of the oasis before giving the rat time to make a rejoinder, entering the shadow of the butte, needed relief from the sun and glare of the day. I sit down for a rest and after a brief spell am able to overcome the lingering waves of nausea. Didn't see anything edible in that oasis, but maybe I can last till the next one. Just need to find the dog first.

Assuming she didn't pass through this bowl and stayed in the dunes, if I just move parallel to the mountains, I'll eventually intersect with the dog's trail... but should I go left or right?

"Can we hazard a suggestion?" The sound creeps around the edges of the rock, pallbearer of that rotten stench.

The rat has crept around the corner and towards the edge of the shadow, beady eyes of its living head shining, a few worms crawling in and out of the eye sockets of the dead one, their glow suppressed in the bright light.

"We may be of some assistance in your search."

"Listen. I'm sorry. I don't mean to be rude or anything, but I have to say it anyway: you reek."

"Well, given our current state, that's only to be expected. In any case, we see you're in a quandary and thought we would offer our help."

"Thanks... but I can handle it myself." My mouth aches with every word. I fish around in the purse for the lipstick.

"Suit yourself." It studies me for a moment and then turns to go. "Though we would suggest going right."

"What's that?" I glance up from applying the lipstick in the compact.

The rat turns back towards me, possibly grinning, though it's difficult to tell.

"Going left would be a mistake," it says in its oily, nasal timbre.

"Why do you say that?" I pucker and stash my things.

It taps its nose.

"Trust us, girl. Unless your 'friend' is a knot of snakes, left is not the path for you."

"Okay. Well, um, thanks."

"Our pleasure." It blinks, half-bowing, a flourish of its good hand. "Now, we leave you in unscented silence."

Then it disappears around the corner of the rock.

"So weird," I mutter, mind wandering back to those infuriating question of acid, madness, and reality.

"And another thing," it adds, heads popping around the corner again, teeth of the skull clattering with the sudden movement, dispatching a fresh wave of foulness in my direction. "Might want to hurry along. The eternity bug headed this way will make tracking difficult."

Then it leaves without another word.

After the rat departs, I step out from the shelter of the butte and scan the horizon. Opposite the mountains, a white haze rises out of the ground, much too high to be a mirage. Must have been obscured by the dune cliff earlier.

A sandstorm?

Aside from this haze, I see nothing else that could plausibly be referred to as an eternity bug. Whatever it is, it must still be many miles away, and it is at the moment impossible to tell how fast it is moving or whether or not it's even approaching.

I set off at a jog, keeping the mountains on my left, gripping the faux-leather strap tight against my chest as my purse jostles around. My wounded leg flashes with pain at the exertion, the bite beginning to seep. For now, I ignore it and push my body on, telling myself I'll treat the wound once I reach the dog, and when I do I'll demand she carry me on her back, civility be damned.

The shore of dunes grow with each painful stride. After a mile or so of jogging, my sneakers read soft, impressionable sand, then I'm clambering up the slope on all fours, and soon enough I spot the ground, the giant paw prints angling off towards the mountains.

Thank you, rat!

I glance appreciatively back down into the crater of the dried lake, the oasis a small, glowing tuft in its center, then I continue on towards the puzzling geometry of the mountains. The haze still looms distant on the opposite horizon, though it appears to have grown, no longer low and clinging but a fuller, roiling mass.

I jog for an hour or more, up and down dune after dune, focusing on the tracks at my feet and now and again catching my breath atop a dune crest and scanning the horizon ahead of me to see if the dog has come into view. At the apex of one such dune, while I pause for a stretch, a curious sound draws my attention. The soundscape of Psyche has until now been as barren as the scenery: steady sifting streams of wind, swelling and eroding, but this element is unique—a droning rumble, distant, only just perceptible. Yet, I can feel it in my bones.

I glance over my shoulder, realizing at once what it must be.

The progress of the sandstorm has been great.

Only now that it has gained on me can I appreciate how massive the storm is: lurching and toppling over itself, ballooning and deflating, crashing and spilling, a macroorganism probing its environment with flagella of grit. I spy an oasis, miniscule in comparison to this beast of sand, crushed beneath the rolling wave, dashed into a spray of fluorescent glitter. Stranger still: there appears to be something inside the billows. Spiny, webbed humps barely crest the top of the cloud. When the sand shifts just so, I can glimpse through the obscuring veil a shadowy forest of stalks and antennae, bulbs and grabbers.

Frantic, I search around for cover but there's nothing at—"

No—several miles ahead, towards the mountains, the ground grows craggy, fields of bone-white rock cleaving the dunes.

Maybe there's a cavern or a crevice I can squeeze into—something, anything.

I break into a sprint—wounds, heat, fatigue, the lingering doubts about reality, all gone. The dog will be lost, I realize, but suddenly nothing matters but reaching the rocks. Maybe they'll deter this thing, whatever *it* is.

Every few seconds I glance back, each time finding the cloud larger, closer, looming higher, and each time puzzling out some new aspect of the creature: toothy orifices, bone-framed lanterns, intricate wind vanes, sand-spewing blowholes. Occasionally, it reels in a boulder and jettisons large chunks of broken rock back out into the Psyche landscape in thunderous crashes. Each time I glance back, the size of the inexorable wall of sand appears to have increased at a more alarming rate. All the while, the rocks in front of me remain aloof. The rumble of the creature swells to an apocalyptic roar. Its head-parts probe and crush the ground with deep booms, slurping up and gnashing the sand and rock.

Feet uncertain on quaking ground, I stumble, face planting in the electrified sand, a flash of red and stars, heat streaming down my lip. Every bone in my body shakes, threatening to wrench apart from sheer vibration.

A brutal angle of rock crashes down several feet away, impaling the desert.

I scramble back to my feet, staggering, the light of the sun fleeing from the ground, turning a blind eye to my doom.

I dash onward towards the lands beyond the shadow

of Armageddon and teeter with each lurch of the ground. Chunks of boulder rain down around me. Something crashes against me, knocks me back down. I roll onto my feet, determined not to be trapped beneath this thing, but when I pop up to sprint onward, my left foot fixes into the ground. As I try to kick myself out, my right sticks as well, legs now immobile up to the knees. The sand surrounding me is shifting tide-like, flowing backwards towards the cloud and the vacuum-pods sweeping over the ground.

By now the air around me has become streaked with eye-stinging jet streams of sand, tangled and inter-locking. Above, the cloud stretches hundreds of meters up into the sky, the spiny wall of exoskeleton visible beyond, pulsing, only meters from annihilating me.

In my last moments, I rip off my shirt and wind it around my mouth and nose, pulling the ends together in a tight knot. A nearby blowhole propels out a stream of sand, arcing up over me and raining down.

Darkness.

Then visions:

CHAPTER 6

She sits in the Oriel window, fingers twirling an unlit cigarette, staring out at the courtyard, the bare tree, the carpet of dead leaves. A gust of wind surges through the wrought-iron-gated tunnel into the courtyard, eddies the leaves, rips insecure cigarettes from the lips of patients, and retreats back out like the tide. Distant classical music echoes through the corridors, an aural ghost in here. Where once her face had glinted with piercings, now these accentuations are absent. So, too, is the metal-studded belt.

After a week of ass-kissing the surliest members of the staff, contributing once or twice during group therapy, and wiping dribble off the catatonics' chins as they drank in the glow of the television, the members of her team had finally promoted her to A-level. Following this level change a couple of great days had followed.

The first thing she did upon hearing the news was put on her sweatpants, tank top, and windbreaker, and take an hour-long, unescorted jog around the grounds.

That had been Friday. Along with this newfound freedom, her appetite increased, as did her mood and energy level, her reading speed, the clarity of her thoughts. Her insomnia washed away. The food tasted better. She'd grown extremely horny and spent the entire evening masturbating in between the tech's rounds, the first time she had done so in a long while. Of course, most of these changes had nothing to do with her level change, but rather the surreptitious lifting of the medicated fog.

Sunday morning, still relishing the perks of her new level, she took another jog in the crisp autumn air. As she was rounding a bend of the woods near the ropes course, the thumping electronic music of Penn's mix tape had sounded through and resonated with the earth. It seemed to vibrate through her legs. She had stopped and stripped off the headphones, glancing around her, out of breath, with the strange sense that she was being watched. Clicking her tongue stud, she put the headphones back on, continued jogging. The wind picked up, blowing streams of leaves past her, pleasant at first, then the wind surged, the world exploded with brittle-veined webbing the color of burnt squash.

She staggered.

The world tilted.

And she blacked out.

She had awoken Sunday evening in the infirmary, wired up to a restless sentry of machines. She tried to fall back asleep, but the beeping of the monitors and the cries of pain from patients in neighboring rooms frustrated these attempts. At last, she abandoned the idea of rest and turned on the television.

A show spotlighting local artists had been airing.

And there he was: Sebastian Bower, talking about Autoscope's upcoming album, a scarf wrapped around his long bird neck. At one point, all three of them—Bower, Penn, and Jing—took part in an interview in the basement practice space of the Compound with its stark, art-gallery décor—"Part home, part club, part institute for the arts," Bower said, showing off the home his inheritance built. The conversation mostly consisted of how Penn and Bower started the group, the influence of Penn's synesthesia on her life and songwriting, Bower's vision for the role the Compound would play in the Detroit arts scene. She remembered then clearly when this had been filmed: several months before the incident and her admission to Glenbrook, several weeks after their single had gained traction on the radio and their music video entered into rotation on late night television—still a few weeks before the official album release. Just that morning before the film crew had arrived at the practice space, Bower had brought in an advanced review of the album. The critic had praised Penn's guitar playing and the other-worldly sounds Bower achieved with his rack of electronics. Of Jing he had only said her playing was "robotic" with drum fills like a "malfunctioning drum machine." The words devastated her. Leif had cracked a joke about it, Bower a meandering argument with an ambivalent point that left Jing confused and even more aggravated, and Penn... she can't remember now what Penn had said.

She had watched on, seeing Bower demonstrate how the various components of the electronics rack worked, constructed over a stand-up piano, a skeletal, precarious kludge of knobs and keys and buttons. He let the reporter experiment with the Theremin component. She inserted her hand and activated an ear-piercing feedback echo. Bower shook his head, chuckling, his smugness palpable as he handily guided the woman away and contained the spreading sonic disaster with the flick of a wrist.

The image cut to them in the lounge, talking about the creative process, Bower describing his own peculiar habits. Most of what he said were lies spread in the hope of adding a mystical element to the group and his own art, and also to prevent others from accurately modeling his behavior. Songs didn't sprout out of him in dreams as he claimed, but were the product of hours and hours of trial and error. Bower was one of the most disciplined musicians she had ever known, but for him the amount of time he spent practicing was a dirty, well-guarded secret. He would wake before dawn every day, go downstairs for coffee and then to the studio, where he experimented for hours until something clicked, often forgetting to eat. He manufactured rumors that he never practiced, that he'd write songs, hand them over to Penn and Jing, and be done with them until show time, wasting the days in drug-fueled orgies.

"A lot of artists say they get their inspiration from this **beep**ing band or that **beep**ing band, but I think my approach has been a bit different, you know? P.C., too. I mean, I just look out at the **beep**ing world, man and pull from there. There's nothing more musical than the sound of snowfall in the woods or wind in the trees," he explained as he and Penn and the reporter toured around the brightly-lit, graffitied tunnels of his home. Jing had disappeared by this point.

Finally, there were several minutes of Autoscope performing before a crowd in the Club Room at the Compound. The sight and sound of them playing—Penn all in white, eyes closed, a curtain of hair hanging over her face, thrashing away at the guitar; Bower in his boots and gold leather pants singing and banging on the piano; and Jing herself in a black mesh shirt, lean and sweaty as she hunched over the drums—brought a shiver down her spine.

She clicked off the television, the air knocked out of her.

It was right at that moment that her left eye ceased processing the world.

First, her body seized up, a ringing in her left ear, which seemed to churn forward in her head, into her vision. A light flared up, every object consumed with a bright, corrosive whiteness.

Then a black more devastating than black: nothingness.

Suddenly able to move again, she clawed at her face, screaming, clambering out of bed and stumbling into the bathroom, her left side colliding with the doorframe, the IV yanked out of her arm in a clean arc of blood, EKG pads ripping off her chest, fluid bags crashing to the floor.

Her screams died as she saw herself in the mirror, saw those big onyx eyes staring back at her, wild and alarmed—but whole.

"I'm fine," she told herself. "I'm-I'm fine. I'm fine. I'm

fine." The self-affirmation trailed off into a whisper, then a twitch of her mouth. She opened and closed her eyes in turn.

"What's going on?" an alarmed voice called from behind. "Ms. Elwood, what happened?" A nurse appeared in the doorway.

"Fine... fine..." *I'm blind,* she nearly said, but feared uttering the words. She turned away from the mirror. "Christ, I'm sorry. I just... panicked when I woke up in here. Didn't know where the hell I was." The lie spilled out of her with unexpected fluidity.

The nurse helped her back into bed, cleaning her arm and reattached the EKG and IV. Jing thanked her, voice placid, flavorless, and was soon alone again. She continued to explore the newfound blindness. It felt as if her head had been cleaved in two.

What the hell is happening to me?

You stopped taking your meds, Jing. What did you expect would happen?

She could almost hear Goldfield's patronizing (but reasonable) explanation. First, the seizures resumed, now hallucinations, practically a repeat of the progression of events she had experienced in the Clouds— but she had only stopped taking the meds a week ago, the day she received her diagnosis. Psychotic relapses after ceasing antipsychotics typically took weeks to months. (Or so the schizophrenia pamphlet claimed.) She was not, however, sure about anticonvulsants.

Maybe it's similar to a migraine. It'll pass if I can relax.

Be Zen, Jing.

It will pass. It will pass.

Be Zen.

I'm just imagining this shit. Everything's fine.

But her vision didn't return, and each passing minute ratcheted up the tension in her body. She called the nurse and requested some books from her room and the tea Penn had brought her. Distraction is what she needed. As the nurse turned to go, Jing said, "I, um..."

"Yes?"

"I need to come clean about something."

"Interesting choice of words. Let me guess, honey: you stopped taking your meds and are feeling guilty about it?"

Jing stared back at the woman, at a loss.

"Happens all the time, Ms. Elwood. Don't worry. We'll get you back on track." She tapped the IV.

Jing wanted to say more, explain why she had stopped taking them and why she had just revealed this information to the nurse—*I'm blind*—but again the words failed her.

I should tell them. There could be something seriously wrong with me. A stroke or tumor or something.

You're relapsing. That's all. This is what Goldfield has been waiting for. You're not going anywhere now—

"Jing?" Waters calls from the bottom of the stairwell.

It takes her several seconds before she turns and looks at the man, her mind excised carefully, surgically from the memory. Dark circles shadow her eyes. It seems that overnight she has lost the bit of weight put on while at Glenbrook. She resembles more the drug-addled musician that had entered the hospital months ago.

"Yeah?"

"Appointment time."

"Coming." She tucks the cigarette behind her left ear, in the process poking herself in the face.

"How are you doing?" Goldfield asks, putting aside her cigarette for her notebook. She is wearing large gold hoops, an autumn-themed sweater and skirt.

"You mean aside from the obvious?" Jing's chin rests in the palm of her left hand, her fingers dancing around her eye.

"We can ease into the obvious if you'd prefer."

"Okay." Her throat constricts. "Well, I haven't felt great. Last night when I couldn't sleep, I caught a program about the band I was in."

"Auto-something-or-other," Goldfield says, glancing back through her notes.

Jing smiles. "Autoscope."

"Right, sorry"—Goldfield looks up, brightening—"so you were on TV? How exciting."

"It was just a local show. Not a big deal."

"Nevertheless, I didn't realize your group had been that successful."

"We did all right."

Goldfield begins to make lengthy notes. "I do remember you mentioning an album."

"Yeah, an album. Several tours, but only one when I was drummer. A song with radio play and a music video, 'The Pineal Eye.'" *Eye. There I said the word.*

"'The Pineal Eye.' Interesting." Her notetaking grows more and more vigorous. "So tell me: how was it seeing your band back together?"

Jing tries to click the tongue stud. Feels its absence. "Painful, surreal. I have trouble believing that was really me. It was some other Jing."

"How long were you guys together?"

"About two years."

"And how was it you came to join?"

"Well, Autoscope had two other drummers before me, the most recent this guy named Kiel. When Kiel became a problem (when his giant ego started to clash with Bower's), Penn called me up—I was in Ann Arbor—couch-surfing, basically; I'd just dropped out of school—and she said:

"'Hey girl, long time no speak, do you know how to play the drums?'

"'No.'

"'Can you learn to play them in like a month?'

"'I guess.'

"'Cool. Feel like moving to Apocalopolis?'"

Goldfield smiles. "Why you? Why not someone who already knew how to play?"

Jing removes her hand from her face and counts the ways on her fingers. "Penn and I played a bit back at school with these two other guys, and she knew we had musical chemistry. I was always learning new instruments back when we played together, picked them up quickly. I suppose those were the main reasons, but I also suspect the two of them were looking for someone that was the anti-Kiel—you know?—lacking the overpowering personality that would be a threat to Bower's ego."

She takes the cigarette from behind her ear, sticking it in the left corner of her mouth by habit, but then consciously shifting it over to the right as she reaches for Goldfield's lighter on the coffee table and burns it. She struggles to get the tip and the flame to meet.

Goldfield watches without comment or note.

Jing settles back in her chair and pulls up a leg, hugging it to her chest. Beyond the small window gray leaves scurry rat-like across the cracked paver stones.

"Penn sounds like a good friend," Goldfield suggests.

"We've had our issues. She can be capricious sometimes, but yeah, I consider her to be one of the best." Her mind darts back to the documentary. "Can't remember if I mentioned this or not, but she has this strange condition."

"What kind of condition?"

"A rare type of synesthesia—music and memory. I thought it was the coolest thing when she first told me about it—well, actually, first I thought she was full of shit, putting me on—but then I saw how debilitating it was. All kinds of simple things I took for granted she can't do when accompanied by music: driving, dancing, movies, video games. She even plays guitar with her eyes closed, and usually walks around with her ears plugged up to prevent stray music from causing her to misperceive reality. When she was a kid she would spend a month every summer with a team of psychologists who would run experiments on her. Made a good bit of money, I think, and a bunch of papers were written about her condition. 'P.C.', that's what they called her in academic journals. Have you heard about her?"

Goldfield shakes her head.

"Anyway, it's sort of her guiding principle in life and music. Since music can be so painful and confusing if produced (in her eyes) incorrectly, she taught herself to play using strange chords and harmonies, very minimalistic. It gave Autoscope a unique sound—that plus Bower's interest in tinkering with electronics. For Penn it wasn't about trying to create something new—just something that looked beautiful to her, maybe to influence others, so they would regurgitate similar songs inspired by and adhering to her same principles. Really it was the tension between their two philosophies that led to our success. I was just kind of lucky to be a part of it."

She takes a drag off the cigarette.

"You know, I have to admit, Jing, that I wasn't at all surprised when I learned about this recent attack," Goldfield says, seeming to sense the appropriate time has at last arrived.

"No?"

Goldfield shakes her head, almost with regret, pausing for a sip of coffee. "It's more likely than not related to the diagnosis; more specifically, my telling you the diagnosis."

"How do you figure?" Jing wraps one arm around her leg, setting the elbow of the other across the knee.

"Many patients after showing signs of improvement from medication and therapy, when given their official diagnosis, reject the judgment of their doctor, stop taking their meds, experience a relapse of symptoms. I've encountered this countless times."

Jing's expression grows murky and distant as she considers again whether her blind eye would be labeled a psychotic symptom. If a hallucination is a perception without stimulation of a sensory organ, then her problem strikes her as the opposite of a hallucination.

A delusion?

"I still don't think we should be toying around with your drug regimen, not when your state of mind has been so stable lately," Goldfield continues.

Jing stares at the psychiatrist for some time, finishing the cigarette.

"What if I want a second opinion?"

Goldfield taps her wedding ring against the nailheads on the armchair trim.

"I mean, you have me on so many fucking meds, labeled with too many conditions—I'm sorry, I don't buy it. There has to be a simpler explanation."

"Dr. Lindgren agrees with me as well."

"Yeah, but she's fresh out of med school; she's not going to clash horns with you."

"What about seeing Dr. Conway? He's a more senior psychiatrist than I."

Jing utters a sigh of reluctance. Dr. Conway had probably once been brilliant, but now has committed himself to purveying any and every kind of alternative therapy in existence. He would probably only complicate matters for her.

Goldfield pauses, thinking, turning her wedding band. "Are you familiar with Dr. Murai?"

Jing nods. She's *heard* of Dr. Murai. In fact, she passes by his darkened office every time she comes to meet with Goldfield, but she has not once seen him there. In fact, the room looks abandoned—chairless, couchless, furnished with only an overturned metal desk and a litter of scrap paper. He had needed more space apparently and so moved to the east wing, otherwise unoccupied and inaccessible to Glenbrook patients.

Jing snuffs out her cigarette in the ashtray on the coffee table. Her aim is off, and she strikes the rim, upsetting the ashes.

"Shit, sorry."

"It's fine," Goldfield dismisses without moving to help. "I'll clean that up later. Anyway, I first consulted with Dr. Murai at the time of your admittance as well as all of the other psychiatrists and psychologists on staff, and since then he has heard about your progress from time to time during staff meetings."

"And?"

"Well, he agrees with my diagnosis, too."

"Okay. Well, I suppose he would agree with you."

"Why do you say that?"

"Because you're feeding him the evidence that fits your hypothesis—of course he's going to side with you."

"You have an argument for everything, Jing. You know, I'm not married to this diagnosis. All I strive for in my work is accuracy and ultimately your wellbeing. If it makes you feel better, however, I can arrange for him to meet with you in a few weeks. He's out of the country at the moment, but after he returns, you can get a fresh perspective from him. How would that be?"

"Fine," Jing says, thinking that the exercise would be pointless: Murai has already been infected by the idea of her being psychotic. "And in the meantime?"

"In the meantime we stay the course." She pulls out the usual checklist and a coldness descends on her voice, "Now, how is your physical health?"

As Jing weaves her way out of the west wing and towards the rotunda staircase, the scent of something far superior than the usual disinfectant catches her attention—garlic, oregano, mozzarella. She tracks down the source of the smell to admissions where Penn, noise-cancelling headphones hugging her head, stands in front of the counter, bemused as the security guard inspects a pizza and bottles of Snapple. The guard pulls off a mushroom, nibbles it, explores the taste, then pops it into his mouth.

"Clean," he affirms.

Penn starts when Jing appears beside her. She is on the verge of punching Jing's shoulder, but then checks herself, taken aback by her friend's appearance. Waters escorts the two of them upstairs, Jing stumbling a few times on the steps and yelping as she rams her ankle into the marble. Once inside the visitation room, Penn takes off her headphones and settles down onto the couch. Meanwhile, Waters sets down in a chair in the corner.

"You want a piece?" Jing asks him.

"Nah, I'm good."

"What's going on?" Penn whispers, handing Jing a slice of pizza

"Crazy couple of weeks."

"Wanna talk about it?"

"Eh."

Penn watches her friend eat. Jing is tentative at first, but is soon wolfing it down, and a sad smile touches Penn's face.

"I would have brought beer or wine"—she glances over towards the tech—"but I'm not confident in my smuggling abilities. Besides, they didn't even let me bring in my lighter as they did last time. Confiscated my cigarettes, too."

Jing nods. "My privilege level has been lowered. And thanks for the thought, but alcohol with antipsychotics is a no-no."

"So, is that why—?" Penn flicks the stud in her own ear.

"Yup."

"You're not going to tell me what happened?"

Jing crosses her legs. "My diagnosis. I may be schizo-phrenic or schizoaffective, something along those lines."

"Jesus, Jing. When did you find this out?"

"Last week."

"I'm so sorry."

"Don't be—"

"You should've called."

"It's a" —she lowers her voice and leans across the coffee table—"a load of bullshit."

"Are you all right?"

"I'm fine. I'm getting a second opinion."

"And this is related to your"—Penn waves her hands around her face—"demotion or whatever?"

"Sort of. I guess I didn't take the diagnosis very well." The words feel like weights in her mouth.

Penn sets her food down and circles the table, sitting on the arm of Jing's chair and wrapping her arms around her.

Waters coughs. "Miss, we have a policy at Glenbrook—"

"My friend's upset," Penn says. "I'm just giving her a hug."

"No, you're not." He stands. "Sit back down, please. Jing could get in trouble; I could lose my job."

"Remember, Penn: high-five rule." Jing wipes an eye.

"How silly of me." She shoots Waters a dirty look as she returns to the couch.

"So awkward," Penn mouths to Jing.

Jing smiles, reaches across the table, and squeezes her hand. "Thanks. This is really good timing, you coming."

"So, what? Did you have a breakdown or something?"

Jing takes up another slice. "Stopped taking my meds."

Penn shakes her head in astonishment. "Why the hell would you do that?"

"I... was proving that they're wrong about me," she whispers with a quick glance towards Waters.

"Just let your doctors handle it, okay? I'd like to see you out of here."

Jing takes a sip of Snapple, a bit of it slopping down her chin. Her hands are shaking. Penn hands her a napkin.

"I'm such a fucking mess." She chokes back tears. "Let's change the subject. It's so tedious: talking about mental health. That's all anyone talks about around here."

"Okay."

"I guess you know Leif called last week."

"Yeah." Penn's gaze lights on her purse, then flits off—quick, but Jing catches it.

"What? What was that?"

"Nothing." Penn's shoulders tighten as if she had intended to shrug one of her exaggerated shrugs.

"That's obviously bullshit. Tell me."

"It's just that your conversation with Leif was partly my reason for coming." Penn relaxes her shoulders, a pained expression lining her face. She pulls from her purse an envelope and a CD in an unlabelled case. "These are for you."

"Is that 'Hypercrystal'?"

She nods. "Leif said you can just fax the signed papers back to him."

"Okay. And why were you debating giving these to me?" Jing's brow furrows as she reaches across the table for the CD and envelope.

Penn withholds them. "Well, the timing isn't great, but I need to tell you something first. I know you're not going to want to hear this, but you'll find out anyway as soon as you listen to the EP."

Jing waits, facial expression blunted.

"We decided to include 'The Blue Hour' as one of the B-sides."

"Okay. Not my favorite, but hardly crushing news."

Penn starts to contradict her, then goes on with her obviously rehearsed explanation, speaking in quick phrases. "It fits thematically and at the same time provides nice musical contrast with the other songs. You might remember the drums you did for them. It was early on, right after you moved here; you were really still getting a feel for things—"

"And?"

"We paid Kiel a flat rate to come in and re-record your drum track."

Jing winces, retreating back into her chair and running her hand through her hair. Again, she tries to click and is again frustrated by the lack of metal.

"I tried to get them to delay recording till your discharge so you could do it yourself, but since that date hasn't been set, Leif urged us to go ahead without you. The demand for our product is... peaking right now, but it probably won't last. Purely a business decision. I would have preferred for you to do it. You're still getting the same percentage of royalties as before—"

The lowest percentage.

"—and I think the result is really excellent. Kiel wasn't just doing Kiel; he was trying to channel you—"

"Oh, I'm sure he was doing his best malfunctioning drum machine impression."

"Jingy..."

"Well, thanks for telling me." She takes a bite of the now tasteless pizza, fighting it down her throat.

"I just want you to be aware of everything that's going on. It's shit timing. I—"

"Yeah, I appreciate you not coddling me. Well, whatever. Raking in the bones, right? That's what matters."

Penn, smoothing back a stray strand of hair, lapses into silence. Jing continues to eat, determined not to let her appetite be spoiled, but her throat remains thick and resistant. Something about the scenario strikes her as eerily familiar.

"You didn't defend me," she says, realizing it all at once, and searching out Penn's eyes.

"What are you talking about?" Penn strokes her slender neck. "You weren't there. How would you know? I defended you. I fought for you."

"No. I mean when we got our first review."

Penn arches an eyebrow, but her silence is telling.

"Just like now, silence is acquiescence, right?"

"Jing, this is…" Penn sounds wary and hurt and confused, but Jing can't stop. In the past she would have let it go. She'd been the queen of letting things go. After she had read the review and was on the verge of tears, and Bower had dove into a nonsensical treatise on musical philosophy, Penn had just stood there, looking away, tweaking her guitar's strange, alternate tuning.

"Just say that you agreed with the review."

Penn's mouth tightens. "In places," she admits at last. "It's just… you were high all the time."

"That's not true. That's so not true."

"No? Jing, the girl that came to Detroit was nothing like the one I knew at college. College Jing was dedicated, thoughtful, sweet. The one that came to Detroit was reckless, self-involved, self-destructive."

"That's so unfair. My mother had just died. You knew that. Not like you gave a shit about what I was going through."

"You think it's unfair? What about the rest of us, Jing? What about *Bower*?"

"I abandoned everything for you"—her face flushes—"I mean, for Autoscope."

"That was our lives. We were in it together, but you treated it like a disposable plaything."

"It sounds like you've really given this some thought."

Penn falls into a brooding silence.

"And Kiel? He's one of the ones you're playing with now? You're forming a new group without me? You're probably fucking him, too."

She doesn't deign to reply.

Jing glances over at Waters, his eyes wide, face ashen. Other employees might have been jotting all this down in their clipboard, but he looked frozen. "Can you leave us alone?" She snaps.

Waters actually flinches, but leaves.

She turns back to Penn, wanting to scowl and continue tearing into her, but finds she can't. It's all gone.

Just like that. A retreating wave. Throughout the fight, Penn had never quite lost her temper, which infuriates Jing even more. It would be so satisfying to wring her beautiful neck.

"I think I should go back to my room or something."

"Okay."

"I fucked things up, Penn."

With only a brief glance at Jing, Penn grabs her purse and headphones, and goes—

CHAPTER 7

Somehow I'm breathing. Shallow breaths. Unsatisfying.

The cloth. I'd wrapped it around my head right before the wave of sand had crashed down.

Grit is weighing against my face. I don't dare open my eyes. Wouldn't be able to reach and clean them if they were exposed to the sand. I must have only wrapped the cloth around one of my ears—the right—leaving the left exposed, now stuffed. Every slight shift of my head creates a lopsided sensation: muted on the one hand, grinding deafeningly on the other.

My body is... fossilized in a bizarre posture—torso twisted, left arm locked into my lower back, the other frozen out and up, legs spread into a runner's stride.

Can't tell if my head is closer to the surface than my feet. I remember I'd been standing upright, but maybe the ground pitched or rolled in the wake of the creature, like hoe-tilled earth, leaving me upside-down or diagonal or God-knows-which-way.

As a test I wiggle the only part of me that seems capable of motion, the right index finger. A light rain of sand trickles down onto my palm, suggesting that either my right side or my head are facing towards the center of gravity—or did the force of my finger's movement push the sand upward onto the palm?

This is getting me nowhere.

I click the tongue stud. *That* at least moves freely enough.

If only I could just wriggle my body. This position, the paralysis—it's excruciating. A little more air and I'd be able to scream.

Be Zen, Jing.

Be Zen.

I try again, moving the finger even more subtly than before, twirling in small, careful circles, packing the sand outward.

Soon my middle finger is moving, too—scraping, circling—and now the sand slides down my palm and wrist. The ring finger joins in. Before long the entire hand is carving out a very small pocket in the sand, the stream of loosened grains cascading down the length of my arm.

Must be lying on my side.

With the rotations of my wrist, I start to carve out an ever-widening cone, then reach an impasse. The right hand has carved out as much space as it's capable of reaching, but my arm still remains trapped, partly as a result of all the extra sand packed down from the hand and wrist movement.

So I shift over to the left hand, starting anew the same process, and before long both hands have formed pockets around them, but to no apparent end.

What else can I do?

I attempt something similar with the feet—without success. I do, however, notice for the first time that one shoe is loaded with sand while the other seems to have come off.

If only I could free my head... but that's far trickier. Each slight movement I make produces a rain of sand, blocking the reciprocal motion: I turn left, can't turn right; I look up, can't look down. I fear disturbing whatever delicate balance my head might be in with the sand. Maybe I'll inadvertently cause a stream of it to flow into my mask and up my nose...

So that brings me back to the hands.

There has to be something more they can do.

They both explore their tiny, new worlds, but it's useless... They scrape endlessly around their grainy environments. The skin under the nails starts to agonize. My fingertips suddenly feel wet.

Fuck.

The frustration betrays a violent exhalation, and the sand compresses, tightening its grip around my chest, further constricting breathing. Can barely pull the air past the back of my throat, but it's just enough.

Time drags on. It's unclear just how much time passes.

Did I sleep just now or have I been awake continuously?

If I did sleep, there were no visions or dreams, just this dank, oppressive embrace.

Stimulation. Any kind of stimulation would be wonderful. The light touch of a breeze on my cheek. A drop of water on my toe. A glimmer of light. Just *something* other than this. I can't really even feel my body... no, my lips are there, and the tip of my nose is here, but beyond that it's dim signals twinkling lightyears away.

I need to move. Need to move this immense, entropy-bound universe that is my body. Need something.

I bite the tip of my tongue and there is a burst of pain and the spill of metallic heat on my lips. An exquisite blossom of life. The sensation sounds out a shockwave to the far reaches of my body, and back bounce responses, signs of life from the edges of the universe.

Maybe if I try to engage a vision, I can transport permanently out of this hell and just watch myself on Earth until the two of us Jings die.

That would be fine. That would be fine.

I concentrate, squeezing my eyes shut even tighter than before.

Anything. Just not this. I won't accept this. This is not me. This is not happening. I'm in Glenbrook. That's reality. Bower's dead. I'm crazy. Penn hates me. That's the truth.

But the visions don't come.

There's no quick way out of this one. No razor to slit the wrists... No. No razor. But death could be quick. I could gag myself on the sand.

As I begin to shift my face, my prayer is finally answered: a sudden flash of light, the blackness beyond my eyelids reddening for a split second.

My breath catches in disbelief.

I imagined it. Must have.

The light rekindles.

Has the dragon come to unearth me?

Then the redness fades once again to black. Moments later it resumes, now brighter than before. But only the left eye. Only the left eye. Why does that seem so significant? In my delirious excitement I can't remember why that would matter.

There's more. A muffled sound. Just discernible. Grinding, shifting sand, very distant.

I risk opening the eyelids a crack, careful to keep the long eyelashes steepled together, praying to the sand gods to spare my eye. A few fine particles filter down, irritating the exposed cornea, but I persevere. All I can make out is a vague phosphorescence. Opening wider, the eyelash steeple gradually parts with bold impiety.

More stinging sand rains down, and a wash of tears obscures my vision.

At last my eyesight clears; I get my bearings. A narrow crevice in front of the left side of my face, formed by two rocks embedded in and buttressing the sand, illuminated at the far end by a single inch-long worm, exoskeleton translucent, innards lunar in their pale fire. Must have just now burrowed its way inside.

The worm clings to the rock edge—from my perspective upside-down—staring at me, intricate mouthparts flexing and clicking, not in the agitated chatter I'd witnessed from its kind before, but leisurely sampling the air. For several minutes we regard each other in stillness.

I shouldn't blink. The movement may draw its attention.

Part of my mind knows this is absurd: it may see me,

but more likely it tastes the chemistry of fear wafting out of my head.

Of my two hands, the right, still positioned above my head, is closer to my eye—I think, I think. If only I could dig my way into the crevice, then I'd be able to just pluck up the worm and squish it between my fingertips.

I start to scrape, ignoring the throb of raw flesh beneath my fingernails.

The worm inches forward, then pauses again to taste the air, the clicking of its mouthparts ratcheting up like a Geiger counter nearing a hot spot. It's only about half a foot from my face, and though it's difficult to tell without a visual conformation, the hand must still be a foot or so away, in another galaxy. What's more, I can only move the actual hand, not the arm, meaning I can't lower the hand into grasping distance. Nevertheless, I continue to claw at the sand. Maybe I can loosen the surface and shift the position of the rocks, so the worm no longer has a beeline to my face.

It inches forward.

With each advancement it pauses, reassessing its position.

I grunt and groan, attempting to frighten it away, but there's so little air, the sound, a whimper, does nothing to deter it.

It inches forward, clicking faster and faster, pitch higher and higher.

My hand tears frantically at the sand. Touches rock. Yes, *the* rock. The one the worm clings to. Seems immobile as I scratch at its surface. Yet I can see the chamber wall before my eye budging somewhat with each prod of my fingers.

The worm inches forward.

I jab at the wall of rock, fingers squeezed together into an arrowhead. I curse. The wall budges. Not enough. Not enough.

The worm inches forward, its clicks a whirring fury.

The thing consumes my field of view. Beyond it, the

back of the rock comes loose, and a flood of sand washes down into the space towards the end of the chamber, the tips of my fingers now visible around the back edge of rock, too far away to be of any help.

It inches forward, all of the mouthparts jittering in synchrony, a vortex of cogs and spicules and grabbers, complex and beautiful and horrible.

I attempt to jerk my head out of its path, but manage to shift only a few centimeters. Not enough. Not enough.

Its flexing mouthparts mow and pluck through my long eyelashes, and I'm left with my last line of defense: closing my eye.

Praying.

A bright orange, veiny darkness. The glowing worm caresses my eyelids, testing it, tasting it.

Then agony and pink and black bubbling blood as it burrows through the eyelid, forcing its light upon me. I shake my head, moan, twist, plead, scream.

Nothing fazes the worm.

It gnaws through the lens, hot vitreous humor spilling out over my nose and down the side of my face.

My skull vibrates as the gnawing worm burrows deeper into my head. A peace settles over me. Maybe it's the relief of letting go, or maybe the worm just devoured the giving-a-shit part of my brain. The sand releases its hold on me. My arms are lifted up into the rancid deathlands, and Death itself faces me, its glowing, bony visage blurry in my sand-stung good eye. It sticks its rotten finger into my left eye socket, harpoons the worm with its long nail, extracts it, and crushes it.

"You must follow us if you can," it whispers as I rub the sand out of my eye with one hand and cover the painful, leaking hole with the other.

An eerie light surrounds the two of us from the hundreds of bugs worming in and out of the walls, and all over my body, illuminating the light rain of loose sand trickling from the ceiling. Many yards in the distance glows a golden orb.

The light at the end of the tunnel.

Beyond.

Death helps me to my knees.

"Your legs do not appear to be broken. You should be able to crawl."

The claw grips my arm. Death's touch is caring if not bony, sullied with the filth of countless corpses, guding me down the cramped, worm-infested tunnel.

I turn to see the tomb that had held me for so long, now just a small indentation in the ground.

"Don't be frightened. You are safe with us."

"I think my brains are falling out," I gasp, hand clasped to the excruciating wound. It makes crawling difficult, but I desperately want to keep everything in place.

"I doubt that," it whispers in its oily voice. "Come. We'll fix you up in a few moments."

"Are you taking me to Heaven or Hell?" The tunnel inclines, a positive sign, but I need to make sure.

"What? What are you talking about?"

"I can't go to the afterlife wearing only one shoe. And my purse. It has a customer loyalty card. I can get a free record."

"Umm..." It sniffs. "Never mind that. We'll retrieve those later. Almost there, poor girl."

We exit the tunnel, and I roll over onto my back. Not Heaven or Hell, just the desert at sunset, smoothed out by the leviathan, beyond the white haze, the setting sun glows marigold. Just discernible above us drifts a cramped panoply of asteroids.

I look over at Death—its furry body, short frame, bizarre long-toed feet with pointed toenails, one of them atrophied and bony, the skin just rotted, black leather webbing.

The rat.

"You have worms," it notes, skull clacking along in agreement, bugs tumbling out of its own empty sockets.

I get to my knees. "Let them eat me."

"Come, that's no way to talk."

"My eye." My voice chokes as I bury my face in my hands, fingers plastered with bloody grit.

The left eye. I remember now. The vision. The same eye that went blind.

"Don't worry. We'll take care of them." I can feel the rat plucking worms from my body.

"Just one tiny worm... I couldn't stop it."

My hand, cupping the wound, wants nothing more than to probe and assess the damage, but another part of me fears knowing, fears touching the deflated eye sac. Maybe, after all, the worm missed the eye, just ate some of the surrounding flesh. Maybe if I just press my hand here long enough, keep the juices and vital matter from flowing out, it will fix itself.

"*One... fucking... worm.*"

"Come, don't touch that." It guides my hand away from the socket. "Let's use this instead." It unwraps the mask wound around my lower face, beats the sand out of it, and begins to wrap it around the left side of my head, having a difficult time with its short, inflexible arms, one of them a reeking, inarticulate parody of life. "That will do for now, but we'll need to treat it along with your other wounds. Perhaps when we find an oasis." Its heads turn to sniff this way and that.

"This keeps happening to me."

"You mean we keep bumping into one another? Yes, that's quite interesting, isn't it?"

"No... I mean... I'm on the brink of death, and then one of you creatures brings me back. I just can't quite die."

The rat squats down across from me. "It would be a neater way to end things, surely."

"You should've just left me down there. I was... it was so close to ending. I could sense that worm getting near the cortex. A little further and I would have been gone."

"Are you so certain you would have died? The body is quite resilient. It might have just lobotomized you, turned you into some mindless zombie. Take us, for example: we should have been dead long, long ago. No, we must do what we can for each other, help each other make the most of the time we're given on Psyche."

"Psyche," I whisper, feeling the shape of the word, despising every contour. "I've had enough of this godforsaken nightmare. Maybe if I die here, I'll return to Earth or wake up or something."

"A nice fantasy, but we believe returning to Earth is a little more complicated than that."

"Returning to Earth?"

"Sure, if that is what you're after, it is more complicated than simply killing oneself."

"So the dragon wasn't lying. There is a way." I click the tongue stud against the back of my teeth.

The rat's paws freeze over the bandage. "Dragon? What dragon?" The skull clatters either in trepidation or from being jostled by the living rat's movements.

"I'm sort of... involved with this dragon. A dog too."

It resumes wrapping my head, slower now. "What do you mean when you say 'involved'?"

"Well, this is going to sound ridiculous... but it forces me into feeding it with this energy stuff. Almost like it's eating bedtime stories but just sort of a rambling one with me as the protagonist and there's no plot and it's really fucking annoying watching me and not being able to just shake me out of this stupor and see out of my own eyes. That's at night, of course. The dragon seems to roam around or something during the day, then find me in the evenings—when it's ready to feed."

The rat angles its nose skyward and sniffs. The burnt sun is bearing down on the horizon, close to setting the mountains ablaze in incandescent rainbows. Everything looks unreal, in this thick whiteness, the edges and colors misremembered—a dream, a memory.

"The evenings, you say."

I lightly pat the bandage over my eye. The pain is all-consuming, but even worse is the empty horror of senselessness. "Yeah."

"That does not give us much time."

"Enough time to do what?"

The rat turns back to me. "To hide from the dragon, obviously."

"Do you mean 'we' as in you two or 'we' as in you and me?"

"Both."

"No"—I shake my head—"I need the dragon, and I'm convinced I can get it to help me. It's threatened to eat me on several occasions, but it won't do it. I'm worth more to it alive than dead. I know it; *it* knows it."

"Whatever it is you think you've worked out about the dragon is irrelevant." It motions towards its decaying left half. "We owe this to a dragon, and we doubt yours is any more compassionate or reasonable. The only thing you can expect from them is erratic behavior with no thought to consequences." The skull clacks as it speaks in its oily, nasal tone. "No, we can guide you to a safe place, somewhere off the beaten path, a place where the dragon is unlikely to discover us. Then we can work on the problem of returning you to Earth."

"And what exactly are *you* getting out of this deal?"

"Why... the honor of knowing and helping a human, of course."

After the rat recovers my battered shoe and purse from the tomb, we set off, trudging side-by-side, which reduces the punch of the odor, a bright flag trailing behind it. The hunched creature alternates between a bipedal hobble and a three-legged hop. Strapped to its back is a kludged together backpack teeming with cactus arms, dried herbs and aromatic grasses, a small garden of flowers planted in a hollowed-out branch, various-shaped stones that could pass for dinnerware or tools, loops of plant fiber stringing together teeth and bones, and a few wooden stakes of varying lengths.

The air is much cooler in the pale wake of the leviathan. With the shirt split and divided among the many wounds and the leftover bits shredded to pieces by the wave of sand, I have little more to clothe me than shoes, jeans, and bra. In this thick haze, I need a mask in order to breathe properly, and so remove the arm bandage and mummy-wrap my head, just the right eye visible now. The arm wounds are still stomach-turning, but the pain is more tolerable than yesterday. The leg, too, walks easier.

How long had I been under the sand?

I pause occasionally, shielding myself from the rat's eyes, to empty out my bra and sneakers, which collect the fine powder of the dust cloud, irritating my ankles and nipples, culturing a membrane of powder-pink blood paste.

The setting sun finally passes below the peaks of the Crystal Mountains, the light arrayed into an infinity of rainbows that circuit and sparkle through the lingering haze. The sight is breathtaking, providing at least a momentary distraction from the pain of the trek and almost making all of this torture worthwhile.

Almost.

The march drags on for hours in this rave-lit gloaming. From time to time my ears prick up, questioning that they had not just heard the scaled-sail billowing of the dragon aflight. Despite this trick of the ears, its glowing eyes never pierce the smog, nor does a fabulous burst of flame dispel the gathering dark.

It can't be terribly safe traveling with such a companion as this rat, which any beast could smell from a long way off. I glance over at the shambling creature, shuddering at the unnerving rhythm of its dead half's clattering bones and loose, squelching flesh.

Where is it taking me, and why should I trust such a foul-looking, -smelling, and -sounding thing? "It's heading towards (if memory serves correct) a much craggier area of the desert, tracking along to the right of the mountains, which are illuminated like back-lit cellophane that's been creased and re-creased. Perhaps it's taking me back to a kingdom of rotting rodents, all awaiting a human to feast on.

I want to ask, but fear making any unnecessary sound, noticing how it carries in the hazy dusk, resounding in unusual ways. So I just continue on in silence, vigilant, shivering.

So many unknowns, the questions carousel around in my head, an echoing memory of my travels with the dog. Except now that I have a companion that can answer my questions, I'm too afraid to break the silence.

Finally the last crest of sun has vanished, though the mountains keep an afterglow vigil for some time. At this conclusive stroke, the cold grows intolerable, and I turtle, head recoiling into my shoulders, arms tucked into my body.

After a time, a familiar throbbing comes to my attention.

The swollen worm hole in my leg has reopened like a hungry orifice.

"How much farther are we going?" I whisper at last, voice shaking with cold, not fear. By now the fear has burned out, leaving a fragile carbonized shell in my mind—perhaps why after so many worrisome and urgent questions have plagued me, I begin with the basest of them.

"Difficult to say." The rat sniffs. "The haze is clouding our olfactory depth. You mentioned a dog, didn't you?"

"Yeah. Why do you ask?"

"The trail is old, but a canine of some sort traveled this way."

"Maybe we should try to find her. She's a little standoffish, but big. Might be able to help defend us against the dragon... if the need arose."

"Well, with any luck the dog traveled towards our destination. We will see."

I nod, rubbing my hands and arms. "Man! It's so fucking cold."

"It would be too risky to make a fire here," it squeak-whispers, features illuminated by the distant neon burn of a floral grove, creating a stark contrast between the white bone and dark fur. "The dragon is probably combing the desert for signs of camp. Even being close to one of these groves is imprudent. If we were the dragon, we would restrict our search to areas surrounding food supplies."

Unconsciously, I pull the lighter out of my purse and rub the flint wheel with the throbbing pad of my thumb, summoning the ghost of flame as a proxy for the heat of bona fide fire.

"So, then, what constitutes a safe place?" I say, clenching and unclenching my fists around the lighter.

"You'll see."

"You're playing this pretty close to the chest, huh, Ratty?"

"We did not fail to notice you were not too keen on us when we first met. We hold no illusions that you would rather be rid of us, so forgive us if we don't tell you everything for fear of becoming inessential."

I frown, continuing onward.

After a few minutes of powder white and darkness and the relentless waves of pain, I speak again. "I'm sorry. I shouldn't have said that about your smell before. In fact, I've been a whiny ass this entire time—and I never thanked you. You saved my life twice now: dug me out of the sand, pointed me away from encountering those snakes."

"Apology accepted, but there is no need to thank us. If you were not human"—the skull clacks with emphasis—"we might not have been so quick to help."

We continue onward as I puzzle over what this means.

At an unknown later the haze begins to clear. The face mask comes off. I wrap it around my chest in a last effort to keep myself warm but settling at least for a modicum of modesty.

After walking several miles through the crisp, clear air, I turn to regard the cloud hovering over the darkened desert—the aftermath of the leviathan.

"We're too exposed here," I whisper.

"Don't worry." It rises on its hind legs and motions towards the horizon, both with its snout and the anthropomorphic hand of its withered foreleg. "You see those outcroppings and cliffs ahead? We should be able to take shelter there, out of sight of the sky."

Soon the sand cloud blurs into the horizon. We pass by a twisting column of rock smooth as ivory. Then another. Soon we are deep in an ivory forest, tumble-weeds of curious tangles and textures scuttling past us, catching on thick brainy folds of yellow lichen. The rock formations continue to grow in size and complexity, arching and spilling into each other, and finally opening up into the base of a boulder-littered canyon, above us a lush vista of stars occluded by the odd planetoid and framed by the tortuous cliff edges. White swirls with purple and gray and starry black. The rock, convex, with rounded facets, catches every sound we make and laughs it back.

Colder and colder, my labored breath turns into thick white plumes. My shivering has amped up to dys-functional, making stealth impossible in this echoing place. Even worse, I'm ravenous and exhausted, sensing again that an incredible amount of time has passed since being pulled out of the sand.

"I need to rest, eat something," I say at last.

The rat stops and sets down its pack, rummaging around and then handing over a small, dried, cube-shaped fruit. "Go ahead and eat this."

The rat sniffs around while I dust off and then gulp down the wrinkly, rubbery-textured fruit, barely tasting anything. It creates an unpleasant sensation in my mouth, difficult to pinpoint, my senses being so blunted from the cold.

"We're not carrying much more in the way of food, but we smell an oasis up ahead. Let's take our repast there and stock up. Afterwards, we suggest climbing to the top of the canyon to scout out a narrower ravine than this one." Its whiskers twitch, nose wrinkling in suspicion. "Our nose will also be much more useful above: the wind down here only announces what is ahead of us and not what may be lurking along the cliff edges."

"What about the dog?" I ask.

"It came this way. That's all we can say for sure."

We trek through the canyon, eyes on those high, shadowy walls. Soon, sure enough, an oasis appears ahead growing out of the side of a cliff base, comprised of a number of familiar flora, fauna, and fungi. As we near it, the rat sniffs deeply, then glances over at me.

"Girl," it says. "We have unfortunate news."

"You mean... the dog?"

"Yes, this is a canine oasis."

I stand there, staring into the thick vegetation crawling with noisy, glowing insects. Stinks worse than the living-dead rat. "I need to check to see if it's..." I want to say "mine," but it's hardly the appropriate word.

The living head nods. The other just gapes idiotically. "Be careful. Don't eat anything. We will gather food for our repast."

I creep inside, mindful not to step on anything moving, but don't travel more than several yards before my breath catches. Ahead of me, lying on its side, body... deflated, the flesh pulled apart and rotting, different types of molds—some filmy, some crystalline—sprouting out of the various tears, the beautiful white fur shedding like autumn leaves, critters chattering away as they weave in and out of its viscera—the dog.

"Christ," I whisper, hand to my mouth, circum-ambulating the giant carcass. When I reach its head, I find gripped in its skeletal paws and crammed into its

worm-riddled jaws an orange fruit emitting a dull glow—
skin grainy, its shape somewhere between a bugle and
an infinity symbol, the mouthpiece also serving as its
bell, extending outward and looping back around to
contain itself but, impossibly, without intersecting itself,
its insides lined with the same rough, orange skin as the
outside.

The beauty of the object mutes that mournful voice
in my head, the one shocked at finding the dog dead. I
move closer to the stinking corpse and the worms,
wrench it from the jaws and back away, brushing off a
few small worms, worms the size of the one that took my
eye, little nothings.

Rotating the fruit, trying to figure out how it should
be oriented, a term pops into my head—a Klein bottle,
one of those curiosities that will entice mathematics professors away from the thread of a lecture and down a
long-branching digression. The figure has no interior or
exterior, only accurately rendered in four dimensions.

Lightweight, completely uneaten, but how? I glance
back at the dog, remembering how it would indiscrimin-
ately scarf up its food. Maybe it was killed by something
right before it took a bite. The dragon?

I bring the orange fruit closer to my face to take in
the dark, resinous aroma—when the rat shouts from
behind, "Do not eat that, girl." Its voice rebounds across
the canyon, circles around us, fades, and returns.

"What?" My faint, indistinct voice sounds alien,
masked by the rat's echo. "Why not? It looks delicious."

"That is a rumination fruit." The rat hobbles towards
me from a clump of shivering gelatinous fungi, pedantic
skull clacking in concert. "It is indeed delicious. In fact
it is the most delicious of all fruits, but it is *under-
nourishing* for our wards as you only lose energy eating
it. Moreover, there is no way to finish it, since there is
no substance to be finished, no beginning and no end,
all rind."

I continue admiring it, inhaling, not quite processing

what the rat just said. The throbbing in my fingertips, leg and arm, the sand burns and the cracked lips, the blind eye, they're all forgotten. "It's so tantalizing..."

The rat snatches it from me and tosses it into the dirt. "This dog must have died eating it. There was probably a smaller, older oasis here, one that bore these rumination fruits. We have seen a number of dogs that have met this kind of end—a weakness in the species. Probably a combination of the bright color, intriguing aroma, and perplexing structure. You see, it is so delicious and so unsatisfying, one taste and you risk being trapped under the spell of endlessly consuming it; the more voraciously you do, the faster you die. Better stick with the puffballs for now. As a rule of thumb, the more sides something has, the more nutritious it is, but never eat anything, anything at all, without first consulting us."

I nod, casting one last wistful glance at the impossible knot of fruit lying in the sand—such a shame to waste it—and then over at the dog's carcass.

Now that the rumination fruit is out of my hands and mind, the weight of the dog's death hits me all over again.

What had gotten into me?

After eating in silence for a time at the verge of the dog's oasis, I stand to tear off a cactus arm, groaning.

The rat narrows its nostrils. "We should treat those bites and that cut. The sooner, the better."

I pause with my drink, watching the rat shuffle past me into the grove.

It approaches a fungal tree, reaches up on its hind legs and using one of its wooden stakes knocks down several chigger-red, wheel-shaped bugs off the branches. It gathers these in its small forelimbs and returns in an unsteady gait.

"What are you doing with those?" I ask, frowning and tossing the cactus arm aside.

"Take your pants off, and we'll show you."

"Pardon?"

"Take off your pants, girl."

I give the rat a withering look.

"We need to apply these spirits of sunshine to your wounds," it explains. "They will help with the pain and healing process. The neurotoxin they release in their bites is a natural anesthetic. Additionally (and quite usefully), chatterboxes cannot tolerate the poison."

"Maybe you should take care of yourself first."

"It's too late for us. The parasites would be of no help. Now, we need to treat your leg first—it is beginning to smell."

I bite back a retort about the rat lecturing anyone on their smell, and comply, shimmying out of the pants-shaped sheets of hardened white sand that were once jeans.

The rat limps over, red insects in hand. It pokes around the wound, now a ghastly carbuncular mound of fire, with streamers of violet branching out across my pale skin. As it touches near the infected bite, faint, intermittent glows appear within.

"What the hell are those?"

"Infestation, just as we suspected. Do not be alarmed."

"A fucking *worm* infestation!?"

"Chatterboxes, we call them." The rat takes the largest of the red parasites, appendages flexing enthusiastically, and places it close to the wound. The creature, about as large as a pomegranate and with a rubbery, unsegmented texture, grips my flesh and sinks its fangs into my wound with its tiny arachnid mouth—a flash of pain, then a cool wave spreading out from the bite. My clenched fists relax as the creature suckles on the wound. The glowing shapes under my flesh accumulate near the surface, then one by one they burrow out, wriggling agitatedly, making pink-pus Swiss cheese of my leg.

I quail while the rat plucks them up and silences them with its long nails.

"Now the arm."

"God, I can't take this."

"Steady yourself. That wound smelled like the worst of them."

The rat inspects both the cut and bite wounds on my left arm.

"Who cut you? Did the dragon do this—or that dog?"

"No, it was... an accident."

It grunts, continuing its inspection. Nothing glows inside my arm when the rat pokes around with its nose, sniffing, and tickling me in the process.

"These smell clean. Last, the eye."

It peels off the bandage and sniffs the hole in my head, the maddening nothingness from which I once would have been able to see.

"This one smells suspicious. We should apply a spirit of sunshine for safety. We don't want any chatterboxes burrowing into your brain, do we? We warn you, though, the neurotoxin will cause temporary slurring of speech and paralysis of some of the facial muscles."

"Just get on with it."

The rat applies another insect, which again sucks enthusiastically at my wound, its red appendages prodding and curling around my face, hooking onto my eyebrow and lip rings. As before, there is an intense pain followed by a cool, relaxing wave, though now I notice the muscles in my face going slack. My leg, too, isn't as responsive as it had been.

"You wehhen't gihhing," I say, then shut up upon hearing the inarticulate sounds. It feels as if half my face has swollen up into a gelatinous cast, a disturbing sense of asymmetry.

"We're afraid talking is very much out of the question for a few hours. Aha!" It plucks a skinny chatterbox out of my eye wound. "Good riddance to you, sir!"

After several more minutes, the rat removes the spirits of sunshine from the wounds and introduces them to its backpack, where they rotate and twist their way past the cacti and dried fruit and nestle against the wooden frame. I ease onto the numbed leg, which now feels a bit like hinged wood longer and thicker than the other leg. After re-wrapping the leg bandage, I pull on my jeans and see to the head wrap.

Above us, a large planetoid crests over the cliff side, just a sliver of it illuminated by the oblique angle of tomorrow's sun. We leave the light of the grove, limping along the base of the slope with reverent, night-time caution. The going is difficult at first as I adjust to the disparate sensation of the two legs, but by compensating for the loss of touch with vision, I at last manage to shuffle in a manner approaching normal. Even so, our passage is chronicled by a volley of echoes.

After a half mile or so of searching for a way up the precipitous canyonside, the rat jerks its nose towards the rear, skull clattering in its trail.

I give my companion an inquiring look.

The skull, glaring white in the darkness, turns back to me, seemingly of its own volition, gaping from empty eye sockets, impressing upon me urgent news. Then the other head turns, peeking around from behind the skull, nostrils wide with redundant alarm.

"What?" I mouth, even this action troublesome and muddled under the effects of the neurotoxin.

It mouths something back, a short word, but one I cannot decipher for the strange way in which rats move their lips when they speak.

"Wha'?" I whisper.

This time it passes a bit of air through its mouth, the lightest gust of a word: "Snake."

I squint down the mottled gloom of the canyon alley-way, carrying on for a mile or so before the nearest bend: a ramble of interconnected, seashell-like boulders; slopes of detritus; the occasional tuft of glowing flora clinging to the remains of some long-dead creature. I scan back towards the way we'd come and see more of the same. Up until now, I've assumed that when the rat mentions snakes, it is referring to something akin to the remains I'd found in the oasis several days ago, but maybe after all it only means Earth-sized snakes.

I creep closer to the rat, into the dense thicket of the rotting stench and whisper: "Whehe?"

"Can't tell. Localization is impossible in this wind, but if we can smell the snake, we must assume it can also smell us. Plus, it will be able to detect our heat. We're blazing beacons standing out here."

I nod, wanting to suggest hiding in a cave or burying ourselves in the sand, anything to conceal our heat signatures. Instead, realizing there is no time to attempt to articulate such an idea in my current state, I gesture towards the talus slope ahead of us away from the mountains, banking on the rat's ability to understand my intentions.

It nods in return, and the two of us scurry cat-quiet up the slope towards the scree where angles of conch lie helter-skelter. We crawl into a rough enclosure of stone like some hollowed-out house—such bizarre, seabed geology on Psyche—and hunker down. I pull out the fang, wielding it two-handed, and the rat slips out one of its pikes. Of course, if the snake doesn't smell me, there is no doubt it will smell out the rat. My best bet would be to distance myself from the rotten creature, waiting for the snake to attack it and then fleeing in the other direction, but I couldn't be so heartless. The only option, then, seems to be self-defense, however ante-diluvian our methods may be.

As we squat here, scanning through a porthole the gorge and the cliffs for any sign of activity, the rat's nose twitches again. "Very peculiar. I know that smell."

I'm on the verge of asking what it means, when movement reels my attention back to the opposite cliff. The shadowy edge has suddenly come alive—shifting and undulating. My breath catches.

Then it ceases, the scalloped edges still, and I release the stale air from my lungs, searching the cliff for more. But the night, the shadows, they obscure all. The rat cowers down, still and out of sight, perhaps having acquired all it needs to know per nasum.

Rubble clatters in the distance, echoing throughout the canyon—long, curious, clapping echoes—but the sound comes from farther off to the side—the reverberation?—I turn and catch more movement, a hundred yards or so distant from where I'd been scanning just before, the scale of the activity immense. Then the dark shape passes into the starlight, the reticulated scales winding down the side of the cliff flashing, spilling on and on, a waterfall of coins. More activity farther below, another protrusion of the shining falls, two light-exposed regions on the cliff, separated by a great distance, between them brewing darkness. About a quarter of a mile separates us and the shifting wall of the opposite cliff, a large distance, but one that a creature of this magnitude could presumably traverse in seconds.

A tugging at my good heel.

The rat is gesticulating towards the rear of our shelter where a path wends up the scree to the cliff face, and there a chimney cuts up the vertical slope. My guide dashes away in a surprisingly effective use of its withered limbs. I crawl out, stumbling, hurtle over a coil of rock, and land in a hobbling sprint, all of my mind focused on preventing the numb leg from tripping. With each racing step my heart races faster. With each stride the slope sharpens, checking my speed. It strikes me what a tragic curse it is to be human and slow. The half-dead rat has already gained the vertical surface of the canyon wall, clambering its way up the chimney—a shallow, kinking crevice. I risk a glance behind and find the opposite canyon wall bare, the snake, those flashing coins, gone.

Where—?

A sinuous river whips across the gray basin, surging and winding between the boulders, the creature giant, out of proportion even with the bizarre dimensions of Psyche—eighty feet long, more—a sleek, black and silver viper.

I push myself on up the slope still forty yards or so from the vertical face. The ground rumbles, and I turn to find several feet from me the scaly body of the snake weaving in and out of the rocks as it climbs, cutting across towards the much smellier rat. For a moment I'm mesmerized by the ripple of muscles and flashing of scales, bronze and blue in the darkness, stroboscopic metal waves that seem to crest forward at a glacial pace. Then, something bursts inside me—rashness, stupidity, I couldn't say—and I dash towards that scaly, undulating wall, fang high over my head. I stab down into the serpent's body, planting the tooth deep into the flesh, wedged in between the scales, releasing an eruption of black blood. The incredible speed of the thing rips the fang out of my hand and knocks me back, stumbling down the slope as the creature snaps around towards me.

Misplacing my numb leg, I tumble and crash into a boulder which booms hollowly like a drum.

Knocked windless, head dazed, I weave up onto my knees. Everything confusing, multiple slopes and snakes dancing and spiraling down into one, the air seems to be ripping apart, a surge of wind blowing up clouds of sand, almost in anticipation of the snake as it lunges.

Bright lights.

Every shadow banished.

Only a second or so for me to react, all I can do is stare ahead at the glistening fangs and wet, velvety mouth, beyond it a foul darkness I'll soon know intimately.

The lights ripple into an intense heatwave.

Heaven rends the night, flinging the snake sideways in a sulphurous burst of wind and flame, leaving in its wake a blackened, sizzling canyon slope, small fires cropping up out of the singed rock, more hell now than heaven.

Struggling to my feet, I glance around, trying to make sense of the scene in my dazed state.

Crashing and squealing, crackling and roaring.

To my left, a dark confusion twists, a giant mass upsetting boulders, sending them bounding down the slope into the basin.

Another burst of flame.

The dragon.

Their ophidian bodies entwined as if in the serpentine sex act, the dragon claws and thrashes at the snake, brutalizing it with lashes of flame. The creatures coil and teeth sink into each other with jackhammer brutality. Tails whip, pound the slope with knee-shaking tremors. I stare transfixed.

"Girl!" the oily clacking of the two rat heads shouting in unison pierce through the nightmare.

Up the sheer cliff face I spot the rat leaning out of the chimney, gesturing wildly for me to follow.

"It is our chance! Seize it!"

I limp forward double-time, scooping up the bloody snake fang and tucking it back into my belt. I mount the scorched slope, blackened rock sizzling to the touch, pursuing the rat, then squeeze into the chimney and begin to scramble upward, upsetting a clattery shower of pebble and dust. It's a treacherous climb, especially with my leg in its lethargic state and the now limited range of vision and flattened conception of the world, impeding my ability to grab hold of the edges of rock—an ill-timed surprise if ever there was one—but I push on in a monkey-scramble, up and up and up.

The battle between the dragon and snake rages on. Horrific bellows, bursts of light, quaking earth. I glance over the side of the craggy chimney to see a jet of magma shooting up out of the darkness, splattering the white walls like splashes of orange black light paint. I'm not sure how the monsters are matched, nor could I say which I'd prefer to rise the victor.

Halfway up, the battle wrenches to a halt leaving an uncertain silence. I don't dare crane my head over the chimney's jagged edge to take stock of the result, but my ears are pricked, waiting for the grinding slither of the snake weaving up the canyonside or the piscine flopping of the dragon's airborne ascent.

Neither sound comes.

Only when I've gained the clifftop and meet the rat there do the two of us peer over the side, watching to no avail for signs of movement below. Here and there, craven fires punctuate the canyon, skulking in the nooks between boulders, without the numbers or means to chase away the shadows. During our vigil, the sky pales, the desert horizon blushes violet, the texture of the immense planetoid above us smeared in a vivid, horror-movie-blood-red augury of morning.

The rat glances at me, hunched and tense. "Perhaps they have murdered each other," it whispers.

Not knowing if it would be better karma for me to shake or nod my head, I click in indecision.

At last with some hesitation we stand, and as if on cue there is a rustle in the air, the swirling up of dust. The rat reels and scampers away, heading for a nearby copse spilling over the side of the canyon like day-glo vomit. The dragon shoots up over the cliff edge, fiery blood spiraling out of its map of wounds, raining down around us, blackening cacti and withering flowers. I attempt to dive out of the way. Too late. The blood splashes across my legs.

I drop to the ground, screaming, rolling, trying to stifle the flames. The rat calls out, and out of the corner of my eye I spot it limping out of the glowing grove, cactus arm in hand.

The dragon coils in the air, then swoops down, crashing into the ground in an explosion of magma. In one glimpse between rolls I see its eyes—mutilated, the side of its snout crushed.

The rat dashes out of the way of the dragon around various sanguineous plumes and at last reaches me, dousing my legs with the jellied water.

Across from us, the dragon flails this way and that, crashing into the oasis, roaring, then half-slithers, half-flies off, writhing in a blind knot across the canyon top, crashing through towers of rock, streaking them with bubbling, orange magma.

Then it's gone.

I sit on a mat of fronds, propped up against a mushroom log, and examine the damage. The burns are not too dire, the worst being my lower left leg, where a patch of skin was melted off with my jeans—another Psyche scar to add to my growing collection.

All the while, the protracted screams and moans of the dragon ring out over the canyons. They simultaneously keep me on edge and reassure me of its distance from our camp; that it's dying. An hour or so passes before the plaints curtail, leaving us to ponder its fate.

After setting up our camp, scavenging materials from the rather meager, destroyed oasis, which appears to have sprouted out of a dead Harvey-sized rabbit, the rat digs a hole and lines it with stones. Then it makes several more trips into the flattened grove for wood and kindling, constructing the material into a small lean-to. It crouches over the pit and begins clacking together two smooth stones from its backpack.

"Umm, lemme." I take out the lighter, easing over to

the pit, and setting the tinder ablaze.

Its nostrils widen as the wood begins to catch. "Incredible. We have seen these in the visions. Many times. But never in person. Warm yourself by the fire, girl."

"Jing," I manage.

"Jing. Sit and rest. We will prepare some food."

By the crackling fire, the neurotoxin wearing off, the pains return one by one, unwelcome but for their reminders that I've survived. I retrace the events of the night, the sand burial, our flight into the canyon. Something is niggling at my mind, maybe something I overlooked, some detail in the blur of activity.

The rat is slicing up several balls of mushroom with a string saw. When it has finished, it grinds up various herbs in a smooth, hollowed-out branch from its backpack, then sprinkles on a bit of cactus juice to make a paste. It slathers this over the mushroom slices, skewers them and begins to grill them over the fire.

Was it something the rat said? It had said many strange things, but... suddenly I remember.

Ward.

It had said something about wards when we'd found the dog. I'd barely noticed at the time, having been so enraptured by the rumination fruit. Ward. Where had I heard that before? Something from one of the visions? A hospital ward or something? Had Penn mentioned it? Henry? Goldfield... no, the dragon! That first evening, it had said something about a ward... my ward... it had *called* me a ward. That was it. But then the rat had used it in a different way, but I can't remember how exactly.

"Rat." I stretch my lips and find the sensation very much returned.

"Yes?"

"You mentioned something about wards earlier when we found the dog. What do you mean when you said that—wards?"

Its heads nod wearily. "We will explain tomorrow

after we have rested. It could be a long conversation. We are very tired."

Soon enough the mushrooms are smoking and a little crisp, a tantalizing aroma wafting off them. The rat hands me one of the skewers. I blow on and nibble at it experimentally. The marinade has a spicy, minty zing like a chutney, blending nicely with the smoky flavor of the grilled mushrooms. I gradually take bigger and bigger bites and am soon gobbling them down. The rat eats slowly, its skull pantomiming the action.

"Thanks," I say at the end of the meal, "those were delicious."

"Never mind. We have actually never cooked before, but we are aware that this is what humans do. After what you've been through today, we thought it might help with your recovery."

"Never tasted anything quite like it."

"You should have a good rest. Once you have recuperated, we must start our journey back through the Memorylands."

Not exactly sure what it means, I cannot argue with the need for sleep. I lie back on a cushion of dead vegetation. Soon the pent-up Earth energy escapes into consciousness, and I'm released from Psyche:

CHAPTER 8

After breakfast Jing loiters beside the nurses' station, smoking a digestif cigarette, sipping coffee from a Styrofoam cup, and studying the billboard to get a sense of her day: her appointment with Goldfield has been canceled, freeing up her morning; the afternoon is packed with group and alternative therapies.

She glances over the weekly privilege table printout and is surprised to find that Henry has been raised to B3.

Jing herself has also been bumped back up to B3 after a week of good behavior, news she learned yesterday at her team meeting before the information was publicized to the rest of Glenbrook. After she'd heard the news, she had collected her piercings and lighter from the front desk and plugged in all the unsettling holes in her body.

As she stands there, Henry steals past, back from the cafeteria, ignoring her as has been his way ever since she lashed out at him in the cafeteria. She considers calling after him but then checks herself. Instead, she snuffs out her cigarette, returns to her room and replaces her sweats with a baggy, black sweater and tight ripped jeans, and exchanges her slippers for her red sneakers. Then, she washes and moisturizes her face, fixes her choppy hair and brushes her teeth. As she performs her ablutions, Henry's voice echoes in her mind:

"Goldfield, Murai, Conway, they're all a part of this. Psychoengineers. They want to sever us from our spirits."

It's been so long since she last spoke with him. Clearly he must have reined in those delusions if he's been promoted to B3. Maybe his recent avoidance of her had been partly due to embarrassment, remembering all the wild things he had confided in her.

She frowns at her reflection. *And I did nothing to help him.*

She'd been dealing with her own issues, true, but that was no reason to be a spectator on the shore while a friend drowned in the murky waters of psychosis.

Mouth clean, she strides over to her desk, pulls a small object out of the top drawer, stuffs it into her pocket, and goes to pay Henry a long-delayed visit.

A combination of preholiday understaffing and an early morning lapse of vigilance has left the nurses' station unmanned. Thus, Jing slips by with no great feat of stealth and finds herself in the men's quarters. She doesn't, however, take two steps before a voice calls out from behind.

"Ms. Elwood, where you off to?"

Christ.

She turns, fighting down a sheepish expression.

"Early morning rendezvous?" Diaz smiles.

Behind her, two other nurses have entered the station, watching intently. So, too, are the more alert of the patients in the dayroom, looking up from their morning papers. The rest stare frozenly or bob their heads mindlessly.

"I was—"

"No need to explain," she says, making a note in her clipboard and quoting the chapter and clause from *The Glenbrook Bible* she was about to break. "Anyway, you have a visitor."

In black tights, high-heeled boots, and a purple overcoat, Rui Elwood is stunning, glossy hair pooling over her shoulders. Taller, fuller-figured than her sister, Rui has their father's nose, Jing their mother's, the only features they share the jet black hair and large onyx eyes. Perched in the same chair Penn had taken so many days ago, she doesn't stand when her sister enters, but studies Jing intently as she walks over to the couch. Beyond her the skyline of Detroit rises out of a stark sea of tangled, leafless branches, into an overcast sky.

"What's up, fuckhead?" Jing plumps down.

"Carl and I are on our way to Marquette," Rui says in English, casting her gaze around the room, pausing on each piece of drab furniture. She mutters something, but Jing can only make out the phrase "a different room."

"Carl?"

"My fiancée." Rui flashes a multi-faceted diamond ring.

"Oh yeah, look at that," Jing says in Chinese.

Persisting in English: "He's a plastic surgeon. It's going to be a late spring wedding in Nantucket. You can expect an invitation in the mail. Should I send it... here or your apartment?"

"You don't want me to be a bridesmaid or anything, do you?"

Rui laughs. "God no. That's what sorority sisters are for, Jinger."

"I guess I'll go if I can bring someone."

"As long as it's not one of your inky girlfriends."

Jing clicks.

"Anyway, since we had a long layover in Detroit, and Carl wanted to take a look around the city, I thought I'd come pay you a visit. So, here I am."

"Awfully considerate of you."

"Can you not speak Chinese?"

"How is Ba doing?" Jing continues undeterred.

"How do you think he's doing?"

Jing shrugs. "We haven't spoken."

"Well, you can imagine."

The two sisters pull out cigarettes, Jing a crushed pack from her jeans, Rui a fresh one from her purse. A wry smile transforms Jing's face as she leans over the coffee table to light her sister's cigarette. "Same brand. Guess we're related after all."

Rui smiles reluctantly, her exquisite defenses dropping, and for a brief moment she resembles the gawky teenager imprinted in Jing's memory.

"He refuses to start seeing anyone else, won't listen to me, but it's clear he needs someone in his life. And this stunt of yours isn't helping. I mean, here you are wallowing around about your band breaking up or whatever when the rest of us have real-world issues to deal with."

Jing turns her lip ring. "I'm not wallowing."

"Well then what do you call this? Clearly there's nothing wrong with you, aside from your pathological need for attention and coddling."

Jing considers a number of potential dramatic responses—mentioning her blind eye or pulling up the sleeve of her sweater to reveal the scar from her suicide attempt—but instead says: "Thanks, Ruirui."

"Sorry, but you need to face reality. Get a job, get married—grow up." Rui has assumed what Jing recognizes as their mother's severe tone. "I could probably get you something in the mail room at my firm, or Carl could maybe find you an administrative position at his clinic—oh no, wait—I think they have a policy against hiring employees with drug records." She smiles critically. "Well, I'm sure I can get you *something*, a short trial period to make sure you can handle the workload. You'd have to remove the extraneous metal."

"Such faith you have in me," Jing says, tapping her cigarette over the ashtray between them. She manages to execute the action without stirring the discarded ash.

"I know you think I'm a bitch and hate me for speaking to you this way, and even though I don't like you very much either, I am your sister and I do love you."

"Well said."

"We'd let you stay on our couch for a few weeks, just as long as you promise not to bring any unsavory people or substances into the house. And, you know, Carl is amazing with tattoo removal. He had a patient whose face looked positively reptilian—"

"I don't need your charity, Ruirui. I have a place. I have money. You know I'm a musician."

"Come on, Jinger," Rui scoffs. "I've heard your stuff."

"Oh? And?"

"That song of yours is weirder than even I would have expected from you and your ilk."

"Well, some people liked it, I mean, not other soulless zombies—"

"And now that that part of your life is over," Rui plows on, "you need to face the truth and finally return to reality."

"Did you just come here to make me feel like shit? Or are you really such a control freak that you have to make sure I follow your own recovery program?"

"I just want to see my kid sister functioning like a normal member of society."

"Well, this is definitely not helping. Is this the way you talked to Ba when you told him he needs a girl-friend? That you don't like him but he's your father and you love him and it will make you feel good about yourself to see him doing better?"

"You have some gall talking to me that way," Rui bursts out in Chinese.

"Listen to yourself. You are Ma rein-fucking-carnated," Jing counters in English, satisfied that she was at the very least able to disturb a geyser of Chinese out of her sister.

"That's rich coming from my institutionalized, dropout, addict of a sister. If you could see yourself now... and the same—" Rui checks herself, her antagon-ism untwisting into thoughtfulness. "But you were probably too young to remember."

"What the hell is that supposed to mean?"

Rui ignores the question for the sake of her own tirade. "Listen. I'm the only stable person in this family, the only one holding it all together, so show a little respect. After the shitstorm you dropped on everybody—and with mom in such a fragile state—it was me who cleaned things up, it was me who made the funeral arrangements, it's me who's making sure dad doesn't go off the deep end like mom did."

"And so modest when it comes time to taking credit."

"You're never going to grow up and learn what responsibility is. That's fine. You know what? Forget this"—she throws up her hands—"I'm done. I've said what I came here to say. If it didn't get through to you, no fault of my own. Just mope your life away." Rui jabs her cigarette into the corpse-riddled ashtray, standing, and smoothing out her coat and hair with practiced poise.

Jing glares at her with a mixture of admiration and loathing. "Okay. See you at the wedding. Say 'Nice to meet you, too,' to Carl for me."

"Here," Rui says, tone still charged, taking a small wrapped gift out of her purse and placing it on the table. "Birthday-slash-Christmas-slash-Get-Well-Soon." Then as she is leaving, as an afterthought, she grabs Jing suddenly, leans over, tugs on one of her ear studs, and kisses her sister on the top of the head.

Hot tears stream down her face as she studies the photo.

This is how Waters finds her when he enters the visitation room minutes after her sister huffed off.

"Jing, Catherine's family needs to..." he starts, then notices her wiping her eyes. "You okay?"

"Just family shit," she laughs.

"She looked tough, but I had my money on you."

He walks over and looks over her shoulder at the photo, the gift Rui had brought her.

"This is where I remind you that wrapped gifts are forbidden at Glenbrook." He hands her a packet of tissue and takes the photo from her to examine the dimensions of the frame. "You could probably smuggle in some razor blades in this thing or, hell, just use the glass as a weapon." He removes the glass, tucks it into the clipboard, and reassembles the frame.

"Sorry, Waters." She plucks out a tissue and hands the packet back when Waters has a free hand. "Thanks."

"That's on me. I let her through without screening. You wanna talk?" He circles the coffee table, sits down in the armchair, studying the content of the picture.

Jing wipes her nose. "I wouldn't know where to begin."

"What's going on in here?" He puts the photo down and gestures towards the two girls and woman standing before a blue-forested mountain shrouded in mist.

"Jade Mountain, Taiwan—family trip forever ago."

"This must be you with the scabbed knees."

Jing smiles. "Yeah. Lanky on the left is Rui. That's my mother in the baseball cap."

"You guys look happy."

"Simpler times, that's for sure."

"You know, I got a kid sister"—he sits back in the chair and rubs his beard—"and whenever we have an argument, I always best her—poor girl—only woman on the planet with whom that's the case."

Jing laughs.

"Must be that much worse having an older *sister*."

"Who's a lawyer to boot."

"Ouch. Probably doesn't get the whole musician thing, does she?"

"Tone deaf."

"Well, if it's any consolation, working here, you see some pretty violent reactions to family visits. And according to Dr. Murai, a high percentage of family visits end in a trip to the Clouds, so I'd say you're handling this visit with aplomb."

She recalls what Goldfield had told her weeks before, how isolation can aggravate psychoses and mood disorders, at odds with what Waters is now telling her. Nothing, it seems, lacks the potential to exacerbate a psychological disorder.

"My advice," Waters continues, "is not to let her get to you. Go down to rec north and work out your frustrations there."

"You mean on the two-note wonder?"

"Go give it another try. Tell me things don't sound better."

"You did it? You called in a tuner?"

"I may have proposed to Goldfield that it could have some therapeutic benefits."

She stares at him for a moment. "Waters... I'm sorry. Last week, when Penn was here—"

"Forget it. Just go downstairs and have a productive morning."

They high-five, and Jing descends to her room to collect her piano books, then down to rec north. As she navigates the maze of hallways, snatches of conversation with Rui burble back to the surface, but they are silenced when she reaches the piano and tests the tuning job. She warms up with some scales, playing each one faster and faster until they're blurring over the stiff keys, and then her fingers find snatches of Mussorgsky's *Pictures at an Exhibition*, which was in a past life to be her thesis recital. Instead, she had dropped out of school and ceased work on it.

She searches hopefully through the piano books and finds that Penn had not neglected to include *Pictures*.

Now, she plays it several mental metronome clicks slower than she would have back at college, exploring for all the weak spots in the piece. Dynamics, fingering, feeling. Later, she'll attack each of the technical weak point separately with hours of glacially-paced practice.

Feeling, expression, these were more troubling for her—they had always been, as one critic had noted. Despite the terrific agility of her fingers, her touch had always been too literal, too specific.

The piece describes the composer's experience viewing an art exhibition, the pictures themselves as well as walking from piece to piece, the latter represented by a "Promenade" theme, a stately melody, with frequent shifts in time signature. As she plays, the theme walks her back to two years ago, the last time she had performed this in one of the claustrophobic practice spaces in the music department at college—*had that really been the last time?* She can *smell* the room—the old wood and varnish of the piano, window cleaner, the greasy odor the brass doorknobs would leave on her fingers—lovely smells, the smells of thousands of hours. Then the music erupts into turmoil—the first picture, "The Gnome"—her memory logically shifts forward to the chaos that had ensued after she had dropped out, painfully bright mornings that seemed to be casting probing beams into nights she would sooner forget, the humility of not remembering what she had done with whom. Her fingers stumble back—*weak spot*—to the reprise of the main theme, her face flushed.

"I think the protagonist's walking a bit too fast," a voice says.

She stops abruptly, scanning the room, searching out every corner, certain someone had just spoken.

But the room is empty.

A chill runs up her spine as she turns back to the keyboard.

She starts playing again, now beginning on a section called "The Old Castle," *the present,* she reflects, the shapes and movement of the music imbued with the same mysterious depths of Glenbrook.

After a half an hour of play, she crashes to a halt at the end of the final movement and stares down at the keys and her thin fingers, mouth twisted in displeasure.

You guys have lots of work to do, she thinks.
Rui, at least, is out of mind.

After lunch Jing brings her meds to the stairwell and downs them with none of the rebellious hesitation of before. She climbs up onto the sill and perches there, reading for a while. When she reaches into her pocket for a light, her fingers graze against something—and she remembers Henry. There's still a good hour or so before group therapy, enough time for a visit if she's more prudent sneaking past the nurses' station this time around.

She hops down, mounts the stairs, and threads through a suite of empty offices to the dayroom. A commotion up ahead—Catherine is screaming accusations about vampire aliens at a stony-faced patient as Waters and another tech flank and creep towards her. Various patients have cleared out of the dayroom, goggling from the tiled hall by the fringe of carpet. Diaz is shouting into the phone, describing the situation with an auctioneer's lingual agility.

Thus, Jing slips past without anyone noticing, then sprints down the hall, but once she is out of sight of the junction, she slows and orients herself. As with the women's quarters, many of the rooms are empty. Others are locked shut, the patients having already gone home for the holiday. A few doors are cracked open, out of which emanate self-directed mumbles or the shuffling of slippers on linoleum: the subdued, disconsolate soundtrack of those with nowhere to go for Thanksgiving. She turns at several intersections, when a distant cacophony grabs her attention. She tracks it to its source: a shut door at the very end of one of the halls, one glass wall overlooking an empty courtyard, the other lined with doors. She approaches, the sounds growing more and more distinct—splashes of drums, piano, electronic hissing—more a battle of instruments than music.

Sure enough, the door is labeled "Henry."

Jing places her ear to the door. She can hear his voice beneath the discordant clamoring—none of it intelligible. Every time she homes in on a phrase, a clash of music derails her focus.

She raps loudly in between bursts of percussion, but her banging on the door melds logically into the disordered soundscape.

No response, of course.

She tries the knob. Finds it unlocked. Enters.

The room is dark, the blinds shut, trapping slivers of afternoon light in the window frame. Henry is seated in lotus position on a small Oriental rug in the center of the floor, eyes wide, whites exposed, his hands upturned in his lap, seeming to gather in psychic energy. He continues to babble towards the open door.

Jing flicks on the lights, shutting the door with a quick glance over her shoulder to make sure no one has followed her down the corridor.

When the light does nothing to disturb his trance, she rushes over to him and shakes his arm.

"Henry! Henry!"

His eyes roll down, pupils wide, gray irises so taut and narrow they seem ready to snap. He gasps, the stream of conversation cutting off, and collapses heavily into Jing's arms.

As she helps him stand and sets him down on the corner of his bed, he blinks at the tattoos on her forearm.

"Jing." He breathes at last.

She strides over to the desk to turn down the volume of the CD player—*Kontakte*, she notices, by the same composer he had mentioned to her weeks ago.

She frowns, sitting down on the opposite, empty bed. "What the hell is this, a séance?"

"Something like that" He rubs his eyes, dons his glasses.

"I came to see how you're doing"—her voice creaks with doubt, eyes narrowing—"say, 'Congratulations,' and give you this as a sort of welcome-to-B-hood gift." She tosses him the lighter she had pulled out of her desk earlier that day.

Henry fumbles to catch it and studies the present, unsure what to make of it. Finally, he sets it aside on his desk.

"You're welcome," she says.

"We... I need a smoke, help me think."

She hands him a cigarette, lights it herself with the gift, used to playing that role in their interactions.

He taps her hand, inhaling.

"Okay"—he rubs his temples—"okay. Back in focus, Henry. Back in focus"—looks up at Jing, the light sparking back into his eyes—"You came. Finally."

"Stockhausen, meditation—seems to me not much has changed, man," she says, taking in the room—books stacked on his desk beside the boom box and CDs—neat and orderly. At the same time she catches subtle signs of how this place might have once looked: tape strips that had removed paint, the ripped corner of a piece of paper still stuck to the wardrobe, hundreds of tack holes spotting the walls and ceiling. Maybe he'd recently purged it of all the psychotic trappings during his im-provement—or deception of his improvement—tearing down the papers of madly scratched conspiracies that had once been strewn across the room—diagrams of neural wormholes, branching trees that link together all the psychoengineers of Glenbrook and beyond. There must be notebooks and notebooks stashed somewhere, brimming with delusional ramblings.

"You left out fasting, Jing, something I recommend for you as well. It allows one to achieve unprecedented levels of purification and facilitates entering into the trance state. While you've been dithering about what to do, I've been having revelation after revelation here. Last month when I confided in you, I probably came across as a bit out there because I hadn't fully grasped the complexity of the situation, but now I know that it was William that has been trying to communicate all this time from the astral plane, using Glenbrook's own weapon against them."

Jing rubs her face, clicking the tongue stud.

"Let me clarify for you," Henry continues. "William has been sending me messages through the Muzak station. However, I was too fixated on the Muzak's use as a tool of suppression—not communication." He squats in front of his bed, fingering open a slit in the mattress close to the bottom seam, then tugs on a thread, widening the hole, and pulls out some papers, handing them to Jing.

Ahh, here we go, she thinks, heart sinking. She hadn't wanted to be right, but she couldn't stop herself from assuming the worst.

"Remember our discussion several weeks ago? About how the editing of the pieces carefully disguises a subliminal signal that closes up our neural wormholes? Well, the reason why they positioned two intercoms in the rotunda and the cafeteria is to cover sonically all the regions the patients occupy. Have you ever noticed that at night, if you listen very carefully, you can just make out the music? Well, its volume and the acoustics in this place were calibrated to fill every inch of every wing of this building, even east wing. It doesn't only cut us off from our spiritual forms, it prevents psychic travel as well—we're talking projecting out of our bodies and into the astral plane—but this is only half the story. The pieces are also played in a set order that William programmed. You see, he must have infiltrated the Glenbrookian workforce from the other side. The Department of Music, that's where the psychoengineers would have assigned him. Only makes sense for them to make use of the talents at their disposal, right? He's been sending me messages about how I can propel out of here—listening to these atonal records, which contain a subsonic psychokinetic frequency that helps me re-dilate my neural wormhole, and to reach a quiet spot on campus, the one place where the Muzak can't reach us."

Jing doesn't respond, just leafs through the papers—detailed maps, etchings, sheets of numbers, notes—a labor of minute handwriting crammed into every inch of the pages.

"Now, in the Muzak, each movement corresponds to a different number, and the numbers themselves make up a separate code, not alphanumeric, but a double encryption. It took me a long time to crack this one. Even though I know how William thinks, he obviously had to be careful and devise something that was nearly indecipherable. Once I realized that, it occurred to me that one of the toughest types of codes to crack is a book cypher." He reaches back into the mattress, digs around, and then pulls out *The Mind of a Mnemonist.* "I remembered this was the book you were reading when I presented you with my findings in the cafeteria, and then it occurred to me that you'd been trying to push the book on me. I thought there must be a reason for it."

Jing, after deliberating where to begin, says, "Well, first of all, thanks for asking if you could borrow this." She takes the book out of his hands as he sits back on the bed. "Second, I didn't intend to say there was any relationship—"

"I know you didn't, Jing. You were being manip-ulated. William was working *through* you in order to communicate with me."

"Henry—"

"Don't write this off, Jing. I've tested these codes. We can go out to the staircase right now, and I can prove to you everything I just said."

"Okay, well... let's say that you did happen to discover some codes in the music—which could be a random coincidence, by the way—it still doesn't make sense." She turns back to the notes while she speaks, wanting to avoid having to look him in the eyes. "If

William were alive and caught in some astral plane Department of Music, why would he be communicating to you through all these obscure channels, especially if he can just use me to speak for him? He could just speak through you, for example."

"He *has* been speaking through me, but I didn't realize he was doing so until he managed to communicate through you. Since Henry and I think the same and our voices sound the same, I could never be certain that it was him speaking through me and not just me talking to myself."

She looks back up at Henry and squints. The muted burbles of the electronic music impregnate the silence between them. "You mean William."

"What?"

"You said 'Henry and I think the same.' You mean 'William and I.'"

"Right, well, sometimes I am William. When he's speaking through me, it's him and not me speaking, right?"

"Henry or William or whomever the fuck I'm talking to, how long have you been off your meds?"

"Six months by now," he says, crossing his legs, inhaling the last of the cigarette and jabbing it out in the desktop ashtray, clean and inconspicuous like the rest of the room. Conspicuously inconspicuous.

"How are you passing the bloodwork? And how the fuck were you just promoted to a B-level?"

"I can't divulge all my secrets to you, Jing. Not, that is, unless I can be sure that you're fully on board with my plan."

She shakes her head. "You're going to hate me, Henry. I'm sorry. I know you're going to hate me for doing this to you."

She drops the papers and book, bolts for the door, about to call out for a nurse, but Henry rushes up and intercepts her, one hand covering her mouth, the other gripping her shoulder—pampered, long-fingered hands,

hands that were bred for piano or the cello, the hands of Schumann.

"You can't do this to me, Jing. I'm close to the end," he says, eyes wild. "I'm not going to let you block my passage out of here."

She slaps the one hand away from her face, furious with him for using his size to intimidate her. "Let me go," she says into his chest.

"Come on, Jing."

"I can't just be a bystander to this. I should have reported you a long time ago. You're lost, Henry."

He pulls her in, whether detaining or hugging her she cannot decide. She wriggles against the invasion of her personal space, but Henry's hold doesn't loosen. He just whispers, his voice deep in his chest, "I know this is confusing and scary, but I'm not going to let you or them block me. I'm only trying to help you because I don't want to leave a friend behind."

"Henry, they need to know. You need help." Her face grows hot, her mind lingering on his hands, how they would wrap finger by finger around her throat, how they would squeeze…"

I'm not going to cry, not going to panic, she thinks. *Be Zen. He won't attack me. It's Henry. He's not a violent guy.*

"No, they don't. This will be our secret. Now come on and sit back down. I just want to show you a few more things. That's all. You've got to hear me out completely before you reject what I'm saying."

When his grip relaxes, she shoves him off her. His head knocks against the door, and she reaches around him, turns and yanks the doorknob—

CHAPTER 9

My eye.

My hand reaches towards my face, then withdraws upon touching the brittle texture of the bandage, crusted with dried blood and sand.

God, I can't do this. It's really gone. The nightmare had been real after all—the live burial and the worm, the dog, the snake and dragon. It just keeps going and going.

A loud crack echoes over the cliff, followed by a dry crash. I start, twisting on the frond mat, and my leg flares up. I curse. When the wave of pain passes, I look again, shifting gingerly. It's the rat—gathering vegetation from the oasis. It's quietly humming the first movement of the *Brandenburg Concerto* No. 3, a strange juxtaposition with this cold morning.

The fire has reduced to a smokeless, wind-abused pile of ash. A god's fistful of asteroids is cast along the horizon.

The rat arrives with kindling and soon begins relighting the fire with my borrowed lighter, its living head focused on the task and the skull a creaking wind vane. Shivering, mindful of the various zones of pain, I crouch before the burgeoning blaze, alternating rubbing my limbs and warming my hands over the fire, ignoring for the time being the potent stench of the rat. Through the charred tatters of my jeans, I examine my leg, with its infected bite and burns, the former still puffed up and sore, but the latter already scabbed and healing.

Incredible.

Only one day—or at least I assume that's all the time that has passed.

How is that possible?

"You're cold," the rat notes, interrupting my thoughts as the flames lick their way into stability. "The fire will only help for so long, as we must break camp soon. However, we may have a solution for you, if you would like to hear it."

"I'll try anything," I say, teeth chattering.

"There is a certain flower, the struggle between light and dark. We have seen rabbits make evening nests of them. Wait here. It smells as if some sprouted up in this oasis." It stands and limps off into the floral grove, which seems to have recovered and expanded overnight, creeping closer towards our camp—or maybe this is a new one that had blossomed out of the rat while it slept and merged with the older one.

While my guide scrounges around in the oasis, I fish the packet of smokes out of my purse, finding only the dregs of tobacco and torn paper in the bottom of the crumpled box. Turning away from the wind, I cobble together a cigarette from the crushed remains, licking the paper into a long torpedo. Smoke leaking out its side, I take a few drags before snuffing it out—the last cigarette on Psyche.

I tuck it back into the box and, wondering what new oddity the rat will emerge with, cast a wary glance towards the oasis, but the rat has vanished from sight.

I stand, shivering, shielding my body with the blanket of fronds I'd slept under, shuffling over to the canyon edge, where a sharp wind cuts, and behold an immense forest teeming in the basin, glowing bright in the purple shadows. The oasis stretches on for a mile at least, spilling up the cliffsides. Spirits of sunshine, chatterboxes (really fat ones), rumination fruits, puff-balls, cacti—the identifiable commingling with novel surprises, organisms strange even to a fleeting abyssal dream.

Another dead snake.

"Here we are," the rat announces, appearing at the

verge of the topside oasis, carrying a stack of towel-sized, velvety black petals. The things undulate in its hands, curling around its hairy limbs.

I meet the rat by the fire, and it lays a petal over each of my limbs. One by one they wrap around and snuggle against my skin, transforming into elegant sleeves and leggings, the material warm to the touch, rippling and adjusting around the edges like a nestling sea slug.

"Curiouser and curiouser,'" I say, wariness dispelled by its soft touch.

Applying more petals to my back and front side, it says, "These must have only sprung up while we slept. Otherwise we would have provided them sooner." Again, the petals hug against my skin, edges joining together along my sides, creating frilly seams that shut out the wind. "How do they feel?"

"Wonderful. A bit more girly than what I normally wear"—I sigh at the sudden relief from the icy needling of the wind—"but thanks."

Gradually my color returns, my bones warm, and the two of us settle down by the fire to a breakfast of fresh-cooked mushrooms.

"What was it, that giant thing eating the sand, the thing that caused all this?" I ask as we eat, gesturing towards my eye.

"An eternity bug." The rat nibbles on its mushroom while the skull gnaws on air. "They are essential to regulating the environment of Psyche, dispersing oases, consolidating and rearranging memories, and gobbling up chatterboxes by the thousands before they are able to grow too large and unruly. They do not eat the sand but filter out its impurities."

At the mention of the chatterboxes, my hand unconsciously slides up to the bandage.

"Do not touch it." The skull shakes in admonishment. "We'll treat all of your wounds once we have finished our breakfast. Now"—the rat shifts its attention back to its mushroom—"these eternity bugs are special in many ways, godlike in the reverence they inspire. We have known many other rats to pray to such things, that they may clear the path to the mountains for them and cleanse their pasts. Pure nonsense, of course—eternity bugs aren't equipped with prayer detectors." It chuckle-squeaks but then, sobering, adds, "However, they do possess an impressive sensory apparatus array: vision, time, air pressure, vibration, animal magnetism, sand quality, electrical valence, the list goes on and on."

"All those sensory organs and it couldn't see me coming?"

The rat misses my sarcasm. "Oh, surely it did. Humans are a rare find on Psyche after all, so it was probably just a little curious to see you up close. But, mind you, not all of these senses are confirmed, just hypothetical..."

The rat continues to catalogue many more of the peculiarities of eternity bugs, but my own mind shifts to other concerns. During a space in the rat's eternity bug lecture, I cut in: "You mentioned 'a journey through memory' or something like that before we slept. What did you mean by that?"

"We believe that if there is a way to get you back to Earth, it can be found in the Crystal Mountains. However, there is a slight problem for us in reaching them. The path into the future"—it points with its good hand towards the west, towards the sparkling mountain range outlined flamingo and salmon pink in the morning sun—"is a long and slow one. By the time you arrive (if you ever do), you will by definition be on death's door. It is said that the base of the Crystal Mountains is nothing but an immense jungle, riddled with the corpses of spirit animals that completed their journey and chatterboxes that have grown monstrously huge, unchecked by the eternity bugs. A faster way may be traveling back through the Memorylands. Still, though shorter, this route is likely even more dangerous."

I stoke up the fire with the snake-blood-stained fang. "So where are these Memorylands?"

It points towards the opposite horizon.

"This makes absolutely no sense. I thought we were supposed to be on an asteroid."

The two heads nod in disjointed agreement.

"Well, assuming Psyche is similar to Earth in that it closely approximates the shape of a sphere, we just need to walk the shortest arc to the mountains, and since the mountains are on that horizon, clearly we should just walk in that direction. Even if its shape is irregular—"

"The shape of Psyche is irrelevant. You see, although the same principles that govern laws of mind and space on Earth also apply on Psyche, they are weighted differently. On Earth, there is greater weight given to Euclidean distance, not the mind's perception of that distance. However, there may be subtle interactions between the two. For example, you may have noticed that (all other factors being equal) the first leg of a journey seems to take longer than a return journey of the same distance on Earth. On Psyche, the mental aspect has much greater weight, such that the first leg of a journey literally lasts a lifetime, and the return goes by in a flash. Also, this greater weight given to the mental aspect on Psyche leads to other kinds of mind-space interactions. For example, our past is the lands we have traversed over. Thus, by walking away from the mountains, we will be traveling through memory—in a manner of speaking."

"What do you mean? Whose memories?"

"The memories of our wards."

I laugh. It seems every other sentence out of the rat's mouth is riddled with alien terminology. "Yeah, we talked about 'wards' before sleeping. I still don't know what it means."

"Right, umm"—it sniffs—"a ward is a being for which

you take psychic responsibility."

I brighten as I recognize the significance of what the rat has just said. "You mean the ward is the one I see in my visions?"

"Precisely."

"But that's me."

"Well, there you have it—*you* are your ward."

"What about you? Are you psychically connected with some rat somewhere on Earth?"

"No. " It stiffens, then puffs out its chest. "We and all other spirit animals of Psyche are the wards of humans. Similarly, each human is connected to a spirit animal, and the two feed off each other in what is normally a symbiotic relationship. However, due to the often harrowing ordeals of Psyche, many humans are rendered spiritless and fall into the depths of mental disorder or death."

"So why don't I have a spirit animal?"

"Well..." it pauses, seeming to debate how to phrase what follows, "we do not want to be the bearer of bad news, but if you are on Psyche and receiving visions, your spirit animal is likely dead."

"Okay... then how am I here as well as on Earth?"

"Of that we are not entirely sure."

"Really? No idea whatsoever? You seem like the authority on everything Psyche."

"We are sorry, Jing. We have heard of humans traveling to Psyche, but have never personally met any before you. For all we knew, it was just a myth that such a thing could be possible. However, we are aware of such schisms as dissociative personality disorder. Perhaps that might explain how you are in two places at once."

"Maybe," I say dubiously. Such a disorder would explain everything if Psyche were not an actual place, an actual asteroid, but instead a mental construct divested from my normal self, inhabited by a dissociated *and* schizophrenic piece of my personality—but if Psyche is an *external* place, then that explanation falls apart. Of course, what evidence other than the word of talking animals do I have that Psyche *is* an external place? I sigh. I can't keep doing this, can't keep retreating back into this exitless, solipsistic maze. "All right. Well, what about Chinese? How is it that you can (and the dragon could) speak Chinese?"

"We cannot speak Chinese. The dragon couldn't either, at least we doubt it could."

"But that's what we're doing right now."

"No, we're not. We're speaking the Deep Language, a language of pure thought."

"Then why do I hear Chinese whenever you open your mouth?"

The rat shrugs, its skull clacking against the living head. "Perhaps that is the language you want to hear. Maybe for you it has deeper psychological significance than other tongues. If you were to very carefully read our lips while we speak, you would find that the movements and sounds don't match—"

It's true, I realize, as I focus in on its mouth, like watching a dubbed movie.

"—such is the Deep Language. For us, we do not hear Chinese or English or any other of your human languages. The Deep Language for us is a kind of"—it wriggles its nose—"olfactory map.

"Now, it is time to examine your wounds. After that we should pack up."

The rat applies the spirits of sunshine to my face and leg. Several more worms flee the latter wound. My eye, on the other hand, is clean—a small miracle. I again express my neurotoxin-impeded gratitude, and the two of us store the spirits in its backpack along with the leftover mushrooms and cactus arms. Then I take a lengthy toilet.

Afterwards, in the middle of gathering food for the

coming journey, I pause to survey the crystal horizon and surrounding desert, when an idea occurs to me: if these creatures—rats, snakes, dogs—I've been encountering are the spirit animals of humans, are (or were) their wards interacting with my Earth self? Once the spirit-of-sunshine neurotoxin wears off, I'll have to question the rat further about the exact correspondence between creatures and events on Psyche and Earth.

Wisps of smoke are curling out of the nearby rock field, bearing the familiar odor of bleak landscapes of pollution and slag.

I take a few steps in that direction, when the rat calls out, "Where are you going, Jing?"

I point towards the smoke. "Ta'e a loo'."

"No need to. We can describe the scene for you based on the smell. The wind is just right this morning." It probes the air with its nose, its expression—though it's difficult to read rat expressions—almost rapturous.

"Thangs, bu' I wanna see mysel'."

The rat shrugs. "Don't be long, and please be careful."

I nod and follow the blackened trail, the ground softened and bubbling, rotted. It winds around seared boulders and melted rocks, leading to a cliff edge overlooking the source of the smoke: the corpse of the dragon, deformed by lumps of cooled magma, igneous rock spores frothing out of its wounds, with a molten, elephantiasis-like appearance, its once wondrous coloring now soiled gray and dun. The surroundings have curdled into a steaming murk, utterly drained of color.

No oasis from this dead creature. Why not? Another question for the rat.

Then something catches my eye, small and jet black standing out among the faded monotones, a little distance from the fuming morass—the sack of leaf for the beast's cigars.

I hobble down the rocky slope into this shallow ravine, mindful of the leg numb and treacherous from the neurotoxin, my body invigorated by the warmth emanating from my new flower suit.

My heart is hammering against my chest. I know it's dead. I know nothing's going to happen. Still, my heart pounds.

I hazard forward, eye on that melting form. When I reach the pouch and stoop down to examine it, I'm surprised to find the very substance I'm wearing—struggle between light and dark. I peel apart the petals and find the interior segmented into pockets, much like my own purse. Tucked in one is a dried aromatic grass with the redolence of cloves, in another the palm-like fronds it used for rolling, and in still another are a number of intriguing opalescent bracelets. I start to pull one out—

A loud *POP!* startles me. I drop the sack, breath catching, and glance up to find a stone bubble has burst, a bright tear of magma crying down the side of the dragon's lumpy corpse.

Did it change position? The head seems to be aimed at me, ready to snap me up into those cruel jaws. I'm certain it had been pointed off on the diagonal earlier. Only a few yards separate us, but I can feel the waves of heat radiating out of the corpse.

I glance back down and find that the sack has sunk into the steaming rot, I reach down to snatch it back up, but too late—vanished beneath the surface. My own feet are similarly bogged down in the ground, which is not liquefied exactly, but spongy and crumbling.

I wrench my feet free and back out of these mauve shadows. Halfway up the slope I realize that I'm still holding one of the bracelets. I tuck it into my purse and hobble-trot back towards camp, frequently glancing over my shoulder to make sure the molten beast isn't clawing up out of the ravine in pursuit.

As I return, the wind rises, pushing streams of stinging white sand across the rock field, momentarily blotting out the horizon, mirroring my own agitated frame of mind. When I reach the oasis, I find the rat squatting over the ground, its right paw tossing stones or bones or something onto the ground.

A game of some sort?

The rat seems to smell me coming, collects its bones—no, teeth—some as large as limes, and tucks them away into its pack.

With a scrutinizing twitch of its nose, it says, "Jing, your wounds are still unhealed, slowing you down. Yesterday, it almost meant our death. We wonder if today we should take better precautions. Would you object to transportation?"

I shake my head hesitantly.

The rat gestures across from me, towards the oasis. As it does so, I become aware of a grotesque slurping reminiscent of the dog's unbridled eating.

"It's called a hippocochlea," the rat says as I turn to look.

Big as a rhinoceros, armored in cobalt blue chitin, the hippocochlea's two pairs of legs resemble cords of wriggling slugs, and where a neck might have extended from a fore-hole in its shell, writhes a knot similar to its feet, though much larger, and splayed apart in order for the feelers to convey puffballs into the creature's body.

"They're quite docile," the rat assures me.

"The hippocochlea's passion for mushrooms makes it an ideal mount, one of the few on Psyche," the rat says as I scale the side of the creature, using its roughly textured armor for handholds.

It hands me up our packs, and I secure them to a portion of the carapace where a series of large pointed fins jut upward. The dorsum is crawling with spirits of sunshine, and while I wrench these off with the fang, the rat constructs a puffball fishing pole using a kelp vine secured to a long, twisted branch with moving stick insect appendages.

Setting the beast in motion is a simple matter of dangling the mushroom in front of its head, just out of reach of its feelers. Thus, it skates forward in eternal pursuit of the puffball while I straddle the carapace, gripping a ridge of pommels and horns. Living nose ever-employed, the rat hobble-scampers about us, avoiding the undulating leg-stalks of my mount. We navigate along the canyon top, through rock fields and bowls and finally into a complex of arches and spiraling pipes and tunnels, a kind of forum for the winds, which whistle and dervish in the open space. Here we rest for a few minutes, while the rat darts from one tunnel mouth to the next, sniffing here and there.

"What is this place?" I ask.

"A way back to the desert, we hope—ahh!"—it gestures towards a tunnel mouth—"this way!"

We enter the tunnel, its cool interior shimmering and nacreous, bearing the sunlight down towards a shadowy curve. A strong, dry wind travels up to meet us, and we pass into darkness. I'm left with the squelch of the hippocochlea and its musky odor, the scratching of the rat's claws on the smooth stone and its busy sniffing. We turn and turn through the dark, descending, then the blackness begins to gray, and the colors of the tunnel wall pulse back to life. Suddenly we round the bend and the passage terminates, beyond it the desert sea, sparkling beneath the warming day. At our feet is a vertical drop of several hundred feet.

"Hold on tight," the rat says and slips over the side, scrambling down through a narrow fissure, grunting and squeaking all the way. The hippocochlea oozes forward, and suddenly we're horizontal, creeping down the cliff face. Butt resting on a narrow ridge of chitin, I press flat against its dorsum, clinging to the various horns and fins, shifting my handholds with every arbitrary meander of the creature. The fishing pole is impossible to manage this way, so I expend bits of mushroom from my purse, tossing them down in hopes the hippocochlea catches the scent.

After a tedious hour we reach the bottom and continue on. Behind us the canyons spread out like the universe's largest murex shell, but soon recede back into sand.

I begin to understand what the rat had meant by "Memorylands." My mind flickers with images, snatches of conversation and soundscapes, wafts of scents—terrestrial, not Psychic. Every swell of sand or towering butte brings with it branches of past events, each laden with vivid blooms of memory.

I glance down at the rat, wondering if it is experiencing something similar. Its one dead side dragged along by the living flesh of the other half, I can make out the rotting organs beyond the ribs and torn flesh, but no bugs. Hadn't it been much more rotten several days ago, with worms wriggling in and out of its carcass?

"How was it your other half died?" I ask. "You said a dragon did it to you?"

The rat does not seem surprised by this question, but the skull rattles in protest. "It was not just any dragon, but the very young one that plagued you. We would recognize its smell anywhere."

I fall silent for a moment, rocking with the strange, skating gait of the hippocochlea, distracted as all of reality unfolds around me. I blink at the startling brightness of the white desert, the shiny blue carapace, the sharp punch of the rat's stench.

"That's"—I clear my throat, struggling for the words, disoriented by what the rat had just said—"a weird coincidence."

It shakes its heads. "You will find that things usually work this way on Psyche. You see, the dragon and we used to travel together. In exchange for protection, we could provide it with our powerful noses for sniffing out danger and food. Plus we could fit into many tight spaces where it could not explore. At that time the dragon was fascinated with memoryfish"

—memoryfish? Where have I heard that before? Something the dragon said? The term distracts me for a moment from what the rat is saying—

"...in tandem with the eternity bugs and other insects. As their name suggests, they are sustained by memories—well-aged visions. For them, the most nourishing memory of all is the trauma, a memory so significant that even after its removal from the desert it continues to thrive and impact the host and ward to which they are linked. At the same time, if the traumas are not removed and consumed by the memoryfish, they could potentially grow so salient as to consume all of the desert, affecting even those not personally linked to the memory. The dragon often brought up this topic during our travels together. In retrospect, the dragon was very careful in what it revealed to us, but we assume it must have developed a theory that it could prolong its longevity if only it could harness the power of the traumatic memory, feeding off it the way the memoryfish do and potentially freeing itself of the need to be connected to its ward. Perhaps what the dragon was trying to accomplish was to manufacture a trauma. In any case, it tricked us into eating an unspeakable fruit—a fruit with a name infinitely long. Soon after, one of our wards died of an overdose, and since then, this half of us has been rotting away."

"But this would have created a trauma for you, not the dragon, right?"

"During that time, our wards must have been intimate. How exactly we cannot say for sure. The dragon was always chary whenever we broached that subject, though such reticence is not unheard of among spirit animals. Many feel it is a betrayal of trust and generally indecent to discuss the matter of one's ward with other animals."

"So, considering the dragon was obsessed with my feeding it, I'm guessing this traumatic memory business didn't work?"

"No. You're probably right. Based on what you have told us, it seems to have found a better way. You see, humans are powerful transmitters of consciousness, but only very little passes into Psyche."

"Is that why I only see fragments from Earth?"

"Yes, you only receive the most psychologically significant events from your ward."

I go quiet again, gripping tight to the pommel as a memory wave crashes over me. White walls, sky blue linoleum, indistinct Muzak—Glenbrook—but from the first-person perspective, unlike how I've always seen the place. Everything looks wrong, with a patina of lightness, new and clean. Bigger. I've never seen this part of the hospital. Must be a memory from my first few weeks there when it was still summer. I'm running, running, running, breath short and light, crying—is that my voice?—towards the bouncy echoes of the string quartet. The surge of memory suddenly retreats back to sea, but the confusion and fear linger.

I remain quiet for some time, thinking about what I just saw. Then I remember we'd been having a conversation. What had we been talking about? Memories, visions... the logic behind what visions I receive from Earth.

"So," I start, rediscovering my voice, "there seems to be some regularity between how much time has passed between each vision. For example, I receive them roughly once a day here, and about a week of time has lapsed between the Earth visions each time I experience them, at least I think that's the case."

The heads nod. "Yes, this is because spirits and humans operate within different chronobiological systems. The human's is circadian, around twenty-four hours, while a spirit animal's is on a weekly rhythm.

Humans obviously intuited this difference when they established the seven-day week."

I take this in, mind teeming with more questions but not knowing where to strike next, then I remember the initial direction of my query, before I had again gotten sidetracked.

"So what exactly do the visions do?"

"They heal and sustain us."

I glance down at the rat as it hobbles along. "Could they heal you?"

The rat hesitates. "It is possible."

"What about my eye? Will the visions heal that?"

"Well, as long as there isn't any mutation and we keep it clean, your eye may regenerate. We must warn you, however, that after such traumas, even when an organ does grows back, it is never quite the same as before. In fact, we knew a rabbit once..."

As the rat recounts the grisly tale of a rabbit whose severed leg regrew as a long chatterbox, I roll up the sleeve of my new suit and study the razor wound. Only several days old. Yet the scab is already flaking to reveal a bright pink line. Is this speedy recovery due to the foods I've been consuming, the energy I've been receiving, or the difference in the passage of time between Psyche and Earth? Perhaps a bit of all three.

"You said before, '*One* of our wards,'" I recall suddenly, interrupting its story, "meaning you have two?"

"Yes, we are or were the host of twins."

Of course! I think. "Stop me if I'm prying, but they're William and Henry, right?"

"That's correct."

"So, in the visions you receive from Earth, you probably see me sometimes."

The rat tenses and stares off into the distance. I pull up the puffball line, and the hippocochlea slows to a stop. After a few seconds the rat's shoulders relax and it seems to grow cognizant again of its surroundings.

"You experienced a memory just now?" I ask.

It nods. "What... were we discussing?"

I lower the puffball, and we continue on. "I was asking if you see me in your visions."

"Ahh, yes. No. Just as we did not understand the relationship between our wards and the dragon's. Henry's stream of consciousness is too fractured and warped to contain any coherent substance. Many years ago, before William and Henry became unbalanced, we had a very clear picture of Earth and were able to pick up a good deal of information about the place, but now it is more like static than a vision."

We fall into silence, and I study the endless waves of glitter arcing around us. I turn back to gauge the distance we've covered and am surprised to find the rainbowed, gravity-defying peaks of the mountains much more distant than they'd been at the start of the day, layers of atmosphere dulling their resplendence.

Lunchtime.

I descend from my mount. We've reached the pinnacle of the highest dune for miles, sprouting blades of sparkling white stone. We haven't encountered any oases since leaving the canyons, and I'd used up all the uncooked mushrooms during our descent, so the cold marinated mushrooms serve as lunch—by now rather slimy. As we rest, a constant phantasmal stream ebbs and flows past my mind's eye. It's a maddening struggle to stay in the present—like trying to clamber up the wet hull of a boat to keep from drowning, each bob in the water bringing my fingers infinitesimally closer to grabbing a hold of that slippery edge.

For dessert the rat offers a Rubik's cube prune—the same type of fruit it had given me during our night flight. Bittersweet and chalky, saliva-inducing, it's as edible as a raw plantain. By the end of it, the thought of more food nearly makes me retch. No idea how I'd devoured one previously without noticing the taste.

"How did you like the dorberry?" the rat asks, noticing the queer smacking of my lips.

"I didn't."

The rat chuckle-squeaks. "It's an acquired taste, but nutritious in moderation. A diet too rich in dorberries will ruin your taste for food... for everything will take on their flavor and consistency."

"Sounds delightful." I take a swig of cactus juice in an attempt to quench my bone-dry mouth. The traces of fruit juice seem to repel the water like a coat of oil.

"Yes, they're just the thing for days like today—long stretches of desert with no sign of an oasis."

"Why haven't we seen any? Oases, I mean. Were they destroyed by that eternity bug thing?"

"Yes, those lands no longer exist, or at least not in the sense that you may be thinking. The past is only full of memories, ghosts, all the remaining traces of the visions of a lifetime, radiating out of the sand." The rat picks another dorberry out of its pack and takes a bite, relishing the flavor. The spirits of sunshine have crawled up to the little garden atop the rat's pack and are flexing their appendages in the warm sun.

"It's... a strange sensation," I say as another wave of memory washes over me.

"The memories, they are beginning to feel burdensome?" it ask, also struggling to speak coherently. Despite sounding exhausted, the rat's voice possesses a melancholy, self-indulgent aspect, lost and distant, much like mine.

"Yeah... it was pleasant at first, but the farther we go, the more *crowded* my mind feels. I've never remembered things so vividly before. In fact, they're not like memories at all. More like the visions."

"We know. Unfortunately, we believe... it will only continue to grow worse. All we can do is try to stay strong." It takes a swig of cactus, using its bad forelimb, the one that had been nearly rotting off days ago.

"How much longer do we have to go before we arrive at... wherever it is we're going?"

"We are not sure. You see"—its living head turns to regard the western horizon, while the skull stubbornly continues to stare off into the past, dangling, grim—"the Crystal Mountains have nearly sunk into the desert. Soon the very tip of the highest peak will be all that is visible. Then, we will have arrived at the start of the journey: the sea."

"And what then?"

"Shush!" The rat's nostrils suddenly widen, ears perking. It raises one hand to its nose, and the other flops up to the skull where a powerful nose had once smelled.

"What?"

"The odor... how unpleasant." It angles its snout into the air and pans its head, sniffing out various streams. I start to look, but in that instant, the rat grabs my arm and yanks me over the edge of the dune ridge. As we tumble down, I only see flashes of sky and sand, sky and sand. Then we jolt to a stop, my face planting into the ground.

"The fuck?" I say, dusting the sand out of my hair and digging it out of my ears.

The rat crouches down beside me and whispers, "Don't make a sound—"

And—*WHUMP!*—we are blanketed in color.

The gaudy net sprouts out of nothing, a brilliant mosaic of shining, irregular shapes saturating everything for yards around us. I look up towards the crest of the steep dune, where the sun is angling down towards us, and find the light refracted through a... pane of glass?

The rat jerks me back down.

"I know that smell," I whisper.

WHUMP! WHUMP!

A light spray of sand mists down upon us.

"Ammonia," it replies, the skull obediently not clacking along, its lower jaw dangling down. A simple word or concept, but to the rat it must be intricately nuanced.

There's a distant squishing and honking—the hippocochlea fleeing.

"What is it?"

"Shh."

WHUMP! WHUMP!

We wait, watching each other and the colors cast around us. They shift and waver, dance and swim, merge and split, at times only beautiful nonsense, but at others serendipitously coalescing like crystal ball visions into shadows of the past or future—forested lakes, industrial skylines, familiar faces—then vanishing. Just as the first color burst fades, another explodes, equally as bright, though more compact, foretelling alternate futures and emphasizing different aspects of the past. It is difficult to judge the overall form of these shadows, stretched as they are over the sweeping curves of the dune. When this one disappears, another follows and another and another. Five of them? More? Maybe just a couple circling the peak, flickering between the toothy shadows of the sandstones. I don't dare look, but I can hear them now, whatever they are, the sand shifting beneath their weight, a wet clicking. The sounds and colors remind me of the crawlspace from my childhood home, a hiding place, my haven for years, until I'd dreamed of the door being splintered open and peaceful dark shattered by a ghoulish light.

Then the colors vanish with a flitter. Above us the dune peak grows hazy in a cloud of sand.

The rat's nose continues to interrogate the air long after the last shadow has disappeared.

"They've gone," it confirms at last. "We are safe."

"What have gone?"

"The memoryfish."

We creep back up to the top of the dune and recover

our things. Strange tracks surround the rat's backpack, my purse, and the opposite slope of the dune, countless perforations, some surrounded by patterns of squiggles as if snakes had been slithering over the ground. The hippocochlea's tracks lead down the dune slope and up another, a distance of half a mile or so, but the creature is no-where in sight.

"What were they doing?" I ask, inspecting my purse to see if it's damaged or anything's missing.

The rat shoulders into its backpack. "Searching for food. Your effects should be unmolested. They were only interested in the memories flowing through us."

I shuffle over the sand in the late afternoon, shoe-gazing.

The rat, several yards away, limps uncertainly on three feet. As we wind up the side of a dune, a narrow stone path springs up—granite. The rat crosses it without notice, but these familiar, welcoming stones draw me in. As I veer off and step onto the path, grass sprouts out of the surrounding sand, and a cool breeze blows across the desert. The vision in my left eye re-flowers— so suddenly I almost lose my balance. The empty dry-ness suddenly grows rich with the tones of spring soil, fresh-fallen rain, flowers, lake wind. Sunlight streams in through the broken, silver-tinted clouds and rocking elm branches above. The dune face shifts into nostalgic terrain: a sloping path by the side of the house, white paint peeling, and a wall of Taiwanese purple-blue rhododendrons heavy with the aroma of honey. An earthworm wriggles over one of the stones, its sleek body flecked with dirt. I bend over to pick it up. It struggles madly as I cup two tiny hands around it. Continuing down the path, I round the corner of the house to find my mother wearing flared jeans and yellow blouse, a pink bandana holding her bone-straight hair out of her sweaty face. I sneak up behind her and clear my throat. Kneeling barefoot in the wood-framed garden plot, she and I are the same height. She turns and squints severely at me behind her huge square glasses, but I can tell this is one of her sunny days.

I smile. "I have something for you. Close your eyes and give me your hand." My voice is bar ly recognizable, light and airy.

She obeys, offering one of her soil-caky, gloved hands.

"Umm, you only get your surprise if you take off your gloves."

She obeys, smirking, eyes still squeezed shut.

I test to make sure she isn't peeking, then drop the worm into her hand. Her eyes remain closed, expression serious. Not the reaction I was expecting. She massages the worm with the pad of her thumb. "So special," she says in Chinese, opening her eyes. "Someone to live in my garden. Which plot should we put her in?"

"Well..." I match her language. "She likes red."

"Does she?" My mother puzzles over this. "Then we have just the place." She guides me towards a small plot of flowers still waiting to bloom, not a mote of red in sight, and sets the worm down ceremoniously at the base of one of the flower's stems. "You know these, Jinger?"

I shake my head. She tells me the name in two languages: red spider lilies, the flower of the other shore. They'll make a silky, red firework show for the worm in late summer.

I'm silent for a moment, watching the worm wriggle into the soil and wondering what she means by "the other shore."

"You mean Canada?" I say at last.

She laughs and pulls me into her. She smells of sweat and soil and a laundry detergent that exists nowhere else on Earth but in this house. "Yes, Canada. That *is* one of the other shores, but there's another I should tell you about. A very *particular* shore. It's not a shore you can visit whenever you want. Only when you're very old and leave this world and cross a great river can you see it. But when you do, all your memories will vanish. They pop like bubbles." She pops my bubble/nose with her finger.

"I don't want my memories to vanish," I say. "I want to remember you and Ba—and Ruirui sometimes."

"Well, you can, but only if you smell this flower. You see, the other shore is full of red spider lilies, and their fragrance, their smell, helps you remember for a time all the things that happened when you were living."

"So you remember and then you forget again?"

"Well... yes."

"Then, maybe we can wait for each other there, and when you start forgetting, I can remind you of everything, and when I forget, you can remind me."

She smiles. "Deal."

Her face flickers, shimmers, then the image vanishes, her voice dying on the wind, the comforting scent ripped away, leaving the painful desert aridity burning my nose. My vision decays to just my right eye. From the crest of a nearby dune, fuzzy and black and insect-tiny, the rat is gesturing for me to follow along. The sky has changed: darker, new asteroids, an early evening star. The shadows have been taffy-pulled, the valleys tenebrous. I wave in return, disoriented by the intensity of hugging my mother after so many years. All her life she had vacillated between the warm, approachable woman in that memory and another that was melancholic and aloof, but towards the end of her life, she had tended towards the latter of these extremes. I stare down at my feet, the battered red shoes caked in a glamour of sparkling sand, ruby slippers, wondering how to return to that memory—I miss those tiny child's feet with their clumsily-tied, thick laces.

I hobble along the peak of this dune towards the rat, following its gradual, curved descent. Behind me the sun clings to the horizon, and the mountains have nearly vanished into the distance. As I watch the reddening sky, the color flickers. Everything coils away, blanches. White surges out of the darkness.

A rhythmic thumping. *Whoosh. Whoosh. Whoosh.* Sweeping windshield wipers.

Murmuring snowfall.

Fainter still drones the tape on the car stereo and David Bowie's lugubrious voice.

Then, in the far distance beyond the windshield, faint embers glow out of the thick white ash—a sentry of flashing traffic barrels.

The car glides towards them.

Beyond, the guardrails have been twisted into coils.

The frozen lake is completely whited out.

All of existence has been reduced to the dim maroon interior of this Taurus, the heartbeat of windshield wipers struggling beneath the oppressive snow, the blinking lights, and the tortured metal sculpture. I pull over and idle for several minutes, heat on full blast, drying out my eyes. I'm still wearing the dress and thick stockings I'd worn to the funeral. No makeup. Would have just run.

I step out into the cold and climb down to the shore, keeping the flashing road barrels in sight so I can find my way back to my car. I hesitate on the edge, taking deep breaths, fighting the allure of the ice, the invitation of death, then shuffle tentatively out, needing to get as close as possible to the spot where Ma had crashed through. That's when the wind picks up, blotting out the lights of the shore, severing my lifeline back to the world. Can't even see my boots on the ice. Shouldn't move. I've turned around too many times and am now disoriented as to the path I'd taken out here.

CRICK!

Though muted by the snowfall, the sound of cracking ice is unmistakable.

CRICK!

I can feel the icy promise in my ankles and shins and knees. A simple language. Every sentence the same.

CRICK!

Can imagine the complex network of splintered ice at my feet, but then... suddenly an ethereal light shines through the TV static of snow. Not the flashing traffic barrels. A rainbow on the shore.

Tentative step after tentative step I approach, leave the frozen lake and find my footprints on the bank, so enthralled with the light that I barely register the fact that I'd just escaped death. As I get closer, I realize it's my Taurus, teeming with what appear to be radioactive plants—electric blue vines choking the wheels, golden moss smoldering the roof, giant fiery blooms exploding from the tailpipe, a pullulation of petals and leaves, thorns and stalks, crowding against the interior windows, blindingly chartreuse and detailed. Unafraid, I open the door to the car and crawl into the radiant jungle, setting down on a seat run through with roots and ivy. I grasp the floral wreath of the steering wheel. The vegetal network yields to my hands, blowing apart from some unfelt billow and then settling back down. Everything is alive around me. My skin prickles and itches and sparks as the flora creeps over my hands and down my arms, such a complex texture and sensation— excruciating and exquisite. I want to scream and laugh and sing. A rising tingle and then electricity jolting through me, muscles quivering. My head blossoms and blossoms, and each blossom creates a new me and withers and bursts the old new me's—like being lost in a hall of magic life-spawning mirrors—until I don't know who I am or where I am or what anything is, each destruction, each creation bone-crushing ecstasy—waves and waves and waves—trapped in some kind of endless time-looping dreamworld—and then I blink and it's over.

The car seat is hot with fresh urine.

The barrels flash

The windows are fogged, the plants vanished. I strip

off my scarf and hat to mop the sweat tracing down my face.

The Bowie tape begins to disintegrate, sputtering between sound and silence, skipping and repeating, skipping and repeating, then is drawn and quartered: lowering, distorted amputations. The whiteness, the car, retreat with this disintegration, clouds scudding off towards the horizon, deforming in the distance.

A hand is grabbing me. Long, lucent hairs sprouting out the back; the fingers bulbous; nails vicious, green-black slivers.

The rat hops back when I recoil from its touch.

"We apologize, Jing," it says, "but you were staring off into space and wouldn't respond."

Darker still.

"I... lost track of time. I think. I'm not sure exactly what happened."

"Try to stay present. You might have fallen."

As the rat speaks these last words, I realize I'd been standing right on the edge of a sheer dune face, a hundred feet high or more. The landscape around me has changed; we must have walked some distance while I was in the dreamlike memory state.

I click my tongue stud. "Umm... thanks."

"Perhaps you should—if it's not too offensive to you—grab hold of my tail. Then we can be sure to stick together."

"Right." I bend over and grab ahold of the leathery tail, barely even registering the disturbing texture. "Good idea."

We continue on this way for a time, up and down and around dune after dune, when I start to notice the fine hairs of the rat's tail lengthening, softening, darkening. The hairs spill over my hands, the desert dissolves, and the fading light intensifies. I tug lightly on the long hair and feel the resistance of a head at the other end. Penn's head. Vomiting in the toilet. In the back-ground pipes the cheery music of *Mario Paint*, the catalyst of this violent reaction. I stroke her upper back until the attack is over, then guide her to the sink—her face is sickly; the expression in her eyes unfocused, dazed—and help her clean up. Penn works up a lather on the lemon vanilla soap and massages her face. I rip open the packaging of a fresh toothbrush and help her to some toothpaste and mouthwash.

When she's finished I guide her back to the bed in my cramped college apartment, switch off the television, and make her some tea. She's asleep by the time I return with the piping hot mug. I set it down on the bedside table and crawl in with her, check for a fever—her skin is cool—then just watch her peaceful face for a while. Outside, the snow whispers, intimate, cloistering. I touch her hair again—almost down to her lower back when she doesn't tie it up—then her face, and soon my nose is brushing up beside hers.

Her eyes open, and I give her the lightest of kisses. Electrifying but too light to taste. She blinks, smiles distantly, and closes her eyes again. I kiss her again. Deeper this time. Her lips part. Our tongues flick together. One finger hooks around my sweater collar and pulls me closer in. Our legs are soon entwined, our hands exploring beneath each other's clothes. Then, piece by piece they're shed. Her body is beautiful—skin taut and smooth, breasts pliant with small hard nipples, a beauty mark beside her bellybutton—but throughout she remains oddly passive—maybe due to the illness. She touches me where I guide her hand to touch. She kisses and licks, bites and sucks what I press to her lips.

It is only afterwards in what is obviously a line she has spoken to countless others, she explains what had happened, how the music had brought on the sickness:

"The discrepancy between the synesthetic imagery and the actual visuals give me a sense of unreality, vertigo, then nausea. Scenes—landscapes from memory mostly, but some I'm not sure ever existed—become superimposed over my senses, generated by particular musical key signatures, and shifting and flowering as a result of the melody and rhythm."

As she speaks more and more, her energy rebounds. She's soon starving, lively, a different person. I make her an egg and tomato sandwich and more tea. While I'm in the kitchen, she sneaks up behind me and pinches my ass, then starts to kiss my neck and rub me through my panties with her nimble guitarist fingers. She spreads me open and fingers me, adding in one at a time, until my legs weaken, and I collapse shuddering and moaning on the counter.

Her food is cold again by the time we finish.

While she eats on the bed, she draws a table showing the synesthetic vistas of the major and minor key signatures. The most commonly used keys correspond with generic scenes—forests, deserts, mountains—but as they grow more and more obscure, the imagery becomes less and less universal, until they are very specific memories of rooms or alleyways from her childhood. The table is packed with information, scientifically beautiful, but after she sketches it out, she crumples it and tosses it into the trash, as if to demonstrate that that is all her visions are—musical mandalas.

The curtain of memory dissolves as I stumble over a petrified plant, falling onto my hands and knees at the base of a dune. I stare dumbfounded at the twisted, black branch angling out of the sand, perhaps the remnant of some ancient oasis.

The rat.

I'd been holding its tail. Must have let go at some point during the memory. I glance around the gathering dusk, the sky a golden crown bejeweled with a showcase of asteroids. The rat nowhere in sight, I scramble up the closest dune and survey the future lands. On the far side I spot it curled up in the sand, twitching and writhing. I slide-tumble down the slope and clamber to the rat's side, fighting off the intoxicating hallucinations fingering at the edges of the present.

I tug on the rat's paw, then lightly smack its living head.

"Ratty, wake up, wake up!"

Unresponsive, limp.

"Come on, Ratty. Don't leave me here like this. I don't know what the fuck to do."

After several futile minutes of trying to revive the rat, I remove its backpack, loop it together with my purse, and using one of the vines, lash it around my belt, creating a tow rope. Then I hoist the creature onto my back. It is heavier than it looks. Even worse is the odor, which stuns me momentarily, seeming to burden me with additional weight. I gag, fall face-first into the sand, the rat crushing me, skull clattering with apparent delight.

"How the hell am I going to do this?" I ask the skull. Too weak, my leg and other injuries have started to flare up.

I dig around in the rat's backpack for the remainder of the cold mushrooms, but they're gone. Had we eaten again? There are just a few dorberries and the fishing pole puffball smeared in hippocochlea slime and caked with sand. I settle for the former. The dry bitterness is somehow not as unpleasant as I remember it being earlier today.

After the short meal I turn back to the rat, occasional tremors fluttering up through its body as if its carcass were riddled with maggots or worse. I grab a hold of its tail and drag it onward, my own body nearly horizontal with the effort. Laborious step after laborious step, my back screams with pain until I crash back down.

I can't do it.

That's when I see them.

On the ground beside me: a wide groove in the sand—hippocochlea tracks.

A memory?

No. How could it be? The memories have only been

of events from Earth, nothing from Psyche.

I scramble after them, up the slope of a dune and find the blue mount idling just on the other side of the ridge, feelers washing the sand in search of mushrooms.

I shout and wave and pull out the puffball fishing pole. The latter instantly grabs its attention, and it canter-slithers over. I hobble away, back down the slope towards the rat, the hippocochlea close behind, speeding up to a sliding lope. When it reaches the base, I pinch off a small piece of mushroom as a reward, then load our belongings onto its dorsum. Using a vine from the rat's pack and a horn jutting out of the carapace, I pulley up the rat. When it nears the top, I shoulder it up the final way, then climb up after it and bind the rat to a dorsal fin to keep it from slipping off. Finally I get the fishing pole back out and lead the creature onward, up the side of the dune, correcting its course when I gauge our location in relation to the last glowing tips of the Crystal Mountains, then lash the pole into place. In case I drift off into memory, the hippocochlea should continue on unfazed.

As we set off, I crawl back, tie myself to one of the hippocochlea spines, then inspect the security of the rat's bindings. It's still twitching, kicking. I set to fastening its feet to one of the chitinous protrusions, so it doesn't kick loose and fall off our mount or swing down and strangle to death. As I do so, they recede from me, transform into knobby human feet dangling over the end of a sun lounger. Bower's feet. Warm summer night. I'm reclining on the chair beside his, a bottle of cold beer clutched in one hand, half-smoked joint in the other. My fingertips and lips are sticky. My boy shorts and bra are wet—chlorine-smelling skin beautiful and smooth and whole in the cyan glow of the pool lights. The night after our first practice, weeks since I'd moved to Detroit. Penn is recovering from musical illness some-where upstairs in the Compound.

"It was a boating accident," Bower says and takes a

swig of his beer. His hibiscus boxers are drip-drying through the cracks of the lounger, and his shaggy hair is plastered over the side of his head in enviably artless curls, his long body utterly devoid of fat. "Both of them gone in an instant."

"Car crash," I say and pass him the joint. Then, nodding beyond him to the gravity-defying orbs of the Compound, "Was this where you grew up?"

He hits the joint. "No, I grew up in Grosse Point, and we had a winter home in Florida."

"Figures."

He flashes a cocksure smile, passing the joint back. "My dad was an architect. He designed this—it was a pet project he'd been working on for some time—supposed to be a modern art museum. He left no instructions behind as to how I should use my inheritance, but practically all of it went into achieving his vision—with some slight modifications with the help of a number of consultants—two and a half years to build. I think it would've made him happy."

"I guess it is being used as a kind of art museum, too—a living art museum."

"Yeah. You play anything other than drums?"

"What exactly did Penn tell you about me?"

"She fed some magic mushrooms to her drum machine and it turned out all along to have been a cursed princess."

I laugh.

"What? Is that not true?"

"I play piano. Violin, too. You name it, I can figure it out."

"Violin... we should use that."

"Lessons were mandatory growing up."

"I hear that."

We clink bottles.

"Are you good?"

"At violin, no. Piano, yes."

"What's the most challenging piece you ever played?"

"Aside from chopsticks?"

"We'll take chopsticks as a given."

I take a drag off the cigarette. "Well, I never quite mastered it: Mussorgsky's—"

"*Pictures at an Exhibition.* Fuck me! I can play bits of it. Never had the patience to work out the whole thing."

I nod, impressed. "Outside of the music department at college, I haven't met too many people that know it."

"You've been running in the wrong circles." He sucks his teeth. "When I was a kid—I was a weird kid—listen to this, Drummer Girl—I wanted to be able to identify every piece of classical music in my dad's library. He had everything. Thousands of records. That's what he did in the evenings. He'd come home, eat dinner with us, then Scotch, put on a record and just zone out. I couldn't penetrate him when the music was playing. So, really young I started sitting down with him and just listening, you know? And he wouldn't talk about the music either. He could tell you what was playing, but beyond that, there was some music-language disconnect. In some other world. Maybe because he never learned to play, never learned the jargon. In any case, when he did speak, I listened and I remembered, and by the end of high school, I could identify any one of those records from just a tiny clip."

"That's not so weird."

"No?"

"You just wanted daddy's attention."

His foot sweeps out and lightly kicks mine, and as it withdraws there's a gentle, perhaps accidental, caress. My thoughts take a turn in that direction, and Bower goes quiet, taking a quick swig. When I look back down at his feet they are no longer Bower's but a memory amalgam: Penn's on my bed in college, the delicate toe-nails painted white; my tiny feet walking in the garden next to my mother's; the deformed foot of a neighbor-hood crackhead crystallized with fungus and cold and rot; Henry's sneakered feet folded into the lotus position;

Ruirui's white sneakers mounting the wet stones of Jade Mountain; the wriggling tentacles of the hippocochlea. All of them, the real and the remembered, move with mystifying coordination, everything multiplied, transformed, the memories no longer cycling from one to the next, but playing simultaneously, overstepping the bounds of consciousness. I recoil, hugging the carapace, neck retracting into my shoulders, as if this might distance my brain and head from my mind and relieve me of this fast-multiplying, perceptual burden. The memory overwork bubbles up, spilling into all the senses, which bleed through, clashing together, a perfect synthesis of vision, sound, taste, touch, smell, emotion, thought— and I scream—a roaring psychic stream, the mind no longer able to contain it, all the doorways bursting open, electrochemical soul-fire lashing outward, down the body, into the viscera and limbs, besieging every cell.

Then Psyche slips away:

CHAPTER 10

Synthetic church bells crackle over the intercom.

The clock reads six-thirty in danger-red numerals. Snow twists and paws at the grated window, fast and fine and virgin white—first snow. Shivering, Jing reaches towards the pile of clothes at the foot of her bed, slips on a pair of wool socks, a sweater, a hoodie, and then nestles there for a few more minutes until the wake-up alarm has ceased. Then she shuffles to the bathroom to make herself presentable for breakfast.

In the conservatory cafeteria, the cognizant patients marvel at the snow pile-up against the exterior of the wall of glass—ponderous, wind-crafted dunes towering as high as the mezzanine dining areas.

Catherine, still disheartened after having missed Thanksgiving with her family for a trip to the Clouds, joins Jing for breakfast. When Jing mentions between a bite of cantaloupe that today is her day to see Murai in the east wing, Catherine's eyes bug.

"Be careful, Drummer Girl," she whispers.

"Why?"

"Don't you know about Dr. Rota?"

"You mean of Wellness Village fame?"

Catherine nods, glancing around. "There was a scandal back in the '80s right before the state took over. A patient accused Dr. Rota of molesting her, and was later found drowned in Serenity Pond." Catherine gestures out into the blue-grey morning, toward the iced-over pond and the frosted cattails. "Afterwards there was a rash of suicides in the Village. Rota faced multiple lawsuits, and Wellness Village was shut down. The scandal ended with Rota's death in his office in the east wing—stabbed in the heart at his desk. 'Suicide,' they claimed"—she arches her eyebrows—"but the list of suspects is endless—a disgruntled patient, Rota's wife, family of the suicide victims, his protégée Dr. Goldfield. Now Dr. Rota haunts those halls, searching for naughty patients who have wandered out of the north wing and lobotomizing them."

"I'll be sure to keep a lookout."

"Yes, please be careful." Catherine reaches out and squeezes Jing's hand with all earnestness. Her eyes wander beyond Jing. "Oh, look who it is."

Jing turns to find Henry standing at the cafeteria entrance, wearing a loose fitting brown sweater piled over his everyday red one, hair even more disjointed from his head than usual. He shuffles over to the food counter and picks out milk and cereal.

"I should go say something to him," Jing says. Tossing back the rest of her coffee, she carries her tray down to the food line. When Henry turns to find a place to sit, their eyes lock, and she hesitates uncertainly for a moment.

"Hi, Henry," she says. "How you doing?"

He sniffles and nods, eyes glazed.

"I..."

"I want to thank you," Henry says to her surprise. "It's good to be back."

"Thank me... You really mean it?"

"You did what you did because you were trying to help me."

She smiles uncomfortably, unconvinced by his sincerity and confused by the alien tone of his voice, so careful and slow.

"I'd been... in this vortex of delusion, but... they got me the meds I need," he continues. His eyes dart upward, then down and meet hers.

He's trying to signal something.

"Okay..." She follows his gaze up one of the columns.

"So, thank you very much," he concludes and

brushes past her to find a table, sitting down by a barren garden plot with a plastic Christmas tree planted in it.

Then it clicks.

The Muzak has changed—Henry had been directing her gaze towards one of the circular speakers embedded in the top of the column—no longer cycling through the disordered *Brandenburg Concertos.*

"Childhood's joy-land,
Mystic merry Toyland,
Once you pass its borders,
You can never return again."

With only fifteen minutes left before her appointment, Jing returns to her room, freshens up, dons a winter coat and hat, and descends back to the grandiose first floor lobby. She shows a pass to the front desk security guard, and he admits her into the east wing.

The halls are empty and clean, much colder than the rest of the main building (as Billie, the nurse on her treatment team, had warned her it would be). The distant echoes of Muzak might have once reminded her of the continued existence of society beyond these abandoned hallways, but ever since last week they'd shut off the central rotunda speaker, and now the only sound is her footsteps. Plants have not taken root anywhere. No vermin flit through the shadows. Through the viewing windows in some of the doors she glimpses bare desks, stripped cots, clusters of medical equipment, a lone piano. She wonders which office was Rota's—and if there was even a grain of truth to Catherine's story. In the stretches of nothingness between the glow of exit signs and the fluorescent-lit intersections, Jing watches for faces looming out of doorways, the milky-eyed ghost of Dr. Rota with a gaping hole in his chest and black blood staining his gray beard. Throughout her walk she is struck with a creeping sensation—not fear of ghosts, but that all of this is very familiar, perhaps because it is essentially a looking glass version of the west wing.

After many twists and turns, she comes upon a string of illuminated overheads framing a door—a hermit's cabin in the wilderness.

Dr. Murai's office.

"We are now going to conduct a psychiatric interview, okay?"

Dr. Murai—a man with luxuriant, shoulder-length hair; thin, graying beard; and wire-rim glasses—smiles at Jing over his notes. He's neatly dressed in a black tie and white short-sleeve shirt. Beside him on the table sets a tube of copper-colored tea, leaves drifting and spinning through the liquid following each sip. They're sitting in an office adjacent to a medical examination room that Jing suspects was at one point a supply closet. Lacking the intimacy of Goldfield's office, Murai's is expansive and sparsely decorated: the metal bookshelves empty, save battered copies of diagnostic medical books and a few mechanical parts and loose wires; tools scattered over his desk; several space heaters purring in the corners; a metal table along one wall showcasing a number of intriguing devices; and a scatter of folding chairs.

"My temporary suite," he'd said with a wince-like smile when they met, "until I become fully integrated into Glenbrook."

The comment had instantly vanquished the tension that had been growing inside Jing—as had the balminess of the room. The sliding windows here grant a view of one of the east wing courtyards, completely barren save one rowan tree, its bright red berry clusters preserved in ice. From this vantage, the east wing seems much more ruined than it had in the hallway. The courtyard walls are crawling with vines. Snow swirls across the courtyard and in through the broken windows of one of the upper floors.

Billie, trim with a bouncy, shoulder-length ponytail, had been present for the physical, which had included examining her left eye with an ophthalmoscope, but Murai had not made any comment about her vision. Presumably the pupil had dilated as it was supposed to. Following that, Billie had taken blood and brought it to the lab, and Murai had seated her at the metal table, shifting his "little hobbies" out of the way to give her room to complete a battery of paper tests which tapped every cognitive dimension imaginable. Throughout, he had read what appeared to be old patient files, sipping tea by the window, periodically checking his watch. At one point she thought she heard muddled echoes of piano—liquid glissandi, meandering chord phrases— but difficult to name the piece. Ravel, maybe. Had they turned the rotunda speakers back on?

Afterwards, she was strapped to various devices and performed more tasks still. All of this had taken nearly three hours, and at the end her stomach had started rumbling to the tune of lunchtime. However, it was at this point that he had gelled her hair and applied the EEG cap. Then he switched on the signal amplifier, opened a program on his computer, and began re- cording, many channels of squiggles erupting into jagged peaks and valleys whenever she blinked or spoke.

"The computer will just be taking readings in the background," he says in a thick accent. "Never know when it might be useful. In the interest of science, try not to move unnecessarily."

"All right."

"So"—he sets the inevitable clipboard on his lap— "Ms. Elwood, what is bothering you? Why did you want to see me?"

"I had this... episode several months ago but don't remember it clearly. Since then I've had trouble sleeping, I've had a few seizures, my period has stopped—but most importantly I want to be discharged from Glenbrook."

"And that's why you asked Dr. Goldfield if you could have another doctor take a look at you? Because she thinks you are not ready to be discharged?"

Jing nods. An eruption of spikes on the screen.

He makes a few notes. "Well, I hope I can help resolve each one of these problems and you can go on living a pleasant life, but first a few questions. Birthdate?"

"New Year's Eve, 1973."

"Your first name is Chinese?"

"Yeah."

"Can I see the character?"

He holds out his notes and pen to her, and she writes a neat logogram in the corner.

"Ah yes, similar to Japanese. Scripture, sutra—something like that."

She nods.

"Your parents, what are their names?"

"Davis and Lili Elwood."

"You're American born?" he asks, noting her responses, eyes lingering on the detailed plant tattoos creeping out of her sweater's sleeve.

"Marquette, Michigan."

"What is the significance of the tattoos?"

"Sorry?"

"Your arm tattoos. Tell me what they mean."

A jungle burgeoning inside a Taurus. "Nothing really."

His face strains as if unwilling to accept this—the wince again, as Jing has begun to label the expression—but he makes a few notes and moves on. "Tell me more about your parents. How did they meet? What do they do? Etc."

"They met in Taiwan when my Dad was stationed there as a military psychologist. My mother was working as a translator at the time. They were married a year or so later. Back in the states. She got her PhD sometime after that. Comparative lit. They were both professors."

"Were? What do they do now?"

"My father still teaches. Ma suffered from mental illness for as long as I could remember, lost her job before I was old enough to know what was going on, had been institutionalized a few times. Several years ago she killed herself."

"I'm very sorry to hear that. What kind of mental illness?"

"Different doctors, different explanations. Schizophrenia was one of them. I always just thought she was sad and a bit eccentric, cold sometimes."

"So... did you seek counseling after she died?"

"No."

"Why not?"

"I have a tendency to try and deal with things on my own."

He nods, scratching on the clipboard, the sound grating. "How did it happen?"

"She drove her car into Lake Superior. The roads were icy, but she was driving extremely fast, certainly faster than she was prone to driving. That was three years ago, December, right before winter break my junior year in college."

"Did she leave a note?"

Jing shakes her head.

As Murai writes, she rubs her eyes, bothered by the bright light of the office. The acoustics in here sound tinny, strident.

"How did the rest of your family cope with this loss?"

"My sister"—she smiles—"took charge of everyone, and my father"—the smile dies—"sort of folded up into himself."

"How is your relationship with him?"

"Strained."

"Succinct answer."

"Yup."

"How is his health now?"

"Fine, I suppose."

"Both mentally and physically?"

"Yeah."

"Okay," he continues, stroking his beard, "what about with the rest of your family? With your sister."

"Yeah. Rui. Pretty rough."

"Care to elaborate?"

"Not really. Ba always doted on her. I suppose I was closer to my mother. Still, I don't think she ever knew me that well, and I guess I didn't know her either. Ma, I mean. I couldn't believe she didn't leave us a note, but at that point we were—I was—we weren't talking anymore."

"Why not?"

"It's complicated, but I think my sex life was a part of the problem. I brought a girlfriend home for Thanksgiving, a tattoo artist I was seeing. It created a huge fracas."

"Okay"—he scratches a note—"I want to come back to this, but let's proceed to the next question first. Your education."

"Well, I was at the University of Michigan, double-majoring in biology and music performance. I finished high school early, had a full ride, but I dropped out not long after my mother died, before my senior year."

"What is your current profession?"

"I'm an unemployed mental patient right now."

Murai flashes a pained smile. "And before you were admitted to Glenbrook?"

"I played drums and various other things in a band. That was really my first paying job."

"What band?"

"Autoscope. Alternative music. We put out an album last summer. One of the songs was sort of a hit. Maybe you heard of us?" she adds dubiously.

Murai shakes his head, with a frown as brief as his smile. "I stick to jazz mostly."

"Well, anyway, we were supposed to go on tour earlier

this autumn. That obviously didn't happen."

"What are your plans for after Glenbrook?" Murai continues with a flood of notes.

"Maybe I'll join another group, move back home, go back to school—I don't know. It's difficult really to make plans when I don't even have a discharge date set. Mind if I smoke?"

"Please. The smoke won't interfere with the machines. Just ash on the floor."

"Okay." She pulls her cigarettes and lighter out of her jeans, not really sure if he was being sarcastic about her ashing on the floor. As it's littered with clipped wires, bolts, and metal scraps, she decides he must have been in earnest.

"Well, I have read through Dr. Goldfield's notes and discussed you a good bit at staff meetings, so I do understand *her* concerns, but let's hold off on that for the moment. Are you worried about your future?"

"The album is still doing well. That and other royalties and advancements should keep me afloat for a while. I just, I don't know..." She trails off, on the brink of mentioning the eye, when she steers back into safe sarcasm instead, decisively lighting her cigarette, "Aside from the occasional seizure, it's been a pleasant vacation."

"Okay. Uh, now tell me about your social life, friends, etc."

"I don't have too many right now." She inhales the smoke, lets it settle inside her. "There's Penn." She exhales at last. "We're pretty close."

"Penn?"

"Penelope Costero. We intersected at college. She introduced me to the other songwriter in the band."

"Any other friends? Boyfriend? Girlfriend?"

She shakes her head.

"Okay." He writes, sipping his green tea. "How about this other member of the band?"

"Sebastian Bower. He just went by Bower."

"Oh, yes. That name I remember." He nods, the mention of Bower's name spurring on an unprecedented flood of notetaking. As the doctor writes, he seems to recede into the distance. Everything appears that way, drifting off, except the room actually appears to be lengthening and heightening as if she were shrinking, her eyes and ears retracting impossibly inward.

No third-person?

Her hand claws at the frayed denim of her jeans, and Murai squints at it. She instinctively relaxes the bird claw, and Murai's gaze drops back to his notes in a controlled way.

"Are you okay, Ms. Elwood?" he asks without looking up again, scribbling with zeal.

She gasps, feeling as if she were operating the breathing mechanisms of her body remotely. "Fine. Let's just continue."

"Okay. Next question. What can you tell me about why you were admitted to Glenbrook?" His eyes dart up, glinting with expectation.

"I... don't remember much." She rubs her eyes at the light, the distance. "I probably had taken a lot of drugs the night before coming here—the night Bower died—but that was the way things were at the Compound."

Murai brightens. "Yes, the Compound. That is the impressive mansion in Detroit?"

"Yeah."

"Have you been following the local news?" He pauses with his notes and turns to the computer monitor, studying the schematic traces of her brain activity.

"No."

"The Compound makes a near-daily appearance. Safety issues, ownership disputes, all rather tiresome by now."

"Is that so," she says distractedly.

He nods. "A real shame. The photos of the interior are quite stunning, but it seems likely its fate is to be demolished. What do you think about that?"

"A real shame," she echoes.

"Now, can you tell me—Bower—how did he die?"

She shakes her head, mind wandering away. "I don't know."

"You do not seem sure of your response."

"What?"

"You are playing with the, umm, the lip ring. I notice you do this sometimes when you are unsure about your responses."

She withdraws the hand from her mouth, staring at the traitorous fingers, now fiddling with a ring of air. "In fact, I do remember a couple of things." As she says this, there is a sudden movement on top of Murai's head, the bulging of a patch of his long hair.

Her fingers freeze.

"Ah, okay. Then please go on."

"There was a show that night at the Compound," Jing says quietly, as if trying to avoid frightening off a wild animal. She examines the top of his head, searching out what she thought she'd just seen.

"And so you took the drugs before or after the show?"

"Must have been after. My contract stipulated that I always play sober. The previous drummer had a substance problem."

Murai nods to himself. "What type of drugs did you take?" Something pushes up a flap of his black hair.

"I don't know." Jing clenches her hand again. "Take your pick: weed, pills, cocaine, X, acid, heroin. All free-floating at the Compound. I assume that night was no different than the rest."

There is a cracking sound, and a slender green shoot pops out of Murai's head, unfurling bit by bit. Startled, Jing recoils deeper into her chair.

"You look uncomfortable, Ms. Elwood," Murai says, his writing screeching to a halt.

"I'm fine... fine," Jing murmurs, voice lost, eyes now devoted to the study of the thing poking out of Murai's head.

"Okay. What exactly are you looking at?" Murai glances behind him at the sliding windows and then back at Jing. As he turns, she notices the back of his head is bloodless, but other spring-delicate buds have begun to needle out of the hole.

"Umm, nothing." Jing drops her gaze and fixates on Murai's face, but in her peripheral vision she continues to monitor the growths unfolding and extending, branching outward.

"There were claims that you were threatening people with a knife that night. Do you recall doing so?"

"No."

"As for Bower, a knife was ruled out as a possible murder weapon. In fact, the authorities are at a loss as to what could have been used. Were you shown photos during the police interrogation?"

"They tried to. They tried to show me."

"Okay." He notes the EEG signal. Several of the channels have begun to erupt into a jagged frenzy. "Umm, next question—"

"Bamboo," she blurts out, finally realizing what it is growing out of Murai.

"Sorry?" His brow furrows. "Bamboo?" As the muscles of his jaw flex when he speaks, she sees the roots of the plant hanging down from the roof of the mouth. They, too, begin to finger outward, poking out of the corner of his mouth, creeping out of the edge of one of his eye sockets, curling around his glasses, and finally bursting out of the base of his jaw. Unfazed, Murai makes more notes in his clipboard, then glances back towards the computer monitor. "What do you mean by that? Is this a new street drug?"

"Um, I... just... I lost my train of thought."

"Okay. Next question," he says, a filigree of roots coiling around his tongue. "You do not remember anything else from that evening?"

"No," she whispers, watching as more shoots of bamboo pop out of the side of his head. The roots creeping out of his mouth and eyes and jaw stretch downward, burrowing in through his flat chest and broad shoulders. No blood, as if Murai's flesh were putty.

"Okay. Have you ever had periods of lost time before this?"

"Yes, especially after my mother's death, I went off the deep end with drinking and drugs, and for a while blackouts were pretty routine; I kind of... sought them out."

The segmented bamboo ripples under Murai's skin, working down his slender arms.

"What about when you were a child?"

"I don't..." She pulls her body deeper into her chair, tucking her legs beneath her ass, hand frozen in front of her face, her voice a whisper. "I don't know."

"Am I making you uncomfortable, Ms. Elwood? If yes, please say so, and we can stop the interview at once, or perhaps you would prefer if Billie were to come back in?"

She shakes her head indecisively, feeling as if she were strapped into a dark ride, waiting to be ferried through the worst of it.

"Okaayy, you should ask your father or sister if they remember any strange behavior in childhood that might indicate blackouts. Every piece of information is important. Helps us fill in the puzzle. Now, have you ever encountered a person that claimed to know you but that you could not remember having met?"

"That was on the test," she says, voice continuing to fade.

"Yes," he winces, "but I want to hear you answer it now."

"No."

"Have you been accused of something you don't recall doing?"

"No."

"Can you read minds?" he says, voice creaking into something subhuman.

"No."

"Have you seen anything or heard anything that others couldn't see or hear?"

Fingerlings of bamboo burst out of Murai's knuckles, fan out, curling around the edges of his clipboard, an auxiliary pair of monstrous hands.

She clicks, heart encased in ice. "No."

Murai shifts in his chair, eyes darting between her and the computer monitor, uncrossing his legs, each movement setting off a clacking of limbs and shushing of leaves. He waters the roots in his mouth with a swig of green tea. "Would you like some tea or coffee or something?"

"I'm fine. Just another cigarette." She pulls out a Camel, though she has barely touched the other one, by now reduced to a history of ash. Directing her eyes away from the bizarre tableau, her shaking hands fail several attempts to light the new cigarette, wedged between her fingers next to the old one. The bamboo hands reach over, pulling the lighter from her fingertips, smoothly lighting her cigarette, and returning the device to her.

"Thanks—" the word catches in the back of her throat.

"Sure. Next question. What about your menstrual cycle? Have you had irregularities before?"

"No."

"Okay. Dr. Goldfield informs me you had an attack just a few weeks ago." He turns a page in his notes, the paper crackling like fire.

"That's right," she says, staring at the wall, at the shadow of Dr. Murai, human shape distorted by the bamboo branching and efflorescing outward: a stained cross-section of neural tissue. As it grows, she can hear it rustling and stretching the skin apart. Next to this shadow slants her own, its head exaggerated by the angle of the light, a maze of wires blasting out of it and coiling together—similarly plant-like. "I'd gone off my meds. Maybe that was why..."

"That is certainly possible." As the shadow speaks,

she can see bamboo shoots jutting out of its mouth, blossoming into a dendritic cloud threatening to eclipse her head.

"Is it connected," she ask, her voice flat and the question she poses to Murai thus devoid of its normal prosodic contours. How her mother had sounded at times. Jing is far away now, both from the room, from her body, mind and emotions, entering into a gray area of consciousness, third-person several times removed. *Third-person makes sense, third-person makes sense.*

"Is what connected? You mean the drugs, seizures, psychosis? It is possible. Your tests reveal you only have mild psychotic tendencies, nothing to raise an alarm about." Murai's voice whirrs with the vibrating of thousands of tiny bamboo segments—a vegetable synthesizer parodying human speech. "In fact, you are within range of what is considered 'normal.' That is, of course, according to the MMPI results. However, the issue is a complex one."

It takes a sip of tea, settling in for a lengthy spiel.

"You see, there is a poorly understood connection between epilepsy and psychosis: many childhood epileptics develop schizophrenia later in life; psychotic episodes sometimes immediately precede the onset of seizure; moreover, long-term use of anticonvulsants have been linked with subsequent psychosis—not to mention long-term use of hallucinogens and amphetamines. In addition to these connections, antipsychotics may actually lower the seizure threshold, and antidepressants have shown to increase the likelihood of seizure. Confused yet?" The arrangement of shadow branches wince and flash a smile. "Uhh, now, while intoxication and withdrawal are associated with brief psychotic episodes and seizures, this does not necessarily explain what happened to you at the beginning of your stay at Glenbrook. The infrequent psychotic episodes are probably related to these tonic-clonic seizures—perhaps as epileptic auras. I am aware, of course, Dr. Goldfield's diagnosis is schizoaffective disorder, and while I can appreciate how she reached that conclusion from the jumble of road signs, at this point I disagree with her assessment."

The shadow seems to have stopped growing, and Jing, taking a long drag on the cigarette, finally turns her head, glassy eyes following with reluctance. They settle on the creature sitting across from her, a leafy explosion of blue-green bamboo, the human putty ripped to pieces, stretched out and drooping in a web of flesh.

"Okay," she gasps and collapses onto the floor, convulsing—

CHAPTER 11

Several layers of struggle-between-light-and-dark petals blanket my body. I smell grilled mushrooms from a nearby, crackling fire and the familiar, now somehow comforting putrescence of the rat. I'm lying in a lean-to of leafy, deep-emerald branches. Beyond, the rat limps to and from a grove of plants unlike anything I've seen before on Psyche—more terrestrial, a forest really, none of it glowing. The sky is a vibrant azure, spotted with planetoids and clouds. Novel notes infuse the wind. Where once it was arid, it is now fresh; once biting, now invigorating. Another conspicuous addition to the Psyche atmosphere is the distant crashing of waves, and therein lies the difference in the touch and sound and rush of this wind—it is wind over water.

I sit up, then cry out as pain flashes down my back. Groaning, I ease back down, and soon the rat shuffles over to my side.

"Jing, how are you?"

"I'm fine. It's just... my back." As I speak, the events of our desert trek come back to me, how I'd set the hippocochlea in motion and had been securing the rat to its carapace. "It's strange. The memories aren't... attacking me the same way they had been."

"No, the hippocochlea conveyed us beyond the wall of memory, though we fear you may have injured yourself. Here, drink this."

The rat hands me a folded leaf cup full of clear water with a subtle, sweet fragrance. It studies my face as I prop myself up and drink the cool liquid.

"Shit, this is delicious!" I down it all in one gulp.

"We want to thank you, Jing. If you had not acted as

you had, we would have been lost in the desert, forever reliving the past."

"Well, call us even, then. Actually, I still owe you a couple more." I nod towards the leaf. Though emptied, the water's fragrance still permeates the air. "Where did you get this?"

"A stream"—it gestures beyond me—"emptying into the sea. This place has everything we could ask for: fruit, nuts, mushrooms, water. It would be wise for us to recuperate here a few days more before we move on."

"Sounds like a plan." I tenderly shift my body from one elbow to the other to get a better vantage. "It's beautiful."

The sand slopes down from the blue forest, ending in a limpid, green sea. To the left water gushes over a high table of black stone, crashes down into a white roil and meanders over rock and sand down towards the waves. In places, great, black-opal cliffs erupt out of the beach, lifting and dividing the treeline into inaccessible copses. The forest extends across the horizon, full of tall, elegant trees resembling bamboo—a blue that shimmers between emerald and deep violet—popping and clattering in the fresh breeze. In the gray distance, several enormous, lofty islands spear out of the water, like blooms of nerves or winter-bare shrubs, vanishing into the atmosphere. The rat sets back on its haunches, living side closer to me, and stares out at the water in peace for a few moments. Its brown coat shines brighter than usual.

"We need to consider... a few new problems," it says at last, casting a sidelong glance at me.

"You mean how we're going to cross the sea?"

"That is, of course, one of them."

"Yeah? What else? What's wrong?"

"We are not sure how to tell you this, but your eye..."

"What *about* my—" I begin, reaching towards the ruined part of my face, but then recoil at an unexpected soft, downy texture.

A bandage?

"Wh-what is that?"

"It's... a flower. It is called the flower of the other shore."

"Is this some new treatment you're applying?" I ask, pulling the compact out of my purse.

"No, it is not a treatment."

I gaze into the cracked reflection. Distorted as it may be, there it is... a red spider lily growing out of my eye socket—an umbel of six flower stalks, each sprouting its own rumpled petals and delicate stamen—a silken firework. That's what I'd been smelling; not the water.

"What the fuck?" I whisper, fingers returning to explore my face. "H-how did this happen? Was it the worm? Maybe it carried a seed with it."

"No. On Psyche insects and florae form by spontaneous generation, not seeds and fertilization and the like. Many of the plants of Psyche feed off consciousness in the same manner as the animals. However, to flourish they also rely on a special kind of crystal, the same substance that makes up the mountains sprouting out of the core of Psyche. The winds eroding the mountains carry trace bits into the sands of the desert, giving the ground its distinctive scintillation. When death arrives, there is a burst of psychic energy, so much that even the faint traces of crystal in the sand interact to create an oasis teeming with insect- and plant-life."

The source of oases.

"But what about the dragon?" I protest. "There were no plants or insects growing out of it."

The rat shakes its heads. "Dragons are born of the stars, not the sea. As a result they suffer from an imbalance of humors. It is why their blood is fiery—and accounts for their insufferably haughty temperaments as well. Ultimately, they suffer a different fate than the rest of us spirit animals: melting into toxic bogs. Does it hurt?"

"No, it actually feels a lot better than it did yesterday—how long has it been?"

"Only one day. We woke atop the hippocochlea, who had stumbled upon a grove of mushrooms in that forest. As soon as we woke we identified the scent of the flower—just not its source. You were unconscious then, but we managed to pull you down and drag you to the beach with our supplies before sunset. When at last we had settled in, we undid your bandages and discovered this... growth. At that time it was just a small bulb. Its function seems to be tied to your mental activity. For example, earlier this afternoon, only a few minutes before you awoke, the flower bloomed. And already it has grown; it may be feeding off your body's resources, particularly your brain. If the roots continue to grow into your cortex, it could damage your mind—an excruciatingly slow lobotomy."

The rat rubs its withered paw in its strong one, living and dead heads staring out at the sea.

"We'd better pluck it then."

The rat wriggles its nose as if weighing the options, then sniffs, nods.

The procedure is painless—just a bit of pressure—and after the plant is removed, my mind is still sharp. As the rat bandages my head with clean rags (the remnants of my clothes), we discuss the second problem: where to go from here. The islands seem our only option. One of them in particular seems much closer and more prominent than the rest, probably the easiest to reach. After tossing around a few ideas, we decide on building a raft and sketch out a diagram in the sand with estimates about our needs: forty to fifty trunks of bamboo and about seventy feet of bamboo-leaf rope. The rat will round up the hippocochlea and use it to down enough trees for our purposes. Meanwhile, I'll be responsible for rope-weaving.

But first is lunch.

The rat prepares barbequed puffballs and roasted nuts (anicca nuts, it calls them). Similar to rumination fruits, the shapes of these nuts—three-sided and yet three-dimensional—seem an impossibility. The rat demonstrates how to crack them—a tilted twist of the hand.

As we eat, I study my new friend—carcass bug-free, its left half not as sunken-in or sagging as it had been before.

"How do *you* feel, by the way?" I ask, taking a bite of a skewered mushroom.

The rat does not look up from its food, its tone somewhat embarrassed: "Well, having you for company has certainly done us some good."

I nod. "I remember a few days ago you said you wouldn't have bothered with me if I weren't human. Something along those lines."

"Yes, well—"

"You're healing. It's obvious. The smell is much improved, too. No more insects, you're moving around without the exaggerated limp you had the first day I bumped into you in the oasis, your withered arm has strengthened. I mean, how far did you drag me through the forest?" I pop open an anicca nut and admire the shiny, pale flesh of the meat inside.

"Not too far."

"But I don't understand how you're healing. It can't be me. I didn't feed you anything, not like how I did with the dragon."

"Oh yes you did. Unconsciously," it says. "The terrestrial energy you give off is almost intoxicating, it's so overpowering."

"Really?" I click, pausing before popping the nut into my mouth. Suddenly, it shrivels into a twisted horror and bursts into a puff of rancid dust in my fingers. "What the hell?"

"We forgot to warn you," the rat says. "There is only

a small window of opportunity, a few seconds, between cracking open the anicca nutshell and eating its fruit. Beyond that, it returns to the sand from whence it came."

I puzzle over my dusty fingertips, but the rat plows onward. "Now, we were saying—your Earth energy—though it is strongest when you direct the visions outward, it constantly emanates out of your head, distorted by the shields of bone and flesh, similar to the sound of your beating heart or the scent of your brain—"

I look up after cracking open another anicca nut. "Wait. Sorry. You can smell my brain?"

"Well, yes, faintly."

"Wow. That's disgusting."

"It's a very useful skill. Every brain has its own unique scent."

Again, the nut withers before I have time to eat it—too many bizarre things coming out of the rat's mouth, each one distracting me anew from eating. I wipe the foul-smelling dust off my fingers and shift back to the mushrooms.

"Anyway, the point is that this Earth energy not only imbues life on Psyche, it sustains it as well. While we are somewhat ashamed to say that our aim in accompanying you on your journey home is selfish, we would not impose on you to feed us directly as the dragon had. Moreover, we would never block your passage home."

"Well I'm more than happy to help; we've made a good team so far."

The rat heads nod, the skull more fervently than the living one.

Later I sit and tend the fire, staring out across the water, listening to the murmur of the stream and the pulsing crash of the sea. In normal circumstances this would be relaxing, except that strange, amorphous creatures bob along on the green waves, flesh webbed in blood vessels, bits of teeth or eyes bulging out, breathing and spouting water out of malformed orifices. Many are dashed and silenced against the scattered rocks that carve out the shore, while others are carried in between them onto the white sands, where they rest, palpitating, until a pseudopod rips free, and they drag themselves up the beach or the mazy cliff-side paths, finally vanishing into the blue-jade forest.

Occasionally I check the bandage over my eye, making sure nothing has sprouted out of it. I recall the most recent vision, the strange parallel in the psychotic episode Earth Jing had experienced and the flower that had been growing out of my eye.

Significant or coincidental? Yet another question to pose to the rat.

There have been other parallels as well: the sand-storm leviathan here paired with an epileptic fit there, the worm eating one eye here and the blinding of one there. Maybe there are others, more subtle, which I've just failed to notice so far.

The rat shuffles up behind me, drops a tree at my side, then turns back toward the forest. Beyond, the hippocochlea rummages around the tree line, head a dim, squiggly mass.

I inspect the bamboo, mind bubbling with questions, but not knowing which one to ask, then decide on: "Ratty, what are those creatures emerging from the water?"

"Recycled spirits," it says, returning to the hippo-cochlea without even a glance towards the grotesque balls of flesh bobbing on the white and green crests.

I shake my head, starting to strip the branches off the trunk of the bamboo. "Of course, Jing, they're recycled spirits. What else would they be?"

In little time all of the branches have been stripped off, and I set to shaving off the leaves. These I interlace into braids a little thicker than my thumb, tedious work.

I manage to weave a yard or so of rope, when my concentration is broken by the hiss of the rat as it scurries towards me across the beach from the trees, leaping over a large teardrop-shaped black opal, no trace remaining of its old limp.

"Jing! Jing!"

I stare, blood freezing at the sight of its wide, flared nostrils, recalling the panicked tone of its voice when the two of us had been fleeing the snake.

"The dragon! The dragon is alive!"

The woods have an accordion-like quality. From certain spots within them, both the desert and beach are visible. Yet, at the same time it appears incredibly dense, folded up, a landscape lacking perspective, with no clear passage through. However, as we move, space seems to unfold and stretch out, complicating movement as I'm not sure whether the direction I take will be met with an obstruction until trying out the route in question. Unbothered by visual confusion, the rat easily guides me through with its powerful nose. Before long, I can smell what it does: the industrial pollution tainting the lovely sea air.

Soon we can hear it moaning beyond a grassy embankment. Crouching down, we sneak up, and peer over the edge.

There in the center of a clearing, leaf-cut sunlight mottling its blackened, moldy body, the dragon drags itself along with its small arms and legs. The side of its head has festered into a misshapen igneous protrusion, disordering its white mane and occluding one of its eyes, while the other eye socket bubbles with rock formations, streaming down to the edge of its jaws in frozen, oily waterfalls. Every now and then, a new trickle of lava blood cries out of either of these wounds, a drop of whitish gold first reddening then blackening as it agonizes down. Stone has sealed up its mouth on the more misshapen side, jagged shards of cracked teeth pierce the rock at odd angles. Through the tight remaining orifice, it grunts and grunts and spurts out the odd test of fire, enflaming a tree or roasting an unsuspecting bug.

"It's so pathetic," I whisper, more to myself than the rat.

The rat stares, starting to shake its head, then stops as its traitorous skull rattles. Steadying the skull with a claw, it says, "You pity it?"

"It was so beautiful once—and terrible."

"It has gotten what it deserves."

"But all it really wanted was to go on living."

"At our expense."

The dragon continues to drag itself over the fine, grassy sand of the forest, occasionally pausing to lift its overburdened, freakish head, frazzled whiskers twitching. In the wake of the dragon snakes a fuming, sulfurous runnel, charring the flora. A sponge on stilt-like spider legs ambles into this rotting morass and bursts into flames as it sinks into the tar.

"What do you think we should do?"

"We suggest moving the raft-making operation several miles down the beach where it is less likely to find us."

The dragon moans plaintively. By now it has lurched past our hiding spot, its image zigzagged into the thick folds of the woods, slogging its way to the water. We trail behind at a distance, slinking in the shadows of the bamboo, through forest layer after forest layer, tracking it for a mile or so, till it reaches the edge of the beach and settles down on the crest of a dune, directing its head towards the crashing waves.

"There's no need to hide. I know you're here," it proclaims into the wind, voice trammeled by the melted contours of its jaws.

The rat and I, stooped behind a large, low stone in

the bamboo thicket, exchange wary glances.

"You may approach, girl. The rat must maintain a respectable distance for my nose's sake," it commands. "Smell is one of the few pleasures left me."

"What are you doing here?" I call out, body still shielded by the rock in case the dragon were to whirl around and unleash a spray of fire.

"Looking for you, of course. There is only one shortcut to the Crystal Mountains, after all. I imagine our mutual, two-headed friend told you as much. But fear not—I have not come to harm you."

"What makes you think either of us would trust anything you have to say?"

"I would not be in my current state if it were not for you, if I had not fended off that snake and saved your life. I know we had a misunderstanding in the past, but you must recognize that I have saved your life twice now and nearly lost my own in doing so. My purpose, however, is not to gripe about your ingratitude, for my existence depends on your survival, just like your rat," it says, turning its head towards the sound of my voice, not entirely, but just enough so I can make out its shaded profile. "As you have likely reasoned out, I no longer receive streams of consciousness from Earth. My poor ward; I have no idea what has come of... them. The only reason I'm still alive is the energy your mind gives off. When you came down to my grave, the brightness of your light, it jolted me and guided me back from the brink of death. I just want to linger on in that light that beams out of you, so delicious and resplendent this close"

—so it's my fault the dragon is still alive? The heat of shame floods my face. Kindly, the rat remains intent on the dragon, showing no sign in its nose or otherwise of the significance of this revelation—

"but I am not a mere parasite. I am a contributor. I feel horrible for having forced you to feed me at the beginning of our relationship—it was pure desperation, you must realize—and have come to express my contrition, to mend my ways, and help you reach the mountains."

It turns more fully towards me as it speaks, face morphing grotesquely, the rocky lumps rising, shifting, squeezing together—a masquerade of a smile.

"How do you plan on helping? It seems you can't fly anymore—and thanks, by the way, for offering to fly me there when that *was* an option—"

"That was never an option!" The dragon flares up, or at least attempts to with its crippled, lumpy form. "No one rides me."

I laugh. "Now there's the old dragon."

"I"—it grits its cracked teeth—"apologize for that outburst. You misunderstand. I only wanted to say that I can be your guide and protector. It would have been unsafe for you to ride on me—you'd have roasted to death."

"The rat has offered to guide me."

"I know for a fact the rat has never been to the mountains. You're stuck here, floundering on the shore."

"As a matter of fact, we have a plan."

"What? No wait, let me guess: building a raft?" it derides. "How much time do you intend to waste on that undertaking? Years will have passed on Earth by the time you've cobbled together something seaworthy. Even then, you would never survive what lurks beneath the waves, and if you did make it across the sea, still the passage into the mountains is filled with all kinds of unpleasantness, and the mountains themselves are an endless labyrinth. It is a daunting journey, but I myself have made it many times. Now, if you accept my offer to help, I can promise to get you to the mountains within just a couple of days—a smooth trip."

"How do you propose to take us if we can't ride you?"

"Feed me. Heal me. Then I can lift and carry you with the aid of some rope."

"We'll manage fine on our own."

The dragon cringes, its tumored crocodile head resuming that mockery of a smile, puffs of smoke spluttering out of its mouth. "*Please.*"

"I don't think so," I say, but part of me lacks the conviction of those words. It *did* save me. Twice.

"Very well. Then I suppose I will just idle here in the fresh sea breeze until I die."

Again I exchange glances with the rat, who, pulling on the frilly sleeve of the struggle between light and dark, gestures back towards the beach camp. Its nostrils are quivering with fear.

Silence reigns as we return to camp, and there, gazing out at the water, out at the islands, I say, "We need to consider our options."

The rat sniffs back down the beach, the way we'd come. Barely discernible from here, the dragon's head pokes out of the forest, smoking, wallowing on the sand at the top of a grandiose slope. "You mean raft or dragon?"

"Yeah."

"Jing, the dragon is a horrible idea. Just look at what it has done to us."

"I know, but at this point we shouldn't dismiss any of our options outright. Besides, it saved me. I can't deny that. You see this?" I pull up the left sleeve of my struggle suit. "I'd been wandering in the desert alone for days and decided to end it. I would have been dead had the dragon and the dog not resuscitated me. At one point I refused to believe that the dragon had anything to do with saving my life, that it had all been the dog. Now, I wonder if I didn't have that backwards."

"If it nursed you back from the dead, there was an ulterior motive."

"I understand why you would only expect treachery

from the dragon, but my value to it is a safeguard. Several days ago, we would have both been snake food had it not been for the dragon's intervention."

"The point is moot, though. It itself said any creature that rode it would burn, and if you fed it and restored it to its former glory so that it could suspend us by rope, it might not find you as valuable anymore."

"Well..." I think for a moment. "Maybe we could cover it in the struggle petals to protect us from the heat, and then have it ferry us across the sea."

"Yes... that may work," the rat admits, worrying its pelt with its claws. "Perhaps listing the pros and cons of each option may be of some use."

"Okay." I snatch up one of the sticks we'd used previously to draw our raft-making plans, favoring my back as I bend down and draw a table in the sand with "Raft" at the top of one column and "Dragon" at the top of the other. "So, first of all, speed. For 'Raft', we could put con, because Christ knows how long it would take to build one."

"And for dragon, pro." The rat heads nod reluctantly.

"How about reliability? I don't expect the raft to try and kill us on the journey, so we'll put a pro next to reliable there, and we don't really know with the dragon: con. Now, what about this thing that 'lurks beneath the waves' or whatever it was it said," I say, mimicking the dragon's trammeled pomposity. "Assuming the dragon didn't fabricate its existence, we have to consider how well we could withstand an attack."

The rat sniffs. "Right: defensibility."

"So Raft? We basically have nothing more than sticks and a knife: indefensible."

"And the dragon?"

"Well, it's covered in rock and may still be able to breathe fire, so perhaps more defensible."

The rat heads nod as I carve the respective marks in the sand.

"Then we have the issue of navigating into and

through the mountains."

"Knowledge," the rat suggests.

Point for the dragon.

"Anything else?" the rat asks.

"Well, it mentioned some 'unpleasantness' in the passage to the mountains. I doubt the dragon could be lying in this case either. There's always unpleasantness to be had on Psyche. The only question is what kind. Once we've reached the island or the passages, presumably the raft will no longer be useful to us, whereas the dragon might be."

"Yes, but conversely the raft will not be a burden while the dragon could very well be."

"Okay, so we'll forget those points."

The two of us look down at the table.

I click my tongue stud. "We're better off with the dragon."

The rat heads nod grimly, then it adds, "This is assuming that what it told us about the trials lying ahead of us is true. If they are lies, however, then there's no need to worry about knowledge and defensibility, leaving just a trade-off between speed and reliability, in which case reliability should be our concern."

"But if the dragon is telling the truth?" I say.

"The dragon is the better bet..." The rat tastes the phrase. "This is foolish. We would just be inviting death in."

"Foolish, yes"—I frown, clearing several surprisingly long strands of hair out of my face when the wind shifts, powdery white with the trace of desert—"but perhaps we can still make it work. In the psychic energy sense, the dragon needs me; as transport we need it. Yet we expect treachery on its part, but it likely doesn't suspect it on ours because we're—"

"Trustworthy saps?"

"Well, yeah," I admit.

"So, we accept the dragon's offer to take us to the Crystal Mountains," the rat takes over, rubbing its paws together, manufacturing mental fire with imaginary sticks. "Moreover, we treat it kindly, build up its trust, and when it lets its guard down, we attack."

"We don't necessarily need to resort to its style of treachery." I pull the snake fang from my belt. Test its integrity. "All we need to do is be prepared to attack in the eventuality the dragon tries to pull something."

"I don't know. Assuming it takes us, I think we should be more preemptive, perhaps striking it when we near one of the islands. Then we don't need to worry about what it may or may not do to us once we've arrived."

"Well in any case, we'll need to arm ourselves."

We decide to wait until tomorrow to approach the dragon, reasoning that the longer we delay the talk and the weaker and more desperate it grows, the more it will need the sustenance I can provide and—perhaps—be grateful for our decision to include it in our group. The rat makes more rope based on my model, but improving the technique: applying a glue made from caramelized dorberry to increase the rope's integrity.

I settle by the fire and focus on fashioning the fang into a spear. I find a bamboo cane of suitable length and unfasten my belt.

—The dragon itself said it no longer receives visions from its ward, meaning its ward is likely dead—

Simply wrapping the studded strap around the fang and tip of the pole is ineffective; no matter how complex a knot I devise the fang conspires to slip out.

—The list of dead people I know is a short one: my grandparents, a cousin I never met, a middle-aged couple that my parents used to have dinner parties with, three high school classmates that died in a car crash—

By inserting the prong of the buckle through a small hole in the fang's venom groove, then hammering this beyond into the bamboo shaft, and finally knotting the two together with the strap—the resulting weapon is quite secure.

—More recently, there's my mother, William, and Bower. The idea that the dragon could be my mother's spirit animal doesn't feel right to me, and I know for a fact that the dead half of the rat was William's spirit animal, leaving Bower as the most likely candidate. He and I were close, and he was also close to William before William OD'd. The rat had warned me, of course, that associations on Psyche do not necessarily correspond with associations on Earth—but it fits—

With the removal of my belt, my jeans officially become useless tatters.

—Bower. My mind returns to the name. He was narcissistic, decadent, but there was another side to him beneath the rock star persona he cultivated—

Fortunately, the desert-side swath of forest abounds in struggle between light and dark, and the rat has already collected several stacks worth of their petals and lined them beside the lean-to, reserves for fresh clothes, sheets, ground mats, and (maybe) riding the dragon. Thus, I move into the privacy of the lean-to and begin designing an outfit made entirely of the undulating petals.

—I remember the old vision I'd encountered on our trip to the beach—Bower talking about his father, our a night that hadn't ended in sex, but in something much more intimate. We had gone into the Compound and played *Pictures* together, him on the left hand, me on the right, disastrously clumsy at first, we had in the end worked out a rhythm, by which time the sun had risen flooding the piano room with a creamy light. Neither of us talked about this after the fact, but it had intensified the bond between us. This aspect of Bower grates against what I know about the dragon, but who else could have been its ward?—

By now the sun is setting in the lands to the left, not

completely disappearing, but just dipping down, a slice of tangerine, occasionally visible through the layered bamboo forest, the sky shifting to that Psyche gold I'd first seen upon waking here as the sun burns across the horizon. Psyche Summer Solstice. The day should take a turn towards shorter and colder now. The asteroids have settled near the mountains, crescent-lit in the brilliant, sustained light, the iridescent aurora of the mountains faint from this distance. The tide, molten silver and gold, has come in up to within a few yards of our encampment, bearing even more of the bizarre recycled spirits, squelching and crawling past us up the shoreline. The forest is alive with an avant-garde concert of clicks and tones performed by the invertebrates.

The rat, somber ever since we've come upon the dragon, goes off to scavenge for more food, but before doing so pauses by its backpack and surreptitiously extracts something. I see a flash of yellowed bone before it's consumed by the black pouch on the rat's belt. The teeth.

Then it disappears into the woods.

I turn back to the matter of raiment. Remove the shorter leggings, study the white and shiny pink scars from my time in the desert, the memories of pain. My arm, too, is healed, the wounds having marred what was once a finely-crafted, exotic garden of tattoos. I fashion a suitable pair of pants from strips of the petals and cover the depressing sight of my legs, then inspect their fit. Some of the more elaborate frills can be coerced into pockets in which I store various bits.

Afterwards I watch the sunset-fired sea for some time, dozing. No visions.

The sound of the rat trudging towards the camp brings me to, and I hop up to go meet it, helping with the burden of mushroom and fruit sacks hanging off the ends of two bamboo bindlestiffs.

"Ah, you've made some new pants for yourself. Lovely," it says cheerily.

A bit groggy, I smile, shouldering one of the poles. "Have a nice, uh, walk in the woods?"

"Most refreshing."

As we set about preparing dinner, the rat hums "Blue Christmas," perhaps something it had heard in a recent vision, piped through the Muzak of Glenbrook. I tag on the lyrics, and it glances up at me, smiling.

When the food is ready, we eat in silence and between bites I practice spear thrusts, careful of my back.

The rat watches me, sniffing with discretion, firelight painting strange shadows on its skull, grinning, scowling, cackling shadows.

"Jing, it is time to examine your wounds." The rat approaches and helps me unwrap the head bandages. Of course, all of the wounds are effectively healed—we both know that. There's only the one...

"It's back," I say before the rat has time to speak. "I can feel it there. Can feel the petals against my skin, spreading outward. You probably knew. You must be able to smell it."

The rat heads nod.

"Christ, what a freak I've become." My face grows hot and tight. Tears accumulate in the corner of my eye— and the base of the flower. Wiping them away impatiently, I say in a charged voice, "What do you think we should do?"

"We are far beyond the realm of our expertise, and in the end, it is your brain. Would you like us to pluck it again?"

"No. No. Just leave it. Guess we'll wait and see what happens."

"We are sorry, Jing," it says, living head bowing. "We have failed you."

"What are you talking about? I'd be dead without you."

"It's possible that this has happened for a reason. Recall that this is all essentially the doing of that eternity bug."

"And?" I blink, and the spider lily with its own nastic motion approximates something similar—at least I imagine it does.

"It was, after all, one of the largest instars we have ever seen—"

I snuffle. "Wait, wait. An *instar*? You're telling me that thing wasn't even an adult?"

It nods. "Years from now it will have fully metamorphosed into an imago. We have smelled only one metamorphosed eternity bug in our life, from miles and miles away, but we could still sniff out the individual golden-and-cream scales of its wings as it lifted off. The ground shook so, we thought we would be bounced off into space or that Psyche would crumble apart. It took many cold years before the white dust storms cleared."

"Where did it go?"

"Well, these bugs are too large to remain on Psyche, so their only recourse is to fly off into space and seek out another planet with which to become symbiotic. Once they have reached their destination, they anchor at a distance, their minds stretch out and splinter, and they curl into themselves and fossilize into asteroids— new Psyches. Just like any other corpse, their bodies soon become riddled with life. It is said that the form Psychic life takes depends on the inhabitants of the planet with which the bug is symbiotic. Their fugues take them away from the sun and out towards other galaxies, other systems. The record of these fugues are plastered across the sky—a lifetime of memories played over and over. In any case, Psyche and other eternity bugs are not leeches. It is said that they gift consciousness to the lifeforms they connect with, that it is the very act of sharing signals between host and ward that is the spark of consciousness."

"So, Psyche, this asteroid, is really just a giant, dead insect?"

They nod.

"And that's why those asteroids seem so close, and

yet we never crash into them. They're just memories, like a film projected into the sky?"

"Planets, most likely, but yes, you are correct—memories superimposed over reality."

"This probably takes the cake as the weirdest thing you've ever told me." Dizzied with the fantastic, I crane my head to look at the sky, at the distant, colorful planetoids.

"Well, anyway, this is the story spirit animals have passed down to one another for ages, a story meant to bring us solace, help us understand our existence. But we digress. The point is this: eternity bugs are lonely creatures; they crave connection; perhaps it was trying to communicate with you."

"Pretty bizarre-fucking-way to communicate if you ask me."

"Well, insects and plants do not speak the Deep Language. They use the Ancient Signs, a darkling system of communication. Maybe this flower is a component of the message."

"Let me get this straight: it buries me in the sand just so, has a chatterbox eat my eye without killing me, and then orchestrates a red spider lily to grow out of my eye socket? I change my mind: *that's* the weirdest thing you've ever said."

The rat shrugs, nose downcast. "When we suffered our own calamity, the only thing that kept us going was the belief that it had happened for a purpose."

I go quiet, feel a sickening wave of disappointment in myself. The rat, in its own weird way, had only been trying to console me.

"Sorry. I... I didn't mean to be so dismissive. Sort of been a rough week."

"Forget it, Jing. We should have a rest."

I keep grasping at things to say to the rat, but the words can't pierce the thick, oppressive silence. Finally, the rat suggests we sleep in shifts to guard against a possible attack from the dragon, and I volunteer myself for first watch. The rat curls up on its mat of petals by the fire and is soon snoring. Judging by how long and soundly it sleeps, I guess it had not rested much during my spell of unconsciousness—an observation that only intensifies the guilt.

Then a sudden pressure builds up in my mind. The terrestrial energy is ready—a full bladder waiting for relief. I let it overtake me, but instead of drinking it all myself, I direct it outward, focusing on the rat just how I'd done before with the dragon, nurturing it with the sustenance it needs:

CHAPTER 12

Waters navigates the van through the rutted snow. Between each labor of the wipers, fluff cakes the windshield. Beside him, in between the jolts of the cratered pavement, Jing, piercings absent, the cheekbone beneath her left eye scabbed and mottled pistachio with an old bruise, stares out the window, defogging with her sleeve every few minutes. Remnants of the city appear through gaps between massive snowdrifts: crumbling concrete frames eyelashed with ice-encased rebar; carbon skeletons clawing out from the nether-world.

"Oh, you gotta hear this one," Waters says, turning up the volume on the stereo, and soon an electro beat from his mix-tape drowns out the sound of the wipers and engine.

"Funky. I like it," Jing says, hooking a smile out of the depths of Waters' thick, curly beard.

A familiar, half-collapsed store distracts Jing from the music. On the other side of the road, the shadow of the abandoned theater looms over the icicled eaves of a row of houses.

And... yes, there it is.

Distant, just visible.

Penn's house, a Victorian Gothic, rising alone and defiant out of the center of an urban tundra, its infirm neighbors now collapsed or burnt down, their remains interred beneath the frozen wasteland. As it slides by through the thin vista between mounds of snow, Jing can spot none of the familiar cars in the driveway. Its dejected façade lends it an air of abandonment. Her bitterness over the EP fight suddenly gives way to concern that maybe Penn, silent for a month now.

They soon arrive at the hospital, a sprawl of layered, frosted concrete, and Waters grows quiet, frowning, as he searches for the entrance to the parking garage.

Inside, they wander from sign to sign, seeking out the radiology department. Though more modern, the absence of people, the whiff of antiseptic and ammonia, and the light piano Muzak remind Jing of Glenbrook. When they arrive, Waters seats himself in a small waiting room while a middle-aged nurse leads Jing to a curtained-off room. There, she slips into a gown and notices the way the nurse scrutinizes the wrist-restraint bruises and the scar in her tattoos before she injects her with a radioactive tracer for Murai's recommended PET-CT scan.

Afterwards, Waters buys her tempura at a cramped downtown restaurant she had frequented in another life. He never mentions that they should keep this part of the day just between the two of them, and his silence on that point is a kind of trust she secretly thanks him for.

As they wait for their food, warming their hands with their tea, he says, "I'm sure the scan won't turn up anything."

She nods. Tries to click, unsure that a negative finding would be reassuring. Gazing out across the street at the snowy rubble of a once-skyscraper, she wonders if an evil black hole in her brain scan is exactly what she needs—an *Aha! This can/can't be fixed.*

The attempt at conversation faltering, Waters swirls his tea, looking stiff, too large for the restaurant, his body better suited for the miles of empty space at Glenbrook.

She sucks on sea-salt-specked edamame, brainstorming about how to ease the tension, and decides music is the obvious sector of their Venn diagram to color in.

"Before today I never came across a mix-tape with death metal and R&B tracks back-to-back."

It opens him up—a self-proclaimed music geek—and from then on, there is a seamless stream of conversation between them. She itches to know if he's listened to Autoscope but modestly scratches everywhere but there.

Waters eats the majority of the edamame, ten gyoza, a sushi appetizer, two plates of tempura, a bowl of udon, and two bowls of rice. Despite his voracious appetite, he offers Jing bits of everything, but she declines, enjoying how he looks when he eats: the chopsticks look like twigs in his hands; the bowls, teacups. He's skilled with chopsticks, which she appreciates, and eats neatly and efficiently. Her mother would have approved.

At home, Detroit home, she would use chopsticks every day—a bowl of rice, stir-fried veggies, and some-times tofu. Strange that until now she hadn't realized how long she had gone without using them.

After they get the check, he asks, "What's that piece you've been working on so much?"

Jing pauses from wrapping her maroon scarf around her neck. "*Pictures at an Exhibition*... just an old piece I never mastered, not with any satisfaction."

"I had a dream you were performing *Pictures at an Exhibition* for the staff, but notes and entire phrases kept vanishing from the score, and all the keys started to stick. I came onto the stage to help, opened up the piano, and there they were: musical notes trapped and twitching in the piano strings like flies in a web. I took it as a sign that I needed to help you in some way beyond just having the piano tuned. There's a music store nearby with a great selection of sheet music. Wanna go check it out? See if you can find something new to start working on?"

Back at Glenbrook, Jing returns to her room to gather up some piano books and with the bag from the music store heads back downstairs. When she reaches rec north, she pulls a wrapped gift from the bag and places it under the squat Christmas tree—the only present there.

With a half an hour still remaining before group therapy, she sits down at the piano to pass the time.

The first few chords she plays sound distracted, as her mind cycles back to the hospital and her conversation with Waters, like some very bizarre first date in which she had been probed by scientists and then treated to a nice dinner afterward—but a first date all the same.

She skips through *Pictures* towards a section that has been giving her particular trouble and plays it over and over again, five measures, discordant, technically taxing.

Repeat, repeat, repeat.

She can only imagine how nightmarish it would sound from another wing of Glenbrook—an echoing blur of madness.

Jing's fingers ache from the repetition, but it calms her, does more for her than any amount of talking or self-reflection could. She expands the loop by several measures, playing the difficult passage in context.

When her fingers lift from the keys, her brow is no longer knitted. She's satisfied.

She widens the loop, kneading in more of the composition, testing for weaknesses in the section she'd been practicing.

"Does she see what's coming?"

"She sees something's coming."

Her fingers stutter to a stop, ears probing the sudden silence, but there's nothing. Voices again. She'd almost taken one of the voices to be her own. Her eyes dart around the room—no one else there.

Must be the peculiar acoustics of the room.

She begins playing again, holding down the soft pedal, casting her attention out beyond the music.

Before long, other patients file in and find seats, watching her curiously, and soon all the tension trickles down her arms, slender fingers kneading everything wrong in her world into the music, transmuting one problem into another, one with a workable solution—a mandala to be swept away.

Group begins with the usual recitation of the Glenbrook philosophy and a review of points from the previous meeting. All of the psychotics attend, including Henry, though he spends the entire session snoozing in one of the chairs in front of a French window half-buried in snowdrift. Her only lighter having been confiscated, Jing bums a light from Catherine.

After they have concluded preliminaries, Dr. Lindgren returns to a recurring topic: strategies for coping with delusions. Throughout most of the meeting, Jing, mind wandering in and out of attention, is careful not to remain totally mum, offering the occasional platitude in response to another patient's story. At one point, however, Dr. Lindgren, in response to one of the Time Traveler's reflections, cites a number of examples of related delusions she had come across in her research—delusions about others, delusions about the self, imagined paralysis or blindness—and ways that other patients have overcome these issues. The phrase "delusional blindness" shines lucent through the dense mist of thought, and Jing shifts in her chair, eyes narrowing, asking if Lindgren can explain what she said in more detail.

"It's a delusion resulting from a psychotic disorder. Often this is part of some larger, more complex framework: for example, the patient may believe the eye was stolen by the FBI in the middle of the night and replaced by a non-functional organ containing a tracking device—or something along those lines.”

"But in these cases the eye—or eyes—they function normally?”

"Well, the delusional patient doesn't believe so—” Lindgren surveys the room, pleased to find all the patients engaged, "—but ophthalmic tests don't reveal any aberrations, and brain scans will show that the patient is processing information in their visual cortex. If they're shown any evidence of its unimpaired functioning, they will typically fabricate an explanation, an appendix to their delusional system: for example, the mechanical eye is programmed to interfere with brain scans and offer seemingly realistic performance output.”

"And this delusional blindness, is it treated with medication?” Jing pursues.

"Typically, yes. Psychotherapy has produced mixed results in treating delusions.”

Jing nods, slouching back in her chair, wondering if she should come clean about her half-blindness to her treatment team. The recent dosage increase of her anti-psychotic medication should have helped alleviate the symptom—if in fact it is a component of the psychosis. At the same time, her willingness to accept the fact that her blindness could be delusional also just seems to be further evidence pointing towards a lack of psychosis.

"What about you, Jing?” Lindgren asks, rousing Jing once again from her thoughts.

"Me?” A wave of paranoia—*you've shown too keen an interest in delusional blindness, Jingy.* "What about me?”

"Why don't you share with everyone about what you've been going through? We rarely *hear* from you.” Lindgren emphasizes *hear* in a way suggesting she's savvy to Jing's strategy of talking without actually saying anything about herself.

Jing glances from Lindgren to her fellow patients, their degree of interest spanning the curiosity spectrum. Henry is awake, she notices—studying her.

"Well, it's all a bit fuzzy."

"Don't be a selfish consumer and give back to the group, Drummer Girl," the Governor says. Several of the patients laugh, and he eats up the attention.

Lindgren raises her hand. "Thank you, Mitch, for sharing your unfiltered thought, but we need to be supportive. We shouldn't push if Jing isn't ready. Perhaps some other time."

"Perhaps…" Jing says, reaching for a lip ring no longer in place.

Its absence stirs her.

"No, you know what? The Governor's right. I'll tell you what happened. It's a relatively short story. I came to Detroit two years ago to play drums for this band called Autoscope. We were on the verge of success, but then everything fell apart. The lead singer died, and they found me passed out by his body. When I came to, it was in the midst of a psychotic episodes in the Clouds." She rubs her wrist, remembering. "Since then, since I recovered from the initial attack, Goldfield advised I stay at Glenbrook so they can continue to monitor my recovery. To be continued…"

The Governor, sitting upright, objects. "I don't get it. In what way are you delusional?"

"I never said I was," she says, blinking, the weight of her half-blindness pressing on her tongue, "but I was at the time I arrived."

"I thought everyone called you Drummer Girl because that was, you know, part of the delusion. Is this band even real? I've never heard of it," he continues to harangue her, turning to the rest of the group for back-up.

"Yeah, it's real, and I am really the drummer. At least I used to be. If you watched MTV at four in the morning you might catch us. The delusions came later, right before I arrived at Glenbrook. According to Goldfield I was—" she chooses her wording carefully, "—purporting that I was outside myself, my body soulless, observing things from a distance, from some kind of purgatory." She looks up and finds Henry staring intently at her, his lips parted. "Third-person. That's what I called it."

Group is followed by forty-five minutes of alternative therapy. Under the guidance of Dr. Conway, a white-bearded guru, the patients meditate in front of specially-calibrated light machines in the sparsely decorated rec west, offering a view of snowy yard scrunched between the conservatory cafeteria and the north wing. As Jing sets there, her mind runs back over group therapy and the question of her quasi-delusions. After ten minutes or so, the running narrative in her head finally silences, leaving only the light, the quiet, the moment—nearly as effective as playing the piano.

On her way back to her room, as she passes by the dayroom, with its covey of catatonic patients, and spots the telephone, her footsteps falter. She considers it for a moment and is soon sunk into the scratched leather chair next to it, headset in hand. She dials Penn first, wanting to hear her voice, at the very least verify her friend is still among the living.

The phone rings ten times before she hangs up.

She tries Leif.

Gets the machine.

Leaves a message, then beeps him.

She pulls out a cigarette and looks around to see if there's anyone mobile and with a light.

No.

She twirls the cigarette in her fingers and considers the phone, mind working back and forth. Finally, she picks the headset back up, fingers first dallying over the keypad, then pounding out the number with memorized speed.

She inhales with anticipation, biting her lip

"Davis Elwood," comes the sound of a man's voice.

Thick Midwestern accent.

"Ba," she says, releasing the air with exaggerated relief.

"Jinger. Hi." She can hear the smile in his voice, the surprise. "How you doing?"

"Copacetic. Happy Thanksgiving and all that."

"Ha ha. Bit late for that, honey, but thanks all the same."

"Ruirui came to see me," she says, throat thick.

"Yeah, she told me when she was here. I take it you heard the *big news*, huh?"

"Yeah, good for her. How do you like her fiancée?"

"Carl? Seems like a cool guy." Something in her father's tone suggests that he would like to add more but that he instead checks himself.

"Yeah, that's great," she says, trying not to be bothered but nevertheless filling in his blank self-critically.

"We all miss you, Jinger." Every time he speaks the diminutive, it pricks her in the chest, seeming to drain her heart a drop at a time. "Wish you could have been here for the holiday. Ruirui was pretty upset after seeing you. Maybe you should give her a call, thank her for going out of her way to pay you a visit. You know, any-time you want to come back home, would love to have you. Haven't touched your room. Still a mess." He laughs.

"Maybe at New Year's."

"Okay, then. New Year's it is. Putting it on my calendar. So, uh, you know, how are you doing?"

"Ba, you already asked me that." She draws her legs into her chest and dances the cigarette on her fingers.

"Yeah, I know, I know, I know. I'm just... I'm just worried about you, is all. I called. A bunch of times, actually, I called. Didn't they get you the messages?"

"Yeah, I got the messages. Should have returned them sooner. I've been meaning to. I think I have some sort of telephone phobia. Sorry."

"Well, you have a knack for letting me worry about you, that's for sure. Did I... did I do something wrong, Jinger? Did I do something to you? I tried to be a good—"

"Ba, stop. Of course you didn't do anything wrong. It's just me. I'm going through some shit—I mean, stuff."

"Would have come and visited, but you know, you didn't call. Thought it must be my fault. All of this. First your mom, now you. A fucking psychologist, I can't even help my own family—"

"Ba, don't say that."

"Well, I don't know..."

Jing freezes again.

"Are you still seeing that girl?" her father says, fighting through a blockage in his own throat. "What was her name? The tattoo artist."

"No, that ended years ago."

"Okay. Okay. You know, maybe I'll drive down this weekend and spend the day there. How would you like that?"

"Wait till the weather improves, Ba. I'll come up to Marquette when I get discharged."

"Well, come soon." He pauses, struggling to find something to say. "Oh, you know, I heard you the other day."

"Heard me?"

"I was working late one night, and when I went to leave I heard this faint pounding coming from somewhere in the building. It was like 'The Tell-Tale Heart' or something, really freaked me out at first before I realized what it was. I tracked it down the hall into the lab. My grad student Melissa was working on her dissertation and had your album blasting over the stereo. I told her that was my girl she was playing. She thought I was messing around at first, but then made the connection between our names. Thought I was cool for about a nanosecond."

Jing smiles.

"If you want, I could probably get you a job up here. You could work, go back to school part-time. I'd even chip in for tuition."

"I'll think about it."

"Okay. I had to offer. You *sound* good at least. Lot better than when I was there in September. I had my doubts about leaving you there. Nothing like I remember."

"What wasn't like you remember?"

"Glenbrook—back when your mother was a patient, when it was still a private institution."

"This is the same hospital?" Jing's grip on the phone loosens. Her mouth goes dry and sour, stomach drops. She remembers running down the halls, running from the sight of her mother frozen with catatonia, arms like tortured branches, face twisted into a rictus of agonized hilarity. There was music playing then, resounding through the halls, bright and cheery music mocking the horrible state of her mother. She'd run for what seemed like an eternity, through small courtyards and twisting hallways, evading anyone wearing white. She had escaped the building and found herself on the back lawn. There was a pond. Rui was there, searching through the tall grass for her, and as soon as she spotted Jing, she dashed over, nearly tackled her in a squeeze. They dropped down to their knees on the grass, Rui letting her little sister cry against her chest the way Jing's mother had done—on her good days. Jing had felt Rui's own tears dripping onto her face and mingling with hers. Then, they'd gone back inside, had hot chocolate together in the conservatory cafeteria, sitting at the exact same table at which Jing would take her meals years later, and their mother's doctor had finally found them, a short, curious-looking man, who distracted Jing with "guess which hand," all the while quietly assuring her that her mother would be fine and back home in no time.

She is so lost in the remembrance, she misses what her father has been saying about the hospital.

"You still there?" he says.

"Yeah, yeah, I'm here." A tremor in her voice.

What was it Murai had said to her? *"You should ask your father if he remembers any strange behavior in childhood that might indicate blackouts. Every piece of information is important."*

"I'm not surprised you don't remember. You were so upset when you saw her there. Maybe it was a mistake to take you along, but you really wanted to see your mom. You remember what you did when she was gone? Wrote her a letter every day, even though she couldn't write back. That summer, before the medication, she was at her worst. Wasn't until they sent her home that you turned back around, back into the old trouble-making Jinger." He sighs. "She kept those letters. After you went off to college, I caught her reading them once. You meant everything to her, Jinger."

"I remember. Bits. I didn't realize—"

"I wanted the best treatment for her, and it was far away, but Glenbrook was highly regarded back then."

"Things have changed a bit, I think."

"Are you getting good treatment there? Do I need to talk to someone for you?"

"No, Ba. Yes and no. It's complicated, but I think it'll be okay. They think..."

"Think what, Jinger?"

"They think I'm psychotic like Ma." A hot tear escapes, her lips trembling.

Staticky silence on the other end.

"Ba?"

He exhales heavily. "I was afraid of that. Rui said you looked good, though—much better than how she remembers your mom looking when we paid her a visit."

Her mind races. Feels she can't say more or the emotions will consume her. She doesn't want that, doesn't want to worry him. She feels a sudden pull, the need to escape. "Well, Ba, I—"

"Anyway, Jinger," he interrupts, deciphering her

intentions and wanting to save her from the need to speak, to betray more, "listen, I gotta run. I got a faculty meeting I'm already late for."

She plays along with the loving lie, grateful. "Yeah. Yeah, okay. Better get back to work."

"All right, Jinger. Call me again soon—and see you at New Year's. I love you."

"Love you—"

CHAPTER 13

The vision severs, the aftersensations of Glenbrook echoing and blinking out—the buzz of the fluorescent lighting, the early evening snowfall, the painful lump in Earth Jing's throat. Unsteadily I rise, gripping the edge of the lean-to, teetering between here and there, then stumble over towards the rat.

Asleep, curled up on its own petal mat on the other side of the fire, one hind leg folded over the nose of its living head. Withered arm inflated with blood, skull mossed with fur, mouth glistening dark eggplant, tight black rot giving way to cords of pink and white and rich yellow gristle—as I watch, more and more flesh and fur germinate out of the remaining rot.

I let the rat sleep several hours more, through the peak of darkness. I sit back down by the embers of the fire, stoke it back up. My struggle suit ripples with delight at the heat. Behind me, the forest wildlife honks and trills, bamboo rattling and rushing in the wind. Replays of the vision seem to crackle out of the fire. The image had been fuzzier than before, like watching a television with poor reception. Reminds me of my first days on Psyche, when the visions from Earth had grown more and more distorted as I had weakened.

Even so, I had learned several crucial pieces of information.

Before being institutionalized, Earth Jing had been discovered next to Bower's body. Unfortunately, Earth Jing's terseness on the subject during group therapy had prevented me from learning anything more useful about that night or the circumstances of his death. Don't know *where* they had found her and Bower—the foot of a wardrobe, the mouth of a rabbit hole, inside a tornado-transplanted homestead—maybe an important part of the puzzle.

Second, all along I've taken for granted that while I observe Jing during the visions, she must experience reality through her own eyes, but given what she said about the third-person delusion during group therapy, maybe that's not the case. Maybe she sees things through my perspective, an observer of herself *all the time.* Maybe she's become habituated to it, similar to her left-eye blindness—at its onset causing great distress, but over time receding to the back of her mind.

I stoke the fire again, mind turning to the final piece of information: Ma was also hospitalized at Glenbrook. This resonates with one of the first memory flashes I'd experienced on the trip to the beach. Must have been a childhood remembrance—Glenbrook during summer. Is it meaningful in some way or just another strange coincidence?

After a few hours, fatigue begins to tug at me. I awaken the rat. As it uncurls and sets up on its haunches, blinking the sands of sleep and Psyche out of its beady, black eyes and wriggling it out of its nose, what seems to be a complex of embarrassment and guilt constricts its nostrils. The feeding. Did it see things as I saw them?

"No activity on the dragon's front," I report.

The heads nod, the left one moving with greater ease than before.

I lie down on the mat in the lean-to, and the rat says, "We thank you, Jing."

"Don't mention it." I gaze up at the roof of the lean-to, the odd sparkling shard twinkling through the thatching, wondering why the rat had built this structure for me and not one for itself. "Now, if you don't mind, I'm exhausted."

"Yes, please rest up. We'll finish out the night."

Maybe knowing the custom of humans to sleep with

a roof over their heads, it had tried to approximate the comforts of home for me.

I smile—and sleep.

A gray morning, damp and cool.

The wash of waves.

Sea mist obscures a rosebud sunrise.

The rat is gone. Its absence galvanizes me out of the syrupy torpor of early morning. I pop out of bed, rush to the fire, and scan the area. The hippocochlea is lumbering through the woods, crashing through the bamboo, disturbing a business of crystalline flies. Blobs of flesh creep up the shoreline, squelching and generally being obscene. The spirits of sunshine have cuddled up together on top of the piles of struggle petals outside the lean-to.

Far off, a mile or so to the south, a plume of smoke rises out of the edge of the woods. I can very nearly make out the dragon's craggy head nestled in the sand, just as it was yesterday evening.

Safe.

Then I catch sight of the rat, sliding through the flattened dimensions of the woods, gathering food from the looks of it.

I add kindling and logs to the fire, stoke it back up, do some stretches as the day brightens. My back feels better today, all my wounds healed, the soreness from the long slog through the desert nothing but faded impressions after yesterday's recuperation. But coupled with this physical rejuvenation is the jittery uncertainty about teaming up with the dragon to cross the sea, which, exposed in the light of morning, strikes me as beyond absurd. However, as I watch the rat emerging from the woods, I'm reminded again of the dramatic healing power of these visions. Though it had once threatened to suck out my brains, had forced me into servitude, the dragon needs me now even more than it did before. The key is to make sure it values what I have to offer. Always keep it needing more. This could work.

"How did you sleep, Jing?" The rat drags a sled laden with fruits, mushrooms, and nuts. At its tail scurries along a dog-sized crustacean, a cousin of a crab or sea spider (or face-hugger)—with peach- and crimson-striped armor, and twelve biramous legs oriented in all imaginable directions, some ending in uniquely shaped claws.

"Okay," I say dubiously, watching the rat depositing the food stores by the lean-to. The creature clacks onto the pile of food, scurries about, then hops down to pursue the rat in its preparations for breakfast.

I head to the stream to fill up two cactus arms and upon returning find the rat hunched over, slicing mushrooms and humming the "Promenade" theme from *Pictures*, and the spider crab creeping up its backside.

I set the drinks beside a log, then approach the pile of food, pluck up a piece of fruit—semi-translucent, purple, the heft of a grapefruit, its surface a landscape of rubbery teeth—and chomp into it. Its interior is divided into hundreds of juice chambers, the skin and cell lining chewy, flavor tart with bursts of sweetness. I chew, watching the leggy creature explore the rat's body.

Then I gag, spitting out a half-masticated, purple mouthful.

The rat heads turn back in alarm.

"Forgot to ask. This fruit, it doesn't do something weird, does it?"

"Why would we bring back poisonous fruits and lump them together with non-poisonous ones?"

"You say that, but to be fair, it seems every other object I come across on Psyche has some kind of weird power or side effect. It's delicious. What do you call it?"

"A monkey brain."

I run my thumb across the short, rubbery feelers of its rind. "Doesn't look very brainy."

"No, perhaps not, but it was not named for its appearance, but rather because it is a favorite of monkeys, the most intelligent of the spirit animals. It is said that eating monkey brains improves one's intelligence—"

"And there we have it—knew it did something."

"—but, we doubt there is any truth to that myth."

"Hmm,"—I take a bite—"monkeys, rabbits, rats... dogs, dragons, snakes, a horse." I chew thoughtfully, trying to recall the different types of spirit animals I've encountered or heard the rat mention. "Bulls, too. I should have seen it sooner."

"Seen what?"

"Presumably, there are five other types of spirit animals in addition to the ones I've met or heard about: tigers, goats, pigs, and—what's the last one?—the rooster."

"You're correct. We are formed throughout a twelve year terrestrial cycle, created according to a scheme of personality archetypes inherent in the minds of humankind, the predominant theory at the time Psyche died thousands of years ago. All of us, all of this"—the rat gestures expansively—"is what the dying eternity bug was able to extract from your ancestors as a model for its own world."

"It's so... *weird*, though. On Earth you guys are printed on flimsy paper placemats at Chinese restaurants."

The more I speak, the more the crab-thing seems to notice me. It hops down off the rat and starts to click-clack over.

The rat pounces on top of the creature, pinning it down with one of its hindlimbs, grabbing a hold of a thick leg in its forepaws and ripping it off. "Well, it is the interpretation of one lifeform by another (admittedly very different) lifeform."

The creature shudders a bit, but makes no sound (indeed, it doesn't appear to have a mouth) nor scurries off in fright. The rat sets the limb over the fire along with several mushroom kebabs and sets a couple of anicca nuts in the hot ash.

"Speaking of other lifeforms, aren't you going to tell me about your new, um, friend?" I ask, nibbling the stone clean and tossing it into the forest.

"Ah yes, how rude of us. Jing, this is a masochistic crab." As the rat makes introductions, the crab spears several pieces of fruit with its legs and begins draining them. "We used to have one as a pet years ago, but they are fickle things: no telling when they will run off." As the fruits shrivel into empty skins, a new limb, shiny, rosy and delicate sprouts out of one of the junctions between the crab's legs. "All you need to do to care for it is provide several pieces of fruit whenever you rob it of a limb."

The armored legs have begun to blacken, the insect meat sizzling and spitting juices along with the mushrooms, the air redolent with barbequed crab and marinated mushrooms.

"So is this crab—I guess it wouldn't be, would it?—someone's spirit animal that you're torturing? Crabs aren't one of the Chinese Zodiac. What about the Western one? Is this some poor Cancer's spirit animal?"

"No, invertebrates are not linked with humans, at least none that we've encountered. The insects, the vegetation—they're based on some sort of genetic memory, perhaps reflecting conditions on the home planet of these eternity bugs. The Western Zodiac was probably not fully entrenched in humanity's collective unconscious when the eternity bug opened the neural wormholes in humankind. Perhaps a younger bug modeled its corpse on such a system or a combination of the two."

"Wait. Did you say 'neural wormholes'?"

"Yes."

"Henry mentioned those to Earth Jing. How would he know about them?"

The rat shakes its heads. "We don't know, but all of

us are linked to the Crystal Mountains via these holes."

The sliced puffballs finish cooking first, and we start to eat, nibbling them on their blackened skewers. Then the rat experiments with tearing off a bit of mushroom and positioning it just beyond the large incisors right before the premolars of the left head. The jaws of the skull begin to move in the tentative way I'd seen last night after rousing the rat, straining open and gnawing at the mushroom, making a gruesome sound, the regenerated sinews and ligaments stretching and popping, most of the food spilling to the ground half-chewed but the rotten, eggplant-colored ribbon of tongue managing to catch some of the food and guide it down the throat.

"Ratty, when I fed you last night, what did you see?" I take an anicca nut out of the fire and set it aside to let it cool.

The rat turns from its experiment to regard me, nostrils dilating.

"Sorry," I say. "I don't know if this is an appropriate topic to discuss, you know, according to your customs."

It nods, popping another bit of mushroom into the skull and letting it struggle to eat. "You have every right to know. It has been a long time since we've experienced anything from Earth so clear as what you gave us. At first, we barely recognized you, what with the shorter hair and the exotic Earth clothes. Your Earth self is also much paler and fatter than you are—"

"All right, ease up, Ratty."

"We saw Henry during a meeting with a group of people."

"What about the perspective?"

"The perspective?"

"Well, if the signal is sent through neural wormholes, presumably within my/her brain"—I wait for nods of confirmation before resuming—"shouldn't I experience the visions through Earth Jing's eyes, not just watching her from a distance? When you would receive visions from William or Henry, what was the perspective like?"

"It is as you say. Your visions have an unusual perspective. We did not realize that we were seeing it exactly as you were seeing it. We thought maybe it was a result of being fed a signal, but you say it is like this all the time?"

I nod.

"Most curious."

"Which means that what I see in my visions is also how Jing sees herself all of the time?"

It nods.

"How fucked up."

The rat clears its throat after a long silence. "What you did for us was very generous, Jing. We know it is a very private thing, the consciousness you receive from Earth. Must be even more so for you."

"Like I said, don't worry about it. I'll do it again when I'm ready."

"You should not feed us too frequently. It's especially dangerous with the dragon nearby as it leaves both of us unconscious and off guard. In addition, doing so repeatedly will weaken you since you are limiting the amount of energy directed into your own body. Given that you have been healing so much slower than we have, it seems clear that you could not keep this sharing up for too long. If the dragon had had its way with you from the beginning, you would have been dead in a matter of days."

"Well, what does it matter as long as I can get plenty of food and water?" I ask, picking up the anicca nut and twisting it open.

"The food and water of Psyche do not sustain our bodies directly as they do on Earth. They feed the mood of our wards, bolster their psychological health."

The anicca nut again bursts into dust as I pause to reflect on this new absurdity. No, not new, I realize, wiping my hands. The rat had said something similar to this many nights ago when I'd been on the verge of eating the rumination fruit that had consumed the dog, except at the time I hadn't understood what it meant by "ward" and had thus dismissed what it was saying.

"It's no wonder, I suppose."

"What is no wonder?"

"When I first came here, I didn't eat or drink anything for days except a cough drop, but I didn't die of starvation."

"No, but the Earth version of you must have been cripplingly dispirited."

I rub my left wrist, mimicking, echoing Earth Jing during the group therapy session. "From the very little I saw of Earth at that time, I would say so."

"That is another consequence. You were not feeding her; as a result you were receiving a very weak signal back from her. Here." It hands me the smoking leg, small claws and other segments branching off it, some still moving. "Try this. Very nutritious."

I shake my head. "I'm more of an herbivore."

The rat insists. "Just have a bite. You'll see, it's quite tasty, and most importantly, it will keep Earth Jing happy and emboldened. She doesn't have to know you are breaking your vegetarian vow."

I take the multi-jointed leg, eyeing it dubiously. Meat spills out of the topmost segment.

"Go ahead," the rat exhorts.

I hear a clickety-clack from behind and find the masochistic crab descending the pile of food, intent on the scene, eyeless though it may be. Pressured on all fronts, I suck out the meat—smoking hot, chewy, savory. As my teeth worry the crab, I consider the significance of what the rat has just said about the relationship between mood and food.

"So what happens when I return to Earth? According to you, my spirit animal is dead. The only thing keeping Earth Jing from falling into a pit of despair is the sustenance I feed her."

"That is indeed a problem. We did not want to bring it up to worry you unduly because we haven't found a solution yet."

"I guess I'll just have to tough out depression. Maybe they can put me back on the Prozac."

The rat wags a finger. "It is not something to dismiss so lightly, and medication may not guarantee your mental wellbeing."

"Well, I don't really have any other choice, do I? I can't stay here. I need to go home."

"Every problem has a solution, Jing. We just need time to work it out. How do you like the food?"

"It's, um, disconcertingly chewy. Not really my thing." I hand the leg back to the rat and try my hand at another roasted nut, determined to finally eat one.

"*Mmmeat.*"

"Pardon?" I say, looking up.

"*I* didn't say anything," the living head says, turning to regard its silent partner.

"*Mmmeat.*"

The sound, flecked with pieces of mushroom and dead flesh, creaks through the skull, dispersing and whistling around its teeth and through the holes in its throat and tongue.

The rat (living) and I regard each other in surprise.

Another ruined anicca nut.

"You never were big on vegetables," the rat says, pulling a long strand of saffron-colored meat out of the masochistic crab leg and dangling it before the skull. The skull nibbles on the meat and before long is chomping and slurping it up with gusto.

"Ratty," I say, and both heads now regard me, the one living and blinking, the other eyeless with flaps of skin hanging off the skull. "I mean you," I add, pointing to the living one. "I'm sorry, I realize I don't even know your names."

"We don't have any. Spirits animals are not typically named."

"Oh, well, this might be confusing now that there are two of you. How about if I give you names?"

"We would be honored."

"Okay, how about Henry and William?"

"No, no, no."

"*NNNooo,*" the skull creaks.

"That would be insulting to our wards, Jing."

"Oh, sorry. Well, okay, how about I just keep calling you Ratty? That's worked out so far. And you, sir, can be Skully."

"I rather like it," Ratty nods.

"Skully?"

The skull turns its horrified, frozen-scream gaze from me to Ratty and back.

"I'll take that as a yes. Welcome back to the land of the living, Skully. I'm Jing."

After breakfast, following Ratty's directions, I hike into one of the more mountainous regions of the forest, where the flattened dimensions are more extreme. I feel constantly as if I'm groping around the intricate details of an alien forest mural, hoping to stumble upon a hidden panel that will unfold a secret passageway. Even when a path appears in front of me, it always twists in unexpected ways, requiring all sorts of curious turns and steps as in some expressionist dance.

Soon I hear the whisper of running water and catch purling glimmers of an underground stream between gaps in the mossy stone forest floor. The water's susurration grows more and more coherent by degrees. Then everything drops away, leaving only the roar of the falls and the spectacular scene of multi-tiered pools, like finely carved disks of turquoise banded in ivory and onyx. I set down my spear and purse on the bank, strip down and lay out my flower petals on the rocks. I rinse and scrub my ripped-up bra and panties, set them to dry in the sun by the petals, then wade in up to my neck, the water cool and refreshing in the heat of the day, growing cloudy as the coating of sand lifts from my skin and washes out of my hair. After a lengthy swim, I return to the bank and lounge on an underwater seat of white-and-black-checkered stone. As I soak, I examine my body, completely healed, the worst of the scars the puffy, self-inflicted one on my left wrist shining when the light is angled just right. Not as devastating a sight as I'd found it yesterday.

I root around in my purse and pull out the half-smoked cigarette I'd rolled days ago. Smoke a bit more of it, eye closed, sunlight shining down on the red spider lily, and feel the head rush of the first cigarette of the day. Every now and then, colorful, glassy meteorites flash across the sky.

After bathing I brush my teeth with a finger, floss and rinse out my mouth in one of the waterfalls. I run the dendrite comb through my painfully knotted hair, by now long enough to brush against my shoulders. I dry off using the black flower petals and wrap new, clean ones around my body. Finally, I apply a coat of lipstick, and as I'm returning it to my purse the dragon's *objet d'art* tucked away in a side pocket catches my eye.

I pull it out and examine it.

Odorless. A brilliant iridescent, at some angles appearing to be streaked with mauve and tangerine, mint and cerise, jet and sapphire, always shifting with the change in the light—a one-sided flat surface twisting to wrap around on itself—a Möbius strip.

Jewelry? What was the dragon doing with these things? Need to ask the rat about this.

Back at camp I find Ratty in the process of giving articulation lessons to Skully. Beyond them, the masochistic crab skitters about, purposelessly busy.

"Say *skuhhleeee.*"

"*Mmmeat.*"

"No, try this: *skuh.*"

"*Mmmeat.*"

"Hi, guys," I say.

The two heads turn towards me. "How was your bath?" Ratty asks, then taking a deep sniff, nostrils narrowed into scrutinizing slits, says, "Where did you get that?"

"This?" I hold up the *objet d'art.* "You know what it is?"

"An unspeakable fruit." The rat rises to two feet and pads over. "You will remember, Jing, we have told you about this. We had been catching whiffs of it now and again but assumed it was some kind of olfactory hallucination, for we have not seen these since our days with the dragon."

"Right." I briefly describe what had happened when I visited the dragon's carcass several days ago. "I was going to ask you about it, but other things have kept popping up, kept taking precedence in my mind. So this is poisonous?"

"After eating it Skully seemed fine, but days later William's signal cut out. Henry's became scrambled and nonsensical. We cannot be sure exactly what it was that happened. Maybe William saw into Psyche and it unhinged him—it is only a guess though." The rat reaches out and takes the fruit, human-like fingers brushing across my hand. Skully bobs around, teeth clattering as the rat moves.

"Ratty, now that Skully is almost fully back to life, is..."

"Yes?"

"Does this mean William is coming back from the dead as well?"

"*NNNooo.*"

Ratty sadly nods in agreement. "Not necessarily, at least not in the way you mean. It may be more related to Henry's belief that William is still alive, as opposed to the possibility that he actually is, or perhaps there is no relation at all. You see, the connection between Psyche and Earth is partly a causal one—for example, the signals of consciousness and nurturance that pass back and forth, or the correspondence of language and music—"

"Language and music?"

"Yes, that's correct. Many aspects of Psyche connect with our wards' experience of music, and the Deep Language is one of them. When we speak, we send the faintest of echoes back to our wards, who hear the sounds as earworms, quite distracting if the ward is particularly sensitive to music."

"Ahh, the dog..."

"What about the dog?"

"It would never speak to me, which I found extremely frustrating."

"Yes, many animals take vows of silence as a courtesy to their wards or out of fear of taxing their wards too much with musical stimulation. So, probably your silent dog was just an example of how loyal that species is towards their wards. In any case, this is one of the direct connections between Psyche and Earth, but there are other connections as well, acausal ones—meaningful coincidences. These are more like rain at a funeral, an eclipse during a mental breakdown. Neither one leads to the other, but when you see them co-occurring, you appreciate their significance, their connection."

When Ratty notes the queer expression on my face, it attempts another tack. "Consider the fact that many things happen to Earth Jing daily, but only a few of those events may have a deep and lasting significance on her. For example, many of the people that surround her are only hostless shells whose spirit animals have perished long ago and can thus have no impact on you, her Psychic form. By the same token, something Psychic may have no correlate on Earth. For example, here you are being chased by a dragon whose ward is likely long dead." It turns back to the unspeakable fruit, sniffing.

"It is most curious that you found this. It could be useful. Keep it with you." The rat grabs my hand and slips the fruit onto my wrist. "We will try to learn more about it."

"Learn more how? The only way we can learn anything definite is if I experiment with eating it as you did. Otherwise, all we have is reasoning. Unless you mean asking the dragon?"

"No, not the dragon. It would, we suspect, only lie. But there are other ways for us to find out. Let us worry about the issue."

No matter which method of transport we end up using (raft, dragon boat, or dragon kite), rope is requisite. Thus, for the greater part of the day, we drive the hippocochlea to pull down tree after tree and weave the blue leaves into sturdy cords. It's not until early evening, when we have several sizable coils, our hands aching with blisters, pleasantly exhausted from the labor, that I go deal with the dragon.

Before I depart, Ratty stops me and says, "Jing. Be careful. The dragon is weak, on the edge of death now, and we need to keep it that way. However, if we were the dragon, we think the easiest way to gain the upper hand would be through trickery—fooling you into feeding it. After all, you saw what you were able to do for Skully in just a small space of time, imagine how effective your power could be if you were to focus it after being fully rested. For now, your presence will keep it alive, but if the balance were upset even a bit, it could mean the end for us."

I nod, collect my spear, and head down the beach, damp wind tangling my hair around my head, petal suit warming up in the dying light. I skirt along the cliff edges and the forest-crowned dunes, glancing through the trees at the recycled souls that have managed to ooze their way into the shade, settling down in the sand, flesh ripping and bones popping as they transform. Behind me, shy but curious, skitters the masochistic crab, segmented legs clicking.

Stony trails of dried blood have veined the slope of the dune atop which the dragon lazes. The surrounding forest has decayed into smoking pillars of carbon and ash. As I approach, the shadow-obscured beast shifts, its orifices and wounds glinting with fire. Halfway up the dune I plant the spear into the ground.

"You have made your decision," the dragon murmurs.

"Yes."

"Well?" As it speaks, the rotten ground beneath a nearby pair of charred trees suddenly cracks, and they begin to sink in slow, listing descent.

"We don't need you. Moreover, we hope you'll move several miles down the beach so you won't disturb our operations. Your smell irritates both of us."

"Operations?"—the dragon chuckle-coughs—"You mean all that racket you've been creating in the woods. Making the raft after all, hmm?"

"That's none of your concern."

"You must think me a fool."

The dragon snorts a bit of flame out of its deformed jaws, not far enough to lick me, but far enough for the wave of heat to curl a few hairs. The ruins and surrounding, insect-riddled forest are illuminated for a flash in the firelight as the orange glow ripples back through the compressed layers of space.

"You wouldn't have come here if you didn't want my help."

"You're wrong. That's all I had to say." I turn to go. The masochistic crab, anticipating my movement, starts to click its way ahead towards our distant campfire.

The dragon shouts, "Wait!"

I pause. The masochistic crab stops, nebbish claws flexing, rotates back towards the dragon, considers me, and then indecisively rubs two of its legs together.

"Come back. We're not done talking. I know you and that stinky rodent are in dire straits."

I turn back towards the dragon. "The only reason I came here is to ask you to leave. I've said my bit. Now I need to get back to work."

"Feed me, and I will carry you."

"I don't think that's a good idea—you dangling us above the water."

There is a pause, the glinting lines of fire flaring. "I'll let you ride me."

"What?"

"I can't fly, it's true—not if you won't trust and feed me now—but I can take you by water, can ferry you to the island. I warn you, though, it will be very hot."

"The last time we entered into a little 'partnership,' you enslaved me, threatened to suck out my brains. I'd be a fool to trust you."

"But I saved you! After our last night together I realized what you said was true: together we could be very powerful. So I rushed back to find you, but, alas, the eternity bug had cleansed the desert. I was desperate to find you again, help you, and I did—just in time. I knew when I saw that snake springing towards you that that was my chance to put everything right, to redeem myself. If you could just see that, if you could just forgive me, I would take you to the mountains and swear to protect you from all the obstacles standing in our way."

Our. Our way. Maybe the dragon is actually starting to think in terms of working together. Team trust. Goldfield would be proud. Still, I can't budge. Not yet.

"Years ago you murdered the rat. Ruthless, unreliable, unpredictable," I list, laughing and shaking my head. "These qualities don't make for a good member of a team."

"What?" It recoils in astonishment. "I did not murder the rat."

"You poisoned it—"

"Lies!"

"—with this." I stretch out my arm. The nacreous bracelet glows golden in the gathering dark, reflecting streaks of burning dragon blood. The masochistic crab, as if responding to my building agitation and increasing heartbeat, begins to scrabble up my leg, but I kick it off.

It sniffs at the air with its asymmetrical nostrils, one torn wide, the other squished beneath a rocky tumor. "What have you got there?"

"An unspeakable fruit."

"Ohhh... yes, the unspeakable fruit. It-it-it's true that the rat ate one and that it happened to be the fruit I offered it, but you must understand that I eat them whenever I can get my claws on them. Why else would I have carried them in my pouch? They're a delicacy. If the rat's constitution was not suitable, I could not have foreseen that."

I sigh, torn. "I need to get back to camp."

"Please, Drummer Girl. Please, don't go."

"I'm sorry. It's not going to work." I stalk off, the masochistic crab leading the way.

Behind me an eerie silence blots out the insect chorus. I'm reminded of a similar scenario many nights ago when I'd turned my back on the dragon, snuggling up against the dog, praying I wouldn't perish in a bath of fire.

"It denies any wrongdoing where Skully is concerned," I conclude.

Ratty wrinkles its nose.

"*NNNooo,*" Skully protests.

The rat (or rats, as I've begun to think of them) has prepared a new marinade, this one composed of leftover glue from our rope-making, mixed with crushed, aromatic grasses, lathered on mushrooms and rock-cracked crab legs. At once determined to make the most of the crab and afraid of being jilted by the whimsical creature, the rat has ripped off four such legs for the meal. By now the leg that had been removed this morning is fully functional, with flexing feelers and claws. The creature isn't at all horrified by having its limbs rent from its body, and the rat again encourages me to mutilate and consume it guilt-free. So I eat one of the legs, hoping that at the very least it will help Earth Jing in some way. After all, after I return, *if* I return, she may never be fed Psychic sustenance again.

"Is it true? Did the dragon eat an unspeakable fruit as well?"

"Yes."

"So, then, maybe it's telling the truth. Maybe this was just an unfortunate accident."

"Or a cunning bit of prestidigitation."

By the time dinner is finished, the sun has set, and I suggest the rat sleep first. Despite the trials of the day, I don't feel drowsy. Need to think more.

As it balls up on its mat and the night grows dark, a new light dawns on the eastern horizon, ghost-like and colorful, smeared across the fog but seeming to emanate from those massive, branching structures. A shifting specter of light. Reminds me of the glowing flora of a Psychic oasis—bioluminescence shining through un-even vegetal sutures.

During the evening, I try another dorberry (tastier and tastier each time I sink my teeth into one), and practice attacks with the spear. Never far from me is the crab, at times dashing beneath my feet as I walk, tripping me up or trying to claw up the side of my leg. Despite its growing affection for me, I adamantly keep it at bay, nudging it away with my foot, swatting it off my body, or giving it a gentle whack with the polite end of the spear. Nevertheless, it fails to take the hint, pes-tering me throughout the evening.

Skully, seemingly unable to sleep after being dead so

long, gapes at me from across the campfire, occasionally voicing its wheezy negations or supplications for meat. Just as the rat skull haunts the camp, thoughts of the future haunt my mind: the sea, the islands, the mountains, the prospect of returning only to die of despair once back home. So many problems to solve, so many unknowns.

Hours and hours pass, and I start to grow weary, when a sound suddenly draws me back to attention.

Drag.

Thud.

Drag.

Thud.

Coming from the forest.

I stand, putting my back to the fire, and as my eyes adjust to the dark, I scan the woods, finally spotting that flattened shape lumbering towards me out of the sylvan passages. Like a moving painting, it seems to be walking in place as it approaches, another strange illusion of the forest, but the sound behaves normally, increasing in volume. Then it bursts into three-dimensions, anchoring in the flickering shadows at the edge of the wood, the melted crags of the dragon head seeming to stare out at me.

The masochistic crab dithers between the two of us, uncertain which it would prefer to bother.

"I need you."

"I know."

"I'm... not ready to die."

Fear. In the end, that's all there is to this dragon. Fear. Of death. Of losing its power.

"But I can take you. Use me as a boat. I will not harm you. When we arrive at the island, I will guide and protect you. That is all."

I wait, letting it fill in the silence with the details of its own paranoia.

"Look at me. I'm too weak to be of any danger to you at this point. My blaze has been reduced to mere sparks."

"I realize that. And since you're so weak, you won't be any help to us in the trials that lie ahead."

"Then feed me so I can serve you. Have mercy. Please!"

The dragon's desperation excites the masochistic crab, and it rushes over. I pause, pretending to consider. The time to budge is close.

"Who was your ward anyway?" I ask, shifting topic. Bower's name dances on the tip of my tongue, but I check myself. It would be all too easy for the dragon to simply affirm my suspicions with a lie, but it would be more believable if it offered the name on its own.

"That's an inappropriate question, girl. You don't understand spirit animal culture—"

"Oh, I understand, but I want you to tell me anyway. A sign of faith."

"It's bad enough my ward is deceased. Please don't ask me to besmirch their memory by revealing who they were."

"I know Ratty's and Skully's. They know mine. *You* know mine. The only piece missing from this puzzle is who yours is—or was."

A red bubble puffs out of one of its eye wounds, pops, and then a stream of lava gushes forth, setting a tree ablaze. "Please spare me this humiliation."

"Just a name. I need to know."

"You... knew him: Sebastian Bower."

"Okay," I whisper, clicking. "If we were to accept you, you would merely serve as a vehicle, and bodyguard if need be." The sentence mirrors what Bower had said to me when I was accepted into Autoscope. *"Drums, other instruments if need be."* I wonder if the dragon notices this.

"That's all I ask for."

Back in Detroit I'd responded differently. A click and a nod.

"Well, I'll see what the rat thinks when it rouses. You

can return to your own camp. I'll let you know our decision in the morning."

The dragon unmoors its stony head from the sand, the creases in the rock exaggerated by the campfire, detailing the tolls of melancholy and defeat. It starts to drag itself back the way it had come—flattening. I return to the fire and sit down on the struggle-between-light-and-dark mat, the crab creeping behind me. I lay the spear across my knees, listening to the dragon as it wearies its way back to its camp. When I lose the sound in the background of insect song, I rouse the rat.

"It's your watch," I say. Then, "The dragon paid us a visit."

It sniffs the air, puzzling out the residue left by the dragon.

"What do you smell?"

"It may genuinely be contrite. Get some sleep."

I smile and settle down, stripping off my clothes and wrapping myself in some large petals. I lie there, watching the starry sky and listening to the crashing waves and the twitter of insects. The leggy clicking of the crab approaches, the firelight casting its long shadow over the interior of the lean-to, then vanishing as I feel the bony thing curl up against my leg, prickling me through the sleeping bag.

I shudder—but let it be.

Before long, visions of Earth return:

CHAPTER 14

"Well, Jing, I can't say I think this is a good idea," Dr. Goldfield says.

Jing's psychiatrist, leaning back from her desk, is dressed in a purple turtleneck sweater, cream-and-black tartan skirt, and high leather boots. She looks wan, her sharpness dulled, perhaps due to the storm that has been grinding down on Detroit, which has kept her living at the staff residence for the past week. At the back of the office, by the overflowing book-shelves, the window is frosted-over, groaning beneath the tugs and lashes of iced wind.

Jing sits in the leather armchair pulled in front of the doctor's desk. She'd caught Goldfield between appointments on a day when they were not scheduled to meet, and from the beginning of the meeting the dynamic had been different: sitting with the desk between them, instead of spread around the coffee table; using the same ashtray; Jing taking the initiative in the conversation and Goldfield put on the defensive.

"I know my treatment isn't finished, but the change will be good for me. I'll go see my father, reconnect with friends. I just don't think this is working for me. I'm not progressing. Four months it will be soon, and... well, I think the best thing for me to do is to quit hiding."

"What you call hiding I"—Goldfield gestures, making a ring of smoke that seems to encircle all of Glenbrook—"*we* call healing."

"When I was a kid and my mother would have one of her fits, I would hide in this crawlspace in our house. It was right by a window seat overlooking the garden, and I was the only one who could fit inside there, just me and all the spiders. To this day I don't think they knew were I'd go." *But I stopped,* Jing thinks, *because of the lights that followed me inside.* "Anyway, I can't help feel that Glenbrook is like my crawlspace on a much grander, more adult scale."

"You realize I've never approved the discharge of a patient lower than A-level."

Jing reflexively tries to click her absent tongue stud. "So raise my level."

"It's not as simple as that. There are still so many issues for us to work through, and all this time there's been this wall between us"—she taps the desk with her ring finger—"things back there you won't trust me to access. I've never felt as if we made the necessary connection, the kind that I can usually achieve with my patients, the kind that does result in progress and breakthrough. At the beginning, during your psychotic episode, you were completely unfiltered, and you shared with me some very disturbing ideas. Do you recall any of that?" She shakes her head in expectation of a negative response.

"Some. Enough."

"I can't help fighting the suspicion that over time you've grown more skilled at concealing things from me. If you have another attack outside of Glenbrook, you may come to serious harm. What if, for example, you were to have an episode while out in this inclement weather? You could freeze to death. And the elements aside, you're an attractive young woman, and the world is full of unscrupulous men that would jump at the opportunity to take advantage of you in those unanticipated moments when you're rendered defenseless."

Despite the temptation to sink back in her chair, she props an elbow on the desk and carefully trims the cigarette tip against the glass lip of the ashtray, glancing up at Goldfield as she speaks: "Well, obviously I'm going to have to make some lifestyle adjustments."

"I hope you will. Years ago, back in the heyday of

Glenbrook when I was still fresh out of school, interning under Dr. Rota, the first patient assigned me was a young woman with more than a passing resemblance to you."

"My mother," Jing guesses. Ever since her phone conversation with her father the previous week, since realizing her mother had been institutionalized at Glenbrook in the early 80s, she had wondered if she had inherited more than just her mother's mental illness...

"That's right." Goldfield nods.

Jing leans back in the leather chair, surprised at the ready breach of confidentiality. The sounds of echo-obscured Muzak wafts in with a shift in the wind, and the two watch each other for a moment, listening to the muddled piano.

"Lili Elwood"—Goldfield extinguishes her cigarette—"I treated her under Rota's guidance. Hers was a very difficult case. So many interesting parallels in symptom-atology with you. Differences as well, of course. Your mother slipped in and out of catatonic states with greater frequency than you and your epileptic fits, but her case has been useful in guiding me in your diagnosis and treatment plan. In one respect, however, I hope your two cases will differ. I pushed Rota to approve her early release, and in retrospect, a more intensive treatment would have been appropriate. I should have insisted on long-term institutionalization—perhaps even on a permanent basis."

"But that's my mother, not me."

"Yes, Jing—"

"Besides—"

"—and I've seen it happen again and again. Patients progress, they're discharged, they return to Glenbrook months later, progress, discharge, rinse, repeat, until eventually they turn up dead in an alley or vanish altogether." Goldfield fingers her pack of cigarettes, but restrains herself.

"I'm not saying I want to terminate therapy or the

meds; I'm just saying I can't physically stay at Glenbrook anymore. I see others around me breaking down at the slightest grievance. It's unhealthy on every dimension of your biopsychosocial philosophy. Dr. Murai doesn't share your bleak view on discharging patients. During our interview he said sometimes patients show improvement after release."

"Some patients, yes," Goldfield admits, "but they're in the minority to be sure, and it varies by diagnosis."

"Maybe I'll be one of those patients. I need to face... people, people from my world, people that matter to me. I need to get back into music and figure out what's next in my life. I need to be back out there, doing something, being a part of society again, letting the world re-temper me. The longer I'm in here, the more difficult it will be for me to reintegrate later on."

"I certainly appreciate this proactive outlook," Goldfield begins, leaning back in her armchair and receding with some relish back into the comfortable padding of Glenbrookian-speak, "but I still have my doubts, and our goal at Glenbrook is not to weaken the patients but, rather, strengthen them, equip them with the mental tools they'll need when they re-enter society."

Jing nods. "Well, I'll still be coming back for out-patient treatment. Won't be totally lost at sea. And if I do have another episode, we can try things your way."

Goldfield considers this. Jing watches her closely, putting out her own cigarette and blinking away the stinging smoke.

"Okay, Jing. If this is what you want to do, you need to fill out a formal request and raise it during next week's team meeting."

"Does that mean you'll vote yes?" Jing asks, detecting in Goldfield's voice an assenting tone bound as it is by webs of bureaucracy.

Her doctor pulls a fresh cigarette from her pack, neatly lights it and holds in the smoke. It almost seems to vanish inside of her—or maybe it never entered.

"Well, I need to consider this some more, and we should wait on the results of your neurological exam. Murai said he should have all your data analyzed by next week, and I think everyone will feel better making their decisions based on his presentation. So for now, let's leave it at a maybe."

Discordant nodding accompanies Goldfield's maddening non-commitment.

After her meeting with Goldfield, Jing slips in late to movement therapy in rec west. The light machines have been swept aside, robot sentinels monitoring from the walls as the patients sway and frolic in improvisatory fashion to cheesy new age music under Dr. Conway's supervision.

I'm doing it, she thinks, raising her arms towards the ceiling and rotating her hips. *I'm going to get out of here.*

"Leave your body, leave your mind," Dr. Conway intones in his high-pitched warble. "Become the music and let everything else wash away."

Patients leap and flap their arms. Catherine's hair is a silvery Chinese fan as she twirls, the floor shakes as the Governor bounds across it, Henry's arms squiggle and wave.

Dr. Conway singles Jing out. "Release yourself, Ms. Elwood. Release yourself."

Jing attempts to obey, attempts to make her movements more ridiculous, more uninhibited.

"Your body does not exist. You do not exist."

She flaps and hops, poses and jerks, and somewhere in the confusion of movement Jing melts into the flock, her body tingling with endorphins.

"Yes! Yes! Yes!" Dr. Conway exclaims.

Afterwards, flushed and out of breath, she returns to her room to collect a few books and goes down to rec north to practice *Pictures.* The dwarfish Christmas tree squatting beside the stage imbues the space with a comforting air, the colorful lights sparkling in the few keys whose gloss has not worn off with age.

As she begins to play, she remembers her lunch with Waters the previous week, his innocent question about *Pictures,* her trivial response. She had originally been attracted to it because of the art exhibition concept, but also the wide variation of moods and styles, and finally because it was such a daunting challenge. When she had abandoned her efforts years ago, it had been with some relief, having only mastered three-quarters of the composition. However, since Penn's first visit and the care package of music and books, and later Waters' nudging, perfecting *Pictures* had day-by-day taken on more importance for Jing. On the surface, it was merely practice—mastering a piece—except that it was more than a piece; it was a phase of her life, a scrapped project, a counterfactual. *Pictures* had been the musical backdrop of her life when her mother had killed herself, after which Jing had dropped out of school, abandoned her work, and fallen into an appalling lifestyle—couch surfing and mooching off of friends, sleeping with strangers, constantly drunk and high. One night, she had stumbled down the steps into a (literally) underground club, packed to the brim, floor sticky with beer, and there on stage Autoscope had performed to a thrashing audience. She and Penn had had a brief shouted conversation at the jam-packed bar afterwards. A week later, Penn invited her to join the group. If Jing had been more resolute, hadn't stopped her work on *Pictures*, she probably wouldn't have gone to the show that night with a boy whose name she can't even remember now, she wouldn't have reconnected with Penn, wouldn't have moved to Detroit, maybe wouldn't have ended up having a breakdown and following in her mother's footsteps.

If only she could trace everything back to that one phase in her life when everything had gone off track.

Just as she is looping back through her mother's past, so too is she looping back through her own.

Pictures is time travel.

Looping.

Looping.

Each time perfecting a small piece of the work, just the trick to achieve mastery.

When her fingers finally lift from the keys, the sky has fermented into a plum wine, and the snowy lawn glows drunk and ruddy-faced. She arrives late to dinner, the sun set on the halls of Glenbrook and the lawn bruised and dour on the tail of its former drunkenness.

She stands at the entrance for some minutes, gaping at the transformed cafeteria, eyes darting from garden plot to garden plot, which had been completely barren since she had been committed, used only as stages for holiday decorations. Now they have erupted with life and color, immense yew-like trees, branches crooking and humping together in tangled plaits, disrupting and up-ending the arrangement of chairs and tables, each knobby protuberance riddled with tumorous, orange fruits. The floors of the mezzanines have buckled and burst, with knots of snaky roots coiling downward to the floor, carrying with them vortices of tables and chairs and dining patients.

"Drummer Girl," a voice says.

She turns to find the Governor standing beside her, on his way out.

"You okay?"

She nods, looking up into his pock-marked face, into his over-dilated, blue eyes, seeing in them the warped reflection of the indoor forest. A floor blooms behind her, his eyes transforming it into tiny, sparkling rubies.

"Listen, I'm sorry about the other week. I was a little rude during group. I'm up and down on these meds. It was nice to have you share."

She shakes her head, rousing out of the stupor, out of the depths of his eyes, and finding his face. "It's okay. Thanks."

They high-five, and when he goes, she turns back and tentatively approaches the fibrous maze, which untangles to permit her entry, the tables and columns and windows twisting to accommodate its shifts.

"*Silver bells, silver bells,*" the Muzak croons.

In each arboreal alcove high above and below in some subterranean alternative space a patient or nurse dines, not on typical Glenbrook fare, but on the fruits of the tree—Klein bottles, she sees, impossible to resolve visually, many with dimensions cubed beyond comprehension, their odor rotten and cloying.

"*Soon it will be Christmas day.*"

Here she finds a plastic Christmas tree sectioned off and spaced out through the growths.

"*City sidewalks, busy sidewalks,*"

A sticky pulp dripping through the knots of wood and pooling on the slivers of walkable floor clings to her red shoes with the desperation of glue.

"*Dressed in holiday style.*"

At the end of her promenade, she finds the bar, where the flora is superimposed over the food. Hands shaking, she pumps out hot chocolate from a carafe and spoons black bean salad into a bowl. Tiny phosphorescent insects swim in her food.

As they swarm over the tray and onto her hands, she nearly drops her food, but just stands firm and whispers, "Be Zen, Jing."

She ascends a spiral staircase of branches and bowed trunks, and finds her usual red table, where she tries to eats her bug-food, which spills everywhere but down her thickening throat.

She closes her eyes, feels the blood pounding through her neck and head.

Turns to look out the window at the darkened snowscape—*snow calms, snow calms*—but whatever is in here has exploded outward onto the lawns, tunneling and curlicuing out towards the Rota Wellness Village.

She abandons her tray, descends, and gets a light from the Time Traveler, his tattooed face smeared with Klein bottle pulp, following the braids of plant-life as they spill out of the conservatory cafeteria and infect the halls of Glenbrook, guiding her to the meds station, where they terminate, coiling delicately, expectantly— and where the nurse gives her a queer look. After downing her meds, she walks the halls, now preceding the spreading wave of life.

She chain-lights another cigarette, then veers off towards a glass umbilical connecting to the north wing, guided by instinct.

As she passes into the north wing hallways, she's met by faint, ethereal piano music reverberating throughout, growing in volume as she rounds the bend onto the corridor off which the rec room is situated, and she at last pegs it for the atmospheric section of *Pictures* called "The Catacombs."

When she reaches the door, she rests her head against the cold wood, eyes shut tight, whispering a mantra to the lugubrious pace of the tune. With her recent dosage increase of anticonvulsants, Jing had been confident that these seizures would finally be put behind her, but now here it comes, this aura, presaging the next attack.

When she opens her eyes, casting them back down the hall, she finds the space empty.

"Thank god," she breathes, placing her hands between her breasts, feeling her rabbit heartbeat slowing. She continues to listen—the music loops back through the same section, brooding but somehow calming as well—and at last her hands have stopped shaking.

She turns to the viewing window.

Within, all the lights of rec north are extinguished save those of the Christmas tree. In the shifting, blinking colors, she spots Henry seated at the piano, right fingers engaged in an extended trill, his posture horrid—slumped and loose-limbed. From beneath his sepia-colored sweater the neatly pressed collar of a toxic orange shirt flaps out like the wings of a radioactive bat. His left foot is depressing the soft pedal, muting the sound to prevent it from carrying. It's the first time she has seen him playing a musical instrument since the Compound days, when he would perform onstage with his brother.

As she opens the door, he ceases playing, retracts his fingers from the keys.

"Go on, Henry. I didn't mean to interrupt. It sounded great." *Just what I needed to hear, what I needed to stop the attack.*

His fingers return to the keys, and his eyes study the lines of music, but he doesn't play a note.

"You okay?" She starts to approach, then her eyes stray to the Christmas tree, to the sole present tucked under it, and she shifts course.

Henry watches sidelong as she crosses the room to the other side of the stage. She plucks up his present, goes to the piano, hands it to him.

"Merry Early Christmas."

He takes the gift from her, glancing up at her face, and then ripping open the paper.

Two copies of Stravinsky's "Concerto for Two Pianos."

"A few weeks ago I had an appointment with Dr. Murai in the east wing. On my way there I noticed an unused piano. Must have been an old rec room. I was thinking maybe we could roll it over here and work on this together, maybe put on a show for everyone." She takes a drag on her cigarette, nearly down to the stub, and leans on top of the piano, trying to gauge his reaction. "Could be fun. I could perform *Pictures*, too. It's nearly ready. I may be leaving Glenbrook—jury's still out on that—but even if I'm discharged, I'll probably be coming back periodically for outpatient treatment. If you're still here, we could practice then. What do you say?" She offers him her hand.

He flips open the book, reading the first few lines of music, nodding to himself, eyes flitting with a mathematical precision.

"Did Goldfield put you up to this? Or Rota?" he snaps.

"Christ, Henry." Her hand wilts.

"Or maybe it was Mussorgsky himself? Or Bach?"

"What?"

"I needed to study the music for myself, make sure I hadn't made a mistake—it's easy to make mistakes these days—but I was correct: Mussorgsky must be high-level—maybe a Director—I don't know—my contact with William is spotty, so it's difficult to obtain accurate information, and I'm uncertain about the chain of command, but Rota must report to Mussorgsky, and Goldfield the middle man between you and Rota, delivering the Director's packages to you—that's how it works, isn't it?"

Knowing there's no sense in attempting to reason with Henry, Jing takes a final drag of her cigarette, jabs it out on the ashtray atop the piano, and gathers up her piano music.

"After they pulled *The Brandenburg Concertos,* I was at first relieved," he continues, watching her sharp, intentional movements, "thought maybe I'd been wrong—it was a clever move on their part—thought that Glenbrook hadn't originally been aware that the Music Department had infiltrated their Muzak programing, and had corrected the problem as soon as they discovered the oversight—didn't matter, though, because they found an even more effective system for stymying me—an agent—*you,* you and your *Pictures,* practicing day in and day out—there are gaps in the music, of course, big gaps—you can't play twenty-four seven—but it doesn't matter—the Department's research must have shown that remembered music is an even more effective psychic suppressant than *actual* music—my brain is full of ear worms, all from *Pictures*, all of them just coded propaganda."

She turns as she reaches the door. "Henry, I'm not an agent of Glenbrook or the Department or anybody. I've only been trying..." Her thought sputters out on her lips, extinguished beneath a weight of insight about his delusion, about how all the constant music of Glenbrook—*Brandenburg, Pictures*—has been a torture for him, a constant reminder of his loss. Of course he hasn't played anything since the Compound days; he hasn't had William to accompany him. All his life the two must have studied and performed together—joint piano lessons, duets at recitals. For Henry, music had never been a solo activity. The only escape he could find was through the atonal, compositions he listened to during his meditations—with no anchoring key, nihilistically broadening the definition of music to the brink of utter meaninglessness.

"To keep me institutionalized," he finishes her sentence for her, gesturing towards the Stravinsky book, "with this, infinitely worse than *Pictures*, brimming with mind-sticky codes—who are you really?—come to think of it, I don't even know if I remember you from the Compound."

She feels a moment of vertigo, standing at the threshold between Henry and the rest of Glenbrook, between falling back into his delusion and fleeing from its grip.

Fighting it, attempting to disprove the veracity of the delusion, to report him, would just provide him with more ammunition. Everything becomes absorbed into his system, twisted to fit.

There's a video playing on the VCR in the day room.

A tree branch has exploded out of the set, its limbs

stabbing into the faces of the patients gathered around it. Jing veers away from the sight and escapes into the stairwell, where only the light of the second floor landing glows. She'd left a book on the Oriel window seat, a Jung biography, but it's too dark and her mind too frazzled for reading. The courtyard, inaccessible from the mounds of packed snow, shines with parallelograms of light slanting down from hallways and patient rooms. Outside is mercifully dead. She focuses on that emptiness, feels herself growing calmer, and is suddenly cognizant of the cold and her fuming breath. She hears a tech doing his round in some distant corridor, the strain of the window against the wind, the pops and creaks of the old building.

Some time passes before she notices the moving shadows on the window seat—long, curling fingers.

Something above her flitters. She turns to look up at the second floor landing, and finds it teeming with growth—alien red ferns, enormous blossoms, the tangling yew branches—creeping downward, over the steps. She glances below and finds the darkness stirring with gray outlines of the same, reaching up towards her. She turns back to the window, shivering, eyes tearing up, gazing out at the mundane sight, but finds all the windows choked with the same bizarre flora, vomiting it down the walls and into the courtyard.

She can hear the stalks stretching and widening, the papery whisper of blossoming, the flutter of the ferns' leaves. She squeezes her eyes shut, forcing herself to take slow, deep breaths, expecting any moment the unwelcome arrival of the seizure.

Be Zen, Jing.

The seizure never comes, and at some point she realizes that she has been mistaken: all of the lights in the courtyard have winked out.

There's a hand on her shoulder. She skirts back into the cold glass, finding a flashlight shining in her face. When her mind solves the weird maze of her vision, she recognizes the tech, a new guy, young and burly.

"Ms. Elwood. Ms. Elwood. Can you hear me? Are you okay? You were staring off into space."

"What? Shit." Her mouth tastes chalky, bitter. "I was… I must have fallen asleep here," she lies. "What time is it?"

"2AM."

Six hours lost.

Her hands have turned icy, and she begins to puff warmth back into them. Her body feels stiff and un-yielding, exploding with pain as she shifts herself.

"I passed by here twice and didn't notice you in the shadows until just now. Shit, you had us scared." The tech gives an aside into his walkie-talkie: "I found one of them. Jing Elwood. Bringing her up."

He helps her down and leads her upstairs over bare steps. Jing stomps her feet, wincing as the feeling comes back in a wave of needles. They navigate through darkened corridors, guided only by the wavering bronze circle of his Maglite—batteries must be near dead. They turn a corner and find the day room, the movie finished, the patients dispersed, everything dark save the beacon of the nurses' station at one end and exit signs glowing deep into various hallway extensions.

Several nurses and another tech have gathered there. A furious Diaz turns on her. "Where have you been?"

"I-I was sleeping. Sorry." She feels awkward entering into the stark light at the station counter. Everything feels wrong.

"And Henry?"

All eyes are on her.

"What about him?" Jing says.

A complex exchange of looks pass between the staff, before Diaz turns back to her, more harried now than angry. "We thought you two must have been together; Henry's missing—"

CHAPTER 15

I awaken again to the boom of surf, the freshness of the sea air—and burnt caramel. I don't want to stir from the comfort of this little nest of black petal blankets beneath the bamboo lean-to, but soon became aware of a weight on my chest, adjusting every now and then with the ripples of the struggle between light and dark. I open my eyes to the sight of the super-numerary-limbed creature nestled on me, pointed crab legs massaging and needling my blanket like a cat sharpening its claws. I peel a petal off me, ensnare it, and fling the bundle from the lean-to.

A thick, cool mist blankets the beach, the islands now totally obscured, the sea a band of steel, and the sun a pink pinprick surrounded by shadowy satellite holes in the sky. The rat is squatting by the fire, braiding more rope, and singeing them in the morning fire.

"Poor thing," it says, watching the crab kick itself free of the light-and-dark sack. "You didn't mean to frighten the human, did you? Come here. It's time to eat, and we are starved."

I approach the fire. "You know, I'm not the bad guy here. You're the one insisting we eat the thing."

"Don't listen to her," Ratty coos to the assemblage of legs as it crawls over.

"*Mmmeat,*" Skully croaks.

"If the crab disturbs you so"—Ratty drops its rope and yanks several legs off the creature, which again shivers with pleasure or pain or both—"you should learn more about its motivations and functioning. It will help you live at peace with it."

"Okay." I set down by the fire and assume rope-making duty.

"For example, it mostly navigates the world via emotion, specifically the intensity of your emotions, but it's blind to whether your feelings are negative or positive." The rat throws the legs onto the fire, while the masochistic crab seeks out the fruit pile station and recharges there. I'm struck again by the improvement in the rat's vitality. Wonder if it knows anything about Henry going missing. He must be safe if the rat is looking so *alive.* "Thus, it will be equally attracted to you if you are ecstatic about or horrified by its presence."

"So if I just stay completely Zen..." I say, braiding the leaves together.

"It will pay you no mind."

Soon breakfast is ready, set out on large fronds. During the meal, the masochistic crab attempts to sneak into my lap. After swatting it away to no effect, I try the rat's method, slowing my breathing and achieving a meditative calm, and sure enough the insect loses all interest in me and wanders back to the rat, scaling its body and nestling into the crook between the two heads.

"Ratty, when—if—I leave Psyche, what will happen to Skully?"

"Skully will slowly rot, unless we can find another way, another human or some other solution to our crisis. Maybe if you could feed us once or twice more before that happens, it will sustain us long enough for us to find a solution."

"Sure," I say quietly, imagining Ratty and Skully in the future traveling on without me, back in the desert, rooting through the oasis of a dead beast, the two heads chatting, maybe with the masochistic crab keeping them company—the image makes my heart ache. "Have you been able to decipher any of the signals you received from Henry recently? I don't want to alarm you, but he's gone missing from Glenbrook."

Both heads turn towards me, Ratty's nose wrinkling

in concern, a piece of crab falling out of Skully's jaws. "No, we are so far from the mountains now, the already weak and scrambled signal is nothing but dim flickering. Aside from that, we've noticed no drastic change in the signal, so perhaps he is okay."

"Okay... but wait—why should the distance from the mountains matter? I thought we were connected to Earth through neural wormholes; distance shouldn't matter, right?"

"Yes and no. The Crystal Mountains are similar to a giant brain, regulating the signals of consciousness, which in part are controlled by proximity to the mountains. Here, we are almost out of range of their control. Have you noticed a change in quality of your visions since coming to the beach?"

"Well, yeah, I just assumed I was exhausted from the journey through the desert."

"We do not think this is the case. After all, spirit animals only start receiving their first sporadic visions in the forest and then more fully in the desert. The disparity in quality leads spirit animals to venture out of the harbor of the forest—the normal course of development. Last night the vision was practically non-existent, but it *was* there. When we are out on the water nothing will reach us."

"But if we lose the signal altogether, won't we just wither out there and die."

The rat heads nod, and Ratty adds: "Yes, our minds will slowly rot. If we can last long enough to make it to the island, we may be back within range. For if we are correct, those islands somehow connect to the Crystal Mountains."

"Do you think the dragon knows this, I mean that I won't be able to feed it when we're at sea?"

"There's no telling what the dragon does and does not know. However, our guess is that it does not."

"But don't all spirit animals know about such things? Isn't this just another basic fact about life on Psyche?"

"*NNNooo.*"

Ratty shakes its head. "No, in fact the first time we heard that proximity to the mountains impacts the quality of our visions, we rejected the notion as absurd. It was an old companion of ours, a rabbit, that introduced us to this idea, but it was not until years later that we confirmed its truth through... other methods. Now, the dragon claims to have been to the mountains, which suggests it has passed this way before, maybe even numerous times. However, if true, we think that such trips must have been made after its ward perished. Remember what a trial it was for us to reach this beach? We were only able to overcome the journy through working together and using the hippocochlea, a wardless creature. That the dragon could complete the same journey alone, in its dying state, suggests it was not riddled with the memory visions in the same way we were."

I eat another mushroom, chewing thoughtfully.

"What do you mean by 'other methods?' It's not the first time you've mentioned that."

"Nothing. Just a bit of nonsense."

"Come on. Tell me."

It pauses, avoiding eye contact, then reaches into its backpack, rummages around, and pulls out the teeth game. "We can... read what Psyche knows."

I smile, wiping my mouth. "Pardon?"

"The teeth—they help us interpret the lingering consciousness of the eternity bug that transformed into Psyche. Over the years, spirit animals have developed a system for reading the Ancient Signs, imperfect though it may be. In fact, the dragon would sometimes ridicule me for rolling teeth, saying that it was all nonsense, and in truth these teeth never seemed to work until after Skully was poisoned. In any case"—it holds up a molar, rotating it to show me the patterns of holes on its different sides—"the method requires four teeth from four different animals: the incisor of a rabbit for caution;

the canine of a monkey for sharpness; the premolar of a goat for perseverance; and the molar of a rat for wisdom (of course). They all must have one (but no more than one) unrotten side. You ask a question, you roll the teeth, and then you read the patterns of rot as numbers. How they land dictates whether you should add the digits, subtract them, multiply them, append them, etc. You keep rolling and combining the numbers until they all roll up blank. That means either the message has ended or the bug's ghost has grown bored of communicating."

"And what do you do with the numbers?" I ask, picking up one of the teeth.

"Well, they're a cypher, one that has not been cracked, because it seems to shift session to session. That is why we are generally limited to asking yes/no questions, questions that can be answered in just one roll. Except that in order to learn which pattern is yes and which no, you have to test the system by asking questions you know the answers to, seeing the pattern of responses, and then you have your key to reading the answers to uncertain questions."

"Sounds a bit like the logic of a lie detector test."

"Well"—it wrinkles its nose in confusion—"Psyche does not lie, though it may not know all the answers. Thus, sometimes we get blanks and other times what we suspect to be maybes or conditional affirmatives."

Considering explaining what I'd meant, making an analogy and not an attack on the dead eternity bug's credibility, I put the tooth down and pick up another sizzling wheel of mushroom, saying instead: "So, what have you asked it?"

"Many things. For example, if our crossing would be smooth."

I take a bite. "And?"

"Mmmeat."

Ratty feeds Skully the final piece of crab. "The answer was frustratingly complex. However, a few of the other questions we've asked it have turned up very clear answers."

"Well, if this is true—I mean, if it works—why have you been concealing it from me?"

Ratty demurs, watching Skully chew. "We were reluctant to share our methods with you because, well, as we said, many think the practice of rolling and reading teeth is unscientific, based on the belief that Psyche is a dead eternity bug, and we had hoped..."

"Hoped what?"

"Hoped that we would leave a positive impression about spirit animals with you. We know that (ahem) some spirit animals have been difficult to deal with. We didn't want you sharing with other humans back home about how primitive our ways and minds may be."

"Well, *you've* been great—I would never speak a bad word against you—but at the same time, if I ever get back to Earth, I'm not going to be sharing anything about Psyche with the people there."

"Why not?" it says, genuinely shocked.

"Because they'll think I'm nuts. I mean, you saw the vision of Earth me: I *am* in a mental hospital. Telling my doctors that there's this giant dead bug in the asteroid belt that burrowed wormholes into humanity's collective unconscious, linking each of us to some archetypal spirit animal journeying across its magical corpse in a cycle of death and rebirth, won't help me get discharged. So no matter what happens here, no matter how fucked up or fascinating, I can't tell anyone."

Both rats are crestfallen. "But..."

"*NNNooo.*"

"Sorry, Ratty, Skully. If I can find a way back home, I'm going to have to pretend this never happened. I figured you would understand this, what with William and Henry and everything."

"We—"

"*Mmmeat.*"

"Shush, Skully! We'd rather hoped you would

become a kind of ambassador to Earth on behalf of Psyche, spread good things about those of us who have deserved it. What happened to our wards was a different matter entirely. You have been here, you have *seen*."

I blink, again the spider lily mocking the movement, almost how Skully used to mimic Ratty before the former had regained consciousness. I pull the last bit of my cigarette out of the purse and light it. By now, it tastes horribly bitter.

"I don't think so. That would be a major... commitment," I say, mind thick with visions of Glenbrook.

"But surely there must be a way to tell others. Don't you have an obligation to do so?"

"I hadn't really considered that. I suppose there may be indirect ways: art, music, literature..." I take a drag, then toss it, grimacing. "What else have you learned from the teeth?"

"Well, many days ago, after we met for the first time, Psyche said you and I would meet again and hinted that you would be the key to reviving Skully. Of course, that was not our only reason for helping you. After years of seeing humans in visions, to meet one in person was an extraordinary opportunity. In addition, after years of rolling teeth, it was the first time we saw that there may be truth to the method. Since then, we have taken every opportunity to ask Psyche more questions about what we should do. We learned about a shorter, more dangerous path to the Crystal Mountains and much more, but many things have gone unanswered. On the subject of the flower it has been mum. However, the dragon seems to be the only way for us to cross the sea."

"So Psyche agrees with us on that point. That's reassuring, I guess."

"Yes."

"*Mmmeat.*"

"We just ate, Skully," Ratty says.

The rat having concluded, I straighten up and stretch. "Well, this has been as weird and educational as ever. I guess it's time we get moving. Shall I go talk to the dragon?" I feel a tremor of anticipation at the words, my stomach fluttering.

Putting its teeth away, Ratty grins unpleasantly, while Skully, already grinning, looks as unpleasantly ecstatic as ever. "You do seem to have a way with it."

I click.

At the base of the dragon's dune, now frozen-over with a black floe of cooled lava, I announce our decision and intention to leave for the islands today. As I speak the masochistic crab fusses the sand at my feet and rubs against my shins.

"I can serve you as a raft, but not in my present state," the dragon says, half in sun, half carbonized shade, its length scrunched by the illusion of the forest folds. "The rock formations accumulated on my body, especially the head, will weigh me down and drown all of us."

"Well, even if you were to serve as a boat, what about the creature in the sea?"

"That creature will not harm me."

"Why not?"

The dragon cocks its head towards me without deigning to respond.

"You can't keep acting like a haughty ass if you want to come with us. You have to be more forthcoming. So tell me, why won't the creature harm you?"

It sighs, exasperated. "Because I am born of the stars, fire-blooded, not of the sea or out of the dead like all the other Psyche riffraff."

"Okay." I click. "Well, what do you propose we do concerning the rock?"

"You and your stinky friend will have to figure out a way to remove them before we can depart." With ease, the dragon has slipped back into the role of autocrat.

Even its position at the top of the dune exudes regality, corroded as its throne may be.

"How the hell are we supposed to do that?"

"I don't know, but if you can't remove them, no one's going anywhere."

Wary against the angle, I circle around well out of the range of its fire. As I approach the throne, the crab latches onto my thigh, wanting to be dragged in humiliation up the slope. "Will you stop it, Crabby," I say, giving it a jab with my spear and knocking it loose. I enter the mute-colored despond, mindful of my footing. Even so, my shoes crack the surface of the ground, releasing gusts of hot ash. Feels like stepping onto another planet. The closer I get to the dragon, the hotter the clime grows. Beads of sweat start to spring up on my brow. I pace down the side of the dragon, examining the bizarre masses of congealed lava blood, tapping them with the fang spear.

"So, do you have any ideas?" I ask.

"*My* solution is for you to feed me. It will reduce all the scarring, and I may be fit enough to fly, then we could get to the Crystal Mountains in a matter of hours. You could be home before nightfall, sipping a glass of wine and smoking cigarettes in the comfort of your bed—"

"What a decadent picture you paint."

"—or are you still pent up in that hospital?"

"It's tempting," I reflect, ignoring the gibe, "but considering that you're blind, flight might not be our safest option." And if you were powerful enough to fly, I think, you wouldn't need us anymore—we'd just be brains for you to eat."

"It is possible—if you really, truly focus—that you can return my eyesight."

I run a hand over the smooth stone, burning hot, a feverish tell of its fiery blood, then quickly withdraw my hand and suck on the fingertips. "You know, this looks like pumice."

"So what?"

"So..." I brighten. "You're covered in pumice."

"Yes. And?"

"Well, pumice has air bubbles inside." I reach down and pick up a saucer-sized drop of blood from one of its burst wounds and examine it. "It should float. Come on."

I bound and roll down the sand dune ahead of the dragon. The crab skitters halfway down but then pauses there, needling the sand and snapping its clawed nubbins, torn between me and what must be a rising state of excitement in the dragon. From the bottom of the slope, I watch the dragon make tentative motions forward and then slide downward after me, more log-like than ophidian, upsetting ash clouds and rocks, plowing over the crustacean (presumably just what the latter was after), and drenching me in a great spray of white sand and black ash. Shaking my hair and brushing myself clean, I continue the few yards to the waterline and hurl the globule of blood out into the sea. It splashes in and as I'd predicted rises back to the surface, bobbing up and down on the waves.

"Well, I know you can't see that"—I startle at a sudden wave of heat and turn to find the dragon's melted head just a few feet away, sniffing, the crab perched on the deformed ridge where its eyes had once glowed, a less elegant mockery of my own deformity— "but it's floating just as I said it would."

"How do I know you're not just luring me in to drown me?"

"Well, first of all, if we're going to start working together, we need to be able to trust each other, right?" I say, approaching, reaching up on tiptoes, and plucking the crab from its head, then backing up to a cooler distance. "Second, you're not going to drown in several feet of water. Just roll in there and see how it is."

It huffs and takes several experimental steps forward, sniffing at the water, craning its monstrous head this way and that.

"Just go straight. You're nearly there."

"Don't rush me." Then as its jaws steam against the first bit of wave: "Oh, no, no, no, most unpleasant and salty."

"Well, don't drink it, you ass."

It advances reluctantly, steaming. "Truly disgusting."

"Have you never swum before?"

"I am a creature of fire and flight. Of course I haven't swum before. I couldn't think of an activity further beneath me than splashing around in the filthy soup of recycled spirits.

"Well, you only have to take us to the island. Then your job is done."

It is by now immersed, rising and sinking with the contours of waves, grimacing with what little capability its rock-encrusted jaws have of expressing emotion, paddling around with its tiny limbs, moving in slow circles as the gigantic pancake fingers of its one ruined claw push it forever rightward.

"No, not like that. Try it like a snake would."

"I'm perfectly capable of figuring this out on my own," it snaps, but nevertheless begins to try rippling horizontally according to my suggestion. "Oh yes, there we are." It laughs, jetting forward, knocking past the floating orbs of raw flesh washing towards the shore. "That's nice, eh?"

"Very impressive." I smile in spite of everything, and the crab digs its legs into my shoulder. "Better turn around and come back. You might get lost if you travel too far sightless." I have to shout as in only a few seconds the dragon has snaked about a hundred yards from the shore. We'll make good time.

The dragon circles back and, following the sound of my voice, crawls onto land, now seemingly disappointed with its limited movement in direct comparison with aquatic freedom.

"Not so bad, after all?" I ask.

"It's... tolerable."

I leave the dragon by the seaside and return to camp to finish readying our things. As we prepare, I tell the rat the news that the dragon is covered in pumice, a rock that floats. Its anthropomorphic fingers pause in their task of securing together various goods. Ratty looks up, nostrils dilated.

"Why, that's the best news we've had in a long time."

I nod, half-smiling, and the two of us flesh out our plan in full detail.

Upon the conclusion of our talk, to the polite end of my spear I fasten a wide cactus pad with the aid of some of the bamboo rope and caramelized fruit paste. The rat constructs something similar with a long bamboo cane. I whittle the other end of its oar into a spear point, but in the process the swivel pin of my razor snaps, the blade whizzing past my face. Though we look for several minutes, there's no sign of it. Ratty mumbles over and over how inauspicious this is. I toss away the handle in frustration and refocus on the rat's spear, toughening it in the fire. The end result is effective, but the loss of the razor has made both of us uneasy.

The rat garbs itself with struggle petals, covering every bit of its body except for its snout and eyes and tail. I mold a face mask and experiment crafting gloves out of the material, finding that while it fits quite well, it hampers my skill with the spear, so I mitten one hand and leave the other free. Finally, I stuff some fruit into my purse and strap it tight around my body.

By the time the sun has climbed to the zenith, we're ready.

We mount the dragon by way of the tail, circling up its entire length from behind to the main body, one hundred feet or so. At its widest the dragon's body spans about ten feet, all of it erupted and fissured into a complex landscape of outcroppings and crevices. We lay out a large number of heat-absorbing petals, creating a carpet of sorts. In one of the crevices we store the supply of food insulated with leftover petals, everything bound together with the rope and fastened to dragon scar. Throughout these preparations, the masochistic crab monkeys about the topography of the dragon's body, relishing the way it sizzles.

"Rat to the rear," the dragon orders with a meaningful sniff once we've finished, and begins to inch down towards the water.

The rat begins to comply.

"You know," I jump to its defense, ripping my mask off, "you don't smell so hot yourself."

"What's that? Insolent girl! If I hadn't intervened—"

"You saved me from the snake because you knew you'd die if I weren't alive to feed you. A gamble you had to take. We all know that. Now, apologize to the rat."

The dragon pauses at the shoreline. "I can't swim effectively with the smell. Water will rush into my mouth—"

"Apologize."

"I..." I can feel the full-body moue shivering down the dragon's spine. "I'm sorry."

The tension disperses as soon as the words pass through the trammeled jaws—or from its brain to our brains via thought insertion, not sure exactly. A nearby wound explodes, giving me a fresh whiff of brimstone as I shield my face from the fire. The rat relaxes its shoulders, nose and whiskers twitching, the sneer melting off Ratty's lips, Skully staring blankly at the sky.

"If you'd please..." the dragon suggests.

"Very well." Ratty scampers towards the stern edge of the carpet and squats down on a stone coagulation before the beginning of the smooth tail.

Spear in my sweaty hand, standing close to the bow of the dragon among the wild grass ruins of its white mane, I spot an unscarred bit of soft flesh, beyond which

I can see the pulsing of a blood vessel the thickness of my thigh. The sweet spot. I point the fang down towards this chink in the armor of rock, ready to strike if necessary.

As the dragon crawls down the sand towards the water, a quick, random thought pops into my mind—why is it moving in this manner?—but then is gone, distracted by the entry into the waves, when the dragon knocks aside several of the floating spirit balls, rocks unsteadily as it adapts to the new environment, and starts to snake its way over the sea.

Soon we are skimming over the waves, a sinuous speedboat, the fresh sea breeze vanquishing the stifling air and drying my sweat. At this speed I can no longer stand comfortably without a handhold, so I clutch onto a rock outcropping at about waist-level with my gloved left hand and brace the spear with my right. Blinded and unable to navigate, the dragon relies on me to shout out the occasional correction in course to keep us headed towards the closest of all the islands. Though the sky is clear, the sun shining, the clouds still hang low over the horizon, obscuring much of the seascape. Occasionally, geysers of smoke erupt out of cracks in the dragon's dorsum. These infection vents sprout up all over the place, and at one point my face is nearly burned by a burst of heat out of the rock I'm clinging to. Thus, I keep my upper body as far from the dragon-hull as possible, holding onto the rock a bit like a helmsman to the boat wheel, swaying with the serpentine movement.

An hour or so into the trip, I start to glimpse strange things below, fleeting, indistinct images that bubble and effloresce—stretched-out animal heads; claws like bony, webbed flowers; eyeballs within eyeballs. At the moment a form strikes me as familiar, it shifts just beyond recognition or vanishes altogether.

"Are you seeing this?" I call to the rat.

Ratty nods, glancing over from its own water studies.

"Dragon, is this thing beneath us the creature you

mentioned?"

The dragon doesn't respond.

"What is it?"

No response.

I look astern towards the rat for support, but lost in thought, it fails to notice. So I continue to water gaze, mesmerized by the nebulous shifting of flesh and hair, scale and bone.

Hours pass.

The dragon, apparently grown weary, slows and allows itself to drift for a time. The rat and I take the opportunity to grill some mushroom and crab kebabs for lunch on an exposed bit of smoking dragon rock. I eat a monkey brain while waiting for the main course.

"Jing," the rat whispers, tamping down a blood flare up, "your question to the dragon from earlier, we have an answer, and we think we understand the danger."

"What is it?" I say in a hushed voice, breaking off a piece of monkey brain and feeding it to Skully.

"It is us—the biospiritual host from which we split off."

"Okay. So what's the problem?"

"Well"—the rat turns a mushroom skewer and fans away the smoke—"we spirit animals are driven by one thing and one thing alone."

"Consciousness."

"Yes. To connect with and be fed by our Earth hosts."

"And?"

"Well, with no signal out here from the Crystal Mountains, even weak vessels of consciousness would shine brightly. On the shore, we were still within range of the mountains, so the creatures were no harm to us, blinded to our lights by the much brighter one of the mountains. Do you see?"

"So this thing may mistake us for the signal it craves."

"Possibly."

"And the dragon?"

"Should be safe."

"Right," I pursue, voice growing quieter, remembering what the dragon had told me this morning—*because I'm a creature born of the stars*—"but it doesn't know the reason why."

The rat's nostrils flex decisively, and it flashes a grim smile. "Ready to eat."

After our meal I stand up to stretch and wander towards the bow of the dragon, the softened, gooey soles of my sneakers sticking and squishing against the scalding deck. I tap it on the head with the paddle of my spear and lower my mask.

"Well?" I ask.

The dragon cranes its head back slightly towards the sound of my voice. "Well what?"

"Well, what's the holdup? Let's get a move on."

"The holdup is I'm exhausted. I'm loaded down with congealed blood rock, a petulant girl, and her smelly rodent. I'm not accustomed to swimming—"

"Okay, well—"

"—and also, I haven't eaten since before I fended off that snake."

"Yeah, I—"

"Tell me. Have you ever tried to swim for many miles in as starved and wretched a condition as the one I'm currently in?"

"No," I rush to complete the thought, "but you did force me to feed you after days of wandering—"

"So, unless you want to feed me now, you will excuse me if I need to take just a few more minutes' rest." The dragon punctuates the end of the conversation with a sigh.

Past midday, the rat and I huddle together, staring out over the water at the distant islands.

"What do you think they are? The islands, I mean."

"We've heard a theory, but not all spirit animals agree."

"Let's hear it."

"Do you remember the appearance of the eternity bug?"

"I couldn't get a very good look through the sand cloud. Cthulhu comes to mind."

The rat sniffs. "We don't understand quite what you mean, but try, if you will, to imagine how such a creature might look after pupation. Very striking: white and blue and a black that is not black but colorful, as if it contained the cosmos—"

"Black opal," I suggest, "like the rocks on the beach and in the folding forest."

"Yes, and sprouting an incredible number of huge wings veined in that black opal and scaled in gold and cream, with a head that seemed to be made of sinus-searing light. More beautiful and terrible than anything we've ever seen or smelled before, but only a glimpse, a whiff, were all we could risk without having our entire sensorium fried. It was like a planet detaching itself from Psyche."

The rat goes quiet, lost in the memory.

"And?" I prod.

"And, well, the dead imago is more bearable on the senses as its awesome beauty has faded, but one can still see in the corpse what once was—"

A wet slap from the starboard side interrupts the rat. I turn to find a fleshy mass curled around one of the dragon's scar outcroppings, steaming against the rock. Many yards long, it stretches on below the surface of the water into darkness, a conglomeration of jointed appendages, spotted with orifices and patches of mutated uncertainty: spiraling ear canals lined with teeth, eyeballs puckered out of lips, tongues protruding out of nostrils. As the pseudopod tightens around the rock, the orifices dilate, and several bony child hands unfold from and stretch out, groping at the air. Beside this first tentacle, another, skinnier and toothier, cranes out of the water and flops onto the dragon, snaking forward, exploring beyond the first. The rat snatches up its paddle spear and presses close beside me. The crab, unafraid of this new addition to the party, scuttles over and rubs up against it.

Skully summarizes the situation most succinctly—*"Mmmeat"*—although either word from its limited vocabulary would've been appropriate.

Ratty extends its staff out towards the crab, scoops it up with the cactus paddle, reels it back in, and sets it aside.

"Dragon!" I shout through the mask, grabbing ahold of my spear and aiming it at the approaching tentacle. "Move! We're under attack!"

"I'm not fully rested yet," the dragon replies, voice rumbling up through our legs.

I jab at the feeler, catching one of its hands. Two fingers come off in a jet of dark blood. Rancid airstreams puff out of the sensory orifices as it recoils, flinging red globules into the air and onto the dragon's dorsum, where they soon bubble and sizzle, filling the air with the reek of burnt blood.

The rat whacks the other tentacle, which withdraws in a similarly unsettling symphony of sound and odor. Another has oozed up behind Ratty and Skully, wreathing around its paw. The rodent spins and stabs down—gushing blood, abattoir squeals—but this one is more tenacious, tightening its hold like a boa constrictor. The rat stabs again and again.

I rush into the blood spray, drive the spear clean through and wrench it apart.

RIIPPPPP!—the pseudopod severs, the stump hosing us down with blood as it retracts back into the water.

"Dragon!" I scream, wiping the mess off my face. "Get us out of here!"

Several more tentacles lash out of the water and onto the side of the dragon with the same fishy splat, then begin to wind and flop towards us. We retreat towards amidships, only to find five more worming in from port.

"I just need to nap a little bit longer," the dragon says.

I stab at the knot of pseudopods, drenching us and the dragon's dorsum with more blood. I retch at the smell of caramelized metal. "Get us out of here now, and I'll feed you."

"I'm sorry. What did you say? It's hard to hear you clearly over all that racket."

Tentacles stream in now from all angles, filling the sky, twenty, thirty, more, each its own unique freak-show interpretation of how a living thing might look.

"Get us out of here, and I'll feed you."

The dragon chuckles. "Very well."

At that, it raises its tail out of the water, whipping it towards the port and starboard sides and in seconds clearing away the tentacles like weeds.

And we jet off.

The dragon planes over the waves for some time, bringing us closer still to the dendritic island and the end of daylight. The clouds creep ever closer, obscuring more and more of the sky, soon leaving us all in an oppressive gray with the faint glow of magma shining up through the dragon's broken, rocky flesh, the western horizon a murky band of orange. The rat and I crawl around the dragon boat as it skims over and cuts through the choppy waters, securing the bags of supplies and readying our oars, knowing that the crucial moment is upon us. The dragon has confirmed the blind spot in its knowledge of Psyche.

"Well, I've brought you two to safety," the dragon announces, coasting to a drift and spitting water out of its mouth. "Now it's time to uphold your end of the bargain."

A fine mist clings to the surface of the water, barely lapping over the sides of the dragon. We approach the bow, the rat on all fours behind me, dragging the supplies behind it with a tow rope, the masochistic crab perched on its back, tattooing the nervous rhythm of its enthusiasm. I grip the spear tightly in both hands, fang pointed towards that big vein running along the dragon spine.

"What are you doing, rat? I don't believe you were invited to approach," the dragon chides, tone bedecked in the full regalia of arrogance.

"We've come to make a deal with you," I say.

"The deal was I swim you to safety and you feed me. I'm waiting for you to uphold your end of the bargain before any more deals are made. If you don't give me what I want, then we float here until we're all dead."

"I can't feed you here." I brace myself against hot rock. "We're too far from the mountains. Maybe at the islands I'll be able to. So what do you say? Take us there, and we'll see."

Then it capsizes.

The force of the roll flings the rat and crab into the air, sacks of food and all. On the other hand, my hold is more tenacious, legs locked into a crevice and body braced against one of the lumpy boulders. Thus, I'm thrown against the rock, the violent, unexpected motion of the roll knocking the spear out of my grasp.

The world inverts: black and blue.

I struggle to swim away from the dragon, but my legs are stuck, the heat of the beast scalding my feet through the thin fabric of my shoes.

Upside down, sinuses screaming as the saltwater floods through the seams of the mask, I stretch up, tugging at my left leg, then the right, then the left again, panicking with indecision about which foot should go first. Out of the corner of my eye, I glimpse the spear floating beneath the silvery surface sheen, twist and strain towards it, but am a second too late, centimeters too far as it slips past my fingertips and floats on to the surface. In that moment I see above me (below me?) the mass of spirits churning and bubbling out of the depths, awakened to my presence in the water, my Earth-rich consciousness a beacon. Twisting cords of blood vessel and flesh, gnashing teeth, clawing hand-things, over-elbowed appendages, strain up, down, towards me. I bend towards my feet, wriggle, kick madly, and manage to yank the left free, leaving behind the sneaker in the rocky dorsum.

Suddenly the water churns and rushes, a bubble wind whipping around me. The dragon completes its roll.

Topside.

I collapse against the dripping, sizzling stone, jerk down the high-collared mask, and gasp for air, forgetting for the moment my trapped right foot. As I stand, burning the sole of my left foot to get my bearings and see if I can spot the rat or spear, the dragon speaks:

"Having fun? How about another dip?"

"Fuck you," I shout back.

"Feed me, and all this ends."

"I can't, you dumb mother—"

It keels over again.

Again my body slams into the rocky protrusion. A hot flash of pain, a burst of heat in my mouth—I hang upside down arms spread wide, dazed by the blow, a strange peace washing over me. The biospiritual-mass pulses above—sky of life, billions of milky eyes watching from the wavering darkness. Pseudopods roil over and twist around one another to reach for me, the deformed claws and paws testing my skin, beginning to encircle my fingers: a parodic *Creation of Adam.* Below me in the rest of the universe, the setting sun transubstantiates the sea into orange alien blood. Transfixed this way, I step outside of time, forget the trapped foot, the spear, the rat, Psyche, just stare into the creature with the thousand welcoming arms.

The dragon rolls upright. I jerk sideways, then rag-doll back onto the rock, vomiting seawater. A severed, twitching tentacle, spurting blood, ripped from its host by the ferocity of the dragon's roll, entwines my right hand. I fling it from me, shuddering, and vomit again.

"Jing! Jing!" floats in a distant voice from the tail of the dragon.

A wooden clattering nearby.

I look over, see the spear, its fang tip glistening, reach out and grab a hold of it, hands clutching slowly and tightly, senses and focus sharpening. Everything centers around this weapon, what I must do. I press my body back against the rock outcropping, rip my right foot free, and reposition the spear, waiting, bearing the searing pain in my naked left foot, tears blurring my sole eye.

This time, when the roll comes, I'm prepared. I feel the tension running down the spine of the dragon, the precursor of movement, and in that instant, power surges through me. I stab the hooked fang into the neck, forcing the spear point down deep as it will go. Magma jets out as the dragon rolls, and now, my legs free, I tumble off its body into the water, diving down towards the submerged Argus and the forest of pseudopods. There I tread water, staring back up at the churning bubbles and magma dappled in the last rays of the setting sun. The blood continues to flood out, coagulating in wide helixes of cooled magma, the dragon twisting and writhing, straining to extract the spear from its back with its ineffectually short limbs or trying to bite it out but unable to twist its spine around enough to do so. Its tail finally whips around and snaps the bamboo in two, unleashing an even greater surge of blood.

I swim out of range of its fiery death field, surfacing several yards from the rat, who's keeping itself afloat atop a sack of bedding. We tread water for several minutes as fire explodes out of the wriggling volcano, the water heaving with the thrashes of the screaming dragon.

Out of the turbid waters, pieces of floating debris bob to the surface.

Little islands of rock.

Blood rafts.

As the fire of the dragon dies and the squirming clew grows more emboldened, we swim towards a nearby chunk of rocky gore, the rat still biting onto a leaf rope towing a floating mass of petal bedding and fruit. I spot the fangless half of my spear floating on the water's surface as we near the raft, veer off course, snatch it up and clamp down on it with my teeth, and swim back double-time. Though solid, the rock is still stinging hot to the touch. Nevertheless, the rat scrabbles aboard with its claws and then assists me up using its bamboo oar.

The dragon's writhing has ceased, discs and curls of its coagulated blood bobbing over the surface. It just floats there, streaks and discs of its coagulated blood bobbling over the surface like black drift ice, barely visible through the steam- and smoke-thickened mist. Choking fires spot the death field, but even in their combined light, the dragon is nothing more than a dark obscurity. I don't understand how I could have managed such a coup-de-grace, even with all the years of exercise and practice drumming. Strange. I remember having the same thought when I'd attacked the snake so many days ago.

By now the pseudopods have honed in on our make-shift raft, popping out of the mist and flailing about with mind-drunk passion. The rat punts off several of these, angling our boat through the thicket, while I whack the appendages, swinging my half-oar like a baseball bat.

As we shout out commands to each other and navigate out of the fleshy tangle of limbs, there's a familiar clicking. Seconds later the masochistic crab scrambles across a skein of tentacles and leaps onto the raft.

The two of us row madly now, taking frequent pauses to beat this feeler or propel the raft away from that one. After several minutes, we have maneuvered out of the largest cluster of them and spend more time rowing and less time struggling free of entanglements. Soon we have made open waters, heading at a good clip towards the island.

We row for several hours more before drifting in the dark, unsure of the direction.

"The water is gone, of course," Ratty says glumly, emptying the seawater out of the various cactus arms it had managed to salvage.

As if waiting for the word, a drop of water plops on the edge of its snout, and it wrinkles its nose at the rich, mineral aroma, wriggling its whiskers. Then Ratty laughs, "Rain!" while Skully turns its hollowed eyes this way and that in confusion. The crab scurries back and forth between the two of us, uncertain whose level of excitement is greater.

We set up the cactus arms to collect the rain as it begins to fall, light and pattering at first and then crescendoing to a drenching downpour so fierce the water seems to be falling from below as well as above. We crane our necks and drink our fill, until both of us and the cactus arms are brimming.

"How auspicious!" Ratty exclaims over the roar of the rain, settling back down on its side of the slick raft. It has removed its costume by now and returned the petals to the pile of supplies. I, too, have removed the mask and glove, and for the first time realize that the rat's fetid odor has completely dissipated, leaving the healthy scent of natural, animal oils. "Which reminds us, Jing," it calls out, "during our trip we may have thought up a solution to your problem of leaving Psyche without a spirit animal to sustain you. It was so silly of us not to think of it sooner, right in front of our noses this whole time. It's the—"

At that moment the raft jostles. A crack.

"Oh!" Ratty shouts.

Startled, I turn and see in the lowlight the rat lying prone, heads looking up at me, Skully's jaw broken and dangling off.

"Oh no," Ratty says with such quiet reserve I almost fail to notice the three shadowy pseudopods that have knotted around its leg and tail.

I leap forward, grabbing at its forelimb. "Ratty!"

The rat slides backwards several feet, claws catching a hold of a fissure in the rock, long nails splintering and popping off. Our vessel begins to tip.

"Oh my," Ratty says in disbelief.

I lunge again, now nearly falling towards it with the upheaval of the boat. My hand closes on rain, the rat vanished into the misty water with a flat splash, the raft rocking aright and bashing me in the face.

I dive in after it, down towards a rising trail of bubbles. Deeper and deeper, I kick and cut through the thick water.

Deeper.

The trail of bubbles vanishes, and I turn frantically, searching this way and that, praying for some trace in the blackness.

There is no underwater forest of pseudopods.

No eyeballs or shifting flesh.

There is no rat.

The rain has slackened, the night air charged, fresh.

After searching, drifting for hours, crying out and yelling till hoarse, I had at last continued on, rowing tentatively at first but then picking up speed when I'd seen a tenebrous snake coiling beneath the surface of the mist. The masochistic crab, disconcerted by my depressed spirits, curls up on top of the perfumed comfort of the light-and-dark bedding. Part of me feels guilty for leaving, feels that I hadn't searched long enough and that perhaps, after all, my escape from the creature could only have been possible with the rat's sacrifice.

As they had on previous nights, the islands light up, faintly and from within, a shifting light, seeping out of the cracks in a muted, prismatic glow. Beyond the closest island, in the foggy distance the others glow as well, maybe a hundred of the things—an alien cityscape, stalks of electric brains.

What does this mean for Henry? I wonder. Had the rat seen this coming?

These questions and doubts revolve around in my mind as I close in on the island. Too dark to make out any of the structural details, at times I can spot creatures aflight, tiny specks darting in and out of the gloomy lights of the upper branches of the structure, flashing.

Stranger still is the sound of the wind wailing across the island—a loud, low moan, shifting in pitch with curious overlapping harmonics, like a chorale played half-speed on a turntable.

Late in the night the raft jolts to a stop against the rocky shore.

I disembark, groping about the slick, dark rocks, clamber up a good height from the waves, and set up camp on the wet ground, laying out a thick roll of petals. After setting the emptied cactus arms upright to collect more rain, I eat a few cold, wet mushrooms. Better forego eating the crab. Can't be sure if a fire would attract the attention of whatever monsters might live on this island. While I eat, the masochistic crab clicks about in the darkness before finally settling down close beside me, as if expecting a pet—or maybe a smack.

Meal finished, I crawl into my sleeping bag tent. The crab prods at the material and even manages to poke a leg through one of the seams, but I knock it back, keeping it outside.

The rain picks back up as I lie in the dark, propping up the petals with bits of broken bamboo, trying to ignore the scratches at the flap. I spend several minutes working on igniting my lighter, which, in my water-logged purse had been potentially ruined during the sea battle. Finally, a flame catches, and I breathe out a sigh of relief. The tent petals ripple and dance in the subtle wave of heat emanating from the small flame. This brief joy excites the crab, who begins to poke with greater ferocity until I'm able to calm back down, and the crab at last skitters off. My mind lingers on the rat, on all it had done for me. Pressure swells behind my eye—and behind the red spider lily. The emotion stirs something in me, and before it seizes my consciousness, I realize what is coming, unexpected but welcome:

CHAPTER 16

At the meds station, Jing collects a single green Klonopin and swallows it on her way to the stairwell. She carries the Jung biography with her, eager to finish the few remaining chapters. Lighting up a cigarette and settling into the Oriel window, she gazes out for a few minutes at the skeletal elder tree rising out of the snow-drowned courtyard, the sky gray, expectant.

She disappears into the book for a time, until the door at the top of the stairwell opens, and Murai in his pressed white shirt and skinny black tie enters.

"We are both of us late," he says, descending. Everything about him is neat, even his Jesus hair and graying beard. "I am, uh, sitting in on group therapy today to give Dr. Lindgren feedback."

As he descends, she recalls the scene from two days ago, another gathering of the treatment team in the stuffy meeting room with its lack of windows, spare furnishing, and buzzing fluorescent overheads loaded with colonies of the insect dead—the inconspicuous bottleneck of Glenbrook. Goldfield, Waters, Billie, and Devon (her discharge coordinator) were all there, waiting about ten minutes before Murai finally arrived, free of alien plant growth.

Murai apologized profusely as he handed out copies of Jing's brain scans to everyone and announced "an absence of anomalies." Following this, he had settled back into one of the chairs around the seminar-style arrangement of tables, sipped his tea and guided everyone over a number of pages of graphed squiggles.

"These are the EEGs I recorded the day of our interview, Ms. Elwood. I apologize for the delay, but it does take some time to analyze and reanalyze the data, and I am currently without research assistants"—he shot Goldfield a look—"but anyway, I think I now have a clear-cut profile of your seizures—if everyone would turn to page fourteen—activity seems to begin in the occipital lobe (a complex partial seizure), which then spreads— flip over one page—into the rest of the brain (a generalized seizure). Now, from my perspective during our interview (during stage one of the attack), I saw what resembled the negative symptoms of a schizophrenic patient: bizarre posture, blunted affect and speech, almost as if you were frightened of disturbing something in the room with us. It was similar"—he turned towards Goldfield, one hand out in preemptive defense and the other stroking his beard—"at least based on the notes you gave me, Dr. Goldfield—to what Dr. Goldfield saw when you first arrived at Glenbrook."

Goldfield had nodded, stony eyes locked onto the graphs. She had grown quiet ever since Murai entered the room.

"Now, Ms. Elwood, I do not know if you remember much about what happened before the seizure, do you?"

Jing had put down the handout. "I... guess it was a seizure aura?"

"This is what I thought. It must have been an intense aura to elicit the kind of behavior we have observed. Would you tell us about it?"

She grew uncomfortable from all the eyes turned on her. "Does it really matter?"

He had nodded. "I wouldn't ask, otherwise. The aura can tell us more about the seed of the attack or the method of how activity spreads and can help support the findings of the EEG, which are more reliable for telling us *when* activity starts, not *where*."

"It was mostly visual"—ghost click—"but also, I suppose, auditory."

"Okay. Start with the visual content. Do you want to, uh, describe it a little more clearly?"

Jing had adjusted her posture, glancing around at the others. All eyes intent on her. "It was focused on you," she had said, voice hushed. "There were plants… growing out of you. Bamboo, or something that resembled it. That's about it. It was horrifying."

Murai had nodded. "Bamboo… right. I remember now you saying that word. Have you seen anything like that since?"

Her heart had skipped a beat. "No."

Murai wince-smiled, an expression she would analyze over and over again in her mind. "Okay, now you said there was also sound, which seems to correspond to the seizure's path. Next in line after the occipital lobes were the temporal lobes, and then it was wildfire from there. That would have been when you lost consciousness." He had stopped abruptly and taken a sip of tea.

Everyone had watched him.

"Is that it?" Waters had asked, flipping over the handout to see if there were more graphs or a more thorough interpretation of the findings.

"Did you want something more? The PET-CT scans are clean. The experience and intensity of the aura account for the psychotic symptoms—her negative symptoms a result of simple terror. It's likely that her antipsychotic meds were lowering the seizure threshold, ironically increasing the prevalence of the intermittent psychotic episodes. I suggest we wean Ms. Elwood off all her other meds, get the seizures under control, and with that, all else will fall." He adjusted his glasses.

Jing had pulled out her cigarettes, thinking that it was a tidy solution… except that it did not take into account everything… but she couldn't fault Murai for that; he'd been working with incomplete information. When she had looked up from lighting her smoke with Waters' lighter, Murai had been staring intently at her, then winked. There was nothing lascivious in the look but, rather, comically exaggerated.

"Are you satisfied with that explanation, Ms.

Elwood?"

Jing had nodded but was careful in her phrasing for Dr. Goldfield's sake. "Maybe we can try it out, focusing just on the seizures. If no psychotic symptoms return, I should be good, right?"

Silent assent had breezed around the table.

"In that case," Dr. Goldfield had said, speaking for the first time since Murai had entered, "I think it's time we move on to the second item of the agenda."

All eyes had turned back to Jing.

Now, as she watches Murai approach and stop on the landing, she says, "I think I'm going to pass today."

"I understand."

"I don't believe I've ever seen you in this part of Glenbrook. I thought maybe you'd been banned or something."

"The ban was temporarily lifted for good behavior. I assumed you wouldn't be attending group and so had Billie direct me to your haunt." He brightens, cocking his head to the side and clapping his hands together. "Very nice spot." Murai leans over to see the view of the courtyard, invading her space, and then takes out an unopened pack of Marlboros, fingers open the cellophane without using the tear strip, and pinches out a cigarette, examining it before putting it between his lips, his movements as sure as if he were attempting to crack open a puzzle box. "Perhaps I can be even a little later arriving to group."

She lights it for him, missing the tip and then adjusting. "Didn't know you smoked."

"I don't." He coughs, tasting the smoke and licking his lips unpleasantly. "You sure you don't want to say your goodbyes to the group? Much more efficient that way."

"Not really. I'd prefer to leave without a fuss. Thank you, by the way. I feel like you've given me the power to walk through walls."

"Well, we still don't know if I'm right, but we have

managed to solve your biggest problem—going home."
He approximates a drag on the Marlboro.

The two lapse into silence, Jing smoking, Murai
puffing and coughing. Throughout, the doctor studies
her, and, discomforted by his gaze, she turns to look out
the window. When she looks back, she finds him several
inches from her, moving a pen in the periphery of her
left eye.

She flinches back against the window. "What the
fuck are you doing?"

"Your eye is still giving you trouble." He backs up,
unoffended, returning the pen to his shirt pocket.

"How?—you know?" she stammers.

"Before our interview, when you were filling out the
various tests, I noticed you doing something odd with
your head, cocking it to the side like so." He demonstrates—a movement, she realizes now, that she has
seen him performing numerous times at the treatment
team meeting—along with the meaningful winking. He
must have been attempting to see things from her perspective. "At the time I put it down to an unusual foible.
Afterwards, during the interview, yet again I noticed you
had trouble when you were lighting your cigarette,
burning the shaft first and then accommodating by
repositioning the lighter down toward the tip of the
cigarette. I noticed it again two days ago. Just now when
you lit my cigarette, you were very careful in how you
moved the flame, but you still didn't quite get it right on
the nose. I find this highly unusual for someone who
smokes as much as you seem to—which you should
stop, by the way. These observations suggested to me an
issue with biscopic vision. Since we were finally alone
today, I could not resist the temptation to test my
hypothesis that you are blind in the left eye."

"You're a... sly motherfucker," she laughs, at a
complete loss.

He frowns, putting out the cigarette and setting the
Marlboros on the sill. "Okay, enough smoking for me.

Not your brand, I see, but you may keep these. Tell me: how long have you been blind?"

"Over a month. It happened after one of the attacks."

"Just the left eye?"

She nods.

"Constant or intermittent?"

"Constant."

"You don't seem alarmed by it."

"I'm not. Well, at first I was terrified, but then it just sort of"—her hands sculpt a bursting bubble—"went out of mind, likes it's not me, like it's not my concern but someone I'm watching. *This* isn't me. *This* can't be happening to me." Jing pauses, watching him, the cigarette on her lips, then says, "Lindgren mentioned something called delusional blindness several weeks ago, but I don't have anything like the weird delusions she mentioned; I just can't see out of it. I don't think the FBI stole my eye and implanted a tracking device there or that it's an alien living in my eye socket or a demonic possession. I just can't see out of it. You're not changing your mind, are you? You're not going to keep me here?"

"No, no, no"—he shakes his head—"it may now call into question my diagnosis, however. A shame: it was such an elegant explanation. And I would rule out delusional blindness. Your bloodwork, brain scans, and ophthalmic exam indicate nothing wrong with the eye itself or your visual processing, so we can probably also rule out any physiological problem. But more tests will be needed. Your attitude towards it, the way you hide it from people, is also telling. I suspect we are dealing with a conversion disorder."

"Conversion disorder?"

"Yes. That is where a patient reports physical symptoms but without any signs of underlying disease. It is psychogenic—essentially, the problem is produced by your mind, potentially due to trauma. When you are unable to deal with your emotions in an effective way, the unconscious takes care of it for you. Typically these manifest as pain, but I have come across cases like yours as well—blindness, paralysis. In fact," he rubs his chin, "this may be the simplest explanation of all: all your symptoms are psychogenic."

"Meaning they're not real?" Jing knits her brow, offended, as if he had just accused her of lying.

"Oh, they're very much real. No one would deny you've been having seizures and that they are a serious problem we need to solve. Same for the amenorrhea and everything else. But they may be somatic manifestations of a deeper-seated issue, one that seems to be worsening during your stay in our lovely institution. Now, I admit I tend to try to avoid overmedicating my patients—one of the main points of contention between Dr. Goldfield and myself—but in light of new evidence we might want to experiment with other regimens that have proven effect-ive in treating these types of disorders. Also, you should probably stay in psychotherapy, maybe with Dr. Goldfield, or someone else, if you prefer—outpatient, of course."

Jing clicks her tongue stud without speaking.

"What does that noise mean? You're unsatisfied?"

"It's just..."

"Just what, Ms. Elwood?"

"My mother."

"Yes, I read her file. Right before our interview, in fact."

"So you know about her diagnosis?"

"I don't see how it pertains to you. Your mother is your mother. You're you."

"Thanks for clearing that up, but... I mean—"

"A genetic component to schizophrenia—you're afraid you've inherited your mother's disorder," he says, unimpressed by the explanation.

Jing nods, ashes.

"It's possible, yes. You're at higher risk of developing a psychosis than someone without a family history of schizophrenia. However, it's also true that you are much more likely to develop a mental disorder generally speaking (anxiety, depression, etc.) than a psychotic one specific-ally. So if we want to bring your mother's disorder into the equation, it still lends greater support to the conversion disorder theory than the schizo-affective one, at least just speaking from a statistical standpoint."

"Oh." They stare at each other awkwardly for a few moments. "Well, thanks. Again."

"No need to thank me. We haven't concluded yet. You've certainly been an interesting case so far, but most doctors don't enjoy playing 'find the symptom' with their patients. Now, I'm extremely late," he adds, checking his watch and patting his pockets as if he did not want to leave something behind. "I hope we never meet again. Then I will have done a really proper job."

"Bye." She suppresses a smile, watching him go and staring at the door at the foot of the stairs long after it has shut. She turns back to Jung and finishes reading the last chapter.

While waiting for group therapy to end, Jing descends to the first floor and takes one of her typically meandering paths through Glenbrook—down empty passages, past abandoned offices, circling around the snow-clogged courtyards, emerging beneath the double-helix staircase in the rotunda. There, before her, is the door secreted away in the back of the staircase, solidly chained, splintered from having been wrenched open. A chill air fingers through the narrow line where the cracked door would not fit back into the frame, seeming to claw at her neck and quaking up a range of goose-bumps.

The muddled echoes of Muzak come to her attention, and she listens carefully, at last recognizing through the acoustic distortion *The Brandenburg Concertos*. First movement of the first concerto. Just an hour or so ago at lunch (in the now unremarkably desolate cafeteria), the Muzak had been stuck on the new-normal loop of Christmas oldies.

Why have they suddenly switched it back?

"Jing."

She jumps and whirls around to find Waters, clipboard in hand, a quizzical expression on his face.

"Sorry. Didn't mean to startle you. Group isn't out yet, is it?"

"No, I'm just wandering around. Somehow ended up here. I still haven't quite figured out the layout of this place."

He nods, chuckling. This could be fodder for the clipboard—but no.

"Hard to believe, isn't it?" she says as he steps past her to examine the damage to the door and frame, his own handiwork.

"Sadly, no." He fails to explicate, and she doesn't ask. "You know, I couldn't help but noticing it's been a little quiet around here—over the past week."

"Yeah, I... the night before, I had a kind of run-in with Henry in north rec. I know I shouldn't be bothered by what he said, but..."

"Not a fan of *Pictures*?"

"You could say that. He said the piano resounded through all of Glenbrook, and he somehow managed to knead that into his conspiracy theory. I... I guess I didn't want to cause any other—"

"It's not true." Waters shakes his head.

"What?"

"You can barely hear the piano from my office, and we're—what—two doors down. The sound certainly doesn't travel farther than the rotunda."

"Really?"

"Henry was hallucinating."

She finds only some small reassurance in this, unwilling to fully accept what he has said. Sound *does* carry throughout Glenbrook, music especially. She'd heard it from as far off as the infirmary, her room, even the ropes course in the woods. And then the Muzak in here… but it's quiet now.

"So are you all ready?" he interrupts her train of thought.

"More or less. Just a few goodbyes to say, papers to sign."

"Would you mind walking with me to my office?"

She arches her eyebrows. "Sure."

"Just got a small favor to ask. Only take a second."

Intrigued, she follows him back into the north wing, where he and the other techs share an office. There's a small window looking into a courtyard she's never seen before, a number of cubicles, both occupied and un-occupied, his own wallpapered with a jumble of film and band posters. He sorts through a stack of CDs and pulls one out. Hands it to her, with a pen.

"Been meaning to ask you to do this ever since you came here."

She stares at the objects in his hands for a few moments, uncomprehending, until he tilts the CD and the glare vanishes from the cover, revealing the familiar artwork, designed by one of the staple artists from the Compound. She opens the CD, pulls out and unfolds the insert, admiring the cartoonish art, a sprawling triptych of an apocalyptic Detroit overrun by alien jungle, with jarring shifts in perspective at once within and outside of the city, the flora and the artificial melding together, climaxing in the nucleus with the Compound, a four-story building of freestanding, tunnel-linked orbs. In the credits section are artfully out-of-focus photographs of Bower, Penn, and Jing, highlighted and defaced with graffiti and miniscule newspaper clippings. She's surprised to find Bower and Penn's signatures already in place next to their photos.

"Just the name is fine," Waters adds, noting her hesitation with the pen. "Nothing sentimental."

Name in place beside the photo, she folds up the insert and tucks it back inside, looking at the cover once more. *Autoscope 1.* A small sticker in the corner reads: "Featuring the Top 40 hit 'The Pineal Eye.'"

Though they're alone, Waters lowers his voice. "I was there... the last show ya'll played. Amazing."

"I know"—she smiles with a touch of guilt at not having recognized him sooner—"I mean not that it was amazing, but... I remember seeing you there." Vaguely, anyway, smeared across the audience.

"Goldfield, Murai, no one else knows, of course. Otherwise, I wouldn't've been put on your treatment team. In fact, I might lose my job here if certain people knew I'd partied at the Compound before." He takes back the CD and pen. "Thanks for this. We're gonna miss you around here."

A moment of hesitation before she turns to go, then she places her hand on Waters' arm, stands on her tiptoes, and kisses him lightly on the cheek. His body tenses as she does so, mind no doubt cycling through the many rules in *The Glenbrook Bible* being broken.

The rest of their goodbye is silent.

Once group ends the patients recess for alternative—Dr. Conway's flower essence therapy—and Jing slips into rec north. Outside, snow spindrifts dance over the ground, occasionally creating brilliant glares in the room. She walks to the piano, sets her book down, and scoots onto the bench. As her fingers touch the keys, as the opening melody unfolds from her, everything around her suddenly takes on an intricate delicacy. Toy-like, tiny, clever. A pseudo-real veneer. When she reaches "The Catacombs," the section of the piece Henry had been playing last week, the veneer of the present washes away. She recalls his strange accusations, all the events that had followed, and those three clear words she had found in Henry's mostly illegible notes...

Pictures concludes flawlessly, but there had been moments where she had only just escaped making an error—a lucky performance. If she were enrolled in school, she could be ready for her thesis recital in a week. During the performance, when she was lost in music and memory, Jing had barely registered the door to rec north opening and shutting, too engrossed to turn. Still, she is not surprised to hear Penn's musing alto.

"That was the piece you were working on back in college, right?"

Jing swivels on the piano bench. Penn is standing near the French window, studying the wall of patient art.

She rises and stretches. "The same."

"I remember how excited you were when you started learning it. Invited me to the recital before you'd even begun practicing, and I said—"

"'I don't know if I could endure it,'" Jing laughs humorlessly, joining Penn at the wall. Catherine's depiction of a vampire alien invasion explodes darkly before them. "Never been more furious in my life."

"Well, it sounded amazing."

"Thanks. I forgive"—she begins to elbow Penn, then stops with sudden realization, turning towards her—"are you *okay*?"

Penn nods.

She's dressed more colorfully than usual. White coat and black jeans, a bright yellow scarf and beanie. What's more, she shows none of the usual symptoms of sensory overload from listening to music—nausea, fever, shuddering, cold sweats—but even so, she looks much thinner than before, pale, the liveliness of her emerald eyes deadened. "Sort of."

"It didn't..." Jing makes a sweeping gesture before her eyes, uncertain exactly how to mime what Penn must experience when hearing music.

"No. Jingy, something weird has happened to me. After our fight, my synesthesia..."

Hearing the first tremble of emotion, Jing puts her arms around her friend, pulling the taller girl's face down into her neck. Hoping to quash whatever pain is there, she gives Penn a firm squeeze, a loose strand of lavender-scented hair tickling her nose.

"I thought you had that stupid high-five rule," Penn says, muted voice alive against her skin.

"Not the first time it's been broken today. Tell me what happened."

"It's gone. I can't explain it. It was like I woke up with someone else's brain inside me. It was so frightening. I thought I was having a nightmare or something. And I couldn't tell anyone, couldn't bear to let the idea spread around, as if doing so might make it real. It used to take me so long to get someone to believe how I saw things, and even then I always noticed a shade of doubt—with you, with everyone—and now to say I can't see sounds that way anymore... I started thinking so many crazy things: maybe I was misremembering that I'd had the synesthesia or maybe I was hallucinating what it was like to be normal or maybe it *had* all been a lie, a lie I'd told myself over and over until I believed it. Those musical landscapes, they were so precious to me. They *were* me, Jingy."

Jing feels hot tears against her skin, the brushing of eyelashes flittering insect wings.

"Maybe it was some delayed reaction to Bower's death and the end of Autoscope and all the changes that came with it. I don't know. I called Dr. Singh—he's the psychologist I used to see in California—and he said this happens to some synesthetes. The brain is always growing and changing. I guess you know all about that now, from being here."

Jing doesn't know how to respond. Just hugs her tighter.

"I started seeing someone," Penn continues.

Jing inhales sharply.

"I mean a therapist."

"Really?"

"I know it sounds stupid. When I was a kid I hated my synesthesia. I was constantly made fun of. Every night, when I said my prayers, the final thing I asked for wasn't for God to watch over my parents or grand-parents or little brother—it was to be able to hear music without seeing things. It wasn't until college when I started becoming comfortable with it, and now I'm seeing a therapist because there's *nothing* wrong with me. How insane is that?"

"It's okay. I get it. Believe me. I get it."

"I thought I had something, a gift, something that wouldn't decay with the rest of me, but it's gone. The world looks and sounds so strange now, like I lost an eye or an ear."

"I'm sorry."

Penn detaches herself and holds Jing at arm's length. Her cheeks dimple. "No, I'm sorry. You don't need this now. With everything that's happened." She wipes her eyes. "This should be a happy day for you. We'll make it a good one."

Jing takes her arm and leads her to the door.

Penn smiles. "I have a surprise for you, by the way."

"A surprise, huh?"

She glances back towards the tree. "A Christmas surprise, no less." The tiny reflections of light spangling her eyes revive something that had been absent a moment ago.

After Jing and Penn bring her suitcases down to admissions, Jing has a quick meeting with her discharge coordinator in a drab room tucked away in the mostly vacant admissions office suite. Goldfield is there, and they shake hands amiably. Then she collects her contraband—straight razor and morning star purse—and she and Penn bundle up and walk unaccompanied out of the front doors of Glenbrook, navigating down the slippery, icy suggestion of steps and a narrow path flanked by snow banks, leading around the side of the east wing to the parking lot.

The air bites.

Their boots crunch in the snow.

Over the expanse of the white lawn she can hear the woods, the shifting susurration of wind in the boughs, the way the frosted branches scrape together, piles of snow plopping to the ground—and Waters *was* wrong; the Muzak is still audible.

"Can you do something for me?" Penn says, former vulnerability gone from her voice. Thick snow has begun to construct crystal cities on her hat and shoulders. "Can you keep what I told you earlier between the two of us? Maybe it'll return, I'll wake up, it'll be like before."

"Okay. I won't say anything."

"Thanks."

They round the bend, the snow banks culminate in a mountain of snow at the corner of the parking lot. In the distance, the snowy humps of the Rota Wellness Village bungalows come into view.

"That's where they found him. Trying to escape," Jing tells Penn as they approach Penn's car.

Penn shakes her heads sadly, and they stare across the grounds together.

"After that first time I came to see you," Penn says, "I returned a few days later, paid Henry a visit."

Jing turns toward her, a little surprised. The two had not gotten along well back at the Compound—what with their widely conflicting musical philosophies.

"You know what we talked about?"

"William?"

"You. He had all these plans built up around you. It was both weird and touching. I had no idea how to respond, and honestly it felt like he could have been talking with anyone. He was whispering, glancing over his shoulder, saying how you had faked your illness to come and save him from the psychoengineers."

As she hears Penn speak, Jing's stomach tightens. That night a week ago, the moment she had learned Henry had gone missing, she dashed down through the dark hallways of the men's quarters, burst into his room, and tore open his mattress. By the time the nurses and techs had caught up with her, she had extracted his notes and explained that she knew how to find Henry—she just needed time and a book from her room—*The Mind of a Mnemonist.* It had taken hours, there were many pages of code, mostly nonsense, but she worked until sunup in an empty office near the cafeteria, at last discovering how the book cypher functioned—triplets of numbers indicating page, line, and letter. The message (whether sent by William or random luck or Henry writing to himself) was directing him to take one of the sealed-up service tunnels from the rotunda to the Rota Wellness Village, a quiet place, where he would be able to propel to the astral plane.

By then it was too late.

She had jimmied her way into the third floor of the east wing after Waters and another tech had discovered his body, and she had watched the police officers and medical examiner desecrating the snow, digging a tunnel through the snowdrift that had buried the entrance of the Rota Center's Town Hall. When they carried out the body bag, Henry's inflexible form poking against the snow-dusted black plastic, Jing averted her eyes, sick. He had frozen to death in the lotus position, a posture that made it impossible for him to be carried back through the narrow service tunnel entrance.

She turns away, trying not to imagine him meditating and convulsing in the cold, beard and glasses frosted, lips blue, Discman malfunctioning.

The girls throw Jing's suitcases into the back of Penn's vehicle—a new SUV, Jing does not fail to notice—and start down the long drive of Glenbrook Psychiatric, over an open white meadow, and through the half-mile of wintry woods, the snow in places banking up beyond the base of the evergreen foliage. Only when they turn onto the main road leading into downtown Detroit beneath the overcast sky, when the wind shifts and the snowfall churn freezes in a moment of uncertainty, does Jing see the alterations in the city skyline—the bizarre form lurking beyond the clouds—and she recalls again those words that she had read in the margins of the notes when she had been working on the code— "William's third-person—"

CHAPTER 17

The warm petals of the makeshift cocoon ripple around my body in the darkness, muting the exterior ambience. Needling me through the petals, the same heaviness weighs down on my body that I'd awoken to on the beach. I smack the mass off me, peel back the covering, letting in the cold air and full, unfiltered soundscape—waves lapping against rock, far off a dull knocking, the slackening patter of rain, the wraithlike moans and creaks of the island tree. I crawl out onto the slick rocks—black, opaline.

A flash of pain in my calf. I look back into the dark tent, expecting to find a vengeful crab pinching me, but see nothing in the gloomy interior. Igniting the lighter beside my bloodied leg, a sliver embedded in the petal glints.

The lost razor blade.

Pick it up carefully, examining it with a bitter smile. Must have landed in the pile of petals the rat had stored by the lean-to, then been tucked away when the sea journey preparations were being made. As I test its divisiveness with the pad of my index finger, the masochistic crab click-clacks back over.

I thrust the creature away with a bare foot, then notice all twelve limbs have regenerated, three of them fresh and delicate.

I turn to search through my supplies and find all of the fruits drained to pulpy flaps of skin. The mushrooms have gone missing. The crab has not just consumed enough to regenerate; it has ruined all the provisions. Last night I'd been so exhausted, I'd forgotten to hide the fruit from the crab.

"Dammit, you masochistic fucker." I reach for it, but when it cowers, shivering with excitement at its expected punishment, I check myself—not torturing it will constitute punishment enough.

I poke around the fruity ruin with a piece of bamboo, searching for anything salvageable, and only come up with three anicca nuts.

I tuck these into the seams of my suit and remember the dorberry and monkey brain I'd stuffed into my purse. I take out the former and bite into it as I brainstorm over how best to put the blade to use.

Maybe combine it with one of the broken bamboo canes, devising a short spear. I pick up various pieces of shattered wood, my mind wandering over the recent vision—Jing's release, Henry's death. Both of them had been experiencing musical hallucinations... hadn't Ratty said something about a connection between spirit-animal speech and music? Had our conversations driven Henry to his death?

I push the thought aside for now. Too late. Too late. Focus, Jing.

I insert the tang of the razor into the blue bamboo shaft. Need to secure it somehow. Need a pin of some sort to insert perpendicularly through the bamboo, crossing the hinge hole of the tang.

What do I have at my disposal? The metallic bits of my purse are all too thick, the keychain too flimsy...

I laugh—and click, reaching into my mouth with both hands and extract the tongue stud. First verifying the position of the tang's hinge hole within the shaft, I pound the pin through the wood with a rock from the rat's sack, with much finger smashing and cursing. It jams in there snug and secure, leaving just a bit of wobble, which I correct with a tight wrap of rope around the tip.

"What do you think, Crabby? You like it?"

I dig out a few more rocks from Ratty and Skully's collection. Beneath them in the sack, the half-rotted teeth nestle. I pull out the curiosities, studying each one in turn.

—William's third-person—

I set them aside. Take up the widest of the rocks to carefully hone the flat tip of the razor blade until it's nearly as sharp as the razor's edge.

When I finish the project, I hold in my hands a two-foot-long bamboo handle with several inches of blade poking out of the end. I practice swinging and stabbing with it.

The crab, responding to my pleasure, scurries up my back and perches on my shoulder, rubbing its pointy-armored crab legs against my face, claws nipping at my ear and spider lily and hair. I shove it off, and it starts preening itself against my shins appreciatively.

I stand and wander inland, rummaging around the shiny, black field—mesmerizing rock, pregnant with roiling nebulae.

—William's third-person—

Rubbish lurks in various crevices. Manmade: corroded plastics, rusted metal, soggy paper. I puzzle over these findings while sorting the flammable from the non. With a hodgepodge of plyboard shards and rotting cardboard and unidentifiable pulpy deformations, I return to camp and construct a small, temperamental fire in the shade of a rock over-hang. It spews a disproportionate amount of thick, eye-stinging smoke. To the crab's delight, I pin it down, rip off a couple of legs (taking no small pleasure in the act) and lay them over the fire.

While the little claws and feelers of the amputated legs shiver ecstatically in the smoky crackle, I examine the teeth and recall how easily the fang spear had sunk into the dragon's neck—a needle into warm butter—preternaturally easy. Ratty never mentioned anything special about snake fangs, but its knowledge of Psyche had its limits.

"Well, here goes."

I cup my hands around the teeth, rather difficult as

the canine and premolar are nearly as large as my hands. I shake them up and say, "Is my name Jing?"

I toss them. They clatter woodenly on the stone and freeze in a peculiar arrangement, all of them exposing their unrotten sides except for the molar, which presents a face of blackened verdigris.

"I guess that's a 'yes'? What do you say, Crabby?"

The crab, who had been sniffing its singed flesh on the fire, investigates and taps the molar.

I scoop up the teeth and ask another question: "Did the rat have two heads?"

I toss.

They clatter and freeze into the same arrangement.

"Hmm."

I try several more questions that should elicit yes answers, all with the same result.

I huddle down as a sharp, chill wind sweeps across the camp. "I'll be damned."

Of course, it might just be the case that the weight of the teeth causes them to land this way no matter what the question. Need to try a few that should be answered in the negative before I can be certain it's working.

Scoop up the teeth again. "Did the dog teach me about the Ancient Signs?"

Toss.

The teeth freeze in a new pattern. The monkey canine bares a ridge of mustard, and the goat premolar turns up bronzed Swiss cheese. The other two gleam white.

"Is the rat still alive?" I ask, continuing the test.

I toss.

Mustard and Swiss.

I slump, the teeth shattering any slight hope I'd been clinging to that the rat had escaped alive.

"The snake fang, did it have a special property similar to these teeth—a psychic conductor or something?"

A rotten molar. *Yes.*

"Was it you that helped me during the battle at sea?"

Yes. Every time I roll the teeth, they freeze as if an invisible hand were slamming down and fixing them in place.

"And again when I attacked the snake. You helped me then, too, right?"

Yes.

I turn to look out towards the water, imagining colossal insect ghosts drifting in the fog. I imagine how the scene must have looked—me standing on the dragon's neck, spear poised, flower fluttering in the breeze, sunset over the sea, massive invisible insect feelers guiding my arms—and shiver.

There are two main pieces of information I need to learn: first, how to get home; second, how to solve the issue of receiving Psychic sustenance after I've returned. "Umm, okay, is there a way back to Earth?"

Yes.

"Wonderful. So how do I return... How should I ask this?" I mutter to myself. "Uhh, do I return the same way that I came here?"

Yes.

So how did I come here? How to suss this out?

Start with what I already know. There was a show at the Compound, I'd gotten high on something afterwards, and sometime after that they found me by Bower's dead body. Hopelessly vague—but *is* that all I know? Something seems to be missing. Can feel it in the back of my mind, clawing its way out of the labyrinth. Another piece of information I'd heard. What is it? A word, a phrase, something that had bothered or confused me when I'd heard it earlier.

In the visions I overheard a number of conversations related to how Earth Jing came to arrive at Glenbrook: in group therapy, the interview with Murai, a one-on-one with Goldfield... also with Penn.

Penn. That was in the first vision, before I really knew anything about this place.

I recall it had been a confusing conversation at the

time.

What was it she'd said?

She'd asked me what Earth Jing remembered about the night of the show.

What else?

Memoryfish. That's what she'd said. *I* had mentioned memoryfish to *her* while I was intoxicated. That was why the term sounded so familiar when the rat told me about them. But how is that possible? How would I have mentioned them to Penn before having heard about them on Psyche?

Also, I'd given her something to keep safe. Something... I would need in order to return.

The realization makes my heart leap, my head tingle, as if I were levitating off of Psyche.

What did I give her?

I know what to ask. Impossible though it may be, I know what to ask.

"Do I need Earth Jing's help?"

Yes.

"She needs something, something I can only get to her through Penn, right?"

Yes.

I exhale, dizzied.

"Am I... in possession of that *thing* right now?"

Yes.

I turn my lip ring, and then see it there in my peripheral vision, encircling my left wrist—the unspeakable fruit.

A kind of poison, Ratty had said—but what if it had been wrong?

—William's third-person—

"Did Skully's ward travel to Psyche?"

Yes.

"Was it an unspeakable fruit that had brought him here?"

Yes.

"It was because Skully ate the fruit, correct?"

The answer is complex, an unfamiliar arrangement.

I frown, wondering what the response means.

"Does Earth Jing need this unspeakable fruit for me to return?" I ask, every nerve electric. Toss the teeth.

Yes.

I pause, not sure exactly how to voice my objections to this, suddenly feeling more lost than I have in all my time wandering around Psyche. The longer I spend talking with this bug, the more reality seems to be crumbling beneath my feet.

"Does she need to eat this?"

No.

"Do I need to eat this?"

No.

"What the fuck? Okay, umm, is it possible for me to give this to one of them—Earth Jing or Penn?"

Another complication of rot and clean.

"I'll take that as a maybe, I guess."

I stare at the teeth for a time, wondering how I should proceed. Eating the fruit seems to have no relation to traveling to Psyche. I examine it more carefully, wondering how else it could be used.

The crab legs, rich and smoky, smell ready. Turning away from the teeth, I pinch the legs off the fire with a struggle leaf, letting them cool on the rocks.

Then I stare back down at the last response. Don't know what else to ask.

I should work on the other problem, the issue about not receiving Psychic sustenance after I return to Earth. Let the other issue digest in the unconscious for a bit.

Again, start with the basic facts.

"Is my spirit animal dead?"

Yes.

No surprise there. Who was my spirit animal, anyway? I hadn't considered the issue until now, but it could be important. I was born the Year of the Ox...

"It was the first oasis I came to, wasn't it? That was my spirit animal's resting place. Right?"

Yes.

"Can I somehow bring it back from the dead?"

No.

What had Ratty been saying right before it was pulled under the water? *"It was right in front of our noses the whole time."*

"Did the rat solve my Psychic sustenance problem?"

Yes.

Again, a thrill runs through me.

"Do I need a new spirit animal?"

Yes.

"Was it supposed to be Skully?"

All blanks.

"What does that mean?" I repeat the question, toss the teeth again.

Blank.

"What the hell? Are you listening to me, eternity bug?"

Blank.

I keep trying, each question meeting with the same clean arrangement.

"Did I tire it out?" I ask Crabby.

Ratty mentioned this could happen. Maybe I should take a break, ask some questions later.

I collect the teeth and set them aside, then continue my meal, ruminating. I have answers now. Just need to figure out what they mean. Every now and then I ask the bug another question, resulting only in blanks—more frustrating than just the typical normal, random rolls I would get if there weren't some ethereal force shaping the patterns.

Finally, I shove them into my purse, frustrated.

By the end of the meal, the rain has abated, the fog withdrawn over the quiet sea and to the far corners of the island. The sun appears late in between a jagged rip in the clouds. Beneath the brightening sky, I study the layout of the island—barren, with sweeping black opal, sculpted like cupcake frosting into spiraling, curlicue-crowned cones and lacy rock domes. Beyond, Yggdrasil bursts into the heavens. Can make out the apex now and from this angle the functional shape is more apparent—a giant insect wing, the scales and membrane long ago rotted off, leaving only the sky-kissing venation. And all these "rocks?" Exoskeleton morphology in close-up. The only signs of activity are those tiny shapes circling the heights, darting in and out of the clouds, flashing in bursts of color when they catch the sunlight at propitious angles. The veins of the wing seem to have erupted in places, leaving gaping holes here and junk spilling out there: frameworks of metal and rust, rubber tubing and plastic paneling, splintered wood, rotted furniture, flights of stairs climbing sideways and upside-down and nowhere, exposed plumbing, dangling appliances. While the dumping yard element explains the presence of the trash I'd found before, it only pushes back the question of how such material came to clog up the veins of the wing in the first place.

Before I break camp, the sun vanishes once more. I floss with some cactus fiber and rinse out my mouth with rainwater collected in one of the cactus arms, then climb down to sea level, where the raft of congealed blood is trapped by the tide in a small inlet, knocking against the rock with the incoming waves. All of the puffballs have found their way into the water, and the crab seems especially intent on pointing out this fact.

I strip to the waist and shock my skin with a splash of cold water. As I gaze out over the fog-shrouded sea, the rain strikes up an encore, delicate and misty. I'm reminded of the lake after the funeral—the memory I'd experienced in the desert. I look down at the scar-rent, floricultural tattoo—and cry.

Through the hot tears, I feel them leaving me—Henry and Ratty, Bower and Ma. I'm back to where I was at the beginning of the Psyche odyssey. Alone and—

Crabby needles my foot.

I pick it up, wiping my eye and the flower. Not exactly alone.

I dress in a fresh assortment of petals, unknot my hair with the comb branch, slick it back out of my eyes, tie it together, and fix it in place with the comb. Then lipstick. Back at camp, I fix the bedroll and cactus arms to my purse. The ragged shoe I toss aside, and create booties out of some spare struggle petals. The snug material soothes the foot I'd burned yesterday. I tuck the short spear into a petal belt, and the crab and I begin our trek across the island.

Ready for war—or whatever it is we're heading towards.

Rainwater pools at the confluence of craggy protrusions and in deep rifts of the exoskeletal formations. The crab cannot help but plan its course right beneath my steps, hoping to be crushed and punished, so I am careful to kick it now and again to keep it both at a respectable distance and content with rejection. After a couple of hours of weaving through the rock garden, I realize the distance to the wing is much greater than I'd first imagined.

Lightning crackles. The banshee wind picks back up. The rain crescendos. Soon it's roaring down. The crab and I stop for lunch in an exoskeletal overhang; I try to eat the anicca nuts, but every time I crack one open, the crab swats it out of my hand, where it writhes into ashes. Eventually, I relent and rip off several legs and eat them raw, an experience I hope never to repeat. After the meal, I wait awhile, hoping the downpour will slacken, but no such luck. Eventually, I position the crab on my shoulders and we set off again. Hours and hours we trudge through the rain, constantly slipping or washing out on rivers of run-off.

At last we reach the base, where a slippery hazard of trash has piled up, and manage to squeeze into a twisty network of splintery, snagging passageways. Above, through a serendipitous vista, I mark our passage out of the rain and into the structure. The dark interior is expansive but similarly chaotic, illuminated by gloomy beams of light borne in on the rippling curtains of fog. Before us spans a gap about fifty meters across, lined with cords and pipes and crisscrossed with overturned catwalks and other time-anonymized, artificial miscellany, none of it assembled for the convenience of human passage—but haphazardly jumbled together. The drumming of the rain is deafening inside. Water gushes through the wing's sutures, bounding and branching down the stinking trash heaps towards the central gap.

I creep forward to get a look at what lies below, navigating over a slanted piece of crumbling concrete and mounting the trunk of a smashed car which extends grille-first out over the edge of the pit.

The crab pinches my neck, and I become aware of my pounding heart. I stop, looking around, wondering what it is that's bothering me.

It's the smell. Even with the rain and all the refuse, the place reeks of ammonia. But there's something more than that, something I can't quite put my finger on. I look down at my flower petal boots, at the rusted metal of the trunk, and my eyes scan up the car body.

Had I seen something?

Yes, there, in the shattered driver side mirror, reflecting back a murky version of me in the black armor with the floral eyepatch and leggy arthropod pressed against my head, a tiny image from this distance, but eye-catching with the brightness of the flower. Even more salient is the mass behind me, a modernist painting of a raincloud, an experiment of bright colors and form.

I turn slowly and see it there, looking past the crab legs on my shoulder and see it there, hanging from the eave above the shower stall I'd just crawled out of. The colorful mass flutters and slims into a stained glass sculpture. It shifts again, spreading outward.

Wings.

As they fan out, it reveals in better definition its long, segmented body. The wings flap, and, emitting a peculiar low-pitched whump, it flits over to a catwalk— closer, now a few yards away—rotating its body to make a careful study of me. Every inch of its glasslike exoskeleton technicolored, the creature has a delicate appearance, threatening at any moment to fly apart into thousands of flashing shards. Must be about seven- or eight-feet long, several long, pointed rostra lancing out of its head. Antennae, curling flagella, and bristly palps like deformed arms complicate its mouth, and countless legs protrude from its thorax. By the time it takes me to resolve these aspects of the creature, there's no doubt in my mind what it could be: the insect the dragon was so obsessed with, the colorful shadows in the Memory-lands—a memoryfish.

Hyperaware of the thrashing of the rain, the rush of the waterfalls, the groans of the giant structure, and the cold silence of this insect, I start to raise the long spear. The convoluted fan of antennae adjust as I move, seeming to triangulate the changing position of my weapon. Flagella unspool, lashing about its carapace-encased head. I freeze again, and the memoryfish stills.

The rain drums on.

I become aware of my shallow, panting breath; the moistness of my hands; a trickle of water running down and stinging my eye, blurring the scene. Blink it away with a few twitches.

Maybe it's distracting me while a second circles around from the back, or maybe its strategy is to make me think another is coming up from behind and then pounce when I turn to look, or maybe—

The masochistic crab begins preening itself against my hair, thrilled by the tension of my body.

The memoryfish launches towards me.

In the instant I have to react, I brace the spear and a bevy of whipping flagella fills my vision. There is a sickening crunch as the spear pierces through the insect's slender thorax and into its abdomen, but the end of the staff is not securely planted, and we fly back and roll several feet, jerking to a stop with the hulking mass crushing my body, and the crab sailing off into the gap.

The creature on top of me is motionless save the twitching of its flagella and sticky palps encircling my shoulders. A gag-inducing liquid, clear and spotted with opaque, geometric bits of gelatin, surprisingly hot, pumps out of it and onto my arms and chest. Its heft has me pinned against the hood of the car. My legs stretch out over the shattered windshield and crushed roof. I try to wriggle free, but as I do so the vehicle see-saws beneath us, tipping down. I freeze, and the car rocks back to equilibrium.

I glance over my right shoulder. My suspicions are true.

We're dangling over the gap. Fifty yards down, the trash and water vanish into shadow. The masochistic crab has latched onto the sheer face of the drop, clinging to the handle of an open refrigerator door hirsute with mold. It scrabbles against the painted metal, sending refrigerator magnets clattering down the sides of the pit. Finally it mounts the door and rests there for a moment amongst the snow-white and teal rot.

Though the creature lacks eyes or any kind of head, I can sense it scanning for me, or maybe just for something living, something that can inflict harm on it. At last, it hops a little, clearly excited by my presence, and all the more by the gripping fear of death that has frozen me to this spot. It steps tentatively towards me, towards the pit—but then stops, understanding the problem. It leaps sideways, doing a quarter twist, latches onto the wall, and scurries around the side, navigating the circumference of the pit face, towards the teetering scale that is this car.

"No, Crabby!" I shout. Even my voice seems to shift the balance of weight. I speak more quietly through gritted teeth, "Crabby, no, don't come. Please don't. Please don't."

If it understands, it disobeys

Be Zen, Jing.

My heart is hammering. Focus on that. Slow it down.

The crab swings along over PVC piping and broken light fixtures.

Be Zen, damn it.

Breathing too fast. Slow it down.

It hops onto the trunk of the car and skitters along over the memoryfish carcass.

Fucking be Zen.

For a moment the crab pauses, and I think it must have worked. In under thirty seconds, I've calmed myself, reached inner peace, embraced nonbeing.

The crab stabs at the dead insect, but when there's no response, its focus shifts forward—it's all in the angling of the legs, I see now—angling towards me.

And Crabby comes.

We tumble down in a knot through the darkness, a sheet of sunlit, mercurial water cascading down with us, undergoing a glittery transformation before my eye. The memoryfish's wings suddenly fan out, and it feels as if we're yanked upward on puppet strings. Coasting. The water flashes past us. I don't know how long the fall lasts, but the scintillation of the water extinguishes in a sudden black wave, then my spine seems to jar into the back of my throat. Lights flicker behind both my good eye and (strangely) the blinded one. After a paralyzing moment, I gaze back up. See the rain continuing to ray out of the rubbish-jagged skylight.

As I lie there, listening to the waterfall, the wings twitch, flapping every now and then, lacking the vigor to lift us.

It takes a moment for me to realize that we haven't stopped moving, but now we're sliding sideways. The skylight tracks upward like a sun rising, out of view.

No, that's not right, I think, groaning as I look towards my feet, at the dead creature that has wrapped itself around me. Beyond it is a reddish glow. All around, just discernible in the near distance are mounds and mounds of trash, crushed houses and cars and felled trees. I reach out for the ground, and my hand comes away with some unidentifiable, rotten slime smelling of death.

There's a loud crash, crunching steel and plastic, shattering glass. I crane my head and see in the gloom the car has stabbed into the ground just above us.

We're sliding downhill, the mass of me and the memoryfish and the crab. Down a trash heap, towards some burning pit at its base. I reach out again towards the sloping surface, struggle for a handhold, but our combined weight is too great. The creature seems still alive, as if the gravity were reanimating it into a final attempt to kill me. I wrench open the spiny palps, only to find beyond them various flagella wrapped around my torso, its clawed legs latched onto my suit.

The furnace is approaching. Maybe ten yards now.

I struggle to free myself from the limbs, but there are too many, their filigreed coils too complex to unravel.

Eight yards.

Then my mind shifts to the knife spear, tucked away in my belt. Manage to worm it free of my belt.

Five yards.

Hack away at the legs and flagella, ripping them from me.

Three yards.

We're gaining speed as the angle of incline increases. Everything's glowing with flame now.

Two yards.

Keep hacking and sawing.

One yard.

I've cut off what I can see, but the creature is still too heavy for me to extricate myself.

We're there. I reach out and hook my arm through the gap of a floor joist canted over the pit edge. The weight of the memoryfish begins to slide off, then catches, jerking me down, straining the rotten wood of the joist. The creature is still hooked onto the purse strap, wrenching down my left shoulder. The crab starts running up the dead creature, but the strain is too great for me to await it. I release the grip of my left hand, and the strap pulls free, scraping down the side of my body and off into the red glow.

I'm dangling there over the edge, the wood cracking.

No heat emanates from the opening. Below is a churning crimson... sky, sea, don't know what it is—the sun shining beyond, below me, flanked not by planetoids but immense, umbrage-darkened biomasses like I'd seen beneath the waves. The dead memoryfish drifts off into the limbo, colorful exoskeleton shimmering in the light, the masochistic crab clinging confusedly to its head.

I kick a leg out, catching an adjacent joist, and manage to wriggle up and away from the hole as the entire floor breaks free and flies off into space.

The crab, the teeth, the rope, extra petals, cactuses, lighter, everything gone.

My eyes snap open to the bizarre sight of the car still balanced on its nose at the apex of the trash mound, beautifully robed in a mantle of twinkling water.

Must have passed out.

I clamber up the slope, slipping on rot and stabbing myself on angles of twisted metal, and reach the car spearing out of the top. Not just any car, either—my Taurus, rusted fenders and all.

The creatures must have carried it off from the desert—a memory.

My vision gradually adjusts to the darkness, and I notice other skylights in the distance, curtains of illuminated water gushing through, thirty yards or so above the peaks of the many waste heaps. Whatever this chamber is, it's vast, stretching for miles in any direction. In the distance, about five trash dunes away, in the shadows between the sky-lights, I can barely make out an immense, swollen structure lined with flat polygonal planes, undulating slightly.

I descend towards another one of those limbo gateways; skirt around the edge; weave between the piles, using the presence of one of the ceiling skylights to keep me headed in the right direction, slogging most of the time through trash-filled slime pits in which floats refuse vaguely familiar to me.

When I reach the base of the fifth dune, the lights come, ghoulish and shifting, the same I had seen shining through the chinks in the chitin.

Night already.

By the strange light, I can see this must be the interior of Psyche's body cavity. The organs long-ago rotted away, leaving behind only the shell, a gorgeous ceiling of rippling domes, of tessellated stars and diamonds and ovals, a maze of scalloping, stretching on and on, all in the black opal.

Knife spear tucked into the back of my belt, I creep out of the water and up the slope. At the top a wardrobe from Glenbrook rises at a lilt like some ancient tombstone, creating convenient cover for me. Peering around its frame, I spot a couple of hundred yards away the giant structure—vase-shaped, the light emanating from within, paneled in colorful hexagons, and connecting to the ceiling. Far in the distance a number of other fat columns enflame the darkness.

I notice what appears to be an entrance, where the surface funnels inward, around where the neck meets the body of the vase, closer to the ceiling than the trash mounds. The opening is crawling with memoryfish, indistinct from this distance, just a quivering confetti. Insects flit in and out, joining or launching from the swarm.

A nest?

I scan the base of the hive, along the talus slope of refuse. My stomach turns to ice when I see it there with its peeling and stained wallpaper half-buried in trash: the window seat from my childhood home and beside it the door to the crawlspace where I'd often hid, light shining faintly from behind the small, closed door.

Creep back down the way I came, circle around through the water and survey the valley between me and the crawlspace. A lake with a few islands of trash, all clear, save one memoryfish, smaller than the one that had nearly pulled me down into limbo. Twenty yards off, head stuffed inside the innards of an overturned piano— my piano, my fucking piano, on which I'd learned to play before my feet could even touch the pedals—creating a discord of snapping strings and clattering wooden action that rattle my heart—sufficiently distracted. Above, the colossal hive teems with the things, a white noise hiss off blurred clicking and vibrating wings. The ammonic redolence rolling of the nest stings my nose and good eye.

I swim the distance, spring up the slope, filmed in muck, tripping on the uneven topography, and fling open the crawlspace door, then squeeze inside feet-first, pulling the door shut behind me—Christ, it's been awhile—down beneath the narrow, sloped ceiling, whose joists I use like ladder rungs, bracing myself on the slick, stinking surface as it drops down at a forty-five-degree angle. At the bottom, the ceiling terminates against the stained glass of the nest wall, the material smooth, with a little give. The razor pierces it easily. Make a small slice, and a strong chemical air wheezes out of the opening. I push my hand through the thick, rubbery wall, widening the hole, then peer through.

Inside is a small, brilliantly lit chamber, a hexagonal prism turned on its side, occupied by what I presume to be a pupa, several feet long, its exoskeleton a milky pastel, not yet translucent, hinting at the brilliant colors that will develop. Tearing the hole wider, I squeeze inside and past the motionless creature, careful not to disturb it. Through the colorful walls of this chamber I make out more pupae in adjacent cells.

At the front of the cell I cut another small slit. This wall opens into a cavern lined with stunningly chromatic wax, paneled in the same hexagonal shapes of this cell— thousands of them, filled with young. Stalactite and stalagmite combs dangle from the ceiling and tower out of the base. High above, the opening expands inward like a bell, the lips crawling with insects. They buzz around everywhere, building on the combs, sealing in the cells that contain larvae. Several of these memory-fish are larger than the ones I'd seen before, perhaps twenty feet long, wingless, centipedal, with additional fat body segments dragging behind them, depositing... chunks of crystal into the empty cells.

At the very center of the nest a multi-faceted, helical tower rises up, atop which rests a massive shifting, white shape. There's something distinctly familiar about it—composed of orbs and tunnels, similar to a space station or a crystal's molecular structure.

The Compound.

And yet, unlike the mansion in Detroit, this building appears to extend up and beyond the nest. Even that's not entirely accurate. It bends *inwardly* beyond, towering in a direction neither up nor down, left nor right, backward nor forward. A kind of vortex of *other* space, beyond which a brilliance shines in and floods the nest. The memoryfish slide in and out of this space pocket, unfazed by its strangeness. Indeed, their attention is locked on the shifting white mass. They scurry over its surface, hover beside it, piercing it with their rostra and sucking it up with their prawn-like mouthparts. Some creatures merely feast, while others fly off and regurgitate the food onto the freshly laid crystal or into the mouths of the hungry larvae.

Unlike the rotting waste in the Psyche interior, this thing looks alive, breathing... malleable.

My thoughts are cut short by a crash in the crawlspace behind me. I turn to see shards of the battered door raining down into my haven once upon a time. They know I'm in here.

My heart skips. No time for deliberation or strategy, I burst through the wax wall and sprint down the smooth surface of the nest into a depression between me and towering dais supporting the memory, aiming my footfalls at the thick, inter-cell junctions.

The buzz of the hive erupts into a madness of skittering and whumping.

One glance back reveals fifty or so of the creatures lifting off from neighboring walls or scrambling down the hive towards me. With one swarm seconds behind me and another starting to spiral down from the top, the only way up will have to be through the interior. I dodge towards another pupa's cell, slicing through the wax and squeezing past the inhabitant. From here, I mount the lower slanting of wall of the hexagonal chamber and slice and shove my way to the next cell halfway up, this one holding nothing but a large crystal chunk, bathed in a citrine hue.

Suddenly the structure rocks with the impact of hundreds of memoryfish colliding into its side. Behind me several memoryfish have begun to extract the pupa and are squeezing inside, nearing the entrance to my cell. All around rostra are piercing through the exterior walls.

Running up the angle of the far wall, I burst into the cell another half-floor above mine.

Empty, emerald, open to the nest, a memoryfish squeezing inside. I dash backwards, mounting up the slope to a higher chamber. Slice through, then swivel back, finding the creature all the way in, stuck, creating a roadblock. I swing my weapon and embed the blade in its brain. Kick into the squiggling clewish mass of its head, my foot momentarily sticking in the complexity of its mouth, then yank both foot and blade free in an arc of goo.

I sprint on and up past a pupa and then shifting course, moving in the opposite direction, a zigzagging climb. Many of them too large, they struggle to pursue along the circuitous pathway or to dig a new route. Beyond the walls, towards the interior of the hive, the kaleidoscope of insects has thickened to a tense disorientation scrambling around the honeycomb tower, their legs and jointed parts a deafening fury. Above wavers the form of the memory, aquatic and distorted through the brilliant layers of the comb tower.

The massive scale of activity is beginning to heat the place, softening the wax, the tower starting to lilt and sway with the hundreds of memoryfish tearing through the fragile walls. Chamber after chamber I scramble through, witnessing in random sequence the full development of these creatures from lifeless transparent crystal, to the milky memory-infused stone, to the grotesque final product.

At last, I cut my way through onto the roof of the tower, the swirling air around me and this memory a hot pandemonium. Beyond, in the other space, the light source, I can just make out the geometric planes of crystal stretching down infinite vistas—a threshold into the mountains. As I approach, the memory structure reacts to my presence. It bends and undulates, a living piece of art unfolding, reaching out and revealing its innards, the furniture and walls and people, sideways and upside-down, oblivious, pulled along the unnatural contours of its movement.

Then the Compound clamps its jaws shut around me.

CHAPTER 18

I'm inside.

A bare, high-ceilinged room, black grand piano angled across in its center, above juts out a free-hanging walkway accessible only from the second floor. Through the windows, I see the pale gauze of the chromatic nest superimposed over early-autumn dusk in Michigan. No sign of the Crystal Mountains.

Wiping the sweat from my face, I walk over to the piano, tucking the gore-covered knife spear into my belt and running my grimy fingers over the keys, pressing down on the sustain pedal to let the notes catch and drift.

A beautiful instrument. Everything in this room sounds exquisite, well-formed. Such a contrast with Glenbrook's neglected spinster in rec north. I close my eye and let the piano's warmth seep inside.

Am I really back?

This is definitely not the present. It's not winter. I'm not seeing things through third-person. Has all of this I've been experiencing—Glenbrook and Psyche—just been some kind of *Christmas Carol* potential future?

No, I think with sudden disappointment, gaze shifting down at my body clad in black flower petals— Psyche is real.

I detach from the piano and leave the room through a connecting tunnel lined with windows and fluor-escent-lighting baseboards. As I walk, disembodied voices and laughter and music bubble out of the silence, echoing through the halls—a familiar cocktail. Hipsters and goths and punks unfold around me out of the emptiness, clumps of them talking and drinking and making out and blocking my way. The piano behind me suddenly springs into life, and for a moment when I turn back it looks as if a ghost had begun to pound away at it, but then a boy with shaggy hair, flannel, and ripped jeans materializes, beside him a tattooed girl in red leather pants chugging along on an acoustic guitar, a crowd encircling them blinking into existence. The former cool, ethereal air has grown hot and close with conversation and smoke, body odor, and hair product. My old red sneakers generate around my feet. Yet at the same time, the rippling struggle boots are still visible. I become aware for the first time in several days of the left side of my head. When I touch the eye socket, my fingers meet the soft petals of the spider lily but also, for a split second, the smooth surface of the eyeball and the long lashes before my reflex response takes over, eyelid flickering open and shut.

At a junction in the hallway, I squeeze through a clutch of partygoers and enter a small bathroom and use the toilet, not aware I needed to until I'm inside. Afterwards, I thoroughly clean my body in the sink, peeling off my breastplate and armlets, and (surprisingly) my jeans and t-shirt, undoing my blue dendrite hair clip, starting with my hair (simultaneously short and spiky and long and draggled), then my face, and moving down to my feet. The water is beautiful, clear, steaming. Then, drip-drying, I turn the faucet to cold and take a long, delicious drink. Finally, I rinse the muck off the various flower-petal armor and, no towel to be found, beat them dry against the wall.

Throughout my toilet I inspect the outlandish mirror Jing: on the one hand, just as I was back then—short-haired, pale, thin, intact; but at the same time the present membrane filmed over this old version—scarred and burned and bruised, body more angular than it had once been, hair falling past my shoulders—and, of course, the flower.

The red spider lily is enormous.

I exit the bathroom and begin to push my way down the tunnel and into an immense lounge, half-indoors, half-out, pocked with pools and hot tubs, completely packed. Beyond us, sunset over the Detroit memoryfish nest serves as a backdrop, an illusion of alien creatures swarming the city, alighting on distant building tops, injecting them with crystal, and sealing them in wax.

Ramps along the walls of the lounge curve up to an indoor balcony connecting with other tunnels and rooms on the second floor. I navigate through the crowd, part of me determined to push past everyone, but another part stopping for a hug or a chat or a smoke. Even so, both parts of me feel I'm needed somewhere. With half the faces familiar, progress is slow.

I hear frequent references to the time. Everyone begins congregating in one direction, towards the sound of thumping dance music and flashing lights at the end of the lounge: the entrance into the Club. My eyes dart to my now-functioning watch. Although I've witnessed similar scenes many times, the impressive size of the crowd this evening suggests the date to be that of Autoscope's final show, the eve of the northeast American tour that never was.

Almost time for us to take to the stage.

I fight against the current of people to the other side of the room, through a seemingly endless parade of metal and ink, ripped tees and leather straps, bird-of-paradise hair, spaced-out and jacked-up eyes. Though I'm moving against the flow, it feels right, almost as if I'm falling into the groove of how I'd behaved that evening.

After squeezing my way through a confusion of tunnels, I finally reach the green room.

The closing door shuts out the chatter and laughter, the drum-and-bass rhythm hushed to a vibrating pulse. I realize suddenly I'm almost shaking with the anticipation of performing. It begins in my legs and hands.

Need to move. If I don't, I could collapse with trembling.

Need a cigarette.

"We're on in twenty minutes," Penn says from the vanity, scrutinizing my costume through the mirror. Wearing a glossy-white corset business suit, stockings, and a flapper headband of feather and pearl—elegant, but alien—she's applying thick swaths of white eyeshadow to match everything else.

My purse rests atop the station beside her. "Needed some fresh air," I say, walking over and rummaging through the bag. Full pack inside.

Beautiful.

I shake one out.

Penn winces as the opposite door opens, emitting a surge of music. Bower enters, on his heels two groupies, followed by Leif, quite tall with a blonde ponytail, and their coke-wizened dealer. The former (and most prominent of the bunch) has already transmogrified himself—luxurious hair plastered over one side of his head in an extreme comb-over, eyeshadow and lipstick sparkling gold, turquoise tribal breastplate dangling over his bare chest, gold leather pants, platform shoes, and a fluffy red boa. The two girls have squeezed into and bound themselves in leather and chain piercings—sex on display. Leif and the dealer, in Diesel Jeans and polos, look as if they've arrived at the wrong party, only their neck and wrist tattoos giving them away.

Bower directs everyone to the couches and coffee table, where the dealer cuts thick lines of cocaine on a mirror.

Meanwhile, I go to the costume rack, and flick through the options before remembering the vision from many days ago, seeing myself in the documentary wearing... there it is—a black mesh top, braless—Christ, what was I thinking?

"Fifteen minutes," Penn chimes.

What else? A pair of baggy, black-and-white clown pants, one leg polka-dot, the other checkered. I think that's right.

"These are beyond absurd," I object.

In front of the vanity, I remove the various Psyche items from my belt and place them on the coffee table, then strip off the t-shirt and flower petals, and reach for the mesh top.

Fully dressed, I sit at the vanity, and with Penn's help sculpt my hair into a roosting raven. While I apply the various cosmetics, I try to go over the setlist in my mind. A number of days ago I had recalled it while trekking through the desert, but now... the excitement has blotted it out. Even so, I've done this long enough to recognize this pre-show amnesia, know it to be an illusion. It's all in my body. Waiting to unfold. I just need to be put in front of a drum set or a piano or a violin and it will gush forth in the memorized sequence whether I want it to or not. At this point my mind feels superfluous.

Bower has dismissed his coked-up groupies, Leif was beeped and has sought out a quiet corner of the Compound to make a call, and the dealer has mysteriously disappeared—the way they do.

Leaving just the three of us. According to her ritual, Penn dons a pair of earmuffs and meditates on the floor, lost in the nirvana of her inner musical visions. Bower paces and recites snippets of lyrics to himself, stopping occasionally to do jumping jacks. And me? I chain-smoke and tattoo rhythms on my thighs.

Finally, the music halts to a wail of applause, the DJ's set ended. I lightly tap Penn on the shoulder, and those deep emerald eyes, embedded in the aspirin-white bars of her eyeshadow, open.

We have a group hug and a moment of silence.

I look up at Bower, and he smiles at me.

Tell him, Jing. Tell him.

It's time.

Autoscope begins in crackling and droning darkness—hedged by scattered applause, hoots—red lights spawning and brightening with the touches of Bower's piano, then colored with Penn's interweaving guitar, progressing from a simple melody to a shifting circle of chords when sudden spotlights like triangular mountains uplift the music into a jangling anthem, the audience cheering and whistling, your hands dancing and bounding over the toms and cymbals—palindromic rises and falls—the theme continuing to build tension for several more minutes before a final spotlight illuminates Bower, who croons in his ever-so-slightly-off-tune baritone, while Penn activates a bone-vibrating bassline on her pedalboard—and the music nails into the viscera—the bizarre, mountainous terrain shifting, higher and higher, so high you're breathless, can't think, can only be impelled onward to the peak and then thrown off on the wind, falling for so long and far that falling feels like standing still, then everything torn down in several atmospheric brushstrokes, leaving in its wake only a fleeting echo emanating out of the amps, but we forge ahead, pulling the audience with us, relentless and pounding drums first, your hand splitting off two ways, each one playing its own distinct, mesmerizing rhythm, phasing in and out, until the math dictates the inevitable coordination, then fanning out again, and I cannot think about it or my mind will obsess to synchronize them—just watch it happen, that's all I can do—Bower and Penn joining in different juxtaposed tunes—rise out of the music, everything becoming unfocused, our Vishnu body multi-tasking many different songs now, Bower's smeared across the keyboard and electronics, impaled on his bass; Penn's guitar drawn and quartered, unscissoring into a tangle of crisscrossing strings; and the crowd transformed into an army of melting, dividing, endlessly cloning doppelgangers, imperfectly split from each other, all gyrating to different tunes; but then the scope becomes too extreme, the crowd becoming a jiggling, grunting blob of peacocked flesh and hair, t-shirts and fishnets, the music transcending into cacophony, notes and pieces and movement blending and condensing, a singularity of music and flesh, all of creation and reality in one terrible catharsis, then an aneurism yanking you back painfully and disappointingly into the unadorned river of blood and nerve and time, claustrophobic breath, flowing along on the music, bandmates shrunken back to their normal postcoital forms as well, Bower playing a noodling bassline on a synthesizer while Penn charges through a minimalistic chord progression, the thin line of reality here hollow and bare and infinitely quieter, the beating of my heart and the drumsticks in my gloved grasp dried into brittle rattles, but even this slump not lasting as soon the spiritual shift recurs and once again the tension and ecstasy, vibrations of sound and light bundle past and future into present oblivion, a florid construction of layers and layers of hyper-notes, anti-melodies, and dark-rhythms, everything touching and interacting, songs overlapping songs—the musical mandala—an inter-petaled bloom of space-time, sustained for what seems an eternity, until we're wrenched free, plunging back into the temporal river, floating, returning, floating, returning, again and again until the music is barreling towards the concluding phrases of the closing number in streaking bliss, only desiring to stay locked inside the safe wonderland of this performance, knowing that after the music ends, there gapes the hole in memory, the split between hero and shade, self and other, mind and body, illusion and reality, what I've come here for; still, there's no worrying away the crashes of the final chords and cymbals, screaming to a halt to enthusiastic applause, simultaneously marking the end of the show and the demise of Autoscope.

The three of us retreat backstage amidst a flurry of activity. Thirty or more people sardine into the green room. After being cajoled to pose for photographs and listening to Bower and Penn say a few lines for the documentary, I slip behind a dressing screen, shed the kinky fool ensemble, and emerge in my half-now/half-then outfit. Barely register the popping of champagne corks in the balmy din, head still ringing from the show. Can still feel the vibrations of the drums in my arms, the surging of adrenaline and the fading electric licks of endorphins.

I cram onto one of the couches. Bum a cigarette from a stranger. Drugs have invaded the coffee table and have begun to single out host bodies among us. Across from me, jammed into a sofa with Leif and out of costume, Penn looks wan—her typical, afterparty self. She passes on the blunt circling around and sips on a beer. Leif is whispering into her ear, and she nods and shakes her head and offers the occasional curt response. Bower, still in wardrobe, voice dominating the room, energized from the performance, is gradually attracting willing groupies to his side.

When the blunt reaches me, I study it for a few seconds—then pass on it. It's half-smoked when it reaches me again, when I reject it again.

A mirror of coke orbits around from the other side of the couch.

Pass.

Glass of champagne spiked with god-knows-what.

Pass.

Foil-wrapped sugar cubes of LSD.

Pass.

The only thing that touches my lips is this cigarette and all of its brethren.

This can't be right. Can't be what happened that night/tonight.

I crawl over the back of the chair, the only path in this human labyrinth. Need air. Need quiet. Need to think. Need to figure this out. I snatch up a bottle of water and my things, then head out.

Full night in the Compound. Everything black-lit, strobed. Head-rattling dance music. The walls creep with spray-painted alien plant life. All those familiar faces from before have been transformed into weird bio-luminescent creatures. I'm jostled this way and that by flailing dancers and pods of scenesters as I navigate to the lounge.

The bubble dome of glass extending above the over-crowded pool is thick with the stroboscopic wriggling of memoryfish.

Take a tunnel to the second floor, circling around over the piano room, now teeming with partygoers, cramped with music and smoke. On to the third floor, ahead Bower's room, an immense suite of sub-nodes and looping balconies. It's locked, the only locked section of the house. Everywhere else up here small colonies of decadence have cropped up. Through a haze of opium and crouching shadows, I cross through a bedroom and over to a balcony, where a couple grinds against each other. Ignoring them, I step close to the edge. A few yards away the memoryfish ripple over some invisible wall in the darkness. Below, the pool glows cyan. The dry night air is laced with autumnal hues, chlorine, and the taint of the nest.

I chug the water, light a fresh cigarette, think.

Now that I'm here, how do I leave the house? If I were to go back downstairs, make a break down the driveway for my car, then drive off into the night, maybe it would prevent me from traveling to Psyche, prevent Bower's death.

Or maybe I'd just be ravaged by memoryfish.

I look back up at the insects, the gauze of the cathedral-lit nest superimposed over darkness.

They're closer by a few feet. The bubble is shrinking.

From the looks of it, the apex has already sliced through the fourth floor.

I flick the smoke out into the night and it passes beyond the memory wall. A creature snatches at it, reels it into its mouth in a puff of embers.

I turn and dash back inside, then out of the room, shoving past everyone on my way downstairs. The basement. Maybe the basement's safe.

Takes me several minutes to get down there. Try to stay cool, but everyone is so blinded by hedonism to the approaching catastrophe, I start to lose it, shoving people aside, waving the razor spear this way and that to clear a path. When I fling open the door to the cellar, the stink of ammonia wafts up. Down in the darkness I can see the glint of busy chitin.

Slam it shut.

I head for the piano room. The surface of the front door and the exterior walls are undulating with the pressure of memoryfish.

I push back through the crowd, trying to get to the third floor again—center of the house, of the bubble.

A hand grabs me by the collar, and I hear the words "harshing my buzz." I jab the polite end of the stick into the guy's face, and then show him the other end. He backs off, cursing, clutching his dripping red mouth.

"Drummer Girl?"

I whirl around and find Leif, Penn's arm drooped over his shoulder, her head dangling. They're blue and orange in the psychedelic lights.

"What the hell is that?"

"Just... self-defense," I say, confused. "Where are you taking her?"

"Burrito's room." Leif jingles the keys.

"Let me help."

"You okay?" His brow furrows.

"Fine"—I tuck the spear into my belt—"just forget it. Some asshole groped me."

When we reach Bower's room, we lay Penn out on the

king bed. I sit down at her side, pushing her hair out of her face.

"I'm a little worried," Leif says, sitting down on the other side of the bed and running a hand through his long hair.

"Yeah, I haven't seen her like this in a while."

"I mean you. Just now."

"I'm okay, Leif."

"You had this wild look in your eyes."

"It's nothing, Leif."

"Jing, we got a long road ahead of us, oodles of shows, and I need to make sure you're going to be okay, going to be able to cope. If you got some shit you need to lay on me, better do it now."

"Don't worry about me. Why don't you get back to the party? I'll take care of her."

"All right." He stands, then hesitates at the doorway. "Beep me if you need anything."

He shuts the door, leaving the two of us alone. Through the glass outer wall, I watch the progress of the memoryfish, listening to them scrabbling their way through the mnemonic surface.

"Jingy?" Penn whispers.

"Yeah, P.C."

"What the hell kind of clothes are these?" She's pleating the cuff of the struggle between light and dark between her thumb and index finger.

I watch her hand for a time, wondering what she's seeing, wondering what Leif had seen. "Just some costume I'm trying out, something for the tour."

"Is that an eyepatch?" She's gazing up at me now.

"Sort of."

"You look frightened." She closes her eyes, wrapping her arm around my waist.

"I am."

"Don't be. The tour's going to be amazing. You're going to be amazing."

"It's not that."

"What's bothering you?"

"Memoryfish," I blurt out. "I don't know how to keep them from entering the Compound."

"Memoryfish," she echoes.

"They're eating their way inside. To the core of the memory."

"Let them eat."

"You don't understand."

"No, I don't. Are you high?"

"No. I can't explain it now. Where's Bower?"

"Probably getting blown in the green room."

A pause.

"Can you do something for me?" I say. I wait. "Penn?"

Her voice floats out of sleep. "Mmm."

"I need a favor."

"Name it, girl."

"Keep something safe for me. Just a few months. Until... the end of the tour."

"The end of the tour."

"Till Christmas."

"Till Christmas."

I take off the unspeakable fruit and slip it onto her wrist.

She falls asleep.

I strip down and step into the granite-walled shower and soak there for some time, my styled hair melting, sweat and purple lipstick and green eyeshadow washing from my body. I clean myself over and over, the multiple, steaming-hot jet streams massage my aching muscles. Earth and Psyche me flicker back and forth, and with them the different flavors of exhaustion: Earth, the sweet ache of the end of a long, momentous day; Psyche, anxiety-fringed emptiness.

What am I doing? I can't shower now. I should be trying to escape, but I feel trapped, a clockwork cog.

By the time I've toweled off, Penn has vanished. I puzzle at the sight of the empty bed, then notice the sounds of the house—or the lack thereof. No music, no drunken revelry. Just the ever-present scratching of memoryfish appendages trying to claw their way in.

I step out into the hallway.

My ears had not deceived me; everyone's gone. A sour, sobering stench fills the empty halls: old smoke, stale beer, wine dregs, vomit, sex. The same must that blossoms out of every dead party.

I worm out a cigarette and wander the upstairs, poking my head in and out of the odd room. Once, in one of the rooms I see the wall, as if made of thick latex, stretching inward on an alarming point. When a rostra suddenly tears through, I slam the door shut, heart jackhammering, glancing left and right.

Down the way I'd come, a prismatic light is shining through one of the doorways—nest light. I sprint the other way, down a link connecting one node of the building to another, and all of the surfaces erupt into a pulsating funhouse. I dash to the other end, dodging out of the way of clawed limbs and other strange appendages as they rip apart the surface.

I've been cut off, I realize suddenly. Only one path remains open to me—down the third-floor hallway.

I know where I'm being led, even before I move in that direction. For some reason—a once-latent flash of memory, I don't know—I'm more fearful of the door ahead of me at the end of the hall than I am of the memoryfish gnawing their way inside. Still, I approach, place my hand on the cold doorknob. A bulky door, more soundproofed than any of the other doors on this level, when it slides open on its rubber gasket, a deep breath of ozone and varnished wood and metal polish and sweat puffs out.

Once the door is open, there's no un-opening it. I jitter inside. Shut it tight behind me. Turn and from the third-floor balcony gaze down at the Club, where we had just played our last show.

The largest of all the rooms in the complex, with a stage, DJ booth, giant dance floor, light machines, bar, and two tiers of balconies wrapping around to the edge of the stage. The music equipment is still set up—my ascetic drum set, Penn's complex of effects pedals and wall of amps, and Bower's tree of electronics sprouting out of a piano.

How long ago now has it been? Feels like it's only been minutes, but it must have been hours. Some trick of memory. Events may have been consolidated and changed.

The place is empty, dim, littered with bottles and cigarette butts, glow sticks and bracelets. The memory-fish haven't begun to eat into this pocket of the memory, but I can hear them beyond the thick metal door. I'm again overcome with a squeamish reluctance—the disaster must be minutes away.

Still, I push myself onward.

My footsteps echo as I descend the metal spiral stairs to the dance floor and cross over to the stage. So unnatural approaching from this direction—like I'm some schoolgirl up next for the recital. On stage, I walk an arced path by my drums, caressing a cymbal, over the neat rainbow of Penn's effects pedals and the complex notations she'd taped beside each one, then over to Bower's piano.

I slide over the bench, its legs squeaking against the wood of the stage, and sit down as I've done thousands of times in reality and memory and Earth visions, before all variety of pianos. Piano recital machinations. My fingers touch the well-worn keys, and I begin playing what Earth Jing has dedicated so much time to in her latter days at Glenbrook. Although at this point in my life I would have had years of rust to work through. The last time I played this piece would have been that night with Bower about two years prior, when we had worked out an impromptu duet with messy results. I'm amazed that *Pictures* flows out with the same fluidity I'd witnessed in the most recent vision—I've been learning with her, detached though I may be. This certainly could not be an authentic detail of the memory.

One of the effects boards still hums with power, eating up the notes of the "Promenade" and blanketing the simple lines in a vast echoing space.

"I think the protagonist's walking a bit too fast."

I hadn't heard him enter, but Bower's self-assured voice doesn't surprise me. Even so, my heart lurches when I hear him speak.

"She's"—I nearly choke on the word—"hurrying along towards her first encounter."

His footsteps approach, crossing from stage right, the same path I'd taken.

"Does she see what's coming?"

"She sees something's coming."

"I had a different interpretation when I studied this." Bower slides onto the piano bench beside me, at the bass end, where the flower blocks my peripheral vision. The air of the night hovers around him—decadence turned. "Lemme take over the left." His voice is slurred.

"You're up."

He seamlessly shifts his hand over mine, and my left drops away. We play on, shoulders touching, and Bower reaches up with his right hand to adjust the effects levels, tuning a knob down to add a touch more warmth to the sound. At the end of the third section, I stop, staring down at our hands on the keys. The final piano note is still ricocheting in the machine, very faint, lost.

I'd heard a sound from above, I'm sure.

Scrabbling and ripping. Bower reaches over and squeezes my hand, turns it over and runs a finger down my palm. When I turn towards him, I still can't see his face for all the hair hanging down, just a thin smile on his lips.

"What are you doing here, anyway?" I ask.

"Was in the green room, passed out, when I woke to

the glorious sounds of the Drummer Girl. It was like you were calling to me. What about you, you creep, playing in the dark for an empty hall in all this goth finery? What the hell kind of a Victorian ghost possessed your clothes?"

He can see it, too.

"Bower, you have to get out of here." My voice is suddenly urgent, cutting through the end-of-night malaise that had begun to fuzz my mind as we'd played.

"Sorry?"

"You have to go. I need to be alone. I'm going through some shit I can't explain. There's no time to. Go out to a diner or something, get some breakfast, come back when the bus arrives; I'll tell you everything then."

His fingers start to intertwine with mine.

"It's so easy, you know?"

"Bower stop." I pincer his hand with my left, try to remove it, but I don't have the strength to fight what's happening. He's going to die doing this.

"If you put on a pair of tight leather pants and go on stage—"

"Bower, come on. Listen to me."

"—girls line up for you. Now, this is convenient," he says, finding the slit of my clothes and running a finger down my left wrist. For a moment, I can't even tell if there's a scar amidst the tattoos.

"But I'm not a buffet guy. You *matter*, Jings. We should have done this years ago, that first dawn by the pool, the first night we really talked. I wanted you so bad, wanted to reach out and touch you then, but Autoscope was just starting to get into the groove and I didn't want to disturb the balance—"

There's that ripping sound again. It rouses me out of the hypnotic spell that keeps settling over me. I stand and knock over the piano bench as I attempt to back away. Bower spills onto the floor, laughing, still in his ridiculous performance outfit. I glance towards the back of the Club, see the church lights shining through the tear in the memory and the prismatic creature wriggling its way inside, antennae twitching.

"Bower, get up." I bend over to pull him to his feet, but he grabs a hold of my shoulders. Skinny as he is, he's strong, and he pulls me down easy enough, clawing his way into my clothes, making fast work even with this alien outfit, hands soon flicking my nipples and squeezing my breasts.

"It's okay," he whispers, lips brushing against my ear. "It's just me. It's just me."

Our lips lock together with that sensation of settling into the groove, and I feel at once the blossoming heat of desire and the cold horror that Psyche-me has lost control of Earth-me. My fingers run down his flat belly and unbutton him and soon he's in my hands burning and pulsing. His hand finds a leg seem and opens it, finds me and opens that, too.

Just a taste, I think.

Just a taste.

It'll be good for our music.

This is all just some wild hallucination, anyway.

That bug isn't really here.

I took acid, went on some weird trip—months condensed into hours. Now, I've returned. We're going to go on tour.

"Fuck me," I whisper into his ear.

For a time all that exists is the movement and friction and our mouths and hands exploring each other. Psyche has vanished, the nightmare ended, leaving me only with the pleasures of the moment, the promise of the future.

Then there's a flittering whump; ammonia-redolent light bursts upon us.

Every one of Bower's muscles tenses. He seems to sprout insect arms and is jerked upward—out of me—half-naked and ludicrous. Beside us the electronics rack rocks with the sudden jouncing from the memoryfish. I try to scramble away, back towards the piano, but am too slow. The rack topples, crashing down on me.

From behind, the memoryfish curls over Autoscope's lead singer, and Bower struggles as the wriggling mouthparts settle over his nose.

For a moment nothing happens. Then a red cloud bursts inside the insect's head and starts to spread throughout its body—a grotesque scraping and lapping, like a dog nosing and slurping into the bottom of its food bowl. Bower shudders a few times, manhood jiggling obscenely, but then just hangs slack in the cradle of appendages as his brains or memories or both are cleaned out through his nose, just the way the Ancient Egyptians did it.

What was that word?

The dragon's word.

Excerebration.

CHAPTER 19

Within the electronics, the piano note, very faint, is trapped along with the flutter of the memoryfish's wings, the jarring crash, and the sucking sound of Bower being robbed of his mind, all picked up by the interior microphone—the aural equivalent of a persecutory nightmare.

The memoryfish releases Bower's body, head intact, but blood oozing out of every orifice, matting down his curly hair. It staggers off drunkenly, brain-thick blood cloud a churning, Jovian storm. A small fire has burgeoned out of the collapsed electronics and begins to eat towards Bower—and me; I'm down there, too, in my red shoes, the Earth me, half-stripped by Bower's hands, knocked unconscious beneath the electronics rack.

I've dissociated.

I stride forward and quash the fire, then reseal my own suit, which had been flapping open in all the vulnerable places.

If I'm unconscious on the ground, that means the memory is over, but if that's indeed the case, what then is this house? The past?

Watching the memoryfish atrocity sauntering onto the dance floor, I'm struck with more bizarre questions: Did a memoryfish really kill Sebastian Bower? What brought it to Earth? The same thing that brought me to Psyche?

A distant thump resounds throughout the Club, followed by the grinding of wood and concrete. At first I wonder if I imagined the sound, barely discernible beneath the piano-infused echoes of the nightmare. But it repeats, louder than before, vibrating up my legs. Warm light streams in through the ground-floor entrance, the tunnel connecting to the lounge and pool.

Another thump, grinding, louder and louder still.

The bright orange light in the entrance shifts and lurches with the sound, that industrial waste, rotten-egg sulfuric stink flooding in on the light, the swaying shadow vague. What finally squeezes through the entrance, fissuring the wall and sending a large wedge of concrete crashing to the floor, is the beast that had ferried the rat and me halfway across the sea. Now, much of the rock that had once encrusted its head has been blasted or torn off and lava seeps freely out of its exposed skull.

I stare dumbfounded.

It senses the drunk memoryfish swaying over the dance floor and licks it with a tongue of flame. Igniting, the insect squeals, attempts to take flight, but crashes into the underside of the balcony and *thunks* back down, writhing and sizzling on the floor. Its exoskeleton pops open, and Bower's ground-up brains press out steaming onto the floor.

"So curious what activating a lantern drum will accomplish, wouldn't you say?" it says, massive body demolishing more of the wall as it squeezes through, scraping off bits of itself in the process, magma spilling out of the holes in its jaws where there used to be fangs and bone.

"How..." I start, backing up along the edge of the stage, slowly, afraid to make any sudden movements, mind a wasp in a jar, flitting about wildly and point-lessly.

"How am I not dead?" it gurgles, more an aside than for my benefit. "I've eaten too many minds." It pokes a grotesquely long tongue out of its ruined jaws, veins glowing with blood, and laps up the cooking brains. As it eats, I hear our voices picked up by the microphone, running together over the echo loop, joining with the piano and the crash into the cramped aural hell. "These taste horrid, but they should be enough..."

"Enough for what?"

Even as I speak, there is a subtle transformation of its body—*regeneration*. Some of its leaking holes patch up the fiery flesh, the structure of its head puffs out from its formerly deflated state, the shine returns to its moldering scales, its wild grass hair ripples into a fuller mane. The meal has helped, but this puffing up looks akin to dressing up a corpse.

There's no need for it to respond, for I know: *Enough* to fulfill the first promise it made me, to do to me what the memoryfish did to Bower.

"I need something fresh if I'm to return to my former splendor and continue with my work. Of all the wards, you've been the most recalcitrant, but also very flavorful. Much more so than your mother, although her mind was lovely in its own way."

By now the dragon has passed through the entrance completely, occupying the entire dance floor, setting parts of it ablaze with its blood, melting the varnish, the nearby glow sticks discarded by ravers bursting with the heat, their neon bubbling cancer brown. I glance towards the entrance and beyond it, towards the pool, glimpse the resplendence of the memoryfish burning, lit creatures darting about in a frenzy.

I turn back to the coiled dragon. "H-how could you have known her? Bower and I hadn't even met before she died. Unless... Bower wasn't your ward."

"Remember the first time we met? The little guessing game we played?"

I think back to the very beginning. "Yeah... when you told me we weren't on Earth."

"Oh no, that was *years* later." It begins to slither towards the foot of the stage.

"Years later?" Two steps back.

"The conservatory cafeteria."

"In Glenbrook?"

"You won several pieces of candy off me—or, rather,

my ward." It reaches the base of the steps and rears up like a king cobra fixating on its prey, still-blind eyes at my level. "Dr. Edward Rota. A great man. He and I were both very ambitious. Rota wanted a bigger hospital, better treatment for his patients, to be a world-renowned doctor—and I wanted more from the visions he fed me, to open my mind. That's what led me to find a path between Earth and Psyche."

"The unspeakable fruit." My mind feels alive. Working quickly, filling in the details before the dragon can speak them—and simultaneously working out my escape route.

"It's no fruit." It chortles bloody fire, which spatters against the stage, charring the wood, catching fire in places. "Just a name I made up. No, not a fruit, it's a desiccated organ—the inner rim of the eternity bug's lantern drum. Difficult to recognize without the membrane wrapping around it and emitting its tell-tale glow and *sound*."

I think back to the leviathan that had buried me in the sand, what I'd glimpsed of it and remember a lantern—similar to an angler fish's lure that shines in the depths.

"Spirit animals are not very enlightened creatures," it continues, body snaking forward, up the stairs of the stage, looming up higher, "as you must know, having spent so much time with a dog afraid to speak and that rat who wouldn't shut up. They revere these eternity bugs with such fervor they would consider it blasphemy to hunt, kill, and consume them. You wouldn't believe the extent of this collective delusion, that this asteroid is a giant dead insect, that you can communicate with its ghost." It barks derisively. "Imagine what fun it was to experiment feeding them various bits of their gods, bits I'd mined from my prey over the years, improvising names as I went, and studying the effects. That was how I stumbled upon this interesting little trick of bringing humans here."

"So you poisoned my spirit animal? And my mother's?"

"Consuming a lantern drum accomplishes nothing, but, yes, the tedious bull was an easy target, as was the dreamy-eyed tiger—"

"But if not by eating it, then—"

"—your mother was among the first. Not *the* first. That honor goes to an addict patient of mine—"

"Whose husband murdered Rota," I say, recalling the story Catherine had told Earth Jing many visions ago. Several more steps backwards, past the piano now and all the wreckage. A clear shot towards stage right.

"Yes." The dragon sounds impressed. "That changed things. My days of experimenting on other animals ended, and I had to develop a system to keep me sustained—to bring numerous patients here, but keep them separated and confused. A lot of juggling that took, and in certain cases, they did find each other or the spirit animals never activated the drums—"

"Activate?"

"It's music that brings them across." It slides more of itself onto the stage, releasing a pool of magma that spreads out towards my trap set, setting the bass drum afire, the parchment crisping then splitting with a *twang*. "Your rat, your bull, your mother's tiger, they all had the unfortunate habit of singing or humming. All I had to do was wait for them to activate it themselves, then find the remnants of the vision memory—in the spirit animal's past—that's where you appeared."

I'm the first to make a move, dashing to the right, and freeing the staff from the back of my belt. Darkness shrouds the backstage, with only the dim dancefloor firelight creeping around the curtain's edges at opposite wings. Then an explosion—the dragon lunges forward, crashing through the wall of Penn's amps and shredding the curtain beyond, attempting to cut me off, littering the backstage with musical-equipment shrapnel. The torn curtain ripples down to the floor.

I bolt forward, dodging past a stream of flame and ducking into the green room. Slam the door shut, but as I propel myself towards the opposite exit, the dragon head batters through the painted wood, molten jaws snapping shut in the space where I'd just been standing. I slide over the table littered with empty champagne bottles, glasses and cocaine-sullied mirrors, hurtling over the couch, and on through the door into the hallway beyond. Behind me, I can hear the dragon wriggling free of the doorframe and pulverizing the furniture in its pursuit.

I spiral up a hallway to the second floor, the house below cracking apart as the dragon first crashes into then rips apart the green room exit, everything paper-fragile, now that the memory has been sucked free. Somehow the piano microphone from the Club is still live, has been picking up every sonic detail, amplifying throughout the house the looping, building crackle of fire and conversation and explosions.

The spiraling hallway cuts through the second floor of the piano room, then twists up to the third floor. The dragon bursts through the tunnel, demolishing the walkway, which crashes down onto the piano with a jarring clang. I hazard a backwards glance, find the dragon struggling to recover as it slithers out of the pitfall and back up onto the second floor, furious expulsions of fire surging before it, wilting the graffitied modern décor into bronze peels.

From the third-floor landing, I catch a glimpse of Bower's room; memoryfish have swarmed in through tears in the walls and night sky fabric beyond the open balcony, bodies singed and melting, scurrying across the ceilings, crashing into walls. The chromatic light shining in from the nest flickers and waves, each pocket of flame below twisted into shade-shifting phantasms through the lenses of melting wax and memoryfish exoskeletons.

Another crash from below.

Glance back to find the dragon gone and the path I took up here destroyed, now just a glowing ember leaf-fall.

I dash down the hallway into the mouth of a tunnel sloping up to the fourth floor, a passageway that had been blocked by the undulations of memoryfish earlier in the evening. Suddenly, the tunnel jolts and ahead of me collapses as the dragon sledge-hammers its head through from the outside. I one-eighty and retreat, flame steamrolling up behind me.

Only one path remains: Bower's room.

I sprint into the mayhem. A shining form of glass and light and fire flashes at me. Slashing wildly, I slice the memoryfish's abdomen, opening a dam of reeking, gelatin-flecked fluid. I slide through the mess, stabilizing myself at the foot of the bed.

Another creature scurries past, head blackened and smoking, squealing, too distracted by its own death to concern itself with me. I reach the balcony and through the shredded curtains of memory, gaze down at the hive, its beautifully-paneled wax scorched, melting, ablaze, a choking smoke billowing up towards me.

I climb onto the guardrail and grab ahold of the ledge above. Beyond the bedroom, the dragon has managed to squeeze into the third-floor junction, dispatching waves of fire in all directions. I hoist myself up onto the bedroom roof and dash through a burning, eye-stinging cemetery of memoryfish, searching out the best path up the building. The only way forward is the splintered and cracked tunnel sloping to the fourth floor.

The roof explodes behind me as the dragon's head bursts through a skylight, and half-crawls/half-flies out of the hole. Cursing, I scramble up the tunnel and leap across the dragon-made gap, spilling down into the fourth floor hallway, breath jarred out of me. I stagger up into a wayward, zagging sprint, colliding with the wall but pushing, fighting back on course and heading towards another spiraling tunnel—but to my confusion, it is no longer the Compound through which I'm racing.

Everything's crystal.

The dragon crashes through the tunnel opening after me, screaming in pain as it scrapes off more rock scar and shatters its jaw.

I round a bend ahead, finding myself in a cavern of lustrous geometry, cool and clean and smelling of the first splashes of rain. Tunnels cut in and out above and below, the gem-like surface capturing my reflection everywhere in the vast space, copied and flipped and reversed and righted—kaleidoscopes of Jing Elwood.

With us, worming over our reflections and generating their own twisted visual echoes, are the giant memory-fish I'd seen in the nest, breaking off and swallowing large chunks of crystal.

I glance back towards the direction from which I'd come and can make out a fractured and rippling beaded curtain of gemstones—carbuncle, topaz, ruby, agate—through the overlapping layers of crystal: the lesioned dragon snaking its way into the tunnel.

Need to move fast.

Distancing myself from both the dragon and the ponderous memoryfish, I edge along a cliff that overlooks an abyss of branching, plummeting deaths. Feel along the walls, looking this way and that, trying to think.

Through the walls behind and in the infinite reflections and false passages surrounding me, I track the dragons within dragons lurching forward, leaking eternities of polygonal magma. A burst of heat from their maws and tendrils of flame curl around the mouth of the cavern, as if passing out of a haywire computer monitor and into real space. One of the memoryfish is caught by the fire jet, bubbles and squeals and clicks as it plummets, silenced with a splatter on the vicious edge of one of the branching drops. The dragon fire lingers within the crystal in citrine napalm dazzling miles up and throughout the mountains.

When the fire blossoms wilt, I continue around the

ledge of crystal. It's light in here, sparkling, even without the dragon fire. Cascading down from above, but of a flavor wholly unlike sunlight. More akin to the bio-luminescence of oases.

Indeed, far up and away, at what must be the limits of the mountains, I can make out a wavering, squirming glow—milky lime. Chatterboxes. The things must be enormous.

The rat had mentioned a giant oasis at the base of the Crystal Mountains, the graveyard towards which all spirit animals are bound. An impassable jungle of giant insects. That needs to be my destination, too.

Nearby there is a disruption in the reflections and distortions—a winding crevice just narrow enough to permit my entry. I squeeze in, gazing up through a tight chimney of rhombohedral protrusions jutting out at irregular intervals, a suitable place to climb. The crystal is slick, but craggy, providing plenty of hand- and footholds, the space tight enough to apply horizontal pressure with my back and ass against the opposing surface.

Up I shimmy.

Higher and higher, pace quickening as I find a rhythm.

Through the farseeing crystal-ball surfaces, I divine the dragon grown near. It pauses at the entrance to the crevice below, trying to squeeze its way inside, sniffing, unusually mum, haunting this chimney in the carbon-mottled jasper of its blood and that hair-singeing fume. It huffs and releases a burst of flame into the crevice. The fireball barrels up the tight passage, and I cower down into the corner of a crystal ledge, covering my head as the heatwave blasts past me, then pop back up and begin a now frantic scramble up the wall. As I climb, the back petal of flower armor, crisped into sheets of cinder, releases and floats down, crumbling apart.

Soon, another wave of fire surges up, but it expires several feet below me; I've out-stripped the range of the weakening beast. The dragon withdraws and slithers off.

Keep climbing, remote viewing the progress of the dragon's snaking, fiery shape, moving up through near-by passages, sometimes crawling so far out of its way that it disappears for long stretches of time, sending towards me only faint ripples of firelight, before re-appearing higher up with only the thinnest of barriers separating us.

My hands are soon raw, feet blundering, and I must stop for rest on a narrow platform, just big enough to sit on. I pant, dripping sweat, my whole body aching from the exertion. Can't even see the bottom now, nor do I see any sign of an exit.

After a few minutes, I begin to stand, when a euphoric energy surges through my body, flushing out the pain and supplanting it with quickness and power, a sense of oneness. A subtle tugging on my left eye socket. The tendrils of the spider lily have latched onto the cave wall, feeding on the crystal, the flower glowing neon red. I caress my blistered fingertips and they spark with pleasure. Turn over my hands and touch the ragged flesh, the pain exquisite.

It's growing, I think, pulling the tendril, which has begun to sprout new glowing blossoms, from the crystal and coiling it around my arm.

I continue upward with renewed vigor, every few minutes the red spider lily injecting glory into my brain and vanquishing pain and fatigue and doubt from my body and mind.

Before long, I find a crevice wide enough to permit me through, beyond it a zigzagging network of tunnels. The quality of the light has changed gradually, above a shimmering glow, bright champagne shattering the alien bioluminescence, dripping and bubbling down as the angle of light changes.

Sunlight.

A slight breeze moves past.

I sprint forward, turning corner after corner, constantly seeking the path of greatest incline, judging the dragon's distant position through the translucent walls. As I run, the sound of my footsteps echoes in a fascinating way, perhaps bounding throughout the crevices of the cave as far as the light, returning to me in fast repeating echo loops or drifting down one path and meeting me down another in crisscrossing sonic lattices. In the hall-of-mirrors visual confusion, where apparent pathways are blocked by tabular crystal surfaces, the nature of the echoes guides me.

Soon the resplendence of above has showered down with stunning heat, blinding me through the miles-thick crystal, repeating a thousand-fold the warped ball of sun on the horizon, like some splendorous Psychic fruit. Thus, I move in blindness, guided by the telling echoes, shielding my one eye, hands and face burning, the skin blistering with the intensity. Then a wave of cold and dark sweep across everything, like some Heaven-sent balm: clouds obscuring the sun. Such waves come and go during the climb. Despite the pain of the sun-infused crystal, when the light is unleashed upon the mountains, igniting the endless chain reaction of burning diamonds, I breathe deeply, mouth parched and dry and bitter, and hold my flowery arm up against the crystal, more and more tendrils and blooms efflorescing with each contact. Then when the cool blanket of clouds roll back over the mountains, I launch onward, marking the pixilated progress of the dragon, lurching and breaking off bits of itself—rock, bone, teeth—in the sharp bends of the tunnels in compounded echoes of rage and pain.

A cold wet wind is soon gusting through the passage. One last bend in the tunnel suddenly opens up to a wide cave mouth in the side of the cliff face. Beyond brews a wall of thick cloud. I approach the edge as the clouds clear, revealing the morning sky, the scattering of asteroids along the horizon, and the miles and miles of seething plant life at the foot of the mountains. The dew-dappled cliff drops sharply, occasional frostwork clusters jutting out and threads of vegetation clinging desperately to the smooth sides. Skyscraper-sized flowers and mushrooms spring out of the ground below, the spaces between littered with a jumbled taxonomy of dead beasts, among them the massive shifting highways of chatterboxes, their gargantuan mouthparts audible even at this height.

The reflection of the dragon's head, swelling as it rounds the corner, bursts into my peripheral vision on a pyramidal tooth of crystal. The creature has destroyed itself squeezing blind through the narrow, jagged tunnels—skull cracked, brains leaking, just a few flimsy links of nerve and corpuscle tenaciously binding its head together. It pitches forward, heaving in wet hacks as if intending to speak but no longer able to articulate anything, emitting disturbing squelches with each lurch.

I edge out onto a narrow ledge moving sideways from the mouth of the cave, all the while watching the dragon through the crystal wall. The fire bursts out of the cave entrance, just feet away from me, but still close enough to singe my flower armor leggings. The petals wilt, releasing me from their embrace, drifting out into the open air, at first afire then bursting in the wind into a shower of embers. Then the beast makes its final sinuous charge towards me and over the cliff edge, tumbling out into space, misled by my scent.

But it does not fall.

It continues to soar outward, a ribbon caught by the wind. There is something morbidly beautiful in the way it ripples through the air, more like a sidewinder than a creature of flight, a jungle horror risen up from some bonfire sacrifice. Then its body whips around, hovering out in mid-air, a hundred yards or so from the mouth of the cave, spiraling, twisting into a giant Celtic knot.

Feeling the bite of the wind in my legs, I watch the dragon and cling to the crystal to avoid being swept off by the gale rushing alongside the cliffs. It continues to twist and float there, fire and blood spilling out of it, flinging in all directions and sprinkling down, head turning this way and that, testing the wind.

Maybe it's lost my scent.

Whatever it is that it's doing now must be burning up its very last bit of vitality—one last desperate attempt to find and consume me. All I have to do is wait it out, wait for it to burn down completely and plummet to the oasis below.

But then the wind hesitates, shifts, and my right armlet, crisped and papery from a few torchings, lifts off bat-like, fluttering out towards the burning phantasmagoria.

The dragon launches towards me.

In the seconds it takes to reach the cliff side, I react unconsciously, the Earth energy surging through my mind, surging through me, so turbulent that everything grows mute and pale by contrast, shredding apart the fragile edges of my mind. For a moment I'm back on Earth, staring at some horrifically altered version of Detroit, but then, feeling my grip on the cliff face loosening I reel my consciousness back in, and cling tight there, rejecting the energy for myself, redirecting all of it outward, and feeding the dragon as it had always wanted.

As it flies towards me, the dragon begins to regenerate again—threads of flesh rewrap around the skull, a wave of colorful scales fans up the length of its body, the stone scars deflate and wash away, bone reconstructs where it had dismembered itself, muscle fills in the holes in its side, and finally the white and celeste eyes dawn in its skull in a brilliant, blinding flash—but its awareness of Psyche is eclipsed by whatever is happening to Earth Jing, snatching with it the control of its flight, the ribbon-like body now just hurtling forward on pure momentum, hurtling towards me. I watch the approaching flame aurora, locking the flood of visions into its mind, unable to flee, knowing that the second I release it, the creature will fly free, killing me anyway and flying off to repeat its game with another unfortunate ward and spirit animal pair.

I shut my eyes and await death, but when the detonations rocks the cliff face and I stumble forward, barely catching myself on the ledge, I find the dragon's trajectory must have decayed, striking the crystal below me. Pieces of burning brain and bone and singed crystal rain down with the giant flaming mass of the dragon, crashing against massive crystal protrusions, rebounding off and continuing down to the jungle below. After a prolonged drop, the dragon's remains strike the ground, where they are ripped apart by a pod of chatterbox whales, its fiery remains coursing through their translucent bodies.

I edge back to the cave mouth and collapse.

Some time passes before I stand, aware now of the heaviness of the flower growing out of my eye and the complex network of roots and other bulbs draping down over my shoulder and chest, and twining around my arm. I walk away from the sunrise, naked body scorched from the magnified rays, but oddly painless, my freakish shadow cast before me through the walls of crystal. As I hobble along, I drift in and out of consciousness, seeing flashes of the other Jing, hair short and choppy, skin pale, smiling, piercings flashing.

When I phase back into Psyche, I find my legs dragging against the smooth surface, almost as if I were growing along the walls of the cave, the red spider lily reacting to the crystal, emerging outward at an alarming rate, roots digging deep into my brain, stealing the parts of me that it needs, deep parts, where the neural wormhole must be. I can feel the transfer taking place, the moment where part of me ceases to exist, where the flower begins to suck me inward, folding down into the wormhole.

What was it Ratty had said? *Right in front of our noses the whole time!*

My new spirit animal has been with me all along, waiting for a safe place to be planted—in the Crystal Mountains, where it can feed on light and crystal and consciousness, unmolested by other creatures, a new addition to an ancient pantheon.

It breathes me in, everything turning inside out—the flower, the mountains, all of Psyche, all of reality—and sings me back out in an exquisite red song.

I flash through the mountains, raying outward. Sense others passing through me, spheres of thought and perception and volition, encompassing me, guiding me to the very fringes of crystal, filling the entire mountain range—a wildfire elecotrochemical storm blasting from neuron to neuron, taking seizure of the entire brain.

As I embody the mountains, I became aware of the corporeal formations of Psyche—feel my desiccated wings; hollowed out insides; dusty, moldering skin crawling with parasites like some animated ceremonial tattoo; feel my young burrowed inside of me, pupating, ready to hatch and begin their own journeys across the cosmos—and wonder if I were to uncoil, if I could still fly off, go with them and seek out a new planet among the impossible spread of stars.

I might shatter if I were to try.

Soon, I become aware of energy coursing through the complex maze of the crystal, incoming and outgoing, and can feel myself unphasing with the ghost of Psyche, being pulled along one such stream into the center of the mountain, the point of egress, where I blink out.

CHAPTER 20

Jing sits up on the mattress in the center of the room, the morning stark with snow glare, runs her hands through her recently-clipped hair, and tests the vision in her left eye as she's been doing every morning since her discharge—still nothing.

Strange being back after Glenbrook. The ghost of regiment still pushes—intercom alarm bells crackling in her mind, the schedule of the day on the bulletin board directing her movements. And there's the Muzak—which has persisted long after she passed beyond the razor-wire-crowned walls.

Seems Waters was right, after all.

She rises, finds a clear spot on the floor between the bookshelf and second-hand drum set, and does push-ups and sit-ups, then pull-ups on the bar in the bathroom door frame. She can only do about half of what she'd been capable of before entering the hospital, but already after having been home for a week, she's seen improvement.

Having worked up a light sweat, she grabs juice out of the refrigerator, showers and, wrapped in a towel, tiptoes past the bed over to the garden window lined with ferns, succulents, and cacti. Autoscope's guitarist had brought them back from the brink of death, nurturing them even after their fight and during Penn's own personal crisis.

She gazes out at the view of the city and frozen river. A garden has blossomed in the derelict building across from hers, bursting through the carbonized frame, teeming with the same fruits she'd seen that day in the cafeteria. Beyond, the snow-covered city is beleaguered with intertwining flora—colossal trees sprouting out of the concrete and vanishing into the clouds, flowering tangles of vines and roots carpeting the streets and winding up building faces, everything pastelized with hoarfrost. Since the moment Jing had seen this landscape on their drive back from the hospital, she's been expecting an attack of incredible magnitude to seize her—but it hasn't come—and as she watches, as gusts of white obscure and clear, the floral network continues to sprout and bloom, elevating roads and houses and shopping centers, rearranging and shifting the city into multitiered, interconnected chaos.

"Jingy?"

At the sound of the sluggish voice, Jing turns to find the quilt on the bed churning. A head periscopes out of it, turning first to the kitchen, then the window. Shutting her eyes against the light, pouting face lightly tattooed with the imprint of sheet creases, Penn smiles, then collapses back into the sea of bedding.

"Coffee?" Jing asks, crossing to the kitchen.

Penn grunts once.

"Cake?"

Two grunts this time.

As she waits for the water to boil, Jing pulls the chocolate cake out of the refrigerator, the one that had read "Congrats Psycho!!!" last night before being reduced to "...Psych..." She narrows the message down even further, wondering if Leif and Penn had been calling her a psychopath or psychotic or if they'd even bothered to consider the distinction. The cake may have been in bad taste, but, well, chocolate is chocolate.

She munches on her breakfast and flips through the large mound of mail obscuring the counter, mostly bills and junk she's been half-heartedly whittling down during the mornings since her return. She happens upon Rui and Carl's wedding invitation: a picture of the two of them posed by the sea among dunes and reeds, his hair jazzed up, hers intricately woven together and draped over a bare shoulder. Beneath this in the stack is a letter from the law offices of Crook and Query: Estate Planning and Elder Law. She rips it open, and her eyes go wide upon reading the check inside.

When she returns to bed several minutes later with a steaming French press and mugs, lips crumbly, the two drink in bed.

"How about you open your Christmas present?" Penn says, sipping her coffee.

"Okay, but—warning—I haven't had time to get you anything yet."

"I didn't really get you anything." She grabs her purse from the bedside and pulls out a small black pouch.

"Jewelry?"

"I don't know."

"So you didn't get me anything and you don't know what it is you didn't get me? You feeling okay?"

"Just open it."

Jing loosens the drawstring and reaches inside. Pulls out a white bracelet.

"A Möbius strip?" she says after studying it for a few moments.

"Does it mean anything to you?"

"No—I mean—it's cool. Thanks. Is-is it food? Smells like cranberry."

"Sorry. I had some Craisins in my purse and the bag spilled. Everything smells like cranberry now."

"Well, what is this? I don't get it."

"Jingy, I'm giving it *back* to you."

"I gave this to you..."

"The last night. You told me to wait until the tour ended. Well, our last date was scheduled for Christmas Eve—"

"Buffalo."

"—so here it is."

Jing's lips twist, seemingly in simulation of the object's contours as she tries to make sense of it or at least remember *something*. She slips it over her wrist, next to the medical ID bracelet—it's a little too loose, sliding down to her elbow.

"Where did you get it?" Penn leans her head on Jing's shoulder.

"Wish I could remember. You know, this reminds me—I've been meaning to ask a favor of you." She looks askance at Penn through her right eye. "Can you give me a ride?"

Penn squints darkly. "Jing, it's all closed off."

"I'll find a way in. You don't have to hang around if you're uncomfortable. I just want a little time inside. I'd drive myself, but"—she flashes her medical ID bracelet—"you know how it be."

She sighs. "Yeah, I'll take you. But... why?"

Jing hooks a finger through the Möbius strip. Turns it. "Closure, I guess."

Several hours later the two drive past large, dirty snowbanks piled on the sides of the road. Jing, bundled up and warming her hands at the air vents, watches the first signs of vegetation appearing as they progress deeper into the city: roots spilling out of smashed shop windows, salt-pink wisteria curtaining billboards, umbrella blossoms eclipsing the winter light. She turns away from the sight and studies Penn instead.

"That check..."

"It's something, huh?" Penn grips the wheel tightly with her gloved hands, squinting beyond the thick snow fractals whirling before them.

"What are you going to do with the money?"

"Use some to finish up the second album. It's what Bower would've wanted. I'd like your help with it."

Jing grabs the oh-Jesus handle as the car crashes down and belly-grinds out of a fissure in the road.

"My bad," Penn says.

"I thought Autoscope was done. Thought you'd

moved on."

"Me too, but I think it's what I'm supposed to do. I think…"

"Think what?"

"I abandoned us, Jings. I think I'm being punished for it."

"Punished by whom? The Almighty Buddha?"

"No." Penn smiles. "An unconscious thing. Different parts of my brain at war. That's what happened to my synesthesia."

"I believe we're talking neurosis here."

"Whatever it is, it's telling me to stay in Detroit, put all my other projects aside until Autoscope gets its proper end… What do you say?"

Jing studies Penn's profile for a second, suddenly unsure of what she wants. "I need to think about it. I promised my Dad I'd pay him a visit—and Ma."

"Dope."

To their left, urban waste gives way to the white sheen of the river; to the right, rows of warehouses now lie in rubble, obliterated by a stories-high braid of roots. Before them, growing out of the city and spanning across the sky looms the claw-like patchwork of frozen vegetation, its fingers vanishing into the steel winter sky—mammoth livid ferns, fiddlehead trees, frilled buttercup suns, bulbous fungi.

Jing has for some time considered describing what she sees to Penn—much as Penn had done years ago with her own sensorial idiosyncrasy—describing the auras of the epileptic fits, the blindness, and this apocalyptic phantasm. Now would be an opportune time, but she checks herself. Lights a cigarette instead as Penn navigates around thorny stalks and barky growths without comment.

After several minutes of silence Penn glances over at her.

"Nervous?"

Jing nods. "Don't know why I should be."

Penn laughs. "Why you should be nervous about breaking and entering?"

"That's not what I mean. The city's dead this time of year. Besides, I'm an ex-mental patient. Worst case scenario you say, 'She had a breakdown, officer, and I followed her here.' Or some shit like that. Improvise as necessary."

Penn glances again, perspicaciously says, "You're afraid you'll remember something about that night, aren't you? That's what we're doing. You're afraid, but you want it all the same."

She takes a drag. "Why not focus on driving, P.C.?"

Bower's Compound is situated east of downtown— once a rundown neighborhood of half-burned churches, collapsed homes, boarded-up schools. He'd had several blocks' worth razed for the construction. The mansion is somehow both at the center of and yet untouched by the alien growth: a tiny clearing in the jungle wall, flanked on all sides by dense blossoms and creepers.

Thick, padlocked chains entangle the grounds gate. Penn and Jing step out of the car, scale the wall, and slog up the long, snowy drive, winding around a wooded hill in an aggravatingly indirect manner, occasionally sinking up to their asses in snow, then round the final bend and trudge up to the immense concrete slab upon which the three-dimensional network is anchored, four stories of nodes and links and boxes, glass, concrete, and metal, tagged with the designs of numerous graffiti artists, all of it interconnected, gravity-defying, set among gardens of pine and bamboo, which sprout up in strategic patches around the hallways and rooms, everything caked in winter, the upper-story rooms and hallways dripping human-sized icicles. It's the first time she has ever arrived here when the driveway had not been packed with cars.

All that remain are Bower's sports car and her old Taurus.

The two mount the steps. The view from the top of the hill is spectacular: the frozen-over river on the one hand and the ruptured Detroit skyline on the other. A flock of geese honk as they pass through a tangle of branches high above. As the plants shift and shiver, ice casings break off and cascade down the structure, shattering against the pavement. The sound is different here: hushed by snowfall, yes, but also rapt with canyon-bottom grandeur. As Jing stands there, the same light tingling that has preceded previous seizures begins to course through her body.

She takes a deep breath.

As Penn had anticipated, new locks had been installed on the front door. They crunch through the snow around the winding porch to the front room.

Jing tests the window.

Locked.

She pulls out her razor, first trying to jimmy it through the window crack to slip the catch, but the blade is too thick. She closes it and hammers at the glass with the handle. It crashes open, leaving behind a jagged-toothed smile. Penn, startled, glares at her.

"There's no alarm system, right?" Jing smiles from behind her scarf.

Penn rolls her eyes, and they both pause to listen.

Nothing but the soft breath of snowfall and the occasional, jarring crashes of ice, which it seems only Jing can hear.

Thus, she continues to hammer until the window is clear, and they climb inside, glass cracking beneath their boots.

The front room with its grand piano and upstairs balcony is cryogenic-chamber cold, the quiet hushed to an eerie extreme by the snowfall. Jing had half-expected to find the place in shambles, the interior scorched, the piano demolished. Yet it's just as it had been the night of the show, littered here and there with paraphernalia, everything now covered in a light patina of dust—the mute herald of forgetting.

Through a long glass hallway overlooking a white garden, they pass into the lounge. Barren save the months-old moltings of the partygoers: smashed bottles, cigarette butts, discarded clothing and wigs, glow bracelets robbed of light.

Jing begins to walk up one of the ramps to the second floor, when Penn speaks, voice reverential.

"I'm going down to root around the recording studio."

"All right. I'm just going to wander around for a bit."

"How about we meet here in fifteen minutes?"

"Sure."

Penn heads down into the basement, and Jing proceeds to the second floor overlooking the pool, now covered, a snowdrift accumulated against the glass screen leading to the patio. She proceeds up to the third floor.

Tries the lights.

Nothing.

She peers into Bower's sci-fi vision of how a bedroom should look. Bleak winter light shines in through the frosted window of the balcony door, illuminating the bed in soft notes.

She walks down the hallway junction, glancing in room after room. On the ground she finds the odd bra, bottles either empty or burst from the freeze, used condoms and wrappers, and various other storied mementoes.

Everywhere she tries the lights; everywhere to no avail.

As before, the sensation comes to her that all of this should have been destroyed, a large section of the hallway tunnel missing. From room to room she wanders, looking in, perseverating with surprise at the emptiness and lack of devastation.

She steps onto the upper balcony of the Club, finding

the stage in darkness, with just the pale December light streaming in from the entrances on the three floors, casting fuzzy spotlights onto the opposite wall, intersecting into a slanting, luminous snowman. The room should have been burned to the ground, curtain torn down, the skeleton of musical equipment at the back of the stage reduced to a jumble of steel and plastic. As she descends to the first floor, removing her gloves and hat and scarf, she gazes at the stage, visualizing how the three of them must have looked when they'd performed that night and on so many other occasions.

She crosses the dance floor, images of fire and destruction glimmering ahead of her, a mirage superimposed over this scene where they'd played so many times.

So unnatural approaching the stage from this direction—*like I'm some schoolgirl up next for the recital.*

As this thought occurs to her, Jing's steps slow—déjà vu—and she pauses there, one foot onstage, the other off.

She finally resumes, walking past the trap set first, stimulating the cymbal with a black fingernail. Its metallic whisper gives her the chills. She turns towards Penn's domain. The wall of amps still stands, but the neat rainbow of effects pedals and her notations are gone. At the other end of the stage rests the piano, with its electronic equipment outgrowths. Beside it a collapsed portion has been hefted aside. That was what had struck her on the head when they'd been having sex, or so she'd been told. White tape highlights where Bower had been discovered a few feet from the piano, at the time in a pool of blood and cerebrospinal fluid— brain removed, to the complete bewilderment of the authorities. Now, the varnished wood shines in the dim light. She walks over, silently skirts around the outline and slides onto the squeaking piano bench.

It all feels so familiar to her. Now, Glenbrook, Autoscope, college, childhood. All linked together by these piano gateways. As soon as her fingers touch the keys, they unlock untold legions of musical memories. Walking through the house earlier, she might not have been able to recall the fourth section of *Pictures*, but now the entire schema of fingers and notes shimmers and pulses with anticipation in her body, waiting for expression, to superimpose itself over space and time, and so do the many occasions she had played the pieces, a brief life of complex action maps, all hanging right on the edge of consciousness.

As she begins *Pictures*, a red light shines in her peripheral vision. She looks up, fingers not even stumbling, and sees that the power of the effects board is on.

Is the power still on in here?

She begins to doubt herself.

Must have been on the entire time.

Her fingers continue, and gradually she becomes aware of the electronic reverberation, murmuring delicately beneath the depressions of the piano notes. The sound builds and with it a memory of Bower.

"Walking too fast."

That's what he'd said.

"The protagonist is walking too fast."

Instantly, her tempo slows, the rhythm clicks with the timing of the echo till the memory of the sound and the present notes strike in tandem, then everything explodes into timeless spectra. Bower is here, talking. They're playing together.

"I woke to the glorious sounds of the Drummer Girl. It was like you were calling to me. What about you, you creep, playing in the dark for an empty hall in all this goth finery? What the hell kind of a Victorian ghost possessed your clothes?"

"Bower, you have to get out of here."

Memoryfish, she remembers thinking.

"You have to go. I need to be alone. I'm going through some shit I can't explain. There's no time to."

Their fingers entwined.

She'd had some kind of a premonition about his death, wanted him gone.

The electronics swell and drown out the piano, a booming drone filling the Club, rattling the drums, the amps, every nerve inside her, everything.

And then something bangs on the inside of the piano. It shudders, and Jing gasps. The wooden flap jerks and shakes and then cracks open slightly. Her breath catches, heart hammering, but she can't stop playing. Her hands are locked into a song reluctant to release her, as from the towering confines of some envious fairytale witch. She can't even tell what section of the piece it is; it is every note and phrase at once, with fifty blurring fingers.

A hand reaches out from inside the piano. Frail, feminine, it clutches at her own hands, then locks onto the Möbius strip around her wrist. It claws at the flesh, working, kneading its way up the tattoos, the scar. Another pops out, tattooed like her own, grabs a hold of her right hand.

The floor beneath the piano seems to drop out beneath her, the faint tingling of the aura rising to a complex sensorial mesh inside her body, not unpleasant for the sensation in itself, but for the helplessness it signifies.

Then the head emerges—upside-down. The hair comes first, tangling around their arms like demonic vines, long and wild and sun-bleached. Then the face, sunburnt and cut and bruised, one of her eyes gouged out, leaving a horrid, gaping wound. Her lips are purple either from lipstick or cold. The piano lid pops up higher, and she sees that this girl—this nightmare transformation of herself—is completely naked, bony, scarred. Strangely, the interior of the piano lacks all of the music-making innards. Instead, it's pure, pulsating crystal, stretching on and on to the limits of vision—a chandelier universe.

The hands of the Jing shade unzip Earth Jing's

jacket and they part the flaps as if doing the breast-stroke. They stroke again, and now the sweaters and t-shirts part, waving out around them like colorful water. Again—but this time Jing screams out as her flesh and sinews and blood and bone stream outward. The girl is swimming inside her now, turning and stretching, positioning herself just right. Beyond them the waves of clothing and flesh circle in a maelstrom while Earth Jing and this new shade merge together, piece-by-excruci-ating-piece. Without the flesh to bind them, the two are almost immaterial, liquid shapes. The projections of their noses and lips, nipples and fingers, touch and ripple and merge.

Then the surrounding space crashes down around them, and Jing collapses.

A voice.

Light slaps to my face.

Hair dangles down, tickling my cheek.

These things guide me out of the darkness.

"Open your eyes, Jing. Come on. Open your eyes." An alto, melodic, bright.

When I open my eyes, Penn sighs with relief, worry creasing her forehead.

"Fuck, Jingy," she says, pulling me into her arms and squeezing me. "You scared the shit out of me."

"I'm okay." My hand is a disembodied piece of meat weighing on her shoulder. I think it's mine. It moves when I think it should. It's mine. Maybe.

Penn holds me out at arm's length, gets a good look in my eyes—my eyes... "I'd ask if you want me to call an ambulance, but I know what you'd say."

"Yeah."

"Was it... one of your seizures?"

"I think so. I... how-how long was I out?"

"A few minutes, I guess. Come on. Put your coat and

hat back on. You're going to freeze. What the hell were you doing?"

"Playing the piano. Did you hear it echoing? The effects board was on."

"The power has been out for months now." She shakes her head, takes my hands, and guides them through the sleeves of my coat. As she does so her eyes go wide at the sight of the medical ID bracelet around my wrist.

"What the hell..."

"Hmm?" I say, still groggy from the attack, fighting for a foothold in reality.

"The *thing* I... you gave me to give... Just look."

I lower my gaze and see the Möbius strip and the medical ID bracelet have merged, the writing on the one now printed in a never-ending, twisting loop.

We step outside into the sinus-burning cold, Penn lugging a box loaded with cables and effects pedals. I light a cigarette. Tastes sharp; gives me a head rush. As we walk down the hill to the gate, the sun comes out for a brief moment, scattering the clouds, the aura vanquished.